THE
UNVEILING

A Novel Series: Volume 1.0

K. L. COLLINS

ISBN: 978-0-9884296-1-1

Cover art: designed by K. L. Collins & illustrated by Yamen Elgamal

Cover design & graffiti art: Tamara Johnston

TheUnveilingSeries.com: designed by Tamara Johnston
& built by Stephen Winsor

facebook.com/TheUnveilingSeries

facebook.com/kl.collins.94

For my mother whose love and
support nurtured creativity.

Acknowledgments

The following people have all been instrumental in bringing this book to fruition: John Baker, Peter Cohen, Roger Collins, Ryan Winsor, Vincent Cummings, David Flores, Sam Flowers, Melissa Hendricks, Norma Henry, Alex Murillo, Greg Steen, Darryl Stephens, my fantastic editor, Jennifer French, and countless other friends and family who have offered their love and support throughout the process. To all of you I offer my deepest gratitude.

THE UNVEILING

1.0

Very few know the truth of
what lies behind the veil.

CHAPTER 1

$\mathcal{T}$he island of Nova Scotia had just come into view as the large chopper made its way up the New England coast. Emblazoned across the aircraft's metallic flank were the two stylized letters "B.I." Slick block lettering, akin to the Braggadocio font, defined a logo that belonged to Battenberg Industries, one of the world's largest and most powerful corporations.

The shark-like copter, with its sleek pewter-colored frame, looked like something out of a futuristic sci-fi movie. It was state-of-the-art technology, the best money could buy. Its fuselage was smooth and absent of seams, which lent toward the most efficient aerodynamics. The rear rotor was encased in a round, metallic housing with a silhouette reminiscent of a shark's tail. As it turned out, some of the world's best engineers could hardly improve upon nature's design.

Inside, the plush craft resembled a compact sitting room that could easily be found on a multi-million-dollar yacht. Instead of standard porthole windows, rectangular panels of thick panoramic glass stretched across both sides, illuminating the cabin. Two sets of upholstered leather, high-back, burgundy armchairs sat side-by-side at the front and rear of the craft. They were arranged like four thrones meant for a meeting of kings and queens. Beneath them, 2-inch wood floorboards ran the length of the cabin, creating a stunning hardwood floor. A teak and glass island in the center served as a makeshift coffee table with a flat screen monitor and a full bar hidden inside. While the cabin was small, its sparse furnishings provided a spacious feel.

Seated in the rear, twenty-four-year-old playboy Maximilian Battenberg gazed down at the gorgeous view. Just minutes before, they had passed over the beaches of Maine on a northeast trajectory toward the Bay of Fundy. In minutes more, they would be at their destination in Nova Scotia.

Below them, a patchwork of cumulous clouds waltzed across sunny, blue skies. Because it was early spring, the landscape was transforming into a plush and vibrant green. Staring down, Max spotted several boats and a few yachts slicing across the bay. He turned to his left where his girlfriend, Brigitte Sturdivant, was seated.

Waking from a brief nap, she stirred in the chair, stretching her arms and rotating her neck.

"Are we there yet?"

"Almost," he answered. Max was doing a decent job of playing it cool even though he didn't feel so relaxed inside. If he had been any more nervous, he probably would have vomited.

Brigitte leaned across his lap to gaze through the window. Then she spotted something below. "Isn't that it over there?"

Max turned to where she was pointing. "Yeah, I think so."

The 140-acre land mass stood no more than six hundred feet from Nova Scotia's eastern seaboard. From a distance, its shape looked like a child's toy, a flat chunk of wood that was being carved into a baby elephant. The legs and tail hadn't yet been defined from the rest of an amorphous body, but the head and trunk were seemingly pointing toward the east.

"Oak Island," Max mumbled.

Much of the island's terrain was covered in a thick canopy of oak trees, from which the island had derived its name. He kissed the top of Brigitte's head and caught a whiff of lavender shampoo.

All day, he had been a ball of nerves. Now that the island was in sight, he could feel the knot in his stomach beginning to unfurl. After nearly two months, here he was flying thousands of feet above what he hoped would be the location of the ultimate prize – the Money Pit.

Oak Island's legendary sinkhole was rumored to be the hiding place of treasures unknown, including artifacts like the Holy Grail and the Ark of the Covenant. For weeks, Max had hoped for a shot at it. If only he could find what he wanted inside.

Sunlight beamed through the chopper's window, as it banked, highlighting the contours of Max's face. He wasn't traditionally handsome, but friends nevertheless described him as striking. Because of his dark, silky curls and olive skin, he perpetually looked as if he had just returned from a month on the beaches of Brazil.

His eyes were by far his best feature: large, almond-shaped and a little further apart on his head than conventional good looks normally dictated. Whenever photographed, Max's windows to the soul shone like pale emeralds, making him look almost unreal.

His nose, slightly large and blade-like, was at the same time aquiline, elegant and aristocratic. Depending on how he tilted his head, Max sometimes appeared as a caricature: a cartoon super-hero or perhaps the villain. The shadow of a scar, nearly one inch long, stretched down the center of his right cheek perpendicular to his eye. The battle wound had healed nicely and could easily be mistaken for a birthmark, as if a painter had lightly brushed it on. The truth was, Max's look, scar and all, drew attention.

Still stretched across his torso, Brigitte gazed down on the island. "It's kind of pretty, I guess. Lots of trees." She looked up at Max. "Is it true Roosevelt came here?"

"Oh, yeah, that's why it's called the Money Pit. A ton of folks have come through and they've spent a shitload of cash trying to get at what's inside. For more than a hundred years they've been coming. FDR, some old time actor — a guy named Errol Flynn, King George VI..." Max smiled a toothy grin. "Now, it's my turn."

Growing apprehensive, Brigitte settled back in her seat. At twenty-six, she was very much the girl next door, but trapped in a supermodel's body. Her limbs were long and slender and her breasts small, yet well shaped. With a sparkling smile and beautiful flaw-less skin, she rounded out a perfect package. Brigitte was every bit the trophy girlfriend, only without a diva's disposition.

"I still don't get why you have to go down in that thing." Her statement hung in the air like a question. "All those people tried, but somehow you think you're going to be the one to find something."

"Will you stop worrying?" Max gingerly swiped hair away from her face. "I want to see for myself what's down there."

"Max, people have died in that thing. You didn't think I checked? There's all kinds of stuff on YouTube."

As a peace offering, he planted a kiss on her cheek. "Then you also know why I want to go down there. The way it's built, there has to be something inside."

"If by 'built' you mean booby trapped, then yes, there's prob-ably something inside. Lost treasure for people with too much is already a bad combination."

"It'll be fine, I promise." Max poked Brigitte in the side, activat-ing her ticklish gene.

"Max, no," she hollered, squirming in her seat.

"Going down that thing'll be like rock climbing, which you know I do quite well."

Brigitte studied his face and then sat back. She knew Max well enough to know her protests wouldn't make one bit of difference. He was a Battenberg after all, and due to boyish curiosity, he would indeed climb down a ninety-foot pit where more than a few people had died. *Men.*

The pilot maneuvered in a half circle, diving toward the location of the Money Pit. They knifed through a blanket of clouds, enabling an unobscured view of Oak Island's eastern shore. Max gazed down, giddy with anticipation. From 8,000 feet the island still seemed small and inconsequential. A single road plunged down the Nova Scotia coast before traversing 600 feet across the water. It wasn't so much a bridge as a dam or causeway.

With the exception of a scattering of structures, Oak Island seemed uninhabited; a white two-story home, a boathouse and a bungalow all faced Nova Scotia's coast. The causeway, once on the island, became a single serpentine road that carved its way northeast through the trees until it snaked off toward the western side of the island where the Money Pit was located.

Max grabbed Brigitte's hand and squeezed it. From the sky, the pit's actual location was easy to miss in a grassy area not more than 300 feet from the northern beach. If it had not been cordoned off, Max would have missed it completely.

Minutes later, the pilot touched down less than two hundred yards from the infamous hole. Finally, Max was near the illusive prize, which he had privately become desperate to find. A mere twenty-three hours had passed since he had received the call from his father's closest friend and confidant, Otto Khrzinsky.

"Max!" Otto had screamed into the phone. "We're here at Oak Island, ready and waiting. When can you get here?"

For a moment, Max had remained speechless. As thrilling as he found Otto's news, his mouth seemed immobilized.

"Max, did you hear me?"

"Yes, Otto, yes. Honestly I don't know what to say." Max laughed into the phone. "I'll be there tomorrow, as soon as I can get a flight." Max hung up, shaking with excitement.

After research, Max had discovered the island was privately owned and explicit permission was required just to land there. He knew if anyone could secure the needed access it was his father, Demetrius Battenberg. In the circles of the rich and famous, the

Battenberg name had grown synonymous with the Rothschilds and the Rockefellers. As a family to be reckoned with, Demetrius had an extremely high level of clout.

The Battenbergs, it was said, hailed from a lineage with ancestral ties to Austrian royalty. In Europe, they had been considerably powerful even among other aristocrats. For reasons unknown, select family members had crossed into the Americas in the mid-1800s. The move, it turned out, had allowed the family to establish a strong foothold in the new world, while across Europe monarchies were simultaneously collapsing.

In the Americas, the Battenbergs had thrived while piecing together a formidable empire. For more than a century, their influence had been far-reaching in both commerce and government. Given the family's history and current social standing, Max was certain he could land on Oak Island if he wanted. The moment he learned of its ownership, he had phoned Otto, who was much easier to get a hold of than his own father. Otto had agreed to see what he could do. In less than a week, a dig team had been dispatched, as dozens of wealthy benefactors had done many times before.

Nearly six weeks had elapsed since Max learned of Oak Island. Some harebrained notion had given him the idea that something he needed, something he desperately wanted, was potentially buried there. He prayed the Money Pit contained the artifact he was so frantic to find. Now, tens of thousands of dollars later, everything was in place for the newest attempt at discovering the pit's hidden treasure.

Above ground, the entrance to the pit hardly lived up to its reputation. In fact, Max spotted it only because of the circular chain link fence around it. In the center of the enclosure, the pit's actual opening looked like an animal's burrow, covered in wild grass and trees like the rest of the island. It would hardly have been surprising if a large snake had slithered from its opening.

From what Max could tell, the pit's entrance appeared to travel horizontally rather than vertically into the ground. The dig captain, upon spotting Max's reaction to the site, chimed in with a strong Australian accent.

"It looks that way because the owner of the island had the pit covered over. Calls less attention to itself that way." The captain appeared to be in his late forties and was, in many ways, the stereotype of a rugged Australian — weathered sun-kissed skin, five o'clock shadow, and curly strawberry blond hair. "It'll take half a day or so to get it uncovered. Or we can enter the way it is now."

On the ground, like a massive picture frame, four logs were embedded in the dirt to form a square around the pit. Max presumed they had served as a platform during previous excavations.

"Let's go in the way it is," Max replied. "No need to waste time."

A day earlier, the captain and his team had constructed a series of metal scaffoldings along with a huge motorized hoist. Within minutes, Max was outfitted with water repellent gear and a protective helmet. The dig captain strapped him into a special harness for his descent. Like many before him, an intricate cable system would lower him into the depths of the pit.

Max wasn't truly qualified for the task, but the only license he needed, at the end of the day, was the Battenberg name. Brigitte, Otto and the dig captain surrounded him on the grassy knoll. Reaching up, Brigitte clasped his cheeks in her hands.

"Promise you won't do anything stupid."

"Bridge, c'mon..."

"Max," she insisted.

Otto smiled, his face still serious with concern. "You heard the girl. We can't afford any mistakes today. Your father'd never forgive me if something happened."

"Neither would I," Brigitte warned.

Desiring to alleviate their concerns, the dig captain smiled a toothy grin. "Every precaution has been taken. In the unlikely event you become submerged, you have a back-up oxygen tank as well as a snorkeling device." The captain pointed to various safety gear strapped to Max's back.

Max reached around and touched the oxygen tank for reassurance. "Yeah, guys, that's why the good captain's here, to ensure everything goes off without a hitch."

In addition to the tank, a breathing tube, like an enormous snorkel, snaked its way along the cable that would lower Max into the ground.

"I assure you today's operation couldn't be any safer. Let's allow Mr. Battenberg to have a look-see and then my men and I can get started."

"An excellent idea," Max nearly sang before kissing Brigitte square on the lips. "Let's see what's inside this thing." Like a military soldier, Max dropped down on his belly and shuffled backwards until his feet slid into the burrow-like entrance of the pit. Halfway inside, his legs fell into the shaft, snapping tension into the cable attached to his harness. Max startled as his eyes sprang open.

"Be careful, Max." Otto and Brigitte both spoke over one another.

"I'm fine, guys. Just relax."

Otto seemed genuinely worried, as if Max were his own child. "Just go in and check things out. Take a few snapshots if you see anything. But I want you back up here so the captain and his guys can do the real heavy lifting. Understood?"

"Yes, sir."

As a child, Max had always feared Otto. In truth, even adults found his appearance off-putting. By all accounts, Otto was fifty-nine, but he appeared ten or fifteen years older. For starters, his hair was frizzy and silvery-white. While he didn't have deep wrinkles, his skin had a weathered quality to it. To top it off, the dimensions of his face were odd. His eyes sat too close together and his long head was pushed in at the nose. Over the years, a struggle with scoliosis had caused him to hunch slightly to the right.

Still, Otto had been a good and close family friend. He had always been kind and over the years Max had warmed to him.

"I'll be fine. I promise." All smiles, Max gestured a thumbs-up before reaching down to the controller at his waist. With the click of a button the motor to the hoist engaged and the cable from which he dangled began its descent, lowering him into the pit. For a brief instant, Max spotted worry on Otto and Brigitte's faces. Then the Money Pit seemingly swallowed him up.

CHAPTER 2

$\mathcal{M}$ax was officially inside, entombed in the Money Pit. The click of a second switch on his tool belt illuminated powerful lights on his chest and helmet. As he scaled down the circular structure, its walls were completely lit on one side.

"I love you," Brigitte yelled down the shaft, her words echoing around him.

"I love you too, babe."

His words bounced about the walls with hers, creating a strange singsongy effect. Inside, the hole was a contradiction of muddiness and solidity. Max walked his feet along the circular wall as the cable lowered him deeper into the island's bedrock.

Positioned at one and two o'clock, there were two tree trunk–sized posts that served as stabilizers. Max stared down as they descended into darkness. Beside them, two large pipes also ran downwards, apparently to the pit's floor. Max knew the excavation plunged nearly ninety feet into the Earth. In the past, the pipes had served as part of the sump pump system to eliminate floodwater. Max took note of their rusty, corroded condition. Their abrasive surface mimicked that of the contoured walls to which they were attached.

Located next to the wooden posts at twelve o'clock, there was a rusted metal ladder. Upon dropping the first ten feet, he flipped a switch that halted his descent. Pausing, he raised a scuba mask from around his neck and fastened it to his face. The high-tech piece of equipment was outfitted with a radio Comlink and polarized glass that enabled him to distinguish details he wouldn't otherwise be able to see.

"How's it going, Max?" Otto's voice was clear as he spoke through the Comlink in Max's scuba mask.

"Everything's fine, Otto. It's like a big well. I'm just checking out the first platform."

Jutting out from the pit's walls were the remnants of the earliest discovered oak platform. Whoever constructed the sinkhole had used oak logs to create a series of floors. Max was scrutinizing what remained of the first one. The majority of the log floor had been carved away, but nearly two inches of wood remained, poking out into the pit.

Max found it comical how the experts argued about the pit's contents, whether or not treasure was buried there, or if the pit was naturally occurring or man made. Max was certain it had been constructed. It didn't take a rocket scientist to figure it out, as too many bizarre aspects had been uncovered about the excavation. When the site was first unearthed, the original platform had seemed odd and out of place ten feet beneath the ground. Then more platforms had been discovered, a new one every ten feet. The oak floors often had foreign substances sitting on top of them. Sometimes, it was a collection of beach stones, charcoal or loose coconut fibers, which were not indigenous to the island. In addition, the soil had been intermittently packed with barriers of putty, as well as metal fragments and an occasional air pocket.

After a brief inspection, Max triggered the hoist to continue his descent. He carefully pushed away from the wall to avoid interference between the cable and the jagged remains of the first oak floor.

At twenty feet, he reached the remnants of the second platform. What wood remained appeared rotted from the pit's constant moisture. Max continued down the shaft, looking up to see the light growing smaller at the pit's opening. Of course, the effect was an optical illusion, as the actual pit, although not smoothly finished, was perfectly cylindrical all the way down. At fifty feet inside, Max felt entrenched in darkness, unable to see beyond the lights mounted on his helmet and chest.

"Max, you okay?" Otto questioned through the radio Com-link.

"A-one, Otto. Tell Bridge I'm fine."

"Will do," Otto replied.

Max reached around and tapped the oxygen tank affixed to his back. He was thankful for the back-up precaution, especially since the air about him seemed to be thinning, or perhaps thickening, Max couldn't tell which. He stared at the walls, which appeared to be sweating like a winded athlete. When droplets began to form on his mask and protective suit, he knew exactly why. On multiple occasions, the pit had flooded and lives had been claimed, just as Brigitte had mentioned — six lives, to be exact.

As the cable lowered him, Max dismissed thoughts of death from his mind. He knew the superstitious believed a curse was on the island. As legend told it, seven lives would be claimed before the pit relinquished its treasure. If ill fortune befell Max, he would be that number seven. Before the thought could get the better of him, Max's feet landed in water, striking the lowest platform at ninety feet.

He shut off the hoist and gazed up, unable to distinguish anything beyond the scope of his lighting equipment.

"Otto, you there?"

The radio was silent a brief moment before Otto's voice crackled through Max's earpiece. "Yeah, Max. You at the bottom yet?"

"Just reached now." Max stared down to see muddy brown water covering a portion of his shins.

"Anything interesting?"

"I'm in water, but it's not even up to my knees."

There was a brief pause before Otto replied with a chuckle. "Brigitte just asked if you could come back up now."

"Give me a minute." Max felt around the pit's deepest floor with his protective boots. The contours of oak logs were apparent.

Already, millions of dollars had been squandered and no one had ever gotten any further than the ninth platform where Max was currently standing. It was here that a mysterious artifact had been found, a large stone tablet inscribed with hieroglyphic-like symbols. Multiple experts had ventured to translate the glyphs, which were a series of circles, squares, triangles, slashes and dots.

Many interpreted the ciphers to mean, "Forty feet below two million pounds are buried." The definition had drawn many people to the island, rich and poor alike, but no one had successfully extracted treasure of any note.

But there were other translations in existence. The Coptic Christians, whose origins dated back to early A.D. Egypt, claimed the symbols meant, "The people shall not forget the Lord. To offset the hardships of winter and the onset of plague, the Arif, he shall pray to the Lord."

Max didn't know which if any translation to believe. For all he knew, the symbols depicted were in a dead language whose translation had been lost to the world.

Adding to the mystery of the stone tablet was a series of boxes that had been located using ultrasound and radar. The supposed treasure chests had been discovered beneath the ninth platform, approximately 100 feet below the surface. No one had actually reached them, but a powerful drill had been instrumental in determining their contents. Scrap metal, it appeared, had been used to form yet another barrier.

There was allegedly a single oak box even lower, at a depth of 200 feet. But the pit, because it had been successfully constructed, or booby-trapped, had thus far rendered this box unattainable.

Max found it hard to believe that he was standing at the bottom of the Money Pit. "There's something beneath the ninth platform, correct?"

Otto's voice crackled through Max's receiver. "My understanding is there are several chests just a few feet below. But you need to let the dig captain worry about that. When you come up, he and his crew can get started."

Max jostled a camera from his pocket and took a few snapshots of the pit's floor. He turned the camera on himself and smiled, capturing his own portrait.

"Max, you there? You're making a certain girl extremely nervous up here."

"Still here. Just taking a few snapshots." Max hadn't yet realized it, but the water level was rising, climbing ever closer to his knees. He fiddled with his scuba mask to ensure it was secure, then plunged his face beneath the surface. The spotlight on his head cut through the water, illuminating the platform of logs beneath him. Then Max felt it, a current of water pushing its way up through the logs. Once again, the infamous pit was flooding.

He stood up straight, surprised to find the water level sitting just below his crotch. "Otto, I'm taking on water down here. I'm coming up."

"Good call, Max."

With the flip of a switch, a gentle yank pulled him off his feet and lifted him up the shaft. Water dripped from his boots, splashing beneath him. Once again, Max began walking his feet along the contours of the pit to prevent his body from swinging unnecessarily.

"How's it going, son?" Otto inquired.

Max could see the water rising beneath him but his pace was swift, enabling him to remain free and clear. When the remnants of platform number eight approached, he kicked off from the wall to avoid becoming ensnared. The cable continued its ascent, but the water remained close behind. Feeling concerned, Max reached for the controller at his waist. He clicked a button to increase his speed and easily passed where the seventh platform had been. Like a camera aperture opening in slow motion, the small circle of light that was the entrance to the pit was growing.

Glancing down, Max saw that the water level was giving chase, covering the oak floor that he just cleared. With his attention diverted from the climb, the long cable began rotating the way a jump rope does when spun in circles. Unable to maintain stability, he recovered too late. Max slammed into the wall, smashing his shoulder.

"Fuck!" He cried out.

Otto immediately came on the Comlink. "Max, is everything okay?"

Realizing that his speed was too rapid, he reached for the controller to slow his ascent. Instead, he came to an abrupt and jarring halt. Disoriented, he looked up at the cable and the attached oxygen hose. Both were snagged in the platform directly overhead.

On the surface, Brigitte and Otto noticed a struggle in the motor that was powering Max's exit from the pit. Tension had developed in the cable, which was growing taut. The entire day, Brigitte had been poised for catastrophe, and the sound of the motor was all she needed.

"What is that?" she demanded.

Otto looked at her, unsure of the answer. The engine was now grinding in its efforts to lift Max.

"Max? What's going on? The motor to the hoist—"

Recognizing the problem, Max punched the stop button on the controller, bringing the laboring engine to rest. "The cable got snagged. I'm trying to free it now." Although he didn't have great leverage, Max pushed himself away from the wall, but the cable remained jammed between the wooden remnants of the platform overhead. He forced his body away from the wall only to swing back into it.

"Max?" Otto questioned, having heard Max grunt through the radio link.

"Give me a moment. This thing's still caught."

Then Max felt it. In its pursuit the water had reached his feet. The creature called panic hadn't fully awakened in him, but it was opening its eyes. Believing that his own weight might free him, Max triggered the hoist to lower himself back into the pit. Instead of coming loose, the cable slowly lowered forming a U-shape as it descended from the snag. With a sense of doom, he watched it dip into the water beneath him.

Brigitte's voice bounced into Max's headset. "Hon, what's going on? Why are you going down again?"

"I'm trying to get loose here." Max punched the stop button to halt the hoist.

After a moment, Otto's voice came on line. "Max? Is the water still rising?"

"Kind of."

"Where is it now?"

"Just beneath my feet," Max lied, as the water crept above his knees. He reached overhead and began wrestling with the offending log.

Otto tried to sound calm but the act wasn't entirely convincing. "Max, if you can't get free I need you to disengage from the hoist and make your way up the ladder. Worst-case scenario, inflate your lifejacket. It'll bring you up with the water."

Otto's words were a comfort as Max reached up for the release connecting him to the cable. He had every intention of following instructions from his father's friend. Suddenly, what appeared to be remnants of the sixth oak platform snapped shut overhead, essentially barring him from an exit of any kind.

"Shit! Fuck!" Stunned, Max reached out to see if his eyes had deceived him. The platform that was supposed to have been removed was fully in place as a ceiling. "Otto, I think we've got a problem." Max's voice was shaky.

"What is it?"

"What was left of the sixth platform... it just closed."

"What? What does that mean, Max?"

The water was at Max's waist and continuing to rise.

"I don't know, Otto. On the way down, they were gone, but one of them just... it just closed."

"Are you above or beneath it, Max?"

"What the fuck do you think, Otto?" Max felt the water rising to his neck and fumbled to make sure his mask was in place. Not knowing what else to do, he reversed the direction of the hoist and the cable began to rise. He hoped it would break open the platform. Instead it became further entangled.

Max turned his face up to avoid the water. Then he was completely submerged. The mask, as it turned out, had been fumbled on the journey up and was no longer properly sealed. Water tickled his face as it trickled through at the sides. He immediately placed the snorkeling hose to his mouth, but was unable to draw in air. The snagged cable had tugged tightly shut, cutting off any chance he had to breathe.

Had he managed to keep his wits about him, Max would have remembered to take the air tank's alternate hose, but he was officially panicked. He tried prying the logs back open, but without leverage, all he could do was push himself deeper into the water. Bubbles shot out from the breathing tube inside his mask. Fear gripped Max like never before as he sucked in combinations of air and water.

He fumbled with the mask to extricate its breathing tube. *People have died in that thing* is what Brigitte had said. He remembered the look of worry on her face and Otto's as he descended into the pit. Somewhere in the distance, he could hear voices through the Comlink, muffled by the water in his ears. Suspended beneath the platform, Max wondered if he might indeed be the seventh death that would break the superstitious Oak Island curse.

In shock, Max began to flail like a wounded animal, pulling at the platform and splashing about. And then he felt it: asphyxiation. He was drowning. Like floodwaters, millions of images and life memories began to rush through his head; scenes from childhood, his first day of college, the night he lost his virginity. While it didn't seem possible, his entire life was flashing before him.

$\mathcal{A}$t the ripe age of twenty-four, there weren't many circumstances that could bring Max to the Children's Museum in Manhattan. Even more embarrassing was his true reason for being there. Despite his reservations, Max had followed his instincts and made an appointment to meet at the museum with one of the world's premiere historians on computing devices.

Dr. Oskar Miklos was of Greek origin, but had grown up in France, where he studied at the Sorbonne. He was fluent in English, French, Greek and German and had completed his doctoral degree at Cornell University. After finishing his studies, he had returned to Europe to find his niche in Athens, studying Roman, Greek and Egyptian antiquities. His expertise on computing began with the Sumerian abacus and comprised a wealth of knowledge on everything leading up to the latest super computer, known as "The Big Brain."

Max checked his cell phone for the time as he approached on 83rd Street. He was fifteen minutes late as he pushed through the entrance to the museum. In the main foyer, he felt transported, as if he had walked onto the set of Sesame Street. Large, overgrown toys were positioned about the main room, all of them the colors of a crayon box. A large green dragon stretched across the floor, its arms propped beneath its plastic head as if it were listening to a riveting conversation.

Max glanced around and spotted Miklos across the room. The doctor wasn't hard to miss, since he was the only adult not playing chaperone to the many young visitors running about.

At sixty-eight, Miklos was homelier than he appeared in the photos Max had found of him online. His hair, which had always been jet black, had transformed and was now a yellowish gray. In addition, he was twenty pounds heavier than he appeared in his online profile. From a distance, he looked slightly younger than the photo Max had seen, but his skin upon close inspection was deeply etched with lines of sun damage and age.

Dr. Miklos was speaking on his cell phone in a very animated fashion. Max could see he was irritated as he rattled off staccato words in his native Greek. He suspected the doctor's salty demeanor was due to his own tardiness, which gave him a moment of pause. In Max's esteem, a delay of fifteen or twenty minutes was acceptable, even for first-time appointments. He approached, interrupting Miklos' phone conversation.

"Dr. Miklos? I'm Max. Battenberg."

Dr. Miklos forced a smile as he quickly ended his conversation. Sliding the cell phone into his pocket, he turned to Max with an empty, regal smile. "Monsieur Battenberg." Dr. Miklos glanced ever so briefly at his watch.

"I know I'm a bit late."

Dr. Miklos frowned to let Max know that twenty minutes was hardly a bit. "Please. Let me show you to the device." Even though he didn't work for the museum, Dr. Miklos turned on his heels and marched from the room as if he owned it.

"How was your trip, Doctor Miklos?"

"Somewhat long. Crossing the Atlantic in this direction is always tedious."

"True." An awkward silence stretched as Max searched his mind for pleasantries. Instead, he decided the doctor didn't merit his politeness. He knew Miklos had been summoned by the offices of Battenberg Industries. Probably, he wasn't too pleased for the inconvenience it had caused in his normal routine.

With no further conversation, the doctor led Max through a series of foyers and corridors until they reached a door with "No Admittance" posted on it. Miklos pulled a keycard from the inner pocket of his jacket and swiped it to open the door. Together they crossed into a private curator's room, after which Miklos turned and snapped the deadbolt shut behind them.

A large Plexiglas box was sitting on a table in the center of the room. Featured inside was the device Max had been seeking. The Antikythera Mechanism was both beautiful and elegant. To the untrained eye, it appeared to be a clock with exposed, shiny metal gears that were either brass or solid gold. A chill immediately ran down Max's spine and the hair on his arms and neck stood at attention.

Dr. Miklos went to a desk by the wall as if looking for something, which gave Max a chance to examine the device. On the face of it, deep grooves etched out what appeared to be a map. Max thought it was a representation of the globe, but as he approached he realized it was much more than that. He could see what appeared to be the sun at the center of the face with dozens of longitudinal and latitudinal lines that ricocheted back and forth.

Another plate was attached on top of the face with at least a hundred different shapes and symbols. It was a map of the sun, planets and stars and it appeared that it wasn't just one solar system, but many. Max surmised that the device functioned like a clock. When the gears ticked forward, the symbols would likely rotate in formation around the collection of suns.

"So, this is it?" Max said as Miklos turned around.

If Miklos had seemed annoyed earlier, he was smiling now. "Voilà the mechanism, Monsieur Battenberg. Normally, it is housed in the fourth floor exhibit they call Gods, Myths and Mortals. Today, however, it is being cleaned."

Max reached out and touched the Plexiglas box protecting the mechanism. He gazed more closely at the strange symbols. "Some of those are zodiac signs, aren't they?"

Nodding his head, Miklos continued, "Are they not phenomenal?" Miklos may not have been enthused to cross the Atlantic for a Battenberg, but the Antikythera Mechanism clearly rejuvenated him. "As you can see the device is quite unique, in particular because it dates back thousands of years, certainly before any such technology ever existed. So they say."

Max hated to admit it, but, up close, he was just as mesmerized as Miklos by the device. "Who do they think built it?"

The doctor frowned, but it quickly morphed into a laugh. "There is quite a bit of speculation on that, Monsieur Battenberg. Certainly, we Greeks have taken responsibility for its manufacture. It was found off the coast of Greece, after all. But then there are those who suggest alien technology was used to construct it."

Max laughed at the notion. "Okay." He was strangely drawn to the device, and actually felt electrified by its presence. He peered more closely, nearly pressing his face against the Plexiglas. "How does it work?"

"Certainly, you are aware it doesn't work, Monsieur?"

Max stood at attention, taken aback by the comment. "What do you mean it doesn't work?"

"Well, everyone is aware, the mechanism is missing a crucial piece. A gear essential for its function."

"But, Doctor Miklos, I would hardly have arranged for you to come all this way to show me a device which serves no purpose. This is useless then?"

A smile twisted onto the doctor's lips. "Hardly, Monsieur, hardly. The device, the Antikythera Mechanism, is one of our world's most important finds. Surprisingly, there are only a few who know this. I figured you to be one of them when I was told you wanted to meet."

Max was still dumbfounded by the news. "So, how do we find the missing piece?"

"If only we knew the answer to this question," Miklos explained. "If the mechanism were operational, I promise it would change the face of the world as we know it. Some presume it capable of unlocking cosmic knowing."

Max could feel his spirits waning. He had no idea what "cosmic knowing" even meant. "And no one's tried to manufacture the missing piece?"

"Sadly, today's technology barely makes a scratch at understanding a device thousands of years old. I'm afraid building this piece is out of the realm of anyone's expertise. Alien theory doesn't seem so fantastical now, does it?"

Max and Miklos had switched places in their disposition. Now, it was Max who was annoyed.

"Well, you're the expert. What do you suggest we do?"

"There are rumors. Stories of the Illuminati or the Knights Templar. Some even say the piece lies hidden in an alternate dimension, so as to prevent the device's misuse. The Bermuda Triangle and other such nonsense." Dr. Miklos toyed with Max, teasing him with his knowledge. "Others say the Knights Templar were as careful in hiding this piece as they were in secreting away Christianity's beloved Ark of the Covenant. A theory that I suspect is quite more likely is the element is buried deep within the earth. Are you familiar with Oak Island, Monsieur Battenberg? It's a small land mass off the coast of Nova Scotia. If I had to bet, I would say this is the location of the missing piece. In the Money Pit."

CHAPTER 4

On the grassy knoll of the Money Pit, Brigitte and Otto were in panic mode, trying desperately to come up with an action plan.

"What's going on?!" Brigitte screamed. "Why isn't he coming up?"

To Brigitte and Otto's horror, the motor intended to lift Max out of the pit was running, but the grinding sound had resumed as the cable fought back against it. The metal line grated on the hoist's aluminum spool, causing the entire assembly to smoke.

There was no doubt Otto was too distracted by Brigitte. Already she was hysterical, making it difficult for him to think. Trying to gather himself, Otto spoke into the microphone.

"Max, are you there? Max!" Otto turned to the captain and his crew. "One of you needs to get down there. Now!"

Max was now five feet under water and sixty feet from the surface. A sense of panicked confusion clouded his judgment, leaving him utterly disoriented. Fortunately, Max wasn't completely without air. There were oxygen bubbles gurgling into his mask, but he would cough and sputter with each attempt to breathe them.

The watery prison was murky, salty and terribly cold. Seawater continued to flood his mask until the air bubbles provided absolutely no advantage. Max knew if he didn't regain his wits, his life would end right there in the Money Pit. In a moment of clarity, he reached down and shut off power to the hoist. Fumbling with the cable and hose, he tried to coax a breath from inside. He managed one inhalation, but the tube locked up, preventing him from exhaling. Max blew the air out into the water, then tried to see through its murkiness.

The platform that wasn't supposed to be there was holding firmly in place. Max felt around with his hands, trying to ascertain exactly where it had closed, hoping maybe to pry it open again. To his dismay, he perceived something he had hoped never to experience. His heartbeat slowed, a result of oxygen-deprived blood. Max knew it wouldn't be long before his already clouded vision would be completely gone.

At this point, a surprising sense of calm overcame him, and he abandoned his struggle with the oak ceiling. For an instant, he floated freely in the water illuminated by the lights on his head and chest.

The walls of the pit seemed perfectly contoured and unusually smooth. Max marveled at their perfection in a wondrous way. Just when his vision began to falter he noticed it—a small, seemingly insignificant imperfection. The flaw shone like a diamond embedded in the walls around it.

Max's vision blurred. His limbs felt heavy, like he was swimming in maple syrup. He pushed himself, drawn by the tiny spot on the wall. Unable to distinguish it by sight, he ran his hands across the walls until he caught the tiny flaw with his fingers. He pushed and pulled at the tiny point, digging his fingers into it. With each second, time seemed to slow, as if he were being frozen by Medusa's cold and magical stare.

Awareness of his body and the pit were now gone. Instead of the thick, syrup-like consistency, the water now felt like clouds buffering him in the air. With only a glimmer of life left in his body, he was still clawing at the tiny point on the wall. Finally, it gave way and pushed through like a doorbell.

For a brief instant, his body floated motionless, his five senses withdrawing into numbness. Just as the oak platform had closed above him, the mysterious Money Pit now offered a new twist. A hidden door directly to his right snapped open into a secret chamber. The sheer force of the water pushed Max inside as if he were being flushed away.

His limp, nearly lifeless body fell to the chamber floor as water swiftly drained from the room. Max, barely conscious, drew in a breath, his first cough erupting into many. He coughed and choked, gasping for air as he spat water from his lungs. Lost in a daze, he gulped air, completely unaware of Otto and Brigitte, who were both screaming into the receiver embedded in the mask on top of his head.

"Max, are you there? Max, can you hear me?"

With each breath, Max could feel consciousness returning to his limbs. His legs tingled as his vision slowly came into focus. Finally, his voice returned, broken and exhausted.

"Yes, Otto, I'm here. I can hear you."

"What's going on?" Otto demanded.

Winded, Max sucked in the stale air of the hidden chamber. "I told you one of those oak platforms closed."

For a moment there was radio silence on Otto's side. "I don't get it. They were supposed to have been removed."

"Otto, the thing is booby trapped. Something else opened up. I'm in some kind of room."

Fumbling sounds came over the microphone and then Brigitte's voice came on line. "Max, will you fuckin' get up here already? Please!"

Having gathered himself, Max glanced at the chamber surrounding him. In some ways, it felt like a cave, but he could see that it had been constructed similar to the Money Pit. Like a jail cell, it was a perfect twelve-foot cube that had been carved from the island's bedrock. A few feet away, a surgically cut oak log with its bark still intact served as a makeshift pedestal.

"What the hell?"

The tree stump must have come from a mature oak. It was three feet tall and nearly four feet in diameter. On top of it sat a single ornate box. A chill ran up Max's spine.

"Max!" Brigitte's voice was urgent. "Do you hear me? Max?"

"I hear you fine, Bridge. You're not going to believe this, but there's a secret chamber down here." Max could hear the microphone being fumbled once more.

"Max, it's Otto. What do you mean, a secret chamber?"

"It's some kind of room. And there's a box!" Max felt giddy with excitement. "It's on top of this tree stump."

"Max, I need you to listen carefully. It's important you don't touch anything. I'm sure the whole place is booby trapped."

Max stared in awe, mesmerized by the box. It was leather, but a series of symbols were embossed in an intricate design. Max had no idea how long the box had been in the chamber, but he assumed it had been a long time, perhaps thousands of years. There wasn't a speck of dust on it, as if the room had been sealed airtight.

"Did you hear me, Max? Promise you won't touch anything. Soon as we get you up here, we'll send a team down to retrieve it."

Max could feel blood pumping through his veins. He was alive. He hadn't drowned, and the very thing he had come for was possibly staring him in the face.

"I'm serious, Max."

Brigitte and Otto were fighting over the microphone. Max had to smile. After some fumbling, her voice came on line mixed with sternness and fear. "Max, you're fuckin' starting to piss me off! Get up here and let Otto handle this!"

Otto's voice replaced Brigitte's in Max's ear. "I get the feeling you're going to do something stupid. I need you to check the pit and see if the log platform is still in place."

"Okay, calm down. I'm checking now." Max walked to the edge of the chamber, then gazed up. The log platform had disengaged and the way out of the pit was free and clear. "That's a negative. The platform's gone."

"If you're still tethered, you should come up now."

Max wanted to do as Otto and Brigitte were asking. He wanted out of the pit that had nearly taken his life, but he didn't trust the chamber. "I hear you guys, honestly I do. But what happens if this room closes up?"

"Dammit, Max," Otto exclaimed. "I'm coming down."

"Okay. Okay. I'm coming up. Just give me a sec." Max vacillated before returning one last time to the wooden pedestal. Something in his core told him this would be his one and only chance to capture the box. On a fanciful whim, he grabbed it.

Max didn't hear or see it coming: without warning a ton of water crashed into the room. The wave knocked the wind from his lungs as it swept him toward the rear of the chamber. As if in slow motion, Max saw the wall of solid rock rushing up before him. The crashing water propelled him forward until blackness overcame him.

Above ground, at the mouth of the pit, Otto and Brigitte stood waiting for the motor to engage and begin lifting Max from the hole. Instead, there was a rumble like a stomach growling deep within the earth. Everyone heard it, but no one had the slightest idea what had caused it.

"Max?" Otto questioned, but his voice was meager, close to cracking.

Otto shared a glance with Brigitte, at which point a huge plume of water exploded the lid off the Money Pit. Dirt, grass and a huge portion of the wooden platform flew through the air as a powerful geyser sprang forth.

Brigitte screamed at the top of her lungs, but her voice could not be heard over the intense roar of water gushing from the pit.

CHAPTER 5

*E*xactly six weeks before visiting the Money Pit, Max awoke in his bed in the city of Chicago. He'd been out drinking the previous night and was both tired and hung over. The outing had come at the spur of the moment after a last-minute invitation had arrived. Max, if anything, was spontaneous, a quality his close friends appreciated. Even though he didn't believe in the zodiac, he'd been told that spontaneity was a trademark of his birth sign, Sagittarius.

His original plan for the prior evening had been to pack for a trip to New Orleans, which was now only a few hours away. But the phone calls had rolled in with invitations to this party or that club. At first, Max had resisted with outright refusals. He even tried not answering his phone. But then Chandler had called with an irresistible proposal. It wasn't so much the event, which was exciting enough. But Chandler was enormous fun, and he and Max had only recently become friends.

The friendship had come about in a very unexpected way. For more than a year, Max had been the functioning president of Badem Publications, one of his father's many companies. The job had come after an array of internship samplings in different Battenberg corporations. With some frustration, his father had finally questioned him about his life and what he planned to do with it. Max ultimately chose to work with Badem Publications.

For nearly sixteen months, he had been responsible for the circulation of several popular gossip and entertainment magazines. Max knew his father wasn't thrilled by his lack of ambition. If Demetrius had had his way, Max would have stepped up for a position in Battenberg Industries, the parent company. Max knew Demetrius was patiently waiting for him to come around and succeed to the Battenberg throne.

As it turned out, Badem Publications had proven more difficult to run than Max anticipated. With his father's urging, he had hired Chandler Paul as Vice President of Operations. He and Chandler had gotten along swimmingly well. In just a few months, Chandler had become a true friend, which didn't come easily in Max's world. Because he was a Battenberg, scores of people wanted to be his friend, but very few actually were.

As far as Max was concerned, hiring Chandler had been a win-win situation. He had a great friend as well as a fantastic vice president. Chandler's publishing world pedigree was impeccable. In a relatively short time, he had worked his way up to editor in one of Manhattan's well-known publishing houses. Without a doubt, he had proven himself an asset to the industry. His presence at Badem Publications allowed Max to play without fear that he might let Demetrius down.

He and Chandler had partied the night before, and now Max was paying the price. He was both hung over and completely unprepared for a flight that was less than six hours away.

Max yawned and stretched, nestled in the sheets of his luxurious sleigh bed. The spacious, contemporary bedroom was painted completely white with high-end furnishings of similar shades. Everything, including the bed, was positioned to offer a spectacular view of a glass-enclosed courtyard.

As intended by the designer, Max laid back and gazed at the atrium that was landscaped as a Japanese garden. There were perfectly trimmed bonsai trees inside and a fountain with moss-covered stones. Max found it a relaxing sight as always, and his aching head pounded slightly less from the view.

Suddenly, his phone's ringtone jarred him back from his daydream. Max flopped across the bed to answer it. It had to be Brigitte checking to make sure he was on schedule for their trip. But upon grabbing the phone, Max noticed the name "Battenberg Industries" flashing across the screen. A sinking feeling overcame him as he pondered whether or not to answer. Of all the interruptions he could have received, his father's office was the most problematic. A call from Battenberg Industries could easily derail his trip.

Deep down he wanted to press "ignore," but his father's hold over him was terribly potent, just as it had been when he was a child. The father-son dynamic sometimes left Max feeling trapped, as if his mother had delivered him from her womb, cut the umbilical cord and then tossed him into his father's clutches. No matter how fervently he squirmed and twisted, he only found himself more entangled in Demetrius Battenberg's web.

Once again, the opportunity was presenting itself for Max to break away and define his independence. In the past, regardless how he tried, he felt incapable of defiance or disobedience of any kind. Even now, there was a lingering innate need in him to prove he was the perfect and pleasing son. But there was a catch, perhaps a vicious cycle: No matter how hard he strived or how well he performed, Demetrius never truly seemed pleased.

Max stared at the phone, listening to its ringtone: "The Star Wars Cantina," from the bar scene of the original "Star Wars" movie. He had downloaded it a few weeks earlier, and people laughed whenever they heard it. But Max wasn't laughing now.

He knew the call was seconds away from voice mail, but answering could prove deadly for his trip. *It's friggin' Saturday morning.* Crumbling like a house of cards as the final chord played, he answered. His father's assistant was on the line.

"Mr. Battenberg, it's Rosalee."

Max sighed rudely into the phone. Before Rosalee even finished, he knew answering had been a mistake. Aware of the passive-aggressive gaffe, he cleared his throat and softened. "Hi, Rosalee, how're you?" It was unintended, but the words came out phony and insincere.

"Very well, thank you," Rosalee replied without skipping a beat. "Your father has requested your presence at the penthouse this morning. Can you be here at 11 a.m. sharp?"

Max checked the time; it was just after 10 a.m. He waited for Rosalee to ask if the time was convenient, but he wasn't surprised when she didn't. His father was after all Demetrius Battenberg, head of Battenberg Industries, often referred to in the media as "billionaire," "mogul" or "tycoon."

Most thought Max fortunate to have entered the world in such a family. But along with the wealth and fame came a sense of pressure and responsibility. Sometimes, there was even danger. He never admitted it publicly, but sometimes Max found it was a burden living up to his name.

His father could easily have rested on the laurels of the legacy name but such behavior was out of character. Every bit the alpha male personality, Demetrius had developed the Midas touch at an early age. While still in his twenties, he had parlayed several of the family businesses into a formidable empire.

Battenberg Industries served as an umbrella company that oversaw the operations of two lesser-known banks, a collection of financial investment firms, the media-publishing corporation

Badem, several fossil fuel companies, and a pharmaceutical development company. Max had dabbled in several subsidiaries hoping to pacify Demetrius, who wanted to identify whether or not Max had any of his sharp business acumen. Results of these tests were still inconclusive.

He lingered on the phone in silence just long enough to make the call seem awkward, but Rosalee didn't mind in the least. She was too competent to be rattled by innuendo or uncomfortable pauses.

"Mr. Battenberg, are you still there?"

"Yes, I'm here. Here's the thing, I'm flying out of town in a few hours. If this meeting's not going to happen, I'd rather we do it another day."

"I've slotted 11 a.m. for you and your father to meet. I'm afraid that's the best I can do for now. Unless I learn to predict the future, that is."

Max didn't know if Rosalee intended her sarcasm to be humorous, but he didn't find it funny. "Can you do me a favor and let him know I need to be out of there by one at the latest?"

"Certainly, Mr. Battenberg."

Max clicked off the phone, painfully aware that his morning had suffered an unfavorable blow. He knew well that his father honored no one's schedule but his own. Eleven a.m. could easily mean noon, 1 p.m. or even "I'm sorry you waited three hours but we need to reschedule." If Max wasn't careful, if he allowed it, he would likely miss his flight to New Orleans. He leapt from bed and phoned Brigitte about the detour.

"Hello," Brigitte sang into the phone.

"You're not going to believe it—"

"Your father called." Brigitte and Max had been together long enough. She understood quite well how the family worked.

"Pretty good, Sturdivant. I may need you to bring a few of my things. Just depends if I get hung up at my dad's."

"Max, you haven't packed? You said you were gonna pack last night."

After a moment's hesitation Max continued. "I was going to when Chandler called. He talked me into a drink."

"You always say you're staying home and then you end up going out."

It wasn't unusual for Brigitte to hunt for explanations or reassur-
ances. But today, there was no time for a discussion, in particular
since Max answered to no one but Demetrius.

"If you don't hear from me in the next hour or so, it'd be great
if you could just pack a few of my things over there. Not sure what
my dad wants, but hopefully we can meet at the airport if I don't
make it home in time."

"Okay, okay, I guess I'll see you at the airport then."

Max could hear the displeasure in Brigitte's voice, but he didn't
have time to coddle her. After hanging up, he quickly showered and
dressed in preparation for the meeting.

$\mathcal{D}$emetrius Battenberg's main home and the head offices of Battenberg Industries were both located in one of the world's tallest skyscrapers, the Chicago Spire. The 150-story building, designed by renowned Spanish architect Santiago Calatrava, had swiftly become one of Chicago's architectural marvels. The glass tower twisted into the sky like a huge obelisk whose sides had been contorted to form a giant screw.

Had his father wanted the top floors of the Spire, he could easily have had them. But security dictated otherwise, especially in the years since 9/11. The offices, which were often referred to as the penthouse, were technically located on the 96th, 97th and 98th floors.

Max had arrived punctually, minutes before the appointed meeting time of 11 a.m. Already he'd been waiting forty minutes in a lounge on the 98th floor. He glanced at the current time on his phone. Just as he suspected, his father was nowhere in sight.

Max stood and paced, repeatedly running a hand through his hair. With each tick of the clock, his naturally easygoing demeanor was eroding into agitation. He crossed to the window, glancing once more at the time. As he stared through the glass he had the distinct feeling of gazing through an airplane window. Although he wasn't at the top of the building, the streets were nearly two thousand feet below.

On the ground, people rushed about on foot, in cars, or on public transportation. All of them were going about the daily events of their lives. This is all Max wanted, to go on with his life. Without thinking, he chewed nervously at the cuticles of his left hand. He felt like a caged animal trapped in a luxury suite on this infernal floor.

Later that evening, the Big Easy's festivities would begin. Max, in his twenty-four-year-old wisdom, didn't want to be late. It was barely noon and Fat Tuesday was officially only three days away. As he stood waiting, an onslaught of childhood feelings overcame him. Demetrius had always made him feel weak, like the consummate underachiever. Max wondered if others saw him as he feared, as a pariah or as the black sheep of the Battenberg clan.

By grade school, Max had already become aware of the "not

good enough" dynamic. He never brought home the trophies or the grades that Demetrius thought dignified the Battenberg name. Secretly, he hoped puberty would bring about the needed change, as if a switch could be flipped, allowing the overachiever gene to kick in. But Max's hormonal changes had only led to more disappointment. Despairingly, he had turned his hopes to future rites of passage such as high school and college. At some point, he hoped he would graduate into the son Demetrius wanted him to be.

Of course Demetrius had no clue that Max, in typical fashion, had arranged and paid for his friends' travel to and accommodations in New Orleans. It was something he did at least once each year, indulging a group of friends by flying them, all expenses paid, to a party somewhere on the globe. In his mind, the generosity made sense, especially given that he had the deepest pockets of the bunch.

A year earlier, the destination had been Munich's Oktoberfest, but the trip had turned out a failure. Everyone had arrived just a day in advance of the festival, and as a result, any chance of enjoyment was destroyed by jet lag. This year, Max and friends agreed it was best to either remain closer to home or in the same time zone if possible. The consensus had been Mardi Gras in New Orleans. Now, because of Demetrius, Max was in danger of missing his own event.

He fought to remain calm, but found himself growing increasingly perturbed. Why, he asked himself, was he still allowing Demetrius to govern his life? With a deep exhale he fell onto his father's white, forty-thousand-dollar couch. From there he glanced about the room at various sculptures and artwork.

Suddenly, Max remembered a childhood game. Just as on the game show "The Price Is Right," he used to appraise the value of items within his line of sight. Several pieces in his father's art collection made the imported sofa's price tag seem like a bargain. Max recalled when *Architectural Digest* ran an issue featuring the offices of Battenberg Industries. Millions of copies sold, with anxious eyes trying to catch a glimpse of how those at the top lived.

Already Max was mulling over Plan B in his mind. If he missed his friends and the afternoon plane, chances were he could board a later flight. In the worst case, he could attempt commandeering one of his father's private jets. But neither of these plans was ideal. He had organized a group excursion and that's how he wanted to arrive, in a group.

Max began pacing. He would glance at the time, get up from his father's pricey designer couch and cross to the wall of windows. After gazing out across Chicago he would return to sit on the couch. He had already repeated the ritual at least three times before becoming aware of it.

Each time Demetrius kept him waiting, Max tried to rationalize that his father was an extremely important man. Running Battenberg Industries was an all-encompassing job, but Demetrius' casual disregard for his time only stirred up childhood resentments. During today's internal struggle, Max heard the lounge door opening. A sense of relief washed over him until he turned to spot Rosalee standing in the doorway.

"I'm sorry, Mr. Battenberg, your father's running a tad bit late."

Max glanced at his phone, not to read the time but more to demonstrate he was in a hurry. "You have any idea how much longer he'll be?" He tried to deliver the question without annoyance, but his agitation nevertheless came through.

"It's difficult to say."

Rosalee's response was dry and unapologetic. At the end of the day, it was Demetrius Battenberg who made people wait. For this reason, Rosalee was not only accustomed, she was impervious to the hints and clues used to illustrate impatience.

Max awaited further explanation of how long he might have to wait, but none came.

"Would you like something to drink while you wait, Mr. Battenberg?"

"No, but thanks for asking."

Max had only seen Rosalee once before, as she had recently been hired. He sized her up as she stood in the doorway. He figured she might be Latina, or Italian perhaps.

She was extremely corporate in a well-fitted maroon, pinstripe business suit. Her skirt was hemmed just above the knee and the jacket cropped at the waist. Rosalee's hair was thick and lustrous, and a deep shade of brown, but she completely downplayed her beauty. Her tresses were neatly tied in a bun, but they were somewhat frizzy around the edges, as she abstained from using lots of product. From what Max could tell, she also avoided makeup, although she was maybe wearing lipstick.

"I'll remind him you're waiting, Mr. Battenberg."

Realizing she didn't have to remind Demetrius of anything, Max offered Rosalee a genuine smile. As fast as she had arrived, his father's first assistant turned and disappeared from the doorway.

Max crossed once again to the wall of windows to take in the spectacular view of Chicago. As one of the world's tallest buildings, the Spire could easily be seen from miles away like a giant dagger stabbing into the sky. The construction marvel made the next tallest building appear like a weed to a tree. The Spire soared toward the heavens, challenging any surrounding structure to a duel in its race for the stars.

Considering the Spire's architectural bravado, Max found it perfectly fitting that his tycoon father lived and worked there. In his mind, skyscrapers like the Spire were the new and improved castles of the twenty-first century, which meant logically that Demetrius was the king and Max his princely heir to the throne.

This, however, seemed a mere fantasy at the moment. Just as Max was preparing to give up hope of the meeting, his father swept into the lounge.

"Max!"

"Hey, pops." Although he didn't mean to, Max glanced at his watch, relieved to now know that he would likely make it to the airport with time to spare.

Demetrius stepped to hug his son, but instead offered a quick pat on the shoulder. He waved Max toward the couch. "Have a seat."

Max thought about his father's aloof nature as they sat. As a young child he had observed Demetrius' stiff body language, but it was only in the last years that he had found the words to articulate how it made him feel, both distant, disconnected and sometimes unloved.

Demetrius smiled at his son before launching into why he had invited him. "I was told you're in a hurry, so I'll cut to the chase. This morning I got a call from my chief of security. He reported 'questionable circumstances.' I think that's the term he used." Demetrius noticed Max perk up. "I need you to be hyper-vigilant unless you're here or at home."

Max listened more intently to his father, suddenly interested in what he had to say and feeling foolish for having been so annoyed. "What's he mean by 'questionable'?"

"Probably nothing. Every week, schemes are hatched in which we're targets. The majority are pipe dreams or what-if scenarios. But every now and again there's one with merit. That's when we're put on notice."

"So what are we talking, Hades or Poseidon?"

Demetrius seemed impressed by Max's mention of the Greek gods. "I didn't realize you still remembered that. It's not Hades. Poseidon at most."

Max remembered the mythological code names quite well. Demetrius had devised them after the deaths of Max's mother and brother, Fiona and Christian. The coded alerts were similar to the Pentagon's DEFCON classification, only with three levels of importance rather than five.

"Zeus," the king of the gods, referred to order and control, indicating all was well with the family's safety and security.

"Poseidon," on the other hand, the god of the seas, was code for the sinking feeling incurred when there were compromises to the Battenbergs' well-being.

And finally, there was "Hades," the god of death and war, brother to Zeus and Poseidon. When in effect, "Hades" meant no Battenberg was to stray from a Battenberg property. Even with this control, there were only a few locales considered secure enough for appropriate shelter.

Max remembered only a few instances when Hades had been implemented: once or twice before the deaths of his mother and brother, and again for several weeks immediately following the accident that claimed their lives. Naturally, Demetrius had suspected foul play, but the investigation had proven otherwise. The car accident had been just that.

On the fateful day, he was six years old and his brother, Christian, had just turned nine. For the summer, their mother, Fiona, had accompanied both boys to a vacation villa in the hills of Aix-en-Provence in the south of France.

At the last minute, her brother, the boys' Uncle Charles, had decided to join them in Aix. In her excitement, Fiona had driven from the villa to the airport to pick up her brother instead of sending a driver. Christian, who awoke early that day, had asked if he could tag along. They'd peeked in on Max, but he was sleeping so soundly that she didn't dare disturb him.

Because it was a gorgeous day, Fiona had grabbed keys to the convertible. The little Peugot was extremely fast and Fiona was an expert driver. She knew exactly at what speeds the car would skid and kept the speedometer just below that threshold. When Max was in the car he would often laugh and giggle as she cornered the narrow, European streets of Aix. For him, it was like a roller coaster ride with his mom at the controls.

Upon their return from the airport, Fiona had crashed. Had the car not been convertible, there might have been a chance of survival. But the area was mountainous with narrow streets winding all the way up to the villa. Fiona's car had tumbled off an embankment, killing everyone.

It was less than an hour later that the nanny pulled Max from bed, rambling about an accident. In his haze, and because he was only six, he hadn't fully understood. The previous night he had drifted off to sleep with no clue that he'd never see his mother and brother again, not to mention the added loss of his Uncle Charles.

In desperation, the nanny had tried for hours without success to get Demetrius on the phone. The following morning, she'd rushed Max back to Chicago flanked by a security detail.

From that day on, Max was anxious. At the tender age of six, Demetrius was all he had. Paranoia had struck him that, as Fiona had done, his father could leave and never return. His fear, of course, further impacted the father-and-son dynamic since Demetrius didn't respect weakness or timidity. As the years carried on, the father grew to resent a son who was in every way still nothing more than a child.

News of this latest Poseidon alert evoked childhood memories in Max. In a peculiar reversion he found himself looking to Demetrius for reassurance or for affirmation that everything would be okay. Instead, Demetrius smirked. All too familiar with his father's ticks, Max knew what his dad was thinking. *He thinks I'm scared. He thinks I'm weak.*

The elder Battenberg continued, "I think you know these threats are typically about me. The chance someone will come after you isn't impossible, but it's slim. Sometimes, the Battenberg name is all they need. In any event, I'm sending a detail to your house to ensure your security measures are up to par."

"It's okay if I leave town, right? I'm on a plane to New Orleans in a few hours."

"Should be fine. But I'd keep my ear close to the ground if I were you. Be aware things could go to Hades at any moment. You'll be the first to know if that happens."

Demetrius studied his son's face, trying to confirm if the seriousness of the message was registering. Max's expression was tinged with concern, leaving Demetrius unsure if he was impressed or displeased by what seemed to be his son's discomfort.

"What's in New Orleans?"

"Mardi Gras."

Demetrius remained poker faced, but Max assumed there was disapproval behind the steely demeanor. His father found his lifestyle less than ambitious.

"Be extra careful. You'll be out of your element there."

After hours of obsessing about being late, Max felt a rush of mixed emotions. Now confident that he would make his flight, he realized he was happy to be in his father's presence. Demetrius was a devoted businessman who worked constantly and was nearly impossible to nail down. From what Max could tell, he was in a surprisingly good mood. Suddenly, he felt grateful for a few stolen moments of his father's time.

But the elder Battenberg wasn't one for idle conversation. Demetrius stood. "I know you're in a hurry so I won't keep you. Have a safe trip. Remember Poseidon." Demetrius moved toward Max, but once again, thought better of hugging him. With another friendly pat on the shoulder, the elder Battenberg swept from the room, off to his next meeting.

A sense of relief settled over Max. He imagined it was how inmates felt when they received parole. With a deep exhale he hurried from the penthouse, rushing downstairs to retrieve his car. Within minutes he was racing across town, anxious to meet up with Brigitte and the rest of his friends. In just a few hours they would be in New Orleans.

CHAPTER 7

*I*t had taken time, but the Big Easy had finally recovered from Hurricane Katrina. Now, some years later, a different kind of flooding had returned, a happy variety. A sea of people undulated through the streets in both elaborate and scant Mardi Gras costumes.

Interspersed on every block were huge tractor-trailers, each of them brightly decorated as parade floats. The one nearest to Max had the head of a court jester built around the cab. Max could barely see the driver sitting inside of the jester's huge smile, which had been built over the windshield. The truck slowly edged forward as a crowd of masqueraders partied on the makeshift dance floor enclosed on the flatbed in the rear.

Each float in the procession had huge speakers blasting music from the front or the rear or both. The volume was ear shattering. Depending on your position in the crowd, the music could be distinguished as separate and distinct. But it would also overlap in other areas into excruciating noise.

Thousands of partygoers paraded forward with tiny baby steps, which is all the crowded streets would allow. As was customary, any woman exposing her breasts was awarded by would-be admirers with strings of plastic beads. It was no wonder the well-endowed girls were much more decorated with the colorful plastic jewels.

Max and his friends, already quite drunk, were tightly wedged in the festive crowd. Too lazy to design full-blown costumes, Max and Brigitte had simply purchased elaborate masks. Perched over Max's face was a sunburst with rays of light built from bright yellow canary feathers. The actual faceplate of the mask was sprayed in gold paint with a design, very much like a motorcycle's visor. The smiling visage could be flipped to the top of Max's head to reveal his true face.

Brigitte's mask, a beautifully painted black and white Yin Yang symbol, sat snugly over her face. Unlike Max's mask, there was a somberness in her quick-fix costume.

In the streets of New Orleans, and anywhere else for that matter, Brigitte drew attention. Her brunette hair shone with auburn highlights in the late afternoon sun. Behind her back, girls swore it was a dye job, but it wasn't. Brigitte's beauty was completely au natural. With just a little lipstick and a touch of eyeliner, she always looked as if she had just left a photo shoot.

As the crowd pushed forward, Max and Brigitte were separated as if pulled apart by a human riptide. Somehow, they managed to remain within eyeshot of each other. Less than two yards behind Max, a group of frat boys spotted Brigitte and mistook her attention to Max as overtures toward them. Even with her face covered, her body was more than enticing. Two of the men yelled, holding up their plastic jewels for her to see.

For Brigitte, the beads were a badge of honor, and she intended to collect as many as possible. In a drunken stupor, she hollered at the top of her voice, "Woooohoo!" and pulled up her tank top to expose her perfectly shaped breasts. In a flash, the fraternity guys circumvented Max, and were navigating toward her through the crowd. They reached her, all smiles, and placed several strings of beads over her head. Brigitte looked at Max but was unable to catch his eye. Instead he was focused on the oddest masqueraders in the crowd.

A large man, roughly 6'4" in height and with a football player's build, was costumed in full Native American regalia. A headdress of eagle feathers sat atop his head and his face was decorated with war paint. His almost naked torso had a harness of leather straps tightly secured about him. Perched atop the man's right shoulder, a tiny midget appeared as if bursting from a boil in the larger man's skin.

Max was enthralled with the makeup job, which looked so real it was disturbing. The entire picture seemed grotesque, like a huge tumor had sprouted from the man's shoulder, giving birth to a sinister demonic presence. The midget, whose face seemed disfigured, turned toward Max, who looked away. Max assumed it was all makeup and special effects, but the scene was visceral, raw and macabre.

Looking around, Max noticed other partiers commenting on the amazing costume. He wasn't sure if it was the large man or the midget who had spoken, but he distinctly heard the word "Manitou." Max had once heard something on the term, which described a folkloric figure among Native Americans. Through amazing makeup, the large man and the midget had embodied the concept of a spirit literally sprouting from the body of its warrior host.

Brigitte was enthralled, watching Max's attention held captive by the strange duo. During this miniscule window of time, she had forgotten the young frat boys who had approached to offer her beads. One leaned in to kiss her neck, catching her off guard as he tried to remove her mask. Brigitte expertly turned her head, readjusting her mask. With no hard feelings, the young man placed another set of beads around Brigitte's neck. But he could hardly linger, as the horde of people drove him forward.

Turning, Brigitte finally caught Max's eye. He was a few feet away and had witnessed the last frat boy bestowing his affections upon her. Brigitte wished she could see Max's whole face, fearing there were looks of jealousy and disapproval behind his mask.

"Max! What's wrong?" she shouted.

He simply shook his head as the crowd jostled him to and fro. Afraid that it might ruin their mood, he hadn't fully revealed why his father had summoned him to the penthouse. The possibility that he, or even both of them, were in danger haunted him. But despite the warnings, Max remained intent on fully surrendering to the spirit of Mardi Gras. He had planned on a weekend of fun, even if the family's warning code, Poseidon, was trying to bend his mind with paranoia.

Brigitte presumed she had witnessed jealousy behind Max's mask. In truth, he was simply too ill at ease to let his hair down. Frowning beneath her own mask, she cut like a knife through the crowd and grabbed Max by the arm. "You're not jealous are you, babe?" Normally, she would have purred these words, but Brigitte was drunk and the crowd was extremely loud. Her otherwise sexy voice cracked from hours of incessant screaming.

Max shook his head no. He wasn't jealous. In fact, jealousy wasn't an emotion with which he was familiar. If the sentiment had been a person, jealousy would have been an acquaintance, someone Max had met once or twice, but had never gotten to know very well.

Throughout life, he had always attended the best schools and lived in the most expensive homes. The moment he was of age, he had also driven the best and most expensive cars. As Demetrius Battenberg's son, he had always been the child to be jealous of and had rarely experienced the sentiment himself on any kind of deep level.

Max had an infinite number of choices available to him in life. It didn't matter if he chose ambition or pretension; the world truly was his oyster. In nearly every aspect he'd been trained to be better, if not the best.

But there were inconveniences deep within Max's being. Intellectually, he understood he was unique, but he never felt superior to those around him. His down-to-earth demeanor was a quality he suspected Demetrius despised about him. He secretly feared that his ordinary nature was one of his deepest flaws.

Max presumed his daily feelings of inadequacy were the main reason for his many travels, to escape the pressures he felt being a Battenberg. There was a misconception that wealth eliminated stress, but Max knew this wasn't true. Money, of course, facilitated things, but it never provided simplicity. There were more toys, more trips, more cars, more houses and of course more problems. It all came at a high price of added pressure and responsibility.

Brigitte stared through her mask at Max in his. So far, they had been together a year. She knew, just like every other high society girl, that Max was a catch. To avoid any confusion she had asked if he was jealous and Max had said no. Even with his face hidden behind a mask, however, she could tell he was stiff and somehow uneasy.

Wanting to smooth things over, she removed her own mask and slid the sunburst mask to the top of his head. Then she kissed him. The truth, Brigitte thought, could never be veiled in a kiss.

Max kissed her softly back, but was unable to cover the paranoia and vulnerability he felt in the crowd. He didn't know if his father had intended it, but the Poseidon security alert was effectively ruining his mood.

Brigitte pulled away with incorrect conclusions bouncing around in her head. She assumed Max was irritated about the frat boys, which he wasn't. Unsure of how to soften the mood, she shoved her half empty hurricane glass in his face.

"Want some?"

He grabbed the glass and drank just as one of their friends, Ted Sanderson, made his way toward them in the crowd.

"Where'd you guys go?"

Max's demeanor softened, and Brigitte was uncertain if it was due to Ted's appearance or to the cocktail. Ted, while he was the same age as Max and Brigitte, was very different from the two. A freckly redhead, Ted had grown up in a working-class family who managed to send him to Yale, where he and Max had met. The two had gotten along well and had managed to keep in touch in the years since graduation.

Ted's face was pleasant and his body in some semblance of good shape. For the most part, he only worked out with high-tech computer equipment, or alcohol, or both. Without asking, Ted snatched Brigitte's hurricane glass from Max and drank from it.

"Dude," Ted screamed, elbowing Max in the side, "look at that!"

When Max turned, a pair of beautiful breasts were staring him in the face. The ample chest belonged to a busty brunette whose T-shirt had turned completely transparent with the large amounts of beer and hurricanes that had been poured over it.

Upon spotting the other brunette, Brigitte immediately felt threatened, even though Brigitte was a much prettier girl. Uncomfortable that she wasn't the center of attention, Brigitte grabbed her boyfriend by the arm.

"C'mon, let's go in here!"

Max turned to see a storefront lit up with a bright neon sign: *Indigo Blue, Psychic, Reader Of Tarot*. A look of disbelief spilled onto his face. "Are you serious?"

"It'll be fun."

Before either Max or Ted could respond, Brigitte pulled them through the crowd and away from the brunette with the wet T-shirt. After sidestepping more than a dozen people, they reached the shop and disappeared inside. Max stared at Ted with unspoken apologies as the door swung shut behind them.

For reasons no one understood, there was a striking change in ambiance. A surprising sense of peacefulness and calm pervaded, blocking out the sounds and insanity of the crowded streets outside. In some ways, it felt like they had traveled through a portal into a different universe.

In the back room, the store's owner and namesake, Indigo Blue, an ageless Creole woman who looked to be anywhere from early twenties to late thirties, rose from the table where she had been sipping a hot herbal infusion. Long, curly auburn hair, she had partially wrapped in a scarf, exploded down her back. Indigo knew someone had entered the front of her store, but when she turned to see, a wave of dizziness overcame her, prompting her to grip the table for stability.

For nearly three generations, her ancestors had closely guarded the special blend of herbs she had been sipping. The slightly bitter concoction contained traces of the hallucinogen peyote, and Indigo knew all too well that consuming large quantities could lead to the sight of things normally unseen.

With her hands gripping the table she waited, hoping to regain balance, but instead the opposite occurred. A wave of nausea overcame her, plunging her into a tailspin. Before she could sit, darkness shrouded her vision. Instead of fainting, which she expected, Indigo suddenly found her consciousness shooting through space with a multitude of celestial scenes rushing into view: stars, planets, meteors, all of them rushing by at lightning speeds.

Upon first instinct, she questioned her judgment, having ingested two cups of the family's secret elixir. Or maybe she had misjudged the recipe by adding too much peyote. Suddenly, from out of the black void a red planet came rushing into view. Indigo had seen photos of Mars, but this planet was different—larger, monstrous even, on a scale that rivaled Saturn or Jupiter.

Completely disoriented, she could no longer feel her feet on the ground or her hands grasping the table. The red planet came rushing ever closer into view. Indigo perceived herself entering the huge planet's atmosphere, and a burning sensation enveloped her as if singeing the skin from her body. The only solace in the agonizing pain was that Indigo could now sense her body once again, with her feet firmly planted on the ground.

In the front of the store, the room was filled with New Age paraphernalia: crystals, beads and various tarot cards. There was an eerie feeling about the establishment that Max couldn't put his finger on. He stared around the room, trying to figure out if it was the lighting or the way the room was painted. After a moment, he decided it was due to the quietude inside, especially compared to the complete chaos just outside the front door.

Ted considered where they were and laughed. "Dude, is this really what we want to be doing? The party's out there."

Max turned to Brigitte, but just as he was about to speak, Indigo burst through the door, still wobbling from the elixir.

Ted found Indigo's appearance startling. Only slightly shorter than Brigitte, she had a solid, semi-masculine build with broad shoulders and a well-defined musculature. A long, black bohemian dress draped down her body and was strangely offset by a royal blue bustier tightly corseted over it.

Ted tried whispering to Max, but was too intoxicated to keep his voice low. "Dude, is that a chick or a dude?"

Indigo spun toward him, tossing her hair to the side. "I am Indigo," she exclaimed. Her voice was husky, but with a deep sultriness to it. She clung to a bookshelf of knick-knacks like a drunk seeking balance. "Why have you come?" Indigo's eyes darted nervously back and forth as she scanned their faces. She laughed, then barked out, "Not one among you is what you seem."

The more Max studied Indigo, the more he believed Ted might be onto something. The medium was striking, but for a woman, her hands and shoulders were inordinately large. From afar, her face appeared elegant and intricately chiseled. Up close, her features were hard, angular and covered with heavy makeup.

Slowly regaining her wits, Indigo began moving like a lioness about the room. Something in her walk was stealthy and regal with hints of power. She approached Ted and studied him briefly before moving to Brigitte, at which point she instantly found herself spiraling again, swaying from side-to-side as if she were inebriated or in a trance.

Steadying herself, she grabbed Brigitte's hands in her own but tossed them aside a moment later. With her right hand she reached out gingerly toward Max, only to withdraw it an instant later as if she had been jolted by an electric shock. Max saw that Indigo began to breathe heavily and her hands started to tremble. Her eyes rolled back in her head and she stumbled back a step.

With renewed courage she lifted a hand once again toward Max and uttered in slow punctuated words, "It is you." When her eyes rolled forward again, there was a look of alarm on her face. She fixed her gaze on Max. "The disturbance is you."

Growing impatient, Ted mumbled, "This is a total buzz kill. Like we're in some crazy scene from 'Ghost.'"

Indigo glared at Ted, silencing him with her eyes. She grabbed hold of Max's hands and her body seemed to immediately convulse. She stumbled back, nearly falling against the wall. She laughed more from nervousness than anything else. "The cycle is ending. The end time for you and your kind draws near."

Ted looked at Max, incredulous. "What's she mean? Rich people."

Brigitte laughed out loud, but neither Max nor Indigo thought the joke was funny.

The ageless psychic, regaining her composure, studied Brigitte and Ted until she realized, "They have no idea."

Max immediately felt tension creeping up his shoulders. The same thing had occurred back at his father's penthouse after Poseidon and danger had been mentioned. "Know what?" Max grabbed Brigitte's hand and motioned to Ted. "C'mon, let's go."

Now steadier on her feet, Indigo moved toward the door almost as if she wanted to block it. She fixed her eyes on Max. "How is this possible?" Indigo studied Max, her eyes widening with astonishment. "You don't even know."

By now, Max was truly aggravated and turned to Brigitte in sarcasm, unable to mask his feelings. "Good call, babe, I'm glad we did this."

With their mood now completely wrecked, an intoxicated Brigitte grew defensive. "I'm sorry. When Marilyn and I went back home it was fun. I just thought..."

Indigo turned, interrupting Brigitte. "Understand this, ma belle. What we provide is truth, not fun."

This time, there was no mistaking that Indigo had firmly planted herself as a barrier to the exit. She glared at Ted and Brigitte. "Neither of you has the slightest idea what you're dealing with." Indigo sneered at Brigitte, "Trust me, you have been deceived." She pointed at Max. "This man is neither who nor what you think he is. If you have the slightest, even most petite notion of what's good for you, I suggest you walk away." Indigo stepped away from the door. "Go on. Leave. Run as fast and far as you can." Indigo spun around to Ted. "That goes for you too, mon cher. Such a friend will bring nothing but grief. To you both."

Indigo's words stung Max. Hours earlier, at his father's penthouse, feelings of insecurity had already been stirred, and now a complete stranger was calling into question his friendship and integrity. Max wondered how he had become this woman's target. He raised his voice in anger. "That's enough!"

Brigitte jumped, never having heard Max speak with such force.

"We'd appreciate if you'd step aside so we can be on our way."

Smiling defiantly, Indigo stepped back into the doorway to block their path. "Such cruelty and domination. Fortunately, the cycle is ending." Indigo, her face painted with a sneer of disgust, turned to address Max more specifically. "Greed for money, power and control, all of it diminishes. It is very near that we shall see the end — la fin! And then your kind will retreat into nothingness."

Losing patience, Max barreled past Indigo. She stumbled into the door, grabbing hold of his wrist to regain her balance. Clutching his hand she continued, her confidence growing. "I sense an error in you. A fault." It didn't seem possible, but Indigo was growing more animated, more confident. "Should you desire, you can bring all of it down, the entire house of cards."

Max yanked his hand from her grip. As he ripped open the front door, the sound of Mardi Gras festivities rushed into the room.

In her deep voice, Indigo screamed over the parade of people outside. "When the time comes, you must fight! Bring about their downfall."

Max pulled Ted and Brigitte into the procession of partiers while Indigo stood in the doorway screaming.

"Distance yourselves from him." Her face pleaded with Ted and Brigitte. "He must do this alone!" At which point, her voice was completely drowned out by the crowd.

Ted and Brigitte glanced back as Max led them deeper into the parade. Indigo was still screaming, but her voice was obliterated by the music blasting from nearby floats. Finally, the psychic fell still, but remained in her doorway watching them depart into the horde. A look of peace and sadness settled on her face as she turned and disappeared back into her building.

The experience was a first for Max and Ted. Unlike Brigitte, neither had ever visited a psychic, nor did they believe in paranormal abilities. But Indigo's antics had rattled them all, leaving each of them off kilter in completely different ways.

$\mathcal{M}$ax was still angry as he shuffled into the procession of partygoers with Ted and Brigitte. Turning, he yelled to Ted over the crowd. "There's something off about that woman."

Ted's face twisted with consternation. "That weren't no woman, chief!"

Feeling guilty that the botched detour had been her idea, Brigitte took a moment to regroup. With their masks still atop their heads, she leaned in to kiss Max's cheek. "I'm sorry," she screamed over the music, "that was totally my fault."

"A psychic drag queen? What the fuck is that?"

A smile flickered on Brigitte's face. "I'm sorry, you guys, I didn't know." Putting on her best puppy-dog face, she continued, "You have to believe I didn't know."

Ted spit out a laugh. "Dude, that's a tough one. You definitely gotta buy drinks to make up for that."

It was clear that Max was still pissed. "Fuck that bitch, telling you guys to run from me. Who the fuck does that? I don't even know her, or him or whatever."

Ted lowered his voice to imitate Indigo. "You must fight them! Bring about their downfall."

"You can't run around saying shit like that. It's slander or defamation. And not that I would, but I should sue her ass."

There was a good chance Brigitte was the most inebriated of the group, but even she was losing her buzz. "C'mon, babe, what're you talking about? We're in frickin' Louisiana for Chrissakes. You have to expect it's going to be a little out there."

At the end of the day, Max knew Indigo's words were of little consequence, but the psychic had bruised his ego. Very few dared speak negatively of a Battenberg out loud, and Max was unaccustomed to it.

Brigitte grabbed hold of his hand and made a silly expression, scrunching up her face and crossing her eyes. Like Ted, she mimicked Indigo's husky, sultry voice. "Such cruelty and domination..." Brigitte laughed playfully as she grabbed Max by the arm. "I apologize.

She's the one who was cruel and domineering."

In the face of Brigitte's silly expression, Max couldn't help but smile.

Brigitte relaxed her face, then tried for the sexiest, flirtiest voice she could muster. "I promise I'll make it up to you."

She leaned in to plant a kiss on Max's cheek, but he pulled her in for a real kiss. When they were done, he released her.

"I'm gonna hold you to that."

Brigitte, a true princess of flirtation, teasingly flipped her hair to the side. "I'm good for it." She had softened the mood and was happy for the tiny victory.

Beginning to feel extraneous, Ted pulled the sunburst mask from Max's head and affixed it over his face. Upon seeing the move, Brigitte cheerfully tousled Ted's hair.

"Sorry, Ted, I'll have to figure some other way to make it up to you."

"Not sure how you're gonna do that, Sturdivant." Ted grabbed her nearly empty glass and slurped down its contents. "But we can start with another round of hurricanes."

"All for that," Brigitte quipped as she raised her voice to a scream. "C'mon, you guys, can we have a little fun, please?"

If anything, Brigitte was resilient. Max loved this about her. The psychic had spooked them, but minutes later Brigitte was in the crowd hooting and hollering as if nothing had happened. Screaming at the top of her lungs, she threw her head back to allow a sexy girl to place more cartoon jewelry about her neck. With a playful wink, the young co-ed planted an innocent kiss on Brigitte's cheek. Loving the attention, Brigitte turned and kissed Max passionately. Unhesitant, he kissed her back.

As they shuffled through the crowd Ted lowered the sunburst mask over his face. "We need more hurricanes, guys."

"I second that," Max confirmed. "Where can we buy some?"

Like floodwaters, the sea of partiers washed through the streets. The pandemonium made it easy to overlook a sole masquerader who was approaching through the crowd. The person, nearly seven feet tall, should have been impossible to miss not only because of his or her height, but also because of the strange and unusual disguise.

A crab-like shell encased the individual's body and was covered in what appeared to be black bottle caps. In their ensemble, the caps gave the effect of scales like those found on a reptile or on an insect's undercarriage. Stretched out along each side of its armor were four elongated arms, as one might find on a spider. The masquerader's real hands held tightly to two long black batons that operated the false arms like marionettes. Together, all eight arms moved in unison as if the upright spider were rowing itself through the crowd.

The menacing costume was entirely black with the exception of its helmet-like mask, which had splashes of red and white to depict a cheerful smiling clown face. It was ironic how the spider's body was dark and threatening, but its face was joyful and exuberant.

Even more peculiar than the outfit was the masked individual's ability to navigate the crowd. While throngs of people crept forward, the arachnid moved agilely against the current of the mob. Its waving arms parted the sea of people, allowing it to move effortlessly through the tightly packed parade.

When the eight-legged creature grew closer, Brigitte spotted it, but only paid it the slightest attention. Other colorful masqueraders were too numerous in the crowd to give it much notice. Then it was upon them, and Brigitte was the first to feel it. Tiny, warm droplets splashed across her face. *Warm beer,* she thought.

Neither she nor Max paid the splatter much mind. Throughout the day, they had all encountered rambunctious jostlings, being pushed, shoved, splashed with drinks and splattered with sweat. What they were feeling now was no different. At least that's what they thought until Ted leapt into them, dodging the way an athlete would the opposing team's offense.

Brigitte screamed as she saw the black spider's four right arms pounding at Ted in the crowd. Whoever was in the costume had a sleek black scalpel in one hand and was slashing at Ted with precision blows. All four of the assailant's right arms were swinging and thrashing about, hitting the people around them. Ted, who was still in Max's mask, had blood streaming down his neck. A cloud of yellow feathers flew about as they were shredded from the visor-like disguise by the spider's arms.

The crowd immediately dispersed as people scrambled to avoid the arms and more importantly the blade. Its wielder, up close, had a stocky football player's build. Whoever was inside had appeared taller, but was actually on stilts, moving with agility through the crowd. With each step, he bounced up and down, striking at Ted with powerful blows.

No sooner than the attack began, the spider was gone. With a quick about face, it hurried on in the flow of traffic. Pasted to the back of its helmet-like mask was another red and white painted clown face, only this one had a sad upside-down smile.

Like everyone else, Brigitte and Max were stunned as the spider rowed forward through the crowd. Resulting from some bizarre mechanism, the mask on the back of its head rotated to the front and was replaced with the same smiling mask they had witnessed on the spider's approach. All eight arms flapped up and down in an eerie wave goodbye. Then the costumed arachnid dropped down off its stilts and merged into the crowd.

"How bad is it, you guys?" Frantic, Ted stared at the blood pouring down his shirt.

Still reeling from shock, Max turned to Ted and gingerly tried to remove his tattered mask. As he pulled it from Ted's face, he could feel his friend's ear peeling back away from his head. To make things worse, Ted's hands and arms were covered in defensive wounds.

"Oh my God, you guys," Brigitte screamed. "What just happened?"

It had taken effort to push Indigo's words to the back of her mind, but the psychic's warnings were rapidly resurfacing. *Such a friend will bring nothing but grief. To you both.*

Max tried to further remove the tattered mask and quickly ascertain the extent of Ted's injuries. "Dude, it's pretty bad. We need to get you to a hospital."

In shock and wide-eyed, Ted stared at his injured hands and arms. "Who the fuck was that?"

"Ted, I don't know." Max removed his cell phone to dial 911. "But we need to get you out of here."

"Max?" Brigitte questioned, her face full of worry. "I think you're bleeding."

"What?" Max examined his arms and chest, which were speckled with Ted's blood.

"Your face, Max, your face."

Directly beneath his right eye, a stream of blood trailed down his cheek like a crimson teardrop. Without thinking, Max swiped it away, smearing blood across his skin. At that moment, an inch long incision opened on his face where the blood had been. Whether intentional or inadvertent, the attacker had slashed Max's face. The area immediately felt exposed as if cool air were gently being whistled upon it.

"You guys, I feel cold," Ted explained dully. "Kind of nauseous too."

All about them, the crowd was pushing forward, jostling them to and fro. Neither Max nor Brigitte could understand these people who were simply parading by a man covered in blood. Perhaps they saw Ted's condition as some strange costume like the Manitou they'd witnessed earlier in the crowd.

Max finally hit "send" on his phone. "Come on, we have to get him out of here."

Together, he and Brigitte formed a barrier around Ted as they led him from the crowd. Max could feel the blood trickling down his own face as an operator finally came on the line.

"9-1-1, what's your emergency?"

Max immediately began rambling into the phone, trying desperately to yell over the crowd, "I need an ambulance. My friend's been attacked."

No one mentioned the strange psychic or her ominous prophecies. But her words had not been forgotten—far from it, in fact. Privately, each one of them thought of Indigo's words and pondered their juxtaposition with this attack. Was it possible? Could there be any truth to the warnings she had uttered?

CHAPTER 9

$\mathcal{M}$aximilian Battenberg was a catch—there was no doubt about that. In a quirky way, he was handsome, and more importantly, he was clever. Brigitte knew a lot of rich kids, and most of them were as dumb as all get out. Because they were wealthy, they had the best education money could buy. But Brigitte knew money couldn't buy personality, and she respected Max for his charisma.

And there was that final selling point that made Max mega-marriage material. He was heir to one of the planet's largest fortunes. The Battenbergs were the envy of the wealthiest people on the globe. Most people dreamt of millions, but Demetrius Battenberg had assets in excess of eighty billion dollars.

Right now, while Max and Brigitte were in their mid-twenties, life was about playing and having fun, flying around the world and living it up. For the most part, that's exactly what they did. When Max wasn't catering to his father or working at the publishing company, he was known to be nightclubbing or schlepping around on his father's planes.

But needless to say, Brigitte hoped they would marry. He had never mentioned marriage, and it was something Brigitte would never push. She knew it was too early in the game. Even so, she felt certain that the thing blossoming between them was true love. With each passing week, they were spending more time together.

In nine months, Max would turn twenty-five. In Brigitte's mind, if she could just hang in there another five years, marriage would just be a matter of time.

Like any other girl, Brigitte had her doubts and insecurities. Indigo's words had effectively caused them to resurface. Something, call it woman's intuition, had whispered quietly in her ear that Max would break her heart. Indigo, in her brazen glory, had spoken those words aloud—words that not only haunted her, they scared her.

Brigitte fought the instinct to think negatively, allowing optimism to endure. After all, in the months since they'd known each other, Max had always been a charmer. They rarely fought, and in fact, they barely disagreed. But there were times when Max needed space, a behavior Brigitte interpreted as purely antisocial.

He constantly assured her there was nothing wrong, explaining that he just needed time alone. It was that simple. The explanation always made Brigitte feel silly, as if her worries were unwarranted. She had never seen or even heard of Max palling around with other girls, but still, she couldn't shake an inexplicable fear.

Less than an hour earlier, Indigo had said to run, and that was precisely what she wanted to do; to break away and run from the storefront, to disappear in the crowd. Surrounded by so many people, there would be no fear. Max couldn't hurt her with everyone around.

When Brigitte mentioned having been to a psychic with her friend Marilyn, she had only said it was fun. She hadn't revealed that the previous psychic had known things that she couldn't or shouldn't possibly have known unless she truly had special powers.

The earlier medium had known about her fear of water, and that it stemmed from a childhood event. At four years old, she had refused to enter the water during her first swim lesson. In infinite parenting wisdom, her father had picked her up kicking and screaming before throwing her in the pool. While it was only seconds before the instructor fished her out, those seconds had seemed an eternity.

Brigitte vividly remembered looking up from the bottom of the pool with distorted figures of people standing above her at the edge of the water. The images had appeared like monsters undulating to the rhythm of the water. On some level, she had never forgiven her father, but the bigger and more cogent point was how this woman, this psychic, had known about it.

Brigitte believed there was something real to the paranormal world of psychic abilities. She had had one example that swayed her toward believing. Now, less than a year later, these new revelations, if true, could confirm both her fears about Max and her belief in the paranormal.

But the tool of denial, when properly used, is a powerful thing. Considering herself a thinking girl, Brigitte presumed to know the difference between thoughts and feelings. Just because she felt scared or insecure didn't mean she really needed to be. More than likely it was just an illogical feeling. Besides, she knew Max was an incredible person. Whenever her heart and head battled, it was usually her head that won.

"How are ya, babe?"

Brigitte looked up to see Max standing above her in the hospital corridor. His right cheek was sutured with surgical adhesive rather than stitches. While the wound was closed, the area was still swollen and red.

"That was fast." Brigitte smiled as she grabbed Max's hand.

"Yeah, well, when they found out who I was..." Max trailed off. "Any word on Ted?"

Brigitte shrugged her shoulders. "They said his surgery might take a while. Whoever that nut job was nearly took off his ear."

"Did the police come yet?" Max stared with cynicism as Brigitte shook her head. "Why is it taking them so long to get here?"

"It's Mardi Gras, Max. I'm sure they've got their hands full. They'll never catch that guy anyway. We don't even know if it was a guy. We never saw a face."

"There are cameras, Brigitte. Maybe he's on camera somewhere."

Max thought of the day's unusual events. Only hours before he left Chicago, his father had warned of dangers lurking in the shadows. Later, on the same day, a psychic had cautioned his friend and girlfriend against his company, instructing them both to flee. Neither Brigitte nor Ted had said anything, but Max knew they were uncomfortable with Indigo's tirade, particularly because it had taken place only minutes before the attack. The more he thought about it, the crazier it all seemed.

Nothing but grief is what she had said. Now, here they were in a New Orleans emergency room; Max's face was packed with liquid sutures and Ted was in surgery. *Fuck!*

Suddenly, the Star Wars Cantina music bounced into the room. Max fished his ringing phone from his pocket to find the name Chandler flashing across the screen.

"Oh, this is Chandler at work." Max pressed the talk button to speak to his newest vice president and friend. "Hey, Chandler, what's up?"

Chandler's voice was masculine, but had a boyish quality to it. "Sorry to bother you, Chief. I know you said no calls."

"No, it's okay. What's up?"

Chandler hesitated on the line. "Did you forget we go to press in two days?"

"Oh, shit. I'm sorry. There's just a lot going on right now."

"I bet, boss man. I just need you to sign off if we're gonna be on shelves this week."

"I know this is going to sound fucked up but I can't really deal with this right now. Is everything copacetic?"

"Yeeesss." Chandler had a habit of dragging out certain words. "I just sent everything to your phone. If you could, an electronic signature's all I need."

"You'll have it in two shakes." Max considered sharing news of their recent ordeal but decided against it.

After a brief silence, Chandler continued. "You back Tuesday or Wednesday?"

"Could be early as tomorrow night. I'll give you a call when I get in."

Chandler chuckled on the other end, but Max wasn't sure why. "After N'awlins, I'm sure you'll be wiped out. But I'll give you a call if there's anything going on."

"Thanks, Chandler."

"Have a hurricane for me."

Max clicked off the phone then turned to Brigitte. "You okay, babe?"

She stared back at Max, filled with trepidation. "How'd this trip get so fucked up?"

He considered his father's warning from earlier that day. In retrospect, perhaps he should have shared Demetrius' concerns with Ted and Brigitte. If they had known of possible danger, they could have been more on the defensive. But they had been warned in the end, even if it was by Indigo Blue.

Max sat beside Brigitte and placed his arms tightly around her. "He'll be fine. I'm just glad he didn't pass out before we got here. You know that was Chandler on the phone. I have a couple of things I have to do for him. It should only take a few minutes."

Brigitte yawned more from stress than fatigue. "Okay."

"I'm going to step outside a sec."

After the day's events, Brigitte wasn't thrilled about being left alone. "Just be careful, okay?"

"I will. I promise." He kissed Brigitte, smarting from pain when his cheek brushed against hers. Reaching up, he gingerly patted the area around the wound. "Forgot about that." Using his phone, he clicked into his work emails. "Call me if there's news."

Brigitte offered a meek smile as she settled back into her chair.

"Be right back." Max moved down the emergency room corridor and passed through a set of sliding glass doors until he was standing in the courtyard of the hospital parking lot. He opened Chandler's emails regarding his work at Badem Publications. One by one, he forwarded the appropriate approvals. Then he took a deep breath. *So much for a better year than Oktoberfest.*

Max stared across the lot, surveilling for assailants that might be lurking in the shadows. The assault on Ted, as vicious as it was, felt infinitely more wicked because of the attacker's villainous spider costume. *Why would a stranger do that?*

Max wracked his brain for an answer. No matter how he tried, he couldn't shake the nagging feeling he had about the Poseidon alert or the prophecies of Indigo Blue. At first indecisive, he glanced from his phone to the sliding glass doors of the hospital entrance. After a minute's thought, he slipped the phone in his pocket and strode across the lot toward the street.

CHAPTER 10

*T*he crowds had thinned, but there were still thousands of people caravanning through the streets. As he tried to navigate the mob, Max was bumped, groped and bustled. His idea had been to quickly venture out and return before Brigitte noticed. Now, he wasn't so sure this was a feasible plan.

He had only been in the crowd for a few blocks when he spotted something unusual. At first, he thought it was a child who had somehow been separated from his family. Upon closer inspection, he realized it wasn't a child at all. It was a small man dressed all in black with the painted face of a mime. The pasty, white makeup had a sad face drawn with an upward curved, black mouth. A lone, black teardrop curved down from the man's left eye.

The tiny person seemed serious and intense, but Max couldn't tell if it was his true expression or just how his face had been made up. Earlier, he had seen a midget incorporated into the strange Native American Manitou costume. Now, another one seemed to be staring him down as he crossed through the crowd.

Not wanting to linger in the mass of people, Max picked up his pace and quickly passed the miniature man. Less than ten minutes later, he was standing before the psychic's storefront.

Max gazed up at the flickering neon sign with the words "Indigo Blue" overhead. *I can't believe I'm doing this,* he thought as he strode to the front door to let himself in.

Entering Indigo's parlor a second time proved an experience eerily similar to the first. It was deathly quiet compared to the commotion going on outside, almost as if the psychic had cast a silencing spell on her space. A bell chimed as he closed the door, a detail he didn't remember from before. Max looked around the room, then took a seat and waited.

After a moment, a cute blonde swished into the room from an adjacent hallway. Her hair was closely cropped in a boy's cut but the look somehow complimented her face in a feminine way. Max could tell there was something effervescent about her personality, but he figured it was just because she was drunk. She was shaking like a child who had a secret to tell.

"My best friend's in there. Indigo's helping with a problem."

Max realized the girl wasn't drunk at all. The bubbly behavior was just her personality. He offered, "Have you been here before?"

"Oh yeah. I discovered Indigo a few years ago. She's amazing. What about you?"

Max laughed, a little uncomfortable. "I guess you could say I've seen her once before."

"She really helped me work through some stuff, which is why I brought my best friend. It was either that or let her keep working my nerves."

Max laughed at the girl's comment. "I also came with friends and Indigo said things... I just want clarification."

The girl's eyes opened wide as if she had just learned the winning Lotto numbers. "Because that's what it's all about, right? Clarity. No worries, you'll get it from Indigo. What happened with your face? Looks kind of gnarly."

Max reached up near the area of his cut. "Oh, just an accident. It's liquid stitches."

"Oh, cool. Didn't know they had those."

Before Max could respond, a girl, who was likely Filipina, exited from the back hall. The bubbly girl jumped to her feet.

"How'd it go?"

It was clear the friend had been crying. She looked uncomfortable when she spotted Max sitting in the salon. "It was fine, I guess. She more or less told me what you said she would."

Indigo entered and froze when she spotted Max.

The bubbly blonde noticed the psychic's reaction, but was too stimulated by everything going on around her. She turned to Max as she pulled her girlfriend toward the door. "Good luck."

"Thanks," Max replied as he looked up at Indigo.

Indigo stood motionless in her doorway to the hall. "I figured you would return."

Max nodded. "I suppose that's the benefit of being psychic."

Indigo remained stone-faced, studying Max as she had done earlier that day.

"You said a lot of things earlier. And I'm not saying I believe any of them. But I'm curious what your problem is with me."

Indigo looked leery as she sized Max up. Her gaze locked on his injured face. "You are wounded."

"Some nut job attacked us. No more than ten minutes after we left here. My friend's in surgery now."

"I see."

Max didn't break eye contact, trying to gauge Indigo's response. It was difficult to tell whether her expression was one of fear or surprise. After a moment, she called out.

"Tommy! Viens ici!"

Seconds later, an older Creole gentleman, maybe 6'4," stepped into the room. The man had a wrinkle-free, caramel complexion, giving him the appearance of someone in his forties, but his short curly hair was full of gray. Max guessed he was likely in his fifties or sixties.

Indigo and the man nodded to one another in a wordless exchange. Tommy evaluated Max, looking him up and down.

"Please come this way," Indigo called out.

Max moved to follow but Tommy turned and stepped defiantly in his path. For an instant Max felt threatened, but then Tommy gently patted him down, checking for weapons, he assumed. Satisfied, Tommy led Max into the consultation room.

In the other room, Indigo still appeared cautious as she took a seat at a small card table in the center of the floor. A large piece of sheer burgundy fabric was pinned to the center of the ceiling and draped down to the outer walls, creating a teepee effect above them. Moorish metal and glass lanterns were tastefully placed about the room with candles burning inside of them. Tommy pulled a chair from the corner and placed it near the only exit, where he sat and stared at Max.

Max planted himself in a chair opposite Indigo, still wondering why he had even come. "Earlier when I was here, you said a few things, warning my friends about me. We were attacked minutes later. Like that girl who just left, I'd like — clarity."

Growing more relaxed, Indigo scooted in closer to the table. "Before, you caught me off guard. Now, we have time. Perhaps I can provide the clarity you seek."

"I'm not saying I believe in this stuff. It's just that you said I would cause my friends grief, and now, one of them's in the hospital."

The day's events by now seemed completely surreal. Indigo gazed directly into his eyes.

"It is you who should be in his place, but you were spared." Indigo seemed impressed that Max had avoided graver injuries. "There are energies gathering in you. Extremely powerful ones. And you will need them, for the weight of the world is upon you. Very soon you alone will have a decision to make. A decision that will decide the fate of many. The question is, what will you choose?"

Something in Max, his rational side, wanted to scoff at the psychic's ridiculous words. Suddenly, he regretted leaving Brigitte at the hospital. "Look, I don't know what you're talking about, it just seemed you knew something was about to happen and then it did. So, you think that attack was meant for me?"

Indigo quietly nodded before glancing at Tommy in another silent exchange. Suddenly, Max felt foolish for returning. The idea that Indigo and the mysterious man were somehow behind the attack was only now settling in. If this were true, he had unwisely re-entered the lion's den of his own volition. At that moment, Max's phone began vibrating in his pocket. He slipped it out to see Brigitte's photo flashing across the screen.

Indigo narrowed her eyes before glancing at Tommy. "Le monsieur nous croit responsable pour l'attentat." Together, she and Tommy shared a joyless smile, at which point Indigo spat out an incredulous laugh. "You believe us responsible for this attack? This you find easier to accept than the truth. You mustn't fall into this trap and allow delusion to be your downfall."

Max returned the ringing phone to his pocket. "I need to get back to the hospital. I probably shouldn't have come."

Indigo continued without skipping a beat. "Before I asked if you knew what you were. It would seem you have no idea. Tell me, have you never wondered where your father gets his riches?"

Max was thrown by the question. "You know who my father is?" While he was far from anonymous, Max had been known to travel without being recognized.

"Who, Monsieur, is of no consequence at all. It is *what* he is that matters."

In a sudden move, Max jumped to his feet and shoved his chair back from the table. Both Indigo and Tommy reacted, jumping from their seats in defensive postures.

"Someone cut my friend up today, and they didn't do too bad a job on me either. I was crazy to think you could shed any light on it."

For the first time, Indigo raised her voice in an aggressive manner. "Your friend means nothing, Monsieur. Nothing at all. I understand you are distressed, but this attack is of little consequence in the grand scheme. I warned both him and the girl to step aside. For them to do otherwise was at their own peril."

Max couldn't mask his frown. He was certain Indigo's antics were about manipulation of some kind. If they hadn't arranged the attack, they were no doubt in it for the money. But Max couldn't figure out what her angle was in the elaborate story she was concocting. She kept insinuating Demetrius was something other than what he proposed to be.

"It's uncanny how creative you've all become. So artful at staying hidden. It would seem you now manage to fool even yourselves."

"Why be cryptic if you have all the answers? Just come out and say what you mean. That's why I'm here," said Max, growing frustrated at the innuendoes.

Growing calmer, Indigo circled behind Max then spoke in a deep tone. "You, mon cher, wouldn't believe me if I told you. But worry not. The universe is aligning. What you wish to know will discover you in an undeniable way." Indigo returned to the opposite side of the table, her eyes narrowing as she glared intently at Max. "You must seek the device — the Antikythera Mechanism. It will help you find the clarity you seek."

"What?" Max turned to Tommy in the corner. "What did she say?"

Indigo slinked across the room and took a lit cigarette from Tommy. She dragged deeply on it before handing it back to her bodyguard. "Ecris-le pour lui, Tommy." As she exhaled smoke, she turned to Max. "I hold no envy for you. In ten thousand years, none have accomplished this task. But you will carry the burden. The Antikythera Device will lighten your load. Find it, and before year's end all will be revealed." Indigo grew solemn and resolute. "Then a choice will have to be made. By you, and you alone."

Max chuckled even though he didn't find anything funny. "Let me guess. This device, this Anti-thing, I need to buy it off you, right? There's gotta be a catch somewhere. What you're not saying is what I'm not paying, right?" Max quickly removed his wallet.

Startled by the sudden move, Tommy snatched his chair and lifted it for a preemptive strike. Max had presumed Indigo guilty of some elaborate scheme, but she was trembling, cringing away from him. If she was acting, she deserved an Academy Award.

Max grabbed a stack of twenty-dollar bills from his billfold. "Is it money? Is that what'll make you answer a question?" Max threw the bills on the table. "You want it, you got it! Now, why don't you tell me something I can fucking use?"

Indigo scooped up the cash and threw it back in Max's face. "Keep it! We don't want your blood money." Max let the bills fall to the table, but Indigo was determined. "I said keep it." She grabbed the money and began shoving it in his hands.

Max couldn't believe what was transpiring. He had felt certain Indigo was working a grift to swindle money from him. Now, she was tossing twenties back in his face.

"You two ought to be ashamed of yourselves."

Indigo nearly spat in Max's face. "When you've learned what you don't know, come back and tell me who should be ashamed." She gathered the remaining twenty-dollar bills from the floor and shoved them in Max's hand. "We'll be waiting."

"I wouldn't hold my breath." Max rushed toward the door, prepared for a struggle with Tommy. The large Creole man shoved a business card in his hand then stepped aside as Max exited. With a sense of relief, Max hurried through the front room and out into the street.

The noise of the Mardi Gras festivities startled him back to the reason he had come to New Orleans in the first place. The vibe in the streets was joyful and celebratory even if Max hadn't fully been able to enjoy it. He turned and watched Indigo's door swing shut and then glanced at the business card in his hand.

The front of the card was a wonderful shade of purplish blue and had the name Indigo prominently featured in the center. Beneath, it simply read "Spiritual Advisor" with her number and address. Max turned the card over and saw what Tommy had scribbled down. Written in beautiful calligraphy were the words "Antikythera Mechanism." Max didn't recognize the name and wondered why the bizarre psychic had suggested he find it.

He shoved the card in his pocket, then turned to reenter the crowd. After barely a block he spotted another small person standing on the curb. Max couldn't believe his eyes. It appeared to be the same man he'd seen earlier in the mime outfit, only now his painted face, instead of sad, was happy and smiling. Max queried his memory, but he was certain of this.

For some reason, Max's sight of the tiny man gave rise to an impending sense of doom. There were three little people all in one day and all in the same vicinity. Max wondered if they might be the same person. Or maybe there was a troupe of small people who had all dressed in mime outfits with sad and happy faces. Max didn't know — was it paranoia he was feeling or simply common sense?

Not wanting to think any further about it, he continued through the crowd. Already Brigitte had called once, and she would certainly be worried. When he returned to the hospital, Brigitte was in the waiting room still sobering from the day.

"Where were you?"

"I went for a walk. I'm sorry, I didn't hear the phone."

It was clear she was still frazzled. "I just found out Ted's in recovery. His surgery went fine."

"Great." Relief washed over Max. "That's fantastic. When can we see him?"

"They said in a couple hours when the anesthesia wears off."

He hugged Brigitte, while they continued to digest the unfortunate events of the day. Max didn't mention he had seen Indigo. The truth was he was embarrassed, and it wasn't as if she had illuminated anything worth sharing.

The following afternoon, Ted was released from the hospital. Within hours, Max chartered a Battenberg plane back to Chicago. In private, they each wished to leave behind the experiences of Ted's attack and their recollections of Louisiana's Indigo Blue. But their efforts to vanquish these memories were futile.

CHAPTER 11

*T*he geyser that sprang forth from the Money Pit lasted only a few seconds, half a minute at most. Brigitte screamed at the top of her lungs as it rained down upon them. Then, before anyone could react further, the plume of water vanished, disappearing back into the pit.

She, Otto and the rest of the dig team stared at one another, dumbfounded and dripping wet.

"Where is he?" Brigitte demanded. She was frantic, but too in shock to properly express it. "Otto, where is he?" Tears began streaming down her face, but it was hard to tell since they were all soaked from head to toe.

Otto tapped the radio headset, which was also dripping with water. "Max? Max, can you hear me?" He needed to ask the question even though he knew the odds were slim that Max had survived such a blast. Otto removed his headset to examine if it was still working.

At this point the dig captain, accompanied by one of his men, sheepishly approached.

"Sir, one of my guys found this." He handed over the scuba mask that Max had been wearing. "Said it nearly knocked him in the head. It must've been ejected from the pit."

The team member nodded to corroborate the captain's story.

Brigitte approached for a closer look at the scuba mask. Upon seeing it she mumbled, "No. No." Her face quivered as she pondered the impending bad news. "I asked him not to go down there. I knew it wasn't safe."

Otto spoke into his headset. To his dismay it was his voice coming through the receiver of Max's scuba mask. Fear crept into his mind as he contemplated how he would have to break such news to Demetrius. If Max was truly gone, it had been on his watch.

Otto snapped into action, barking out commands to the dig captain. "I need your team down there now. And we need medical ASAP."

Frowning, the dig captain responded. "Sir, all due respect, I can't send my men down after that. Not till we assess what happened."

"That's Demetrius Battenberg's son down there. You want to be the one who didn't act fast enough to save him? Now get your fucking men down in that pit so we can see what the hell happened."

The dig captain knew it was improper protocol to go in after such an event. But Otto was right; he didn't want to be the man who failed to act in time to save a Battenberg. He looked at his men.

"Come on, guys, finish getting suited up. I'll go in first."

Seconds before the eruption, Max had decided not to follow Otto's instructions. Instead, he had picked up the ornate leather box. As it turned out, Otto had been right. The chamber was booby-trapped in a particularly unavoidable way. Without sign or warning, thousands of pounds of water had been released into the chamber.

Max felt rather than heard or saw the wall of water as it swept across the room. It knocked him off his feet, propelling him toward the rear of the chamber. He had been too afraid to leave the box behind, and now, he was about to pay the price. He saw the rock wall coming toward him but could not twist away. Max clenched his eyes shut. He felt a bang to his head and a knock on his shoulder, then the same to his elbow and knee. He had anticipated his whole body impacting the wall, but it never did.

Disoriented, he had a distinct feeling of motion, as if he were moving rapidly through some sort of tube. He had opened his eyes but rushing water had forced them shut.

Somewhat unaware, he had drawn in a breath only to have water enter his lungs. For the second time, he'd felt the effects of oxygen deprivation, and once again his consciousness was beginning to fade.

Above ground, the dig captain and team were suiting up to enter the pit. The cable used to lower Max had quickly been recoiled and refitted for another trip inside.

Otto and Brigitte were both a mixture of fear, turmoil and anxiety as they watched the dig captain motion thumbs up and begin lowering himself into the pit.

All nerves from the earlier debacle, Otto continually questioned the dig captain during his descent. "What do you see now?"

Despite the dangers involved and Otto's arrogant manner, the dig captain managed an impressive sense of composure. "So far, nothing but the expected."

Not especially religious, Otto was now praying that Max was still alive. "What about now? You see anything now?"

As the dig captain was about to speak, Otto heard instead Brigitte shrieking, "Oh my God!"

Otto flinched, figuring if she couldn't control herself that he would have to ask her to sit in the copter.

Brigitte hollered again, jumping up and down and pointing at the beach. "Oh my God!" Tears were streaming down her face.

Otto could not hear the dig captain over Brigitte's antics. He followed her gaze downhill toward the water. Otto's mouth dropped open. "Jesus Christ."

Max was soaking wet, bruised and shivering. He was stumbling along the grass, clinging tightly to a leather box.

At the sight of Otto and Brigitte he broke into a run and then collapsed, exhausted.

They didn't waste a second rushing to his side. Younger and faster, Brigitte was the first to reach him. She dropped to her knees, grabbing Max in her arms.

"Thank God you're okay."

Seconds later, Otto arrived, slightly winded. "What the hell happened down there?"

Max was still clutching the leather box. He relinquished it, rolled onto his hands and knees and vomited salt water into the grass.

"Give him room, girl."

Brigitte glared at Otto before releasing Max to stand. She stroked his back as he coughed to catch his breath. Finally, he spoke.

"I don't know." Max was disoriented. "Do I still have the box?"

"Yeah," Otto answered, "You still have it. Give it to me." Otto removed the ornate box from underneath Max. "Come on, help him up."

Max continued his account as they helped him to his feet. "The room flooded. Somehow, I have no idea, I got washed out to sea." Max cracked a brilliant smile of resilience. "Let's open that thing... see if it's what we came for."

"Max, that can wait," Brigitte protested, "You could have fucking killed yourself."

"I'm fine, Bridge. But that water's fucking cold." Max's senses were slowly returning. "Why are you guys all wet?"

Brigitte couldn't decide if she wanted to hug or smack Max.

In spite of his trauma, Max was impatient. "Otto, if you're not going to open it, I will."

"That you found this is huge, Max." Otto fidgeted with the box but was unable to unlock it. "It is not, however, obvious how you open the thing."

Brigitte had been completely focused on Max. Now she turned her attention to the ornate container in Otto's hands. "Give it to me." Reaching out, she removed it from Otto's grip. Even though it had been in the water, its leather surface glistened in the sun as if it had been cured with essential oils.

Brigitte's long and delicate fingers handled the box, turning it over as she fully examined it. She located a long, wiry pin that had been inserted to hold the lid in place. "Wait a minute. Here we go." Using her finely manicured nails, Brigitte slid the pin out and opened the lid.

Max gingerly took the box and peered inside at its contents. "Jesus Christ."

The three of them gazed into the leather case, which was dry as a bone and lined with luxurious, burgundy-colored silk. Centered in the cloth was a flat, golden dial roughly eight inches in diameter. The piece glistened so that Max was sure it was 24-karat gold. At first glance, it seemed like an ultra thin compass. Dozens of symbols were etched into it with precision, just as they had been on the Antikythera replica in New York's Children's Museum. For several seconds, all of them were speechless.

Finally, Otto spoke. "Looks like an astrolabe."

"A what?" Brigitte questioned.

"An astrolabe. A navigation device sailors used before the compass. Muslims also used them for astronomy, to figure out when and in which direction to pray."

Max was shivering or perhaps shaking from giddiness, he wasn't sure which. "Oh shit, you guys. This is it. It's got the same markings as the piece I saw in New York."

"Mr. Khrzinsky?" It was the dig captain's voice coming through Otto's receiver. "It's the strangest thing. There's no sign of Mr. Battenberg anywhere down here."

Smiling from ear to ear, Max removed Otto's headset and placed it on his own head. "Captain, Max Battenberg here, freezing his ass off. Pack up, man. We're done here."

The captain's voice was riddled with confusion. "What? Wait. What?"

Max returned the headset to Otto and then placed the golden dial back into the box. He laid a wet kiss on Brigitte's equally wet cheek. "I told you everything would be fine."

"Dammit, Max." Brigitte offered a playful jab in Max's ribs. "You scared the hell out of us."

"Ouch, careful, Bridge. Can we go now?" Max chided, and the three of them headed toward the Money Pit to pack up their things.

Otto stepped to Max, stopping him in his path. "It's better if we keep this to ourselves for now. If this is the missing piece it could very well belong to Greece."

"Should I call my contact?" Max looked at the box. "He should know if it's the missing piece or not."

Otto shook his head. "It's better if we wait. Believe me, this could get complicated. Just give me a few days."

Max turned to Brigitte, who simply shrugged in agreement. "Okay. We'll sit on it until you figure things out. Just let me know when you do."

Otto and Brigitte grabbed hold of Max, assisting him on his way back to the copter. With a smile on his face and the leather box in hand, he finally felt worthy of the Battenberg name. Unlike anyone before him, he had conquered the Money Pit, extracting a piece of its treasure. And as soon as he received the green light from Otto, he would uncover precisely what the Antikythera Mechanism was all about.

$\mathcal{M}$ax returned from Oak Island incredibly happy to be back home. During Mardi Gras, Demetrius had issued a series of security cross-checks to ensure there were no potential weaknesses in the armor of Max's house. Max couldn't believe that upgrades had been necessary. He already considered the previous safeguards extreme, but they had nevertheless been enhanced in light of the attack on Ted and the Poseidon alert.

Over the years, Max's ultra-modern home had evolved into a mini fortress equipped with cameras, alarms and panic rooms throughout. Electronic keypads limited access to this or that room while strategically placed monitors enabled observation of different parts of the property at all times. Even though he thought it was overkill, Max had to admit he felt entirely safe in his space. Not even Brigitte had all the codes to move freely about the house. Max knew she wanted them and maybe one day, as they grew closer, he would give them to her. Maybe.

He keyed in his entry code to gain access to the front foyer. After tossing his bag on the floor, he collapsed against the wall. *What a day*, he thought, before heading upstairs.

Inside, the house was a quintessential bachelor pad — contemporary concrete and glass, quadra-level and exquisitely furnished. Just as in Demetrius' penthouse, modern pieces of furniture could easily have doubled as art due to their sculptural design. Each piece was thoughtfully placed throughout each room, many of which had retractable walls to create wide-open areas or to delineate private spaces when desired.

When Max thought of the series of events leading up to the Oak Island adventure, their details seemed whimsical, farfetched, even insane. A kooky psychic had insulted him with carnival antics and prophecies about the unknown. And Max, in his own lack of wisdom, had listened, setting off in search of a legendary device. Just hours before, he had nearly drowned, not once but twice, and his body was now aching and bruised.

Against Otto's and Brigitte's wishes, he had refused medical attention. He was simply too exhilarated for such a detour. In the end, he was sure he had retrieved something of value from the Money Pit. This endeavor many had spent centuries toiling to do but all had failed to accomplish.

It didn't really matter whether or not Indigo Blue was the real deal. Powers or no powers, she had successfully manipulated him into action and something positive had been accomplished.

Ted and Brigitte had also been affected by her ramblings. He didn't like to think of them being in danger, especially because of him. But Ted had been attacked. Privately, all three of them wondered about the prophesied warnings.

Indigo had suggested Max was in the dark about something, but he had no clue what that might be. Immediately before he stormed from her shop, she had yelled, *When you've learned what you don't know, come back and tell me who should be ashamed.* The accusation still rang in his ears.

The truth was Max knew there were secrets and hidden agendas in his family. For starters, there was the Battenberg initiation, a coming of age ceremony that always took place on or immediately following a Battenberg's twenty-fifth birthday. For centuries, the Battenbergs had practiced this tradition, but details of what transpired during the ritual were still veiled in secrecy.

The initiations, he suspected, were just one item on a long list of clandestine Battenberg affairs. In some ways, he compared his reality to the concentration games he sometimes stumbled on in the newspaper, where two seemingly identical photographs were displayed and the reader was challenged to identify how they were different. The areas of disparity were never obvious until you found them. The same seemed true of his own life, which felt ordinary until the details were examined.

Max was convinced that Demetrius, like a magician, had a variety of cards hidden up his sleeves. It was probably impossible to run Battenberg Industries without an arsenal of well-played tricks. But Max never spoke of his suspicions about Demetrius' dirty dealings. When such thoughts crept into his brain, he would quickly push them aside or dismiss them as foolish paranoia.

He assumed such fears about nefarious behavior were due to the family's colorful history. There were labor disputes, constant threats on the family and innumerable lives affected in the crossfire. Add to that the deaths of his own mother and brother, and Max was left with such a heavy burden that he didn't dare try to distinguish or evaluate any of it.

For years he had yearned for Demetrius to fill the empty void that was left by his mother and brother's deaths, but that had never occurred. At the time, no one had fully explained to six-year-old Max what had happened. A car accident is all he'd ever been told. How could he feel enlightened when Demetrius, who was so cold and impersonal, was constantly keeping him in the dark on the things that really mattered?

Since his childhood, Max's mind had been riddled with seeds of doubt about such matters. During the incident at Mardi Gras, Indigo had watered those seeds. Then she suggested he find the Antikythera Mechanism and he had listened. In the past, he had wasted time and energy on infinitely more foolish things.

Otto had requested he hold off on calling Dr. Miklos. Max had agreed, but he was feeling impatient. His entire life, he had been given instant gratification. Now, he had been asked to conceal a newsworthy accomplishment he was proud of, and humility was not his forte.

Otto had dubbed the instrument he had found an astrolabe. Max prayed it was the missing component to the Antikythera Mechanism. Perhaps its worth had been exaggerated, but Max nevertheless knew he had recovered something of value to the archeological community. First, Otto would have the leather box carbon dated to determine if it was from the same period as the larger device. From there, they would see.

If it were the missing component, the world would soon discover the device's actual function. The moment he had the green light, he would phone Miklos to announce that the golden dial had been recovered.

Max had researched the strange device many called an ancient computer. He had to admit its existence was at best peculiar. The Antikythera Mechanism had been constructed of a complex series of gears not unlike those found in ancient clocks. In some ways it did chart movements through space and time, as it could accurately track astronomical markers. Max learned it had likely been used to predict the occurrence of eclipses, which were often seen as bad omens in ancient times. One of the mechanism's dials was even used to predict the exact dates of Greece's Olympic games.

The superstitious, like Indigo Blue, believed the mechanism had other uses that science refused to consider. They alleged the device could also be used to track astrological markers and the ebbs and flows of the energies associated with them. Believers in the zodiac thought the position of the sun and the moon dictated times and places of important events. Immense time and energy was spent charting these periods so followers could determine when to make meaningful decisions like war or peace, or the best times to marry, divorce or conceive. In simple terms, such charts had become the horoscope.

Max knew his sign was Sagittarius, the Archer, but he didn't give much credence to astrology. Whenever he read about his own zodiac he found it mildly interesting, especially when there were parallels or coincidences to his life. But he had also found the same phenomenon of other people's horoscopes relating to him.

All things considered, Max figured he was about to make big news. But he hoped he could make the device operational before creating a clamor. Since Dr. Miklos had claimed the device capable of cosmic knowing, Max intended to find out just what that meant.

After showering, he stopped in the kitchen to grab munchies. A note on the refrigerator read, "Made lumpia last night. There's a tray for you in fridge. LC"

With a smile on his lips, Max spoke the name aloud. "Cora."

He opened the refrigerator and removed a foil-covered tray. Inside were neatly arranged rows of Filipino-style egg rolls that had been left by the house manager. Max popped one in his mouth and placed a handful of others in the microwave. He grabbed a fizzy drink and other choice snacks before settling on the L-shaped couch in his den.

Across from the door was a huge picture window. Lights from the street below danced across the room as he grabbed a remote control. Triggering a button on the remote, a large flat screen descended from the ceiling, covering the large window and plunging the room into darkness.

Max powered on the television and began surfing stations. A moment later, the chime of his phone rang through the room's built-in speakers. He pressed a button on the remote to answer the call.

"Hello."

The television's volume automatically faded to mute; microphones were placed throughout the house so Max could speak hands-free.

"Hey, you back?"

"Hey, Chandler. Just got in an hour ago. What's up, man?"

"I don't know. I was thinking I might go to the Library later if you're interested."

Max hesitated. "I don't know. Not sure tonight's the right time."

Without seeming pushy, Chandler continued, "Bring your bike. I'll let you in the back door if you text me."

Max took a deep breath as he contemplated. "Brigitte's coming by later. Let me see what she's up to first."

Disappointment rang in Chandler's voice. "All right. You change your mind, shoot me a text."

To end the call, Max pressed another button on his remote. There was a brief delay before the television's volume returned to its initial level.

Snuggled comfortably on the couch, Max continued flipping channels as exhaustion set in. Within minutes he was asleep, but it was a restless slumber painted with surreal and disturbing dreams.

On some level, he sensed with his conscious mind that he was in a strange, ethereal state. He desired to wake and banish his dreams to the netherworld, but his subconscious was in control.

Max was oddly aware of his body splayed across the couch. He willed his eyes open, still unsure if he was asleep or awake. The large flat screen was still on. Then Max saw him: one of the midgets from New Orleans. The man was standing in the room, his face covered in the white mime makeup. Dressed like a miniature James Bond, the man wore a finely tailored black suit with a matching black shirt and tie. But this time, there was no expression drawn on his white face.

Max wanted to scream for help but felt too paralyzed to do so. With a blank, almost robotic expression the midget approached. Too sluggish to escape, Max scooted clumsily across the couch. In the back of his mind he wondered how the intruder had breached his security, but then the conscious part of him remembered it was just a dream. He resolved to strike the small intruder, but when he tried, his limbs felt as if hundred-pound weights were attached to them.

With impressive strength the white-faced midget grabbed Max, restraining his attempts to struggle. Max watched him pull a tiny, circular red sticker from the lapel of his suit. He slapped the sticker in the center of Max's forehead between his eyebrows. The tiny circle adhered to Max's skin, and within seconds it began to burn. Max tried to yell but couldn't.

A tall blonde woman, also dressed in black, stepped into his den. Max had never seen her before, but he figured these interlopers were somehow connected to the Poseidon alert his father had warned him about. And then he felt, as if he were awake, a palpable and real fear.

A moment later, Brigitte was standing there, gently nudging him. "Hey, sleepy head."

Max cracked open his eyes, relieved to hear her voice. With a deep stretch of his arms he answered back, "Hey, how are you?"

"Better than this morning. You should've heard me when water came gushing from that hole in the ground. I'm pretty sure Otto wanted to kill me."

Max looked around, utterly disoriented. He was certain he had drifted off in his den, but Brigitte had awakened him in his bedroom. He quickly rushed to the nearest mirror to check for the sticker on his forehead. There was no sign of anything on his skin.

"What's wrong, babe?" Brigitte questioned, noting Max's confusion.

Max wracked his brain, trying to recall leaving the den for his room. He couldn't. "I guess I'm just tired. I thought for sure I fell asleep in the den."

Brigitte smiled, with a touch of concern on her face. "You sure you don't want to see a doctor?"

"Sleep's all I need, I assure you."

Brigitte studied Max, but didn't find anything noticeably different about him. "I'm thinking you should stay in tonight. And you shouldn't be alone if you're not gonna get checked out. I can blow off my dinner with Marilyn."

Max spit out a laugh. "Bridge, I'm fine. You don't need to blow off dinner. You and Marilyn, I'm sure, need some good gossiping. Just please don't mention what we found today."

"I won't, Max. I'm not even thinking about that. I'm actually trying to forget most of what happened today."

Jumping to attention, Max tickled Brigitte. "Stop your worrying,

Sturdivant."

Struggling not to chuckle, she squirmed before squealing with laughter. Max hugged her tightly, sensing remnants of her distress.

"I'm sorry I scared you... but it was worth it in the end, right?"

Brigitte pushed Max away with a look that answered his question—it was definitely not worth it. "We have to be at Nobu in an hour. You sure you're okay to be alone? Maybe you should come, too?"

Max contemplated the question. "No. I'm going to rest."

Brigitte planted a kiss on his forehead then stood. "If it's not too late, I'll call you when we're done."

Max blew her a kiss as she marched from the room and skipped down the steps.

Grabbing a remote control like the one in his den, he activated a flat screen monitor affixed to the wall. He pressed a few buttons until a tiny window popped up on screen, showing Brigitte as she exited the building. He launched a search function and scanned the surveillance footage to see what had transpired between his falling asleep in the den and awakening in his bedroom. After a brief search, he saw himself marching zombie-like up the steps into his room.

In a way, he felt foolish for even watching the surveillance tape. No patch on the forehead. No midget in makeup. No blonde woman in black. How could any of those things have been possible anyway? Battenberg security measures were too intricate and too sophisticated. He dismissed the strange dream from his mind. Perhaps his near-death experience had evoked it.

Then he remembered Chandler had called. Now, he had a choice to make. Max needed to decide whether or not he was actually going to stay home.

CHAPTER 13

*A*fter Brigitte's departure, Max piddle-paddled around. He watched TV, checked his work voice mail, talked on the phone, surfed the internet, all the while trying to decide if going out was sensible. He was tired after all—apparently tired enough to sleep-walk from the den to the bedroom. At the same time, he was giddy with excitement. Even if he couldn't discuss Oak Island, he could still celebrate.

Feeling slightly refreshed from the odd nap, Max stepped into his enormous walk-in closet. To call it a closet was an understate-ment. The room was in fact larger than most people's bedrooms, with everything inside perfectly organized like a small boutique. On one wall, a suit rack held dozens of suits, all of them sorted by color. In the center of the room, a table of neatly folded sweaters was on display, and just below that sat a rack of shoes. On an adja-cent wall, jeans were displayed almost exactly as they would be in a department store.

Max navigated through the closet and quickly dressed in black jeans, black boots and a black T-shirt. He moved to his coat rack and pulled off a black leather motorcycle jacket. Crossing to a mirrored wall, he evaluated himself. He looked good in black, great in fact. Satisfied, he descended to the garage and input the proper codes to access his vehicles.

As the outer garage door was opening, Brigitte phoned. "Hey, babe," she sang into the receiver. "You still up?"

Max could hear in her voice that she was buzzed. "Sounds like you two had a good time tonight."

"Just missing you. At dinner, I started thinking about what happened today and I got emotional all over again."

"Bridge, I hope you didn't say anything."

"No, Max, but thanks for your concern. I was thinking about other stuff like you almost not coming home with us."

"Whoa, whoa, just cool your jets. I'm fine, you're fine, every-thing's fine."

"I left early. Marilyn kept asking a lot of questions."

"You home now?"

"Yeah. I just wanted to say good night."

"I know, it was a long day. Just try to get some rest, okay?"

"I will. I love you."

"Love you too."

Max hung up. Because he knew Brigitte wouldn't approve, he didn't reveal he was going out. He would spend an hour or two indirectly celebrating the Oak Island discovery, and then he would return for a decent night's sleep. He glanced about the garage at his two current cars: a jet black Range Rover and a burgundy Porsche Boxster. Instead, he pulled a black helmet from the wall and crossed behind the Range Rover to where a black Ducati motorcycle was parked.

Seconds later, perched atop the Ducati, Max raced out onto the streets of Chicago. On occasions like these, he preferred the bike. For starters, he was impatient and deplored traffic but could move unimpeded on the Ducati through busy streets. He also enjoyed anonymity, as he could scarcely be recognized with a helmet and black visor covering his face.

It was still early May with a midnight chill in the air. A brisk wind cut through his clothes, reaching his skin as he cornered through the back streets. Fortunately, he wasn't traveling far.

Fifteen minutes later, he pulled into a dark alley, the bike vibrating beneath him. The asphalt had recently been sprayed and was glistening with a thin film of water. Along the entire block there were a series of back door entrances. Max coasted toward the end, where there was a nook for large trash bins. This night it was empty. He shut off the Ducati and wheeled it into the space, hiding it from view. Satisfied, he retrieved his cell phone and sent Chandler a text message that read, "I'm here."

Even in the absence of garbage bins, Max could smell the residue of trash; a strong and pungent odor made him impatient for Chandler to open the door.

During the wait he noticed graffiti spray-painted against the wall roughly three feet from the building's exit. It was in black paint and looked as if it had been sprayed on with a stencil. The image was of George W. Bush's face. For the most part, it was well defined except where paint had dribbled down the wall. Sitting on top of the ex-president's likeness was a large crown with a single word spelled out across it in black capital letters: *RIZICK*.

Max assumed the graffiti had just been applied since the wall appeared recently painted. He wondered if "RIZICK" might be an underground band and the stencil some kind of concert promotion.

Before he could give it any further thought, the door to the Library opened and there stood the infamous Chandler, Max's new friend and employee. Max could hear music thumping from the club's dark hallway.

Chandler was extremely pale, but with flawless porcelain skin. There was a slight red tinge to his cheeks, and his brown hair looked soft and floppy. Although slighter than Max, he had a nice physique and was dressed in a light blue v-neck T-shirt, which revealed a rather hairy chest.

"Get in here, it's chilly out," Chandler barked as he pulled Max inside. He grabbed Max's helmet as Max slipped off his motorcycle jacket. "Let's get you to coat check."

Once inside, Max and Chandler made their way through a series of shadowy hallways, which were peppered with men. At coat check, they were greeted by a small line and Max wondered why. A muscular man at the front had just removed his coat and was now taking off his pants. He stripped to a black leather jock strap then began carefully folding his clothes. The man behind the counter took the garments and placed them in a clear plastic bag.

Incredulous, Max turned to Chandler. "Why're they taking clothes off? Is this a special event tonight?"

Chandler was dismissive and matter of fact. "I guess it's underwear night. Don't worry, you know you don't have to strip if you don't want to."

Max offered a half smile. "Okay. I'll wait for you over here."

Chandler poked Max in the stomach. "Suit yourself." He took his coat. "I'm glad you came out."

While Chandler waited in line, Max stepped into an adjacent

hallway. Men of all shapes and sizes were circulating back and forth in various states of undress. Max smiled as some of them passed. In the back of his mind Indigo's words whispered, *You have been deceived. This man is neither who nor what you think he is.*

A handsome man with brown skin and curly, black hair started to pass, but Max caught his attention, causing him to double back. The sexy stranger spoke with a slight accent.

"How are you tonight?"

Max wasn't shy, but his response was awkward. "So far so good. The night's young."

The man extended his hand. "Antonio." Antonio shook Max's hand and continued to hold it.

"You have an accent, Antonio. Where are you from?"

"Buenos Aires. You gonna tell me your name?"

Max contemplated the question, unable to decide if he was put off by Antonio's aggressive manner. Poking his chest out and standing a little taller, he confidently answered, "Ian. My name's Ian."

Although the name wasn't entirely correct, Max didn't feel he was being completely deceptive. Ian was an alter ego composed of the last three letters of his name, Maximilian. He had used this moniker before. He finally withdrew his hand from Antonio's. "So, do you live here or are you just visiting? From Argentina, I mean."

Antonio stepped in closer to Max. "I live here now."

Before Max could respond, Chandler was at his side. "Already found a friend?"

"Yeah. This is Antonio. This is my friend Chandler."

Chandler smiled at Antonio, looking him up and down. Had the Argentinean been a model in one of their publishing layouts, Chandler would definitely have signed off his approval. With an even larger smile, he urged Max and Antonio forward. "C'mon, boys, we're going in."

Together all three men turned and headed down the long, dark corridor. Music was thumping in the main room as they entered. Max spotted a glass booth high above the floor. Inside, the DJ was spinning cutting-edge house music.

A small laser show, peppered with strobe lights, was also going on in the otherwise dark room. Red and blue lasers shot back and forth above everyone's heads. Max glanced around the room. Ninety-five percent of the crowd were men and half of them were in their under-wear. The other half were in tank tops and sleeveless T-shirts, each flashing skin and bulging muscles.

The majority of patrons were meticulously coiffed with perfect haircuts and many had contoured eyebrows. In that respect, Antonio didn't fit in. His appearance was raw and unrefined with thick, jet-black eyebrows framing his dark eyes. The Argentinean reached out and touched Max's arm.

"So, Ian, I haven't seen you here before."

Chandler turned, at first surprised but then remembering Max's alter ego. "Ian doesn't come out unless you twist his arm."

Max laughed heartily, somewhat ill at ease. "You guys want a drink?"

Chandler frowned at Max's offer, jealous in a way that Antonio was receiving his attention. It was the first time in a long while that he and Max had hung out, and already he'd become a third wheel. The three of them crossed to the bar where a small crowd was wait-ing on drinks. Max hoped a cocktail would relax him.

When they stepped in line, Antonio stood close. Within seconds the crowd pressed forward, pushing the men together. Max could feel the contours of Antonio's body pressing against his. Just a few feet away, two men were engaged in a passionate embrace. Max turned toward the stage where male go-go dancers moved to seduce. As they crept ever closer to the bar Max found the whole scene titillat-ing. He turned, his face barely inches from Antonio's.

"What're you having?"

Antonio watched Max's lips as he answered. "A brandy, please." His voice was masculine and deep.

"A brandy it is." Max leaned back to ask Chandler what he wanted, then ordered their drinks. Once they'd been served, the three of them made their way to a quieter corner. Sensing that Chandler was feeling extraneous, Max leaned over and whispered, "You okay if he hangs out a while? Seems like a nice guy."

Chandler could barely stop from rolling his eyes. "Of course you're pulling the minute you arrive. We were friggin' at coat check, Ian."

Max noticed the sarcasm in Chandler's use of the name.

Glancing Antonio's way, Chandler continued, "Looks like Antonio

Sabato, the junior of course, sounds like Antonio Banderas, and his name is freakin' Antonio. How can I say no to progress?" With a coy wink, Chandler laughed, pretending to high-five Max while Antonio was looking away. Then he retrieved his vibrating phone from his pocket and read a newly arrived text message. "Oh shit, another friend's at the back door."

"And here I thought you only did that for me."

"Be right back." Chandler turned to Antonio. "Don't let him leave, okay? I'm coming back." Then Chandler disappeared into the crowd.

Antonio smiled, showing off a perfect set of teeth. "I didn't chase him away, did I?"

"Not at all. He's off to fetch another friend." At the beginning of the night, Max had been uneasy with Antonio's flirtations, but the alcohol was putting him at ease. In order to hear over the music the men were now standing close to one another. From time to time Max could feel Antonio's lips brushing against his ear as he spoke.

"Have you ever been to Argent—"

Max leaned in and kissed Antonio before he could finish his sentence. Antonio's lips were soft and his breath was sweet and tinged with the taste of brandy. After a brief moment, Max broke away.

Antonio looked surprised, but pleased. "I was wondering if I'd get to do that."

Max laughed. "Another brandy and maybe you will again."

Antonio smiled and retrieved his wallet. "Next round's on me. I'll be right back." With a skip in his step, Antonio returned to the bar.

Max removed his phone and quickly sent Chandler a text, wanting to know his whereabouts. Chandler always responded right away no matter what he was doing. Nearly a minute later, Max's phone beeped. He laughed when he read the message. "Busy right now. Get back n a few." Max wrote back that he was still with Antonio, but would find him later. The moment he hit "send," Antonio returned with drinks.

"Here you are." Antonio handed Max a cocktail.

"Thank you," Max replied, then turned the glass up and downed the whole thing. A shiver ran through his body as the liquor coursed down his throat. "Didn't want to carry that around all night. C'mon, let's go downstairs."

Initially, Antonio had been the aggressor, but Max was taking control. He took the Argentinean and pulled him through the crowd into the nearest stairwell. Together they descended into the darkest bowels of the club, where a series of catacomb-like corridors led back and forth like a maze. As his eyes adjusted, Max discerned the silhouettes of people in all sorts of sexually compromising positions. Before he could process it all, Antonio stopped dead in his tracks.

"Oh shit." Shaken, he abruptly pulled Max into a corner. "My ex is here."

"What?" Max couldn't tell whom Antonio was referring to since he was facing the wall.

"He didn't handle our breakup very well. Made him kind of nuts."

"Like he's stalking you nuts?" Max could see Antonio was squinting to determine who was standing in the corridor. The idea that Antonio might be setting him up came to mind. *Keep your ear to the ground,* his father had warned. Now, here he was with a complete stranger and no one but Chandler even knew where he was.

"I already filed an order of protection, but I don't want him to see me." Antonio grabbed Max by the shoulders and traded places with him so Max had his back to the wall with a view of the corridor. "I'm sure that's him right behind us. Can you see him?"

Max had been skeptical, but now Antonio had him pinned against the wall. The alarms in his head quieted when he noticed a man lingering and looking their way.

To reassure Max, Antonio continued, "If you don't mind waiting a minute or two, I am sure he'll go away."

Max could feel the heat of Antonio's breath on his neck. Even more telling was the South American's heart, which was racing in his chest. Antonio was scared. He pushed Max farther into the wall and lowered his voice to a whisper.

"What about now? He still there?"

Max squinted and could see the strange figure looking their way. Then it happened. A burlap bag snapped down over Antonio's head and he was yanked from Max's grip. Antonio screamed out but the cry was immediately stifled as if he had been punched in the gut. Suddenly, Antonio was gone.

Stunned, Max stepped forward on adrenalin and instinct. He yelled, "Hey!"

It was so dark he hadn't noticed the attackers' approach. Two men grabbed hold of him as well, and a burlap bag descended over his head, blocking out his already limited view.

"What the—"

Max's words were choked off when a strap in the burlap bag was pulled tight about his throat. The move cut off his air and restricted his vocal chords. He struggled to free himself but realized he was no match for what might have been three very strong men. Before he knew it his arms were yanked behind him and bound.

Demetrius had given the Poseidon alert, warning him to be aware of his surroundings. Instead, he had gone to this public place and compromised himself. Gagged and bound, Max felt his feet leave the ground, making any kind of struggle impossible.

As club music thumped in the background, he felt his assailants carrying him up a stairwell. A profound sense of doom washed over him. Suddenly, the cold air of the night hit his skin and Max knew with finality that he had just been abducted from the club.

CHAPTER 14

*I*t had been only a year since Max's graduation from Yale. He wasn't sure how, but Demetrius had learned of a tryst he was having and hadn't reacted well to it. His name was Gary Richards, the first man to spark Max's attention away from the opposite sex. Before Gary, sexual contact of any kind with a man had never been considered. At times, Max still wondered how Gary had awakened something in him that he hardly knew existed.

In a twist of irony he had met Gary through Shelly, a girl he'd dated at Yale. Shelly had asked him to be her escort to a friend's wedding in California. They had flown out together and were staying in a hotel with other invited guests. On the day of the ceremony, everyone had dressed in their best attire before going downstairs to their cars. Because he and Shelly had forgotten their gift, Max had returned to the room to retrieve it.

As it turned out, Gary had also left something in his room, which was adjacent to where Max and Shelly were staying. He and Max had taken an elevator together. Inside, Gary had stolen glances at Max. Each time, Max had looked away.

He had been uncomfortable, but there was something intriguing about the stranger. He was tall and rugged with brown, puppy-dog eyes and his hair was so dark that it looked like polished onyx. He smiled, showing off a set of slightly crooked teeth, but the imperfection only added to his appeal. It looked like Gary was blushing when he spoke.

"It's funny we both forgot something in our rooms."

Max didn't fully comprehend the comment. There was nothing funny — perhaps coincidental, but not funny.

But Gary didn't stop there. He gave Max a once-over, taking in his appearance from head to toe. There were mirrored walls in the elevator and Max even thought he saw Gary look at the reflection of his backside. After the evaluation, Gary looked Max directly in the eye.

"You look pretty sharp in that suit."

Max squirmed just a bit at Gary's forwardness. "Thanks, man."

"What kind of suit is that?"

Max awkwardly returned Gary's stare as he answered. "Hugo Boss."

The next thirty seconds were a blur to Max. He couldn't remember what words were exchanged; maybe he had blocked them out. But as the elevator doors opened, he and Gary were kissing passionately. He couldn't believe how the intimate contact made him feel. He and Shelly enjoyed an excellent sex life, but kissing Gary was different. Max felt as if a switch inside of him had been flipped to the on position. In that moment, he wanted to know more about Gary.

They hurried to their rooms. With a devilish smile Gary offered a suggestion.

"Open the adjoining door."

Max didn't reply. He swiped his key card in the access slot, then rushed to unlock the room's neighboring door. When he pulled it open, Gary was standing there, his arousal more apparent than ever in his suit.

The two men grabbed each other tightly, their hands groping up and down their bodies as they kissed. A tsunami had been set in motion, and there was no stopping it. Max felt amateurish with Gary, who unzipped Max's pants. Gary reached down and slid down Max's boxer-briefs, which left him completely overwhelmed.

"What are you doing?"

Gary smiled again, playing Max like a familiar instrument. "What's it look like?"

Gary dropped to his knees and took Max in his mouth. Max moaned as beads of sweat began to rise on his forehead. It was by no means his first sexual act, but the sheer taboo of doing it with a man added to the excitement.

During the interlude, time became disjointed. Max wasn't sure how long it had been when he thought he heard a key card being swiped in the lock at the room's entrance. He pulled Gary to his feet and shoved him back in the adjoining room. He quickly closed the door, snapping the lock shut as the outer room door swung open.

Shelly entered just as Max was fumbling to fix his pants. She had just missed it. He could hear Gary locking the interior door on the other side.

Shelly stood in the doorway and watched as Max zipped up his pants. "Babe, what are you doing?"

He was nervous and breathing heavily, trying not to appear like a kid caught with his hand in the cookie jar. Given the circumstances, it was difficult. "I'm so damn horny. I thought I'd finish myself off."

Shelly frowned, feeling a little uncomfortable with Max's revelation. But then a smile came to her lips. "I suppose we have a few minutes." She crossed to Max and began kissing him passionately.

Max wondered if she could taste Gary's kisses, but she didn't seem deterred. Within minutes, they were tearing at each others' clothes, passionately engaged in sex against the adjoining door.

Gary listened on the other side as the door vibrated to their lovemaking. Realizing he would be missed, he didn't linger, stopping only to grab his forgotten greeting card before returning downstairs.

Neither Gary nor Max spoke a word to each other for the remainder of the day. At the wedding reception, Gary managed rather covertly to slide his business card into Max's pocket. When Max saw the card, he had mixed feelings about keeping it. On one hand, he felt awkward about what he'd done, but he had also been raised a Battenberg. The privilege of such an upbringing provided Max with a sense of entitlement that he could enjoy whatever his heart desired without the worry of repercussion or collateral damage.

In the past, he had often dated multiple girls, but he was always clear with everyone involved that he was not exclusive. But this was different. He wasn't interested in dating Gary. What was he supposed to do with his card? Suddenly Max was confused.

On more than one occasion, he contemplated tossing the business card in the trash. What they had done haunted him in the best and worst of ways, and Max was titillated each time he thought of the interlude. A week later, he was still experiencing sexual tension, at which point he simply broke down and called. Gary didn't seem surprised.

A month later, he and Gary returned for a weekend at the same California hotel. For hours at a time they would lock themselves away. Before he even realized it, Max had begun an affair. They met every few weeks in various cities about the country. The trysts continued for several months until one day Max received a call while Gary was in the shower. In the middle of repacking, he had seen his father's number flashing on the screen of his phone. Max was upbeat when he answered.

"Hey, dad, what's up?"

"I think it's time we talk, Maximilian."

Max knew there was something negative brewing. It was only when he was displeased that Demetrius used his entire name. "Okay. What's up?"

"You realize the Battenberg name has become synonymous with an empire? Thanks in part to me, my father and his father before him." Demetrius' voice was stern and gave Max flashbacks from childhood. "I need you to stop what you're doing."

"Dad, I'm sorry," Max blurted, "but what're you talking about?"

"Where are you right now, Maximilian?"

Max faltered at the idea that Demetrius might know where he was or, even worse, what he was doing. He said nothing.

"I've worked tirelessly building the family name and you will not tarnish it or bring scandal upon it. I won't allow it."

Max feared he knew just what Demetrius was getting at, but he couldn't relent just yet. There was still a chance that his private life was in fact private. "I wish you'd just say what you're talking about."

"Don't play games with me, Max."

Puzzled, Max looked about the room, searching for surveillance devices. He crossed to the window and pulled the draperies shut. "What? Are you having me followed?"

"You're not clever enough for this. If I can see what you're up to, everyone can."

"I don't want to discuss this anymore."

"It stops today. I need you to promise me, Max."

"Okay, I get it. I heard you. Let's just drop it."

Max was feeling defensive and angry. He didn't wish to argue any further, for it was pointless. His father controlled too many things—didn't know any other way to be than in control.

Demetrius remained quiet on the line and Max understood his silence. His father was a shrewd businessman who drove a hard bargain. He treated personal issues much like he did professional ones. He had a mental checklist, and once checked off, he was already on to the next thing. Max recalled the conversation and remembered something he hadn't thought of in years. Before hanging up Demetrius had mentioned, *One of these days, you'll know what it means to be a Battenberg.*

CHAPTER 15

While it seemed an eternity, Max's dramatic club removal had barely lasted ninety seconds. Once outside, he had been carried forty or fifty feet before being thrown into the back of a vehicle. Max coughed and choked from the bag that was tightly noosed around his neck. Utterly in shock, he had failed to struggle even after his restraints had been removed.

He couldn't see a thing but felt as if he had been thrown upon a leather bench. He did notice classical music playing in the background and that the air felt comfortably warm. The next voice he heard belonged, strangely, to Demetrius.

"I'm aware, but I've made it clear that's not my issue."

Hearing his father's voice was both soothing and terrifying at the same time. On one hand, he realized he was no longer in danger, but why would his own father kidnap him? Now, it was Demetrius he had to confront, and in some ways that seemed worse than the things he'd been imagining.

Max could feel the burlap bag being unfastened. His throat opened and he gulped in air. When the sack was removed, he realized he was in the back of Demetrius' limousine.

A man named Logan, who Max only knew slightly, had removed the burlap bag and restraints. He smiled at Max. "Hello, Mr. Battenberg."

Now he was being offered smiles and hellos.

Seated on a leather bench across from him, Demetrius had his legs crossed and was calmly talking on the phone. He nodded to Logan, who stepped from the car and closed the door. Demetrius looked Max's way but was expressionless as he continued his phone conversation.

Finally able to get his bearings, Max noticed they were parked in the alley where he had left his motorcycle. Outside, Antonio was being detained by one of his father's security details. As rumor had it, the majority of his father's men were from one of three places: former military, FBI or CIA. Typically, when they arrived on the scene it was only a matter of minutes before they were in complete control. Tonight had been no different.

Logan joined the men detaining Antonio near the club's exit. One of them handed the Argentinean a sheet of paper. His new South American acquaintance looked scared and perturbed, but Max knew he would cooperate. When Demetrius was involved everyone always did. The paper was surely a nondisclosure agreement, and Antonio would sign it. That was part of Logan's appeal. Demetrius had immediately been impressed by how convincing his assistant could be.

To Max's surprise, a flatbed tow truck with his Ducati already on the back turned the corner, exiting the alley. Demetrius still hadn't acknowledged Max, who sat, ill at ease, glancing around. Max had been in his father's cars before, but he had forgotten how plush they were. By simply entering the limo, Max felt he had left Kansas for the more colorful Oz. He studied the wooden rack holding crystal glasses and decanters that sparkled like fine Tiffany diamonds. The finely polished wood shined as if encased in glass. And somehow the lighting in the limo was flattering to everything inside. Demetrius had given Max a generous trust fund, but the son's lavish lifestyle in no way compared to what the father enjoyed.

As his father's call dragged on, Max grew more and more self-conscious. He longed for Ian to step in and receive the reprimand for his crimes, but this wasn't Ian's world and his alter ego had never been tasked with handling Demetrius. Even at twenty-four, Max felt like a five-year-old in trouble. There hadn't been a trial but he was nevertheless being forced to await the sentencing phase.

His phone chimed with a text message. Max knew it was from Chandler. He removed the phone, happy for a distraction, but Demetrius raised a hand to indicate displeasure. Max took a deep breath as he placed his phone on the shiny table beside him. Whoever the message was from, it would have to wait.

Demetrius' voice was strong and imposing. "I don't like where the election's heading. I'm sure you understand the problems we'll have if things don't go our way. Remember there's a pipeline through that country." Demetrius listened, then cut the other person off. "Keep the oil flowing, all right? Even if it's just for another year or two." His tone lightened, but his face remained heavy and serious. "I give you carte blanche. Do whatever you have to." Demetrius shut off his phone and placed it on the table beside Max's. "Have you fucking lost your mind?"

"I was just thinking I should be asking you the same thing."
Although his words were bold, Max felt sheepish, hoping Demetrius
hadn't gotten word of the type of club he was in. His father apparently decided to ignore his impudence.

"Just a few weeks ago I asked you to keep your ear to the ground.
The same fucking day you're attacked by some nutjob, and then this
is where I find you today?" Demetrius gestured at the seedy alley-
way outside. "It's sloppy, Max. Fucking sloppy."

"Dad..." Max struggled to find the right words.

"Not now, Max. I don't have time for stories." Demetrius pressed
a button beside him and within seconds, the limousine was on the
move, turning onto the street outside the alley. "I thought I made it
clear when I first learned of your tastes that you have to be savvy
with your plans regardless of what they are."

"I am not a child anymore."

"You sure about that? Because that, back there, was extremely
careless. There's so much you have to learn." Demetrius removed
a brandy bottle from the limousine bar. "Would you like a drink?
I'd say you need one."

Max's gut reaction was to say no, but Demetrius was right. He
did need one. "Yes, please."

Demetrius poured a drink for his son, and another for himself.
"I wish you'd keep in mind how busy I am."

"Your guys choked me back there. Did you know that? Not
to mention the spectacle of pulling me out that way. It was
embarrassing."

Demetrius laughed. "Embarrassing to who?"

"I have a phone. You could have asked me to come out."

"We're Battenbergs, Max. Discretion is of the utmost importance, in particular when your cravings are of such an exotic nature.
Establishments of that sort are not for our kind. Our breeding dictates
this. Something you repeatedly ignore in defiance of our pedigree.
It is you that embarrasses, it is you that brings shame."

"Why are you here? I'm twenty-fuckin'-four, about to be twenty-five. And you're still following me like I'm some kind of a
runaway."

Demetrius chuckled as if the whole thing were a joke. "I needed
to prove a point. Show you what happens when you're reckless.

Apparently, you didn't learn that in New Orleans."

Max turned and looked out the window, disgusted.

Undeterred, Demetrius continued, "Now, thanks to you, Hades is in effect."

Max was perplexed by his father's statement. "What're you talking about?"

"You let your guard down, Max. Otto asked you not to mention Oak Island."

"He told you we found something?"

"Word is out that you recovered something. But someone on that island couldn't hold water. Either you, your girlfriend or someone on your crew."

Having figured that his father would be proud, a satisfied air settled onto Max's face.

"Thanks to your foolishness and indiscretion we've all been placed in a predicament."

Max was stunned by his dad's reaction. "What? I thought you'd be happy about this."

"Not so grown up now, are you?" Demetrius paused to drink from his glass before continuing, "If what you found is indeed the missing component to that device, there are powerful people who'll go to great lengths to make sure neither of us ever use it."

With each word Max was growing more confused. "You're talking like you know what it can do."

"You have no idea what you've done, Maximilian. The Antikythera Device is voodoo. Witchcraft. You've placed us on the precipice for something so silly."

Max simply stared at Demetrius in bewilderment. Just like Indigo, his father was speaking in riddles. "How'd you know where I was tonight?"

"When Hades is in effect, it's my job to know where you are at all times."

Max studied his father, who had the best poker face of anyone around. "If I didn't know better I'd think there's some kind of GPS implanted in me."

Demetrius raised an eyebrow ever so slightly, as if to say touché. To someone unfamiliar with the Battenberg patriarch, it would have barely been noticeable. But Max caught it.

Sipping from his brandy, Demetrius continued, "Perhaps you're catching on. I had Logan retrieve you because things have turned. Hades, Max. After what happened to your mother and brother — " Demetrius faltered, something he rarely did. "In spite of your actions, it is my goal to keep you safe. You think you're clever, but you know so little of this world and how you fit into it. Probably it's why you run the streets, exposing yourself and the family name to such foolishness. You have no idea what you've gotten yourself into, or what it takes to keep this family strong."

Max studied his father's face with a bit of bravado. "I know you don't always play fair. And you pull strings to make things go your way."

"If I pull strings, Max, it's to make things go *our* way. Not mine. I might not be the one who made this family powerful, but I have strengthened its hold. And I am going to make sure to keep it that way."

Max turned and gazed out at the street. "I'm not like you. You know that."

"Because I've sheltered you. I'm beginning to wonder if I've done you a disservice. Our methods are efficient and they allow us to fit in."

This wasn't the type of reprimand Max expected. His father actually seemed quite calm. But somehow, the conversation still seemed distressing. He wasn't quite sure what his father was getting at, and the uncertainty of why he was there, why he had been humiliated, was beginning to make him antsy.

"You're speaking in riddles. Can you just tell me what's going on?"

This time, Demetrius turned and gazed out at the passing streets. "Like I said, you know so little of this world and how you fit into it. But this is your lucky year. Very soon, it will all be clear. I have moved up your initiation." Demetrius turned and fixed Max in his gaze. "It will happen this week. Arrangements have already been made."

Max was completely caught off guard. He had assumed his father raided the club because of the type of establishment it was. Now, Demetrius was talking about something completely unrelated: his initiation. Could that have been why?

"But it's only a few months away. Why move it up now?"

"You did this, Max. With that dreaded Anti-k Device. Seeking it has set forces in motion. It's become clear I won't be able to keep you safe. Not until you're initiated. Right now, you're in the wind and that has to change. It was necessary."

Max stared at his father, still miffed by the night's conversation. He found the irony peculiar and unfortunate. Demetrius, who was normally cold, distant and unavailable, had finally given enough of a damn to rush into the night with an entire security detail only to find Max groping and being groped by a complete stranger.

"So, that's it? You're not going to explain anything more about this."

"That's how it works, I'm afraid. These traditions aren't to be tampered with."

As Demetrius finished his sentence the limousine pulled up before Max's house.

"Once you're initiated, we'll talk again. That's when things will begin to make sense. I promise." Demetrius pushed a button on his console. A drawer beneath the leather bench disengaged and rolled out, revealing a silver attaché case. "Take it," Demetrius instructed.

Max leaned over to pick up the case, but it was so heavy that he nearly fell over when he tried to lift it. "What the hell's in that thing?"

Demetrius smiled. "Open and see for yourself."

Max stared at his father, wondering what on Earth could be in the locked case. "What's the combination?"

"Right now, the last four digits of your social."

Max keyed in the code and popped open the case. Inside there were five shiny pieces of gold bullion lying side by side. Light from the limousine's cabin reflected off the bars, illuminating their faces. Stunned, he looked up at Demetrius.

"What's this for?"

"You'll need them at your initiation. That's all I can tell you right now."

"You keep saying that." Max stared at the gold bars. Each must have weighed at least twenty pounds. "You've got to help me understand a little more than what you're saying."

Demetrius frowned, silently letting Max know things didn't work that way. He reached in his jacket and removed a leather wallet from which he pulled a credit card with Max's name on it. "This is yours.

In two days, you'll go to O'Hare. At 8 a.m. sharp. Your driver will know which terminal. Place the card in the first automated kiosk you come to. A boarding pass will print with the location of your initiation. For security reasons those details will be withheld until the last minute."

Max's expression gave away what he was about to say. "You realize this is kind of creepy, Dad."

When Demetrius responded his voice was loving, but his tone held immense gravity. "If you're unsettled, Max, you should be. I hope you understand that."

"I get it, it's serious. It's Hades. But I don't understand because you're not telling me anything, which is starting to freak me out."

"You'll put the case in a larger piece of luggage. I've made arrangements so you won't be stopped." Demetrius placed a hand on his son's shoulder and showed a sensitivity Max was unused to. "Normally, under Hades, you'd be home bound or provided a security detail, but we can't do that now. The terms of initiation are clear. Plan nothing. No prearranged cars, no planned trips. Everything you do should be spontaneous. Am I clear?"

"Yes." Max could feel his defiant nature bubbling to the surface but he squashed it down. "I got it."

"One more thing. It's important that you fast until the initiation's complete."

Max was dumbfounded by the instruction. "Excuse me."

"You heard correctly. A period of fasting is vital to the initiation. It's crucial you don't eat until it's over. Do you understand?"

"Actually, no, I don't. How many days do you expect me to do that?"

"As long as it takes. I want you to promise, Max. You can do water, limited juice from fresh fruits or vegetables, but that's all you're allowed. A fast is integral to the process. You have to swear to it."

"All right already." Max didn't believe himself capable of the restraint required to fast, but he would try. "You could have warned me about this sooner."

"We'll speak again when you return. By then at least some of this will make sense. And we can proceed from there."

Once again, Demetrius pressed a button on his console. Within seconds, one of his guards opened the limousine door. Max stepped out and the guard accompanied him, lugging the metallic case of gold to the front of his house. Max punched in his security code to disarm the alarm. As he moved to enter, the tow truck arrived with his Ducati on the flatbed. He turned and instructed the guard.

"Have them offload at my garage."

The guard nodded, placing Max's case inside the doorway. Max locked and re-armed the door before descending to the garage to assure that his motorcycle was safely inside.

When Demetrius departed, Max returned to his den and plopped on the couch. He was more than exhausted. He was wrung out. From start to finish, the day could not have been any stranger. After helicoptering to Oak Island, he had nearly drowned in the Money Pit before recovering the mysterious golden dial. Intruders had seemingly invaded his dreams. Then his father had him abducted to provide him with a case of gold bullion so he could attend his initiation. And Demetrius' declaration that they were in danger had only made things worse.

Just weeks earlier, Indigo had predicted all would be revealed, and now Demetrius had more or less reiterated the same thing. *Things will begin to make sense, I promise,* were his father's exact words. Max felt almost overwhelmed by the fact that Demetrius and Indigo both knew infinitely more than they were willing to reveal. Independent of one another they had each promised clarity in the future. Sadly, Max was hardly comforted by the synchronicity.

Slipping off his shoes, he remembered the text Chandler had sent from the club, which seemed ages ago. He opened and read the message. "Where r u? Did u leave?"

Max sent a reply saying he was home and would call in the morning. As he prepared cursorily for bed, he hoped and prayed the next days would be without the intense drama of the last.

CHAPTER 16

The following morning, Max awoke feeling as if the entire previous day had been a dream, or perhaps a nightmare. Before New Orleans, Max's life had been more or less charmed and carefree. In some ways, the events of Mardi Gras had served as a turning point, but Max could hardly say it was for the better. It started with Indigo. In her strange and peculiar glory, she had disparaged the Battenberg name. Max wasn't sure why he had been so troubled, but the insane accusations had hit a note with him. As time passed he felt increasingly foolish for having reacted so aversely. People spoke ill of the Battenbergs daily, often times in public. It came with the territory. Wealth and power had placed targets on their backs and Max knew this.

He also knew because of his cognitive science major at Yale that people often protested when elements of truth were involved in harsh criticism. Why, if he didn't believe in psychics, had Indigo struck a note? More importantly, why had he sought the Antikythera Mechanism? Max still didn't know the answers.

According to Demetrius, his find had triggered a Hades alert. Now, the entire family was in jeopardy, but no one was hurrying to explain why.

Max crawled from bed and stepped into his state-of-the-art shower, hoping that it might rejuvenate him. He turned on the jets. Water splashed from three separate showerheads, one spraying warm water, the others hot and cold. After a brief delay, the three-jet assembly began rotating, dousing Max's entire body with stimulation.

In the back of his mind, he hoped the water would serve to cleanse not only his body but also his conscience. He didn't think of himself as dishonest or a cheater, but essentially he had become both. Each time he invoked his alter ego, "Ian," it was to deceive someone: mostly Brigitte, sometimes his friends and always himself.

On occasion, he felt grimy for his actions, but relinquishing his desires was never easy. As a Battenberg, he could scarcely remember a time when he hadn't gotten what he wanted.

In his heart, Max knew when his actions were improper, but he rationalized them as he saw fit. And college had only worsened the situation; Yale had been like a different planet for Max. It was the closest he had come to being out of his father's view, free to do and say as he pleased.

New Haven, Connecticut felt like freedom, not only from Demetrius but also from the daily pressures that came along with being a Battenberg. Max loved his time away. His entire freshman year, he had enjoyed his freedom just as most college students did. He played, sometimes studied and spent the entire first year deciding on a major. When he announced cognitive science to Demetrius, the choice had been received with a frown.

Max was nevertheless fascinated by the subject matter, whose primary objective was the creation of artificial intelligence. Through psychology, philosophy, anthropology, sociology and linguistics, Max toiled to comprehend the inner workings of the brain. Little did he know the groundwork was being laid for the creation of Ian, an alter ego who allowed Max liberties he would otherwise never enjoy.

At first, Ian had appeared quite innocently when Max chose to conceal he was a Battenberg. In the beginning, his aim hadn't been to mislead but was rather an exercise in defining his independence.

Over time, he realized there was a certain comfort living in Ian's skin. As Max Battenberg, so much was expected. Ian was simply allowed to be. Not a Battenberg, not a rich kid, not a disappointment, not a celebrity, just Ian. Ian knew how to relax and didn't have to apologize for his imperfections. Ian was empowered. Ian was free. But then everyone at Yale had realized he and Max were one and the same. With his secret identity revealed, Ian had vanished, only to be swiftly forgotten at school.

In the following years, Max perfected how to use an alternate persona. He couldn't ever allow his world to collide with Ian's. If he did, the usefulness of the alias would once again be lost. Not long after graduation, he rolled out an upgraded version of his pseudonym. The new and improved Ian had little to do with innocence and was more about stealth and subterfuge. Through Ian, Max could behave badly or satisfy his most ridiculous desires, often without guilt or at least consequence.

Max truly did care for Brigitte. It was possible he even loved her, but his ability to have whatever he desired made it difficult to commit. He supposed the issue of his lagging career also stemmed from the same struggle — he was still not prepared to fully make up his mind as to what he wanted.

Ian, on the other hand, lived by a very different set of rules and cared very little about the things that Max hoped to disavow. At the start, Max had wrestled with the concept of two lives. The reality of Ian versus Max was difficult if not impossible to reconcile. After all, his and Ian's desires were often diametrically opposed.

In some ways, Ian had always existed. Like the Frankenstein monster, he resided in fragments of Max that hadn't fully been assembled. At Yale, Max had acquired the tools of assembly and then lightning had struck, bringing Ian to life.

Deep down, he knew the alias only existed as a result of his own flaws. But over time, he had grown comfortable assuming less and less responsibility for Ian's thoughts and feelings. Finally, at some point, Ian developed his own secret life.

Max stepped from the shower and stood nude before a mirrored wall. Washing had cleansed his body, but it did nothing to assuage his soul. Approaching the mirror, he examined his finely sculpted physique, scrutinizing the smoothness of his skin. The night before, he had accused Demetrius of implanting a GPS chip in him. The accusation had been in jest, but the more Max thought about it, the more it made sense. From his glance, Demetrius had nearly admitted to it. But where was it?

Max knew the fleshy part of the buttocks was a likely hiding place, so he twisted his body for a better look. He examined his legs, and his arms, and then he saw it. Just a minuscule imperfection near his left armpit. Max ran a finger over the spot and felt a tiny, nearly imperceptible bump.

"How long have you been there?" he questioned. Before he could think further, his ringtone rang through compact speakers embedded in the bathroom wall. Max strode across the tiled floor and hit a button on a keypad near the door. "Hello."

Chandler's voice replaced the chime piping through the speakers. "What happened last night?"

"Oh, man, you won't believe it." Max crossed to the door, pulled down a robe and wrapped it around his naked body. "Let's just say I probably shouldn't have gone out."

"I figured you left with that guy."

Max thought of the outing, still perplexed by the night's events. "We did leave at the same time, but not together. It's a long story.

My dad showed up."

"Oh, shit, you're kidding."

"Yeah, some family shit he needed to talk about." Max exited the bathroom, but could still hear Chandler through speakers that were strategically placed throughout the house. "It looks like I'm going out of town tomorrow."

"Already? You just got back."

"Yeah." Max hardly felt the need to explain his absences. When call waiting beeped in, he crossed to another security keypad on the wall. A small LCD screen was flashing the name Brigitte. "Hey, that's Brigitte buzzing in. Can I call you back?"

"Of course."

Max clicked Chandler off to pick up Brigitte's call. "Good morning." Max sang more than spoke the greeting.

"Hey, sweets, you sleep okay last night?" Brigitte sounded rested and upbeat.

Max hesitated, wondering if it were a trick question. Then he lied. "Yeah, more or less. What about you?"

"Drank a little too much at Nobu. Kinda hung over."

"My dad did a drive-by last night."

"You're kidding. That must've been pretty late if it was after we talked."

Max could hear Brigitte chewing gum on the line. "You know he has his own schedule. He wants me to go on a trip tomorrow."

Brigitte remained quiet. Max knew she found the news disappointing.

"Where to?"

"Not sure yet. It's some confidential thing."

"Well, how long will you be gone?"

"Don't know that either. Guess I'll find out when I get there. You know what my pops wants, he gets."

"Yeah... I guess."

Max could hear Brigitte's insecurities rising to the surface. As a form of damage control he asked, "You want to grab lunch? Say in about an hour?"

With Max's invitation, Brigitte's tone lightened. "Can you pick me up?"

"I'll be there in an hour."

Max hung up and quickly dressed while mulling over the insanity that had become his life. Lately, few things seemed to be going his way.

Dressed in jeans and a T-shirt, he skipped down the steps and nearly collided with his house manager. "Oh, shit, I'm sorry, LC. I didn't know you were here."

"Good morning, sir. You know how I prefer an early start. I wanted to confirm if the new cleaning crew is doing a satisfactory job."

"So far so good. It was all sparkling when I got home last night."

"Wonderful, sir. I will check that your kitchen and bathrooms are properly stocked with supplies. If so, we will probably move forward with the new staff."

"Perfect. Thank you for the lumpia by the way. As usual, they were delicious."

"You couldn't have finished them already."

"No, but I'll probably have a few more before the day is done."

"Oh, sir..." Cora Batoon was a small Filipina who had been on the Battenbergs' residential staff since Max was a young boy. While in her early teens, Cora, whose full name was Corazón, had left the Philippines with her family for a new and exciting life in Milan. Already fluent in English, Spanish and Tagalog, she had quickly attained fluency in Italian and French.

While still in college, Cora had subsidized her expenses by occasionally cleaning houses. The agency that she worked for had incidentally assigned her to a villa where Demetrius and Fiona were staying with their newborn Max and their three year-old Christian. Fiona had quickly taken a liking to her for her multi-lingual capabilities and her upbeat disposition.

For the following two years, Fiona had asked for Cora whenever they were in Italy. As time went on, Cora had gained their trust. Her services had eventually been requested during the family's visits to France, Belgium and Spain, where she could easily double as interpreter. When she completed her business degree, the Battenbergs had made it worth her while to remain in their employ.

In a year's time, she had graduated from housekeeper to house manager, and currently supervised several Battenberg properties.

At Max's request, she had added his private residence to her roster. Aside from Demetrius and Otto, there were few people Max had known longer.

Cora's thick black hair was styled in a short bob that framed a round, pleasantly proportioned face. Her smooth olive complexion hardly defied her age, which was ten years more than her thirty-something appearance. Large, brown sympathetic eyes beheld Max with maternal pride. "Are you on your way out, sir?"

"Yeah, I'm traveling this week. I have a few errands to run."

"Very good, sir. I'll make sure everything's in order here."

"Thanks, LC." Max added. He had never given up his childhood nickname, which stood for "Lady Cora."

With a cursory hug, Max stomped down the steps toward his garage. Within seconds, he was zipping through traffic for a quick detour across town. There was still one thing he had to do before his lunch later that day with Brigitte.

CHAPTER 17

$\mathcal{A}$cross town, Max slipped his car into a spot in the underground parking structure of a mid-rise building. Instead of the standard elevator, he crossed to a locked metal door and opened it with a key on his ring. Inside was a single elevator door. He boarded the private lift and exited a dozen floors up. Seconds later, he strode into the plush waiting room of a private medical office. A forty-ish redhead was seated behind a nurse's station. She lit up at the sight of Max.

"Mr. Battenberg! How are you today?"

"I'm fine, Phyllis. Is he in?" Max flashed a semi-charming smile.

"Of course." Phyllis looked down at her computer, searching. "I don't see you on the schedule though. Is he expecting you?"

"Actually, no. I was just hoping to grab him for five or ten minutes."

Phyllis was very efficient. She quickly typed into her computer, then awaited a reply. After a few moments, she smiled at Max. "He's in the office. Just head on back."

Phyllis' response brought a smile to Max's face. "Thank you, Phyllis, you guys are tops."

Max crossed around the desk to a hallway leading to the back office. Before he made it down the corridor, a door swung open. A stocky South American doctor named Iago Bettencourt stepped out.

"Mr. Battenberg."

Max grinned. "Doctor Iago, how are you?"

Doctor Bettencourt's accent was not unlike Antonio's accent from the club. At age fifty-eight, he had aged gracefully. Salt and pepper hair and finely etched crow's feet lent credibility to a man who still possessed the looks of a Hollywood leading actor. Dr. Bettencourt shook Max's hand. "I'm just fine. What brings you in today?"

"I was hoping you could do me a favor." Max seemed slightly embarrassed by his request. "There's something I need removed."

The doctor stared into Max's face, examining his flawless skin.

Max offered a bashful smile. "It's not on my face."

Doctor Bettencourt was shrewd, which is why Max had chosen him. The doctor quickly ascertained the issue was of a more personal nature. "Got it. Please, step into one of the exam rooms, I think three is open."

Doctor Bettencourt followed Max inside. Once the door was shut, Max lowered his voice nearly to a whisper.

"I found something and I need your help."

Doctor Bettencourt stared quizzically at Max. "Why are you whispering?"

"I have a question first and I want you to be honest."

"Of course."

"Doctor-patient confidentiality, that applies all the time, correct?"

"Absolutely."

Max watched Doctor Bettencourt nod his head in agreement. "I'm pretty sure you know why I came to you that first time."

Doctor Bettencourt smiled warmly. "Of course. There was an issue you didn't want your father to know about."

Max nodded. "Which applies even more today. He can never know what I'm about to ask you to do."

Doctor Bettencourt remained hesitant, trying to understand where Max was going with the conversation. "I'm sorry, has there been a problem with information—"

"No, no, not at all. I just need to know the same privacy will be extended, even if there are pressures from the outside."

Doctor Bettencourt's interest seemed piqued. He further assured Max with the same warm smile. "Mr. Battenberg, as you know, I am not only ethically but legally bound to keep your business with me entirely confidential. Nothing has changed in this regard. So, tell me what is it you need removed?"

With his voice still at a whisper, Max continued, "Last night I learned there's a chip in me. It's GPS. I'm not sure how long it's been there, but I want it removed."

Doctor Bettencourt seemed relieved by Max's revelation. "Coming from someone like yourself, this is not at all unusual. You'd be surprised by the number of parents who are doing this nowadays."

"I need it out. And I'd prefer if no one but you knew about it."

"This is no problem." Bettencourt hesitated again. "Although something like that I'm sure is for your own protection.

"It's a leash. I can see the value for a child, but it was used inappropriately last night. I want it out." Max took note of the doctor's response, which now seemed reluctant. His demeanor left Max feeling uneasy.

Upon noticing Max's reaction, Bettencourt continued, "Let's remove it then."

A few minutes later, Doctor Bettencourt had a shirtless Max positioned on the exam table. He swabbed at the tiny bump on his left arm. After two shots of local anesthesia Bettencourt took a fine scalpel and made an incision. It took less than a minute to lift out the tiny implant. Max heard a pinging sound as the doctor dropped the implant in a glass Petri dish.

"Consider yourself unleashed." Bettencourt placed a small bandage over the incision. "That'll be sore, probably the rest of today. By tomorrow, you'll barely notice it."

Max pulled on his shirt. The implant was covered in a tiny layer of flesh and didn't look anything like he expected. He studied it before asking, "Is there any way to clean that up?"

"You want to hold onto it?"

"Are you kidding? I have to. My dad'll know something's up if I don't. I'll carry it until I need privacy, then I can leave it behind."

Max removed a necklace from beneath his shirt. Dangling from it was a miniature vial in which he could place the implant. Years ago someone had given him the pendant with cocaine in it.

"Very clever, Mr. Battenberg."

Doctor Bettencourt squirted a solution over the implant. It immediately dissolved the layer of flesh. The doctor tweezered the minuscule chip from the Petri dish and examined its construction more closely.

"An amazing piece of technology when you think about it."

Before Max could respond, his cell phone rang. He looked down and saw the name Brigitte flashing. "Oh shit, I'm late. Thanks, Doc. I have to bounce." He held out the tiny pendant jar so Dr. Bettencourt could drop the GPS implant inside. Max fastened the tiny container and shook the doctor's hand. "Thanks, doc." While hurrying into the hall he picked up Brigitte's call. "Hey, babe, I'm almost there. I had to make a pit stop."

Within minutes, Max was maneuvering through traffic, fidgeting from the ache in his arm. Twenty minutes later, he pulled up in front of Brigitte's house. Her place didn't compare in any way to his high security lair, but rather the Spanish-style bungalow was charming. It sat back from the street and was obscured by a large hedge that wrapped around the front yard. As he exited the car, Brigitte came running and nearly jumped into his arms.

"I can't believe you're leaving already."

Max kissed her briefly, but passionately. "How do you think I feel? I just found out myself last night."

Brigitte took a moment to consider what might be her own separation anxiety. "How come you don't know where you're going or when you're coming back?"

"Because it's my initiation, and so I don't know anything about it."

"What? I thought that wasn't happening until your birthday."

"Yeah, well, join the club."

Part of her wanted to protest, but Brigitte knew Max had to do as Demetrius asked. While she didn't know anything about the clandestine family tradition, the secrecy behind it was common knowledge. "That's huge, Max. You're going to find out what the big deal is."

"Yeah, I suppose so." Max studied Brigitte but was tentative when he spoke. "I need to ask you something. Last night, my dad said the word got out about the dial we found. You didn't tell anyone, did you? Like Marilyn."

"Of course not, Max, you asked me not to."

"He said someone leaked it and it's triggered a bunch of shit."

"Then it must've been Otto or a member of your crew, 'cause it wasn't me."

Max ran a hand through his hair and sighed. "In theory, all those guys signed nondisclosure agreements." He studied Brigitte's face, but she remained steadfast in her denial. "Anyway, the way my dad tells it, my safety and even yours could be at stake because of it. With all that shit that went down in New Orleans, I figured I'd better tell you."

"Fuck." Brigitte stared at Max, chewing her bottom lip and full of concern.

"I know we didn't talk about it, but whoever did that to Ted may have thought it was me behind that mask. We all know that."

Flabbergasted, Brigitte raised a hand to her mouth. Like Max, she understood the reality of his statement, but she hadn't wanted to consider the ramifications. What if he truly had been the target?

"Probably it's a good thing I'm going out of town, right?"

Brigitte threw her arms around him more out of fear for Max than for herself. "Oh Max. I should be asking if you're excited, I mean this is your initiation. But jeez, this has got to be nerve wracking."

"To be honest, I just want the whole thing to be over."

Brigitte unfolded herself from Max. "You wanna grab lunch or is that also too risky?"

Max knew Brigitte was being sarcastic, but then he remembered. "Fuck!"

She looked up, completely startled by the outburst. "Max, what?"

"I forgot, I can't eat. I'm supposed to be fasting."

The declaration puzzled Brigitte. "Why?"

"Because of the initiation. It's something my dad asked me to do."

Brigitte stared quizzically at Max. "So, what? You're not supposed to eat anything?"

"Just juice. Of course, I feel hungrier than ever now."

"How long does he want you to do that?"

Max shrugged. "That's a good question, but another one I don't have the answer to."

Max could see Brigitte squirming. She wasn't thrilled about his departure and all of the mystery surrounding it. He adored her, but he sometimes found her insecurities daunting. After a brief silence, she finally spoke.

"Don't forget Marilyn's twenty-fifth birthday party. It's next week if you think you'll be back."

Even though he wished he could answer, Max had no idea. "I hope so." He hugged her tightly. "As soon as I'm able, I'll let you know."

"You better." Brigitte tried to smile through the uncertainty. "I promised her we'd be there. She's convinced you don't like her since you never show up at her to-do's."

Max kissed her tenderly, knowing his kisses put her at ease. "You tell Marilyn I like her just fine."

She leaned into him and slid her hands down his back. Max knew the tactic. Brigitte was trying to seduce him. If successful, she knew he would stay another hour or so. Max pulled away and smiled, letting her know the plan wouldn't work this time.

"There's no sense in you not having lunch just because I can't.

But I don't want to sit and watch you eat while I'm having juice."

"Okay. I guess I'll go eat then. I am pretty hungry."

"I think I'll just go home and pack." Trying to generate enthusiasm, Max continued, "Maybe get some juice along the way."

"You sure you don't want me to go with?"

"No, I'll call you later." He hugged Brigitte tightly.

"Just be careful, Max. If your father thinks it's really not safe..."

"I will." He offered Brigitte a quick peck on the lips and returned to his car. Kissing his hand one last time he blew her a kiss. Brigitte watched as he pulled from the curb and disappeared down the block.

During the drive home, Max took out his cell to call Chandler. His VP picked up on the third ring.

"Hey there, Battenberg."

"What's up, man?"

"Just heading out to lunch."

"Everything cool?"

"Absolutely. All is well in the house of Badem. I thought you might be in today."

"The best laid plans, my friend, the best laid plans. I just left Brigitte's and I have to get home and pack for a little impromptu trip."

"How long are you gone this time?"

"Not sure. But I'll be checking in when I can."

"Is Brigitte going?

"No, not this time." There was an awkward pause before Max continued. "Look, man, I'm sorry about last night. My dad showed and," Max shivered from the memory, "there's just a bunch of stuff going on. Probably, I'll be pretty low-profile for a while."

"Such is the charmed life, I suppose."

As Max approached his house, he reached over and typed a code into a small remote on the passenger side visor. The garage door opened. "Like I said, I'll give you a call when I figure out my itinerary."

"Sounds good, chief. I'll hold things down while you're away."

"Dude, I can't believe I have to pack again." Smiling, Max slipped his Range Rover into its parking spot. As he exited the car, the garage began closing.

"Poor, poor Battenberg."

"Sucks being me, huh?" Max chuckled as he headed up the interior stairwell and keyed in the entry code for the house. Once inside, he typed an access code into the touch pad and transferred the call. Chandler's voice began piping through the house speakers. Max set the phone on a counter as he skipped up the steps to his bedroom.

"I'll talk to you later, man."

"Travel safe, my friend."

"Will do. I'll speak to you soon."

After the call, Max pulled a piece of luggage from his closet and vacillated about what to put inside. Choosing what to pack was difficult without knowing a final destination.

He packed a variety of things: a suit, shorts, jeans and a sweater. Max crossed to the nightstand beside his bed and, from a nest hidden beneath it, removed a matte black asp baton. Considerably heavier than it looked, the foot-long asp extended out another eighteen inches. With a quick snap of his wrist, Max watched it unlock into a formidable two-and-a-half foot weapon. He swung it several times like a bat and listened as it whistled through the air.

Satisfied, he collapsed it until it was a foot long again. He stepped back into his closet and slid the asp into a secret compartment of his bag. If the luggage were scanned, the asp would appear to be part of the retractable handle.

When he was finished, he fastened the bag and crossed to a set of drawers built into the wall. From the top drawer he removed his passport and the credit card Demetrius had given him the night before. After a brief hesitation, he shuffled through a small stack of photographs in the drawer. He came across one of him at six years old with his brother and mother. It was taken on the beach in France just a week before his mother's accident.

Max stared at the photograph. He and Christian both had pails with small plastic shovels. The sand castle they were building looked more like an erupting volcano. Max loved this particular photo of his mom. Even though it was just a piece of paper, the warmth of her smile emanated off it like the sun. He scrutinized her straight, light brown hair and her large eyes, which he had inherited. He slid the photograph into his passport and stuck everything in a compartment of his bag.

Max stepped to an adjacent closet where the metal case containing the gold bullion was stashed. He opened it and bent down to lift the heavy case, wondering just what purpose the gold could serve at his initiation.

Finally prepared, he placed the bags in the hallway. Part of him resented his father's influence so that he didn't appreciate being asked to make the trip. But another part of him was excited, even thrilled by the top secrecy of everything going on. Demetrius had promised answers and Max was anxious to know them.

Emotionally drained and weak from the fast, Max settled in, venturing out only once to buy fresh juice. When darkness fell, he set his alarm to try for a good night's sleep. In less than twenty-four hours he would learn the ultimate destination of the initiation. If Demetrius and the psychic were right, the first layers of truth were about to be revealed.

CHAPTER 18

$\mathcal{T}$he following morning, Max awoke to his alarm. He showered, dressed and waited downstairs for one of his father's drivers. It had been pre-arranged that a Town Car would pick him up and shuttle him to O'Hare Airport.

Max felt slightly nervous as he lifted the metal case of gold his father had given him the night before. He knew it was illegal to carry anything valued over $10,000 without declaring it. But Demetrius had said he would make the necessary arrangements, and Max trusted his father had done so.

The trip to the airport was uneventful. In fact, Max slept for a large portion of the ride. Like most Battenbergs, he didn't travel with average citizens. On rare occasions when commercial airlines were used, the Battenbergs were typically shuttled straight to the tarmac for boarding. For reasons unknown to Max, the journey to his initiation had been deemed safer on a commercial airline.

He followed his father's instructions while the driver waited curbside in front of the terminal. He removed the special credit card and placed it in the airline kiosk. After keying through several screens, he nervously awaited his destination. Part of him hoped for a boarding pass to some ancient European city. A tropical island would also have been satisfactory. When Mexico City popped up on screen, Max's heart dropped. *Mexico City!* He thought of the traffic and pollution there. It was hardly safe, as attempts to abduct wealthy people occurred in Mexico on a regular basis. He had visited only once before about fifteen years earlier, but his memories were of poverty and filth.

He remembered a group of children rushing up to Demetrius as they exited a luxury hotel. It was a band of panhandling street kids who had made it to Demetrius before the guards could intervene. Several of them, only slightly younger than Max, had shoved their soiled hands into his and Demetrius' faces. It was only seconds before the guards intervened, but Max had already been spooked.

As he pondered the location, the kiosk asked for the number of bags he was planning to check. He keyed in two and waited for his boarding card to print. An airline representative approached, looking down at a small handheld computer. He asked Max about the two bags he was checking.

"It's all under control," Max replied as he returned to the Town Car, where he read off his flight information to the driver.

Every Battenberg car was equipped with an onboard computer, similar to but infinitely more sophisticated than OnStar. The driver keyed in Max's itinerary, then pulled away from the curb. Once particulars of the trip had been entered, the driver was issued clearances to shuttle Max as close to the plane as security measures allowed. He would be among the very first to enter and leave the plane.

Eight minutes later, Max arrived at the terminal's VIP lounge, where the chauffeur oversaw the handling of his luggage. Private handlers would take his bags with the concealed case of gold and load them on the plane.

Max thanked the driver and headed to the lounge to await boarding. His entire life he had traveled in these exclusive circles, but he never lost his fascination with airport VIP lounges, which were great for people-watching.

The lounge at O'Hare felt like a hybrid, part day spa and part swanky restaurant. Upon entering, he was greeted at the front desk beside a barrier wall to the actual lounge. The large room divider of opaque glass prevented paparazzi or other nosey onlookers from spying to catch a glimpse of the lounge's elite members.

Behind the glass partition, a large open space looked out onto the tarmac. A series of couches, coffee tables and booths were sparsely placed throughout the area for passengers to sit and relax while servers circulated with complimentary drinks and hors d'oeuvres. A full service restaurant was located to the right of the open area with a fully stocked food bar.

Max often wondered how or why people made it into the exclusive circles of airport lounges. Sometimes, it was celebrity and other times, wealth. Additionally, airlines favored businessmen; frequent travelers amassed mileage awards that often catapulted them into the VIP lounge.

Max surveyed the large area and figured there were approximately thirty passengers lounging. He noticed a few poorly disguised celebrities in large hats and sunglasses. It was always actors and musicians who attracted attention in their supposed efforts at anonymity. There were also a dozen or so distinguished men and a handful of women, dressed in finely tailored business suits, many of them reading the *Economist* or the *Wall Street Journal*.

Max was scanning the room for a good seat when he caught the attention of a young woman smiling from across the room. He returned the smile, then awkwardly crossed to an island of three armchairs surrounding an oval coffee table.

The woman followed Max with her eyes. She looked to be Hispanic, perhaps Mexican. Whatever her background, she had quite a bit of European blood. Her skin was a golden caramel tone, but her blond shoulder length hair was bone straight and layered in a precision cut. Max could tell she had paid dearly for the coif that intentionally looked messy. While the color didn't appear natural, the blond was not a dye job either. It was a sun-kissed shade that was likely darker in the winter. Whoever the woman was, she looked exotic and unique.

Max found a seat, then further perused the room. His attention wandered back to the exotic traveler who was at least pretending to read a Spanish magazine. Each time Max glanced her way, she managed to look up and smile. He fidgeted, rubbing the area of his arm near the incision. His discomfort had improved since the implant's removal, but the area was still bothersome.

The stranger and Max continued a cat and mouse game of who's looking now until boarding was announced to Mexico City. Full of intrigue, Max watched the woman gather her things and exit the lounge as she headed toward her gate. He grabbed his carry-on and followed. It appeared they shared the same destination. He retrieved his boarding pass as she approached and inquired, "Going to Mexico City?"

Max barely detected an accent, leading him to believe she might not be Hispanic. "Yeah. I suppose that's where you're headed."

She nodded. "You traveling on business or is your trip pleasure?"

Max found the question rather forward and decided to flavor his answer with ambiguity. "A little bit of both actually. It's sort of an impromptu trip."

The attractive stranger smiled. "I guess you could say my trip here was impromptu. Mexico City's my home."

Now that they were conversing at length, Max could better hear her accent. It was only slight but seemed more British than Spanish.

"You have an interesting accent to be from Mexico."

"Boarding school in London. My family was quite determined for me to be an international woman of mystery. My name is Amalia by the way."

Max half frowned and half smiled. From what he could tell, her parents had done a decent job, as her demeanor exuded quiet sophistication.

"Nice to meet you, Amalia. My name is Max."

Both Amalia and Max shifted their carry-on bags to shake hands. Max found it intriguing that she allowed her hand to linger just a smidgeon longer than conventional.

Together, they chatted during the brief transition from the lounge to the plane. Max found her actions, although friendly, extremely difficult to read.

Is she flirting or is this Mexican hospitality? Suddenly, Demetrius' words, *I need you to be hyper-vigilant,* echoed in his head.

While he sometimes didn't show it, Max was shrewder than Demetrius gave him credit for. He considered the circumstances of the Hades alert and his pending initiation. Without thinking he fidgeted with the tiny microchip around his neck. He knew how Demetrius operated. Someone could easily be on the flight to maintain a watchful eye over him. Perhaps it was Amalia. As far as Demetrius knew, he still had the microchip tightly tucked beneath the skin of his left tricep. If he were ever going to remove it from his person, he would have to do so cautiously. Otherwise, Demetrius would certainly devise new and improved ways to keep him on a leash.

He and Amalia boarded the plane and were escorted to their seats on opposite sides of the cabin. Both had purchased fares that afforded secluded pod seats. If desired, the chairs converted into beds that were surrounded by cubicle walls. Max was still tired and hoped to sleep during the ride.

Less than thirty minutes later, they were in the air, and Max quickly converted his seat into a bed. When he wasn't napping he thought of the Battenberg initiations, and was full of wonder about what would transpire.

And why Mexico City? Max supposed enough time had passed for him to give it a second chance, but he didn't like the secrecy.

Why had the ceremony been moved up six months? When he thought too long about the circumstances of his departure, he grew anxious and nervous. Part of him wished he had come with Brigitte, Ted or even Chandler. He could use a friendly face, but his father would never have allowed a companion of any sort.

After what seemed a short time, the flight staff woke Max and requested that he lift his seat into the upright position. They were landing. He was pleased the flight was ending and trying to amass more enthusiasm about his return to Mexico City. He hoped the hotel would be away from the city center in a place where the air wasn't so polluted.

As they deplaned, Amalia approached with her carry-on bag. "How long you in town for?"

Max was determined to keep his responses ambiguous. "On an open ticket for now. Probably a week, maybe less, maybe more."

Amalia handed over her business card. "If you need a guide, or just want to know a place to go, give me a jingle. Where're you staying?"

Amalia's line of questioning left Max wondering if she truly was one of his father's spies or even a Hades intruder. "That's very kind, but I'm not sure how hectic my stay will be. If I get a chance I'll definitely give you a call."

"Great," Amalia responded, "Perhaps I'll see you around."

As they filed through the airport, Amalia made a beeline through customs and immigration. Max watched her zip by a customs official. Before he had even reached the queue, a fortyish, pleasant-faced Mexican national stepped into his path. The slightly plump man smiled warmly.

"Mr. Battenberg?"

Max turned and smiled. He knew someone would be meeting him, but figured it would be at baggage claim on the other side of the immigration line. In a general sense, meet-and-greeters weren't allowed in this area, but of course Demetrius had been able to make it work.

"Bienvenidos. My name is Elízar Sanchez. I work for Battenberg Industries here in Mexico City." Elízar's accent was thick, but his English was good.

"Oh great. I figured someone would meet me on the other side."

"My understanding is you have special needs for your bags. Everything's been arranged, and they will be offloaded to a car that is waiting for you outside."

"Wonderful."

"If I could please have your passport."

Max handed over his passport. Within minutes they were whisked through customs. Elízar had been dispatched to facilitate. Demetrius loved the word "facilitate." For him, it was a way to describe a variety of things most people weren't permitted to do. Elízar was there to enable Max's entry into Mexico City to include five bars of gold bullion.

"So if you'll just follow me," Elízar instructed.

While other passengers exited to baggage claim, Elízar turned and led Max toward a set of double doors. A sign above them read, "No Entrar! Solamente La Gente Autorizada."

Max was quite fluent in Spanish, so he knew this was not a proper exit. Still, he followed Elízar through the doors, and no one questioned them. In minutes, they were in a large SUV being shuttled to a small but luxurious resort hotel called "El Agua Del Oro" or "the Goldwater Hotel."

The Goldwater was a little-known, exclusive resort situated off the beaten path in a mostly residential neighborhood. The hotel rarely advertised and made it virtually impossible to stumble onto in a random search for accommodations, which is exactly how the guests at the Goldwater wanted it: exclusive, clandestine, unknown.

When their SUV pulled into the large circular driveway, porters met them at the entrance. Max chuckled when a young man bent down to pick up his bag containing the gold. As he rose up the true weight of the case pulled him back to the ground. Elízar barked out a few words of Spanish and the porter ran off and quickly returned with a luggage cart.

Elízar attempted to load the case of gold, but he turned to Max upon realizing how heavy it was. "Señor Battenberg, what on Earth do you have in this thing?"

Max simply smiled. "You wouldn't believe me if I told you."

The young porter was enthusiastic as he wrestled the case from Elízar's hands and placed it on the cart. Elízar smiled, happy to be rescued from the task. Each bar of gold weighed approximately twenty-eight pounds, so the case was at least a hundred and forty pounds.

Spring had only just begun and the temperature was already in the low eighties. During the drive from the airport, Elízar had run the air conditioner at full blast, but now they were standing outside, Max's clothes were growing damp with sweat. Due to the smog inversion layer, Mexico City was hotter than it should be but, thankfully, Demetrius had chosen the hotel well. It was at a slight elevation and away from commercial areas, so the air was qualitatively better and easier to breathe.

Satisfied, Elízar removed his business card with a toothy grin. "Señor Max, again, bienvenido. You speak Spanish, no?"

"Claro qué si," Max responded.

"Then I'm sure you will have an excellent time here in Mexico City." Elízar handed over his business card. "Here is my card."

Max glanced down, instantly recognizing the logo of his father's businesses. It was a pair of thick lines that were intertwined at the bottom similar to rope. Just above, the lines split off in opposite directions, eventually turning upward to form a triangle. If you didn't look carefully, the logo was quite simple. Upon close inspection, it became clear that the ropes were in fact two snakes intertwined at their tails. Each slithered away from the other to form a triangle above. Tiny details of the snakes' heads were distinguishable: each had a simple dot and a line for the eyes and mouths.

"You call me if you need anything," Elízar instructed. "No me importa if it's big or small, you call, okay?"

"Thank you, Elízar. I do have a question."

"Dígame, Señor. What can we do for you?"

"Is there anything you can reveal about my stay here? I'm not exactly sure what my father has planned."

Elízar shrugged, a huge smile plastered across his face. "As far as I know, you're here for enjoying Mexico City, Señor. Unless otherwise instructed, that is your goal. Have you been before?"

"Not for a while. The last time, I was nine or ten."

"If you have time, there are pyramids just outside the city. Teotihuacán is spectacular — as fine if not better than Egypt. I suggest you visit if you find the time. You need a guide, you let me know."

"Thank you, Elízar. I'm sure I'll be in touch."

Elízar surprised Max when he leaned in and hugged him. "Hasta luego, Señor Battenberg. Maybe we'll talk tomorrow."

"Great. I'll be sure to give you a call if I need anything." Max watched briefly as Elízar exited the hotel. The porter nodded for Max's approval to continue to the room.

Of course, Demetrius had arranged for Max to stay in one of El Agua Del Oro's best rooms. It was a penthouse suite with a phenomenal view of the city. There were marble floors in the main suite and bathroom, and the room was contemporary with imported European furnishings.

Max tipped the porter, then plopped down on the bed. *What am I doing here?* He flipped on the television and surfed a few stations.

Bored, he picked up a tourist magazine. Thumbing through the pages, he came across an article on Teotihuacán. Pictured was a huge complex of streets, temples and two large pyramids. Max flipped the page and saw the Pyramid of the Sun, whose base was identical to the Great Pyramid of Giza. A short distance from there was the smaller Pyramid of the Moon. Max was stunned by their appearance. The complex looked powerful and untouched by the elements, almost as if it had been built in his lifetime. But Max knew better. The pyramids of Teotihuacán dated back at least two thousand years.

Flipping through these pages, he knew he would have to visit. Two years before, he had spent a week in Egypt and had been awed by everything Egyptian, from the artwork and architecture down to the mysteries of their technology. It was fascinating to him that modern ingenuity couldn't explain or reproduce much of what the Egyptians had accomplished.

The magazine article evoked similar emotions in Max. The next day while awaiting his initiation, he would definitely follow Elízar's suggestion and travel to Teotihuacán. There, he would witness an up-close-and-personal view of the complex.

A new feeling of excitement arose in Max. Maybe the trip to Mexico City would have an added benefit. He closed the magazine and pulled out his cell phone to inform Brigitte of his safe arrival. When she didn't pick up, he left a message. Sensing a second wind brewing, Max contemplated whether he would actually stay in his room.

CHAPTER 19

*I*t hadn't quite settled in, but Max was alone. It had been weeks, even months, since he remembered being solo. For Max, a social creature, the feeling was odd and uncomfortable like ill-fitting pants. Since high school, he had populated his world with hordes of people and events. This helped him cling to the feeling of busyness as Max, if anything, wanted to be titillated by adventure and activity.

During his college years and since graduation, he had dated a string of girls and the occasional boy. Between the girlfriends and friends, the people who wanted to be friends, the security details, the parties, or work and family, Max was always in the company of others. This year was more than a quarter over, and he was only now finding solitude due to a high-stakes security alert and a clandestine family ceremony.

The unusual circumstance actually allowed him a moment to breathe. There was finally time to ponder all the things going on in his life. But the more he thought of the previous night's conversation with Demetrius, the more he allowed paranoia to creep in. With the Hades warning in effect, Max couldn't help but feel as if he had been shoved out of Chicago in a whirlwind of secrecy.

Nothing can be planned, Demetrius had stated. Then he reaffirmed that Max should be unsettled by the slew of things going on. The last time he recalled his family in this state was when his mother and brother had died nearly nineteen years earlier.

Max knew he shouldn't leave the Goldwater, but he had no intention of staying cooped up awaiting the initiation. *And I'm hungry as hell.* In order to fight the boredom he made several more calls, but couldn't get hold of anyone.

Already stir-crazy, he descended to the concierge, mindful of Demetrius' instructions to plan nothing. He would simply figure out travel options for a day trip to the pyramids of Teotihuacán. Later, he could decide how and when to go.

At the front desk, a dark-haired gentleman nodded to Max. "Buenas noches, señor." He was roughly Max's age, but deep acne scars marred his skin. "How can I help you?"

"Teotihuacán. I'd like to visit while I'm here."

"Oh, Señor, the pyramids are very popular. If you like, I can arrange a private car. There are also taxis and a shuttle that leaves daily from the city center. Which do you prefer?"

Max didn't truthfully know the best option to choose. "Let me think about it."

"At your leisure, Señor."

While he rarely used public transportation, Max liked the idea of sightseeing in a crowd. He could travel anonymously without the fanfare of fancy cars or some security detail breathing down his throat.

"What about nightlife, my friend? Any places with a cool vibe, not too trendy?"

The concierge smiled from ear to ear, then spit out an idea. "Oh, Celebracíon is the place, Señor. There is great food, beautiful girls, and not just Mexican girls. Whatever you like, you'll find at Celebracíon."

"Celebration, huh?" Max thought of the unique, golden dial from the Money Pit. "Actually, the name's kind of fitting."

"Is your first night in Mexico City, no? Celebracíon will be very fun." The concierge winked. "Mucho fiesta. You need a car, you let me know."

"Thank you."

Max returned to the room. After a quick shower, he dressed and slipped from the hotel through a side exit. He had to acknowledge, the Goldwater was a beautiful hotel both inside and out. The grounds were lush with vegetation but perfectly manicured. Without drawing the least bit of attention, Max departed the hotel grounds and hailed the first taxi he could find. Within minutes, he was whizzing across town to Celebracíon.

He settled in the bouncy cab's back seat, observing how today's Mexico City differed from his memories. He had to confess it was nothing like he remembered. Many of the buildings were distinctly European in design and the general aura felt infinitely more sophisticated. His visit held promise.

He took in the boulevards and avenues, all densely packed with buildings, people and pollution. In Mexico City, antiquity and modernity co-existed like oil and vinegar, mixing but not coalescing into one. The capitol city provided colonial architecture, cobblestone streets and an array of new world skyscrapers. The city's infrastructure was contemporary, but it felt chaotic at the same time. Max hated to admit it, but he did feel out of his element. In the United States and especially in Chicago, it was extremely likely that either he or the Battenberg name would be recognized. Now, he was sitting in the back of a rickety cab, staring out at the city streets, packed and bustling with people. The driver glanced at the rearview mirror and spotted him in the backseat, oblivious to his identity. The idea of blending in made Max feel small and inconsequential.

He perhaps grasped for the first time how insignificant he was. What difference did it truly make whether he lived or died? Life, he saw, would continue with or without him. It was a sobering realization.

In Chicago, the opposite seemed true. As a Battenberg, he was very much in control. When he stepped into the offices of Badem Publications, employees scrambled about, trying to make their best impression as either useful or hardworking. His staff feared him, but also wanted to impress him at the same time. It was tough not to feel overly important when people reacted so strongly simply because you entered the room.

Demetrius had requested he fast, abstaining from solid foods of any kind. He did feel a tad lightheaded even if his stomach had ceased growling hours before. This time spent alone simply expanded the concept of a fast to include the absence of social nourishment that he normally enjoyed in the company of others. In some ways, social abstinence felt liberating. But it was also a little frightening since Max would have time to confront his own thoughts.

Gazing upon the busy streets, Max contemplated his love life. He loved Brigitte and could even see himself settling down with her. Not in his wildest dreams did he imagine meeting a more suitable partner. But could he live up to such an incredible woman and all that she offered?

Routinely so busy, he rarely gave any deep thought to his relationships. On occasion, the boundaries blurred between himself and other men, crossing the line into blatant bisexuality. To explain this away, Max was quick to lay blame on Demetrius. In his mind, it was his father's cold and impersonal disposition that had crippled him with a yearning for more intimate male connections. Deep down, he realized this was probably a gross rationalization, but it suited him nonetheless to beat up on his father's parenting.

Already burdened with a muddled personal life, Max scarcely cared to acknowledge the uncertainty he harbored about his career. For more than a year, he had struggled to run Badem Publications without totally abandoning it to Chandler's prowess. On some level, he enjoyed the work and had thus decided not to toss it aside as he had done with countless other endeavors in the past. At the same time, he didn't experience the kind of passion he thought a man should feel for his job.

Potentially, many careers existed for Max within the variety of companies that Demetrius owned, but this left Max feeling even more puzzled. He no longer wanted to squander his time or additional sums of his father's money creating something he would some day allow to fall by the wayside. Fortunately, he had found Chandler, who was infinitely more qualified than he in the publishing business. In a perfect world, where people got what they deserved, Chandler would have been his boss and Max the employee. But Max was lucky to live in a world where the Battenberg name trumped what was fair.

When the cab came to a stop, Max was startled back to reality. He hadn't noticed their arrival at Celebracíon.

The driver turned to him. "Estamos aqui, Señor."

Max pulled a few pesos from his pocket and handed them to the driver. Upon exiting, he turned and took note of the venue. The building was tasteful and unassuming. In many ways, it seemed like a large, beautiful home—a commercial space in disguise.

Without checking his I.D., a bouncer waived Max inside. Apparently, he fit the image of the club's desired clientele. Max strode through the foyer, immediately recognizing that Celebracíon was everything the concierge said it would be. Its roomy interior was a contemporary lounge and held no connection to the image projected from outside. The décor was slick with modern furniture and perfect mood lighting. And the crowd was young and full of hipsters as promised.

At the front desk, a pretty woman smiled and asked, "Para comer?"

"Solamente bebidas por favor."

The hostess was petite but well proportioned. "Would you like to sit in a booth or at the bar?"

"Which do you recommend?"

"If you're solo, absolutely the bar." The hostess winked at Max with a smile.

"The bar it is."

Max followed the hostess around a barrier and was seated at the bar. He immediately knew he'd made the correct choice. The room had multiple levels and his seat at the bar overlooked all of them.

The hostess offered a coy smile. "The bartender will take your order whenever you're ready."

"Thank you."

Max winked as she turned and retreated to the front. He spent a few seconds scanning the crowd. More than half of the patrons seemed American or European. These were the rich and famous not just from Mexico but from across the globe. They were immune to recessions and depressed economies. When prices and unemployment skyrocketed, it was the local populations that suffered, and not these folks. Max supposed this was the case no matter what city one was in.

He was intrigued by the venue. He turned his attention to the menu, wishing he could eat. By now his stomach was growling again. He flipped through the menu and confirmed his suspicions: the prices at Celebracíon were exorbitantly expensive.

He looked up, remotely surprised to see Amalia, the woman from the plane, across the room in a crowd of what seemed to be attractive locals. He still suspected Amalia might be a plant sent by Demetrius to keep an eye on him. He studied the menu before ordering a virgin Bloody Mary from the bartender. He sipped the cocktail, feeling awkwardly extraneous in the crowd. Suddenly, Amalia was approaching from across the room.

"I thought that was you. Didn't take you long to find Celebracíon."

Max smiled. As much as he wanted to deny it, there was something incredibly charming about her. "Yeah, the concierge at my hotel steered me here."

"Must be a nice hotel if they sent you here."

"I guess. It's just corporate lodging really."

Battenberg training had taught Max to remain vague and unclear. If Amalia wasn't his father's spy, she could still be posing as the innocent stranger, gathering information for some other hidden or nefarious agenda.

"Sounds like you're an important person."

"Oh, I don't know. Depends on who you talk to." Max was switching into defense mode.

Amalia raised her glass to Max. "I'm here with my brother and some friends. You're welcome to join if you like."

"That's very kind, but I have a big day tomorrow. I'll probably head back early."

"Claro, claro. Well, enjoy your evening."

"You do the same."

"Amalia!" One of her friends screamed from across the room.

The man approached through the crowd. As he drew closer, Max became aware of the striking resemblance between him and Amalia. *Must be her brother.*

The male version of Amalia could have been her twin. He was exuberant and obviously buzzed as he stumbled up to the bar. Amalia smiled as she placed an arm around him.

"Esta mi hermano, Jorge Salazar."

Max greeted Jorge with a smile and a handshake. "How are you, Jorge?"

"Bien, bien. Qué tal, muchacho?"

Max nodded to Jorge. "I was just about to order another drink. Can I get you guys anything?"

"A Kahlua and cream would be fantastic," Jorge quipped shamelessly.

"What about you, Amalia?"

"Nothing for me. I'm afraid I'm driving."

Taking note of the continued grumblings from his stomach, Max hailed down a bartender and ordered a Kahlua and cream for Jorge and two more Bloody Marys to quiet the hunger in his belly.

"Where do you go later?" Jorge questioned. "If you want, we are going dancing — bailando a la discoteca!"

"Maybe another time. I have your sister's card."

Jorge shrugged, matter of fact. "Suit yourself."

Before Max could respond, Jorge jabbed his sister in the gut. "You ask him, güapita?"

"No, Jorge, todavía no."

The bartender approached to place three cocktails before Max. Max handed Jorge his drink, then clanged his own glass against it. "Prost." He tipped his head to acknowledge Amalia then drank from the virgin Bloody Mary. The tomato juice was salty as it slid down his throat and crashed into his empty stomach like water dousing a fire.

Jorge took a gulp of his own drink then turned to Max without hesitation. "So, you're Maximilian Battenberg, right?"

Max was caught off guard by the question. The anonymity he felt in the cab seemed to be eroding. "Yes. That would be me."

Jorge elbowed his sister in the arm. "I told you, guapa." Jorge's cocktail splashed on his shirt as he tried to steady himself.

Amalia nodded to her brother. "I owe you another cocktail, Jorge. But I don't think you need it right now." Amalia turned to Max. "He bet me you were Max Battenberg. I suppose that does make you un hombre muy importante."

"Like I said, it depends on who you ask."

Amalia brushed the engineered messiness of her coif out of her face. Max watched her carefully and thought of his girlfriend back at home. Brigitte's beauty and charm remained superior to any woman he knew, and her position as frontrunner for his mate remained unchallenged.

Jorge was growing more and more buzzed with each sip of his cocktail. He turned to Amalia and shoved her playfully. "You should ask if he wants to go to the club with us later."

"I did, Jorge."

Jorge turned to stare into Max's eyes. He slurred his words when he spoke. "Wow, they really are that green. I always thought your eyes were Photoshopped. You sure you don't want to go dancing?"

"Sorry, I can't. I'm here on business." Max was beginning to lose patience while growing increasingly uncomfortable that they had figured out his identity—or perhaps they had known it all along. "If my schedule opens up I have your sister's number."

Jorge nodded his head. "Sounds good. I'd love to say I partied with Maximilian Battenberg."

Amalia took note of the degrading dynamic between Max and her brother. She pulled him aside and whispered a few choice words in Spanish. Jorge looked as if his feelings were hurt when he turned and held his hand out to Max. "It was nice meeting you, Señor Battenberg."

"You guys have a good night." Max waved politely as Amalia and Jorge departed to rejoin their friends. He quickly downed the remainder of his Bloody Marys to satiate the hunger gnawing at his entrails. Satisfied for now, Max placed a fifty-dollar bill on the counter and turned to exit Celebracíon. For his own peace of mind, he would need to return to the hotel, away from the prying eyes of anyone else who might recognize him.

Outside, he flagged down a cab for his trip back to the Goldwater. Under other circumstances he would likely have stayed to party with Amalia and her brother. Their pursuit of fun appeared no different than his usual endeavors. But Max was too unsettled. In spite of himself, he was running a zillion possibilities through his head. For the time being, he would lay low, at least until he could make sense of his initiation and the associated dangers behind the alerts.

He returned to the hotel with a deep sense of relief, then quickly phoned Brigitte to wish her a good night. They exchanged pleasantries a while, then Max hung up and readied himself for bed. Within minutes, he was asleep with the television blaring in the background. Shortly thereafter, the dreams followed.

Max had been sound asleep, he knew that much. But there had been a transition into some bizarre fugue state. He had become aware of himself on a bed in an unfamiliar room.

Is this my hotel room? Max perceived that he was somehow awake, but just as in the odd dream-like incident at his house, he was completely unable to move. A burning sensation stung the inside of his nose. The discomfort, both sharp and concentrated, was confined to a single area. When the sting vanished, Max immediately recognized what had caused it. A needle had just been removed from his nostril.

Because of where she was standing, Max hadn't immediately noticed the tall blonde positioned beside him at the edge of the bed. She fully withdrew the strange looking syringe from his nose, then handed it off to the midget beside her. Like before, the diminutive man's face was covered in white makeup.

Max felt his heart stop as terror immobilized it like the rest of his body. A deep panic overcame him as the midget approached. The small man removed a tiny, red sticker from a cartridge affixed to his belt. He placed the sticker on Max's forehead directly between his eyebrows. Within seconds the spot began to burn, just as it had done in the dream at home.

Max sprang up in bed, punching at the air where he imagined the midget to be. Shadows danced across the room as he took note of the stillness surrounding him. There was no one at the side of the bed. No midget, no woman, just quiet all about.

Max glanced at the television. He didn't remember turning it off, but the screen was dark. Feeling creeped-out and disoriented, he touched a finger to his nose. There was no soreness or discomfort that he could discern. Max wondered why he had again dreamed of the strange couple. He stared at the clock; it was 5 a.m. Max shrugged off his strange reverie as a sign of anxiety. Within minutes he was fast asleep again, attempting to steal just a few hours of peaceful, dreamless rest.

CHAPTER 20

*T*he next morning Max showered, dressed and hustled downstairs. He spotted a large breakfast buffet and considered how ridiculous it was that Demetrius had asked him to refrain from eating. *What on Earth for?* Max had imagined hazing in the family initiation and, indeed, it had begun.

He downed some juice and returned to the concierge desk, where a different man from the previous evening was on duty. Before he could speak, Elízar appeared.

"Señor Battenberg! Buenas dias."

"Elízar, how are you?"

"Muy bien, señor, muy bien. I dropped by to make sure you were being looked after. The concierge mentioned you'd like to see Teotihuacán."

"I'd love to see the pyramids. I was thinking to get a shuttle from the city center."

Elízar frowned when he heard this. "If your father learned of this, he'd think I wasn't taking good care of you."

"You're taking great care, Elízar. The shuttle's not a big deal." He intended not to do anything planned.

Elízar threw up his hands. "You prefer the bus, you take the bus, Señor. I'm here to provide what you want."

"I tell you what. How about you drop me at the shuttle, and when I'm ready I'll call you to pick me up?"

Elízar smiled infectiously. "I like this plan. The car is parked, Señor. I will bring it around."

"Thank you, Elízar. Ten minutes, please."

Max grabbed his day bag from his room and met Elízar at the hotel entrance. Twenty minutes later, they were standing at the shuttle stop to Teotihuacán.

"Okay, Señor, you sure I cannot take you all the way?"

"This is fine, Elízar, but I appreciate the offer."

The friendly guide reached in his bag and produced a bottle of water. "In case you get thirsty, Señor." He handed the bottle to Max, then quickly shook his hand. "Llamame cuando estas listo, Señor. Call me when you are ready and I pick you up, okay?"

"Thank you, Elízar." Max opened his bag and placed the water bottle inside. It settled next to his wallet, a set of travel brochures and the asp baton. If anyone tried to attack in Mexico, Max would be ready.

Max zipped the bag shut, then turned to see fellow passengers entering the bus. Most were foreigners with a sprinkling of Mexican tourists. He didn't care much for tourism itself, but he did wish to see the pyramids. He waved to Elízar, then double-checked to ensure he still had the man's business card. He knew after a long day of sightseeing that he'd be more than happy for a ride back to the hotel.

During the bus trip, Max mostly kept to himself, only smiling here and there when he overheard interesting or funny conversations. If something along the route was architecturally or historically important, the driver would come on the P.A. system and point it out to the tour. He spoke in perfect, strongly accented English.

"On your right you will see the two Basilicas of Guadeloupe."

Max and the other tourists took note of the two structures, the old and the new. The original basilica's construction began in 1531 and was not completed until 1709. Its architecture was baroque in style with towers in each corner and a large dome for a roof.

Beside it, just hundreds of meters away, stood the modern basilica, built between 1974 and 1976. The latest architect, Pedro Ramirez Vazquez, had also constructed Mexico City's Aztec Stadium. The newer basilica's resemblance to the stadium was evident in its coliseum-like shape, and the roof peaked like a circus tent just off kilter from its center.

The driver didn't stop the bus, but slowed to a crawl. "Both the new and the old basilicas were built to commemorate the day 'Our Lady' the Virgin Mary appeared to a Mexican native named Juan Diego Cuauhtlatoatzin. As history tells it, when a young Juan Diego explained to his tribe what he saw, he was asked to prove it." The driver lifted his foot from the gas pedal and the bus nearly came to a stop. "Then our Lady appeared to him once more. She asked him to gather roses in his cloak and carry them to the tribal leaders. Later, at the tribe's council meeting, he opened the cloak, allowing the roses to fall to the ground. There in the fabric was Our Lady's image. That very cloak hangs in the new basilica if you wish to see it. It is this event that gave rise to Christianity in the region. For the Catholic community, this is the most visited spot, second only to the Vatican."

After the detailed report, the driver punched the pedal to the floor. The bus jerked forward, gaining speed on its final leg of the journey. Minutes later, Max spotted a portion of the pyramid complex in the distance. Teotihuacán was approaching him in all its glory. While the pyramids weren't like those of Egypt, they were equally captivating in an entirely different way. They were step pyramids. Rather than smooth triangular facades, Teotihuacán's pyramids each had four graduated levels.

The bus driver came on the microphone again, delivering a speech he had likely recited many times before. "Señoras y Señores, arrivamos a Teotihuacán. Even today the experts are unsure of the origins of these pyramids, whose construction is believed to have begun in 300 B.C. No one, not even the best archeologists, have a clear idea who built them." The driver slowed as the pyramids came more clearly into view. "The Teotihuacános, it seems, just disappeared. Very much later the Aztecs discovered the complex and named it Teotihuacán. In their native language of Nahuatl this means City of the Gods. The Aztecas worshipped the grounds here, calling them sacred, using them for pilgrimages and religious ceremonies."

From the bus it was impossible to fully see the site, but Max was already satisfied that his visit to Mexico City had been worthwhile. In a peculiar way, there was an awesome energy to the picturesque view of Teotihuacán. The Pyramid of the Sun loomed against the hilly background at a height equivalent to a twenty-one-story building.

The driver crept into a parking spot before coming on the speaker system one last time. "Señoras y señores, bienvenidos a Teotihuacán." He opened the bus doors. "Enjoy your visit."

Everyone stood and filed down the narrow aisle to the exit. The ride hadn't taken long, but Max and the others were impatient to see the pyramids from a personal perspective. He stepped from the bus, crossed the parking lot and passed by a large visitor center until he reached the Calzada de los Muertos, or as it was called in English, the Avenue of the Dead.

Directly across this road was Teotihuacán's third largest pyramid, the Temple of Quetzalcoatl. Max marveled at the construction, whose impressive carvings of animal and warrior heads were artfully placed all about the structure. The intricacy of the stonework wasn't apparent until you were very close.

Max removed a brochure on the complex and read: *Quetzalcoatl is the Aztecs' Nahuatl word for 'feathered serpent.' There are many Mesoamerican cultures that worshipped a feathered serpent deity but Teotihuacán was the first documented to do so. The location has also been used as a center for sacrifice, as the remains of more than two hundred people have been recovered from various burial sites in and around the temple.*

Max flipped the page and saw just how expansive the complex was. From the point where they entered the Avenue of the Dead it would be over a mile and a half to the other end. The ancient road, which was wider than an airport runway, stretched all the way to the complex's second largest pyramid structure, the Pyramid of the Moon.

On the left, about three quarters of the way down the calzada, was the complex's largest and most magnificent Pyramid of the Sun. Teotihuacán's principal pyramid structure was ranked the third largest in the world, second only to the Pyramid of Cholula, also in Mexico, and the Great Cheops Pyramid of Giza, in Egypt.

Due to their sheer size, the Pyramids of the Sun and the Moon both appeared closer than they actually were, especially the former, whose hulking mass loomed like a mountain against the sky.

Max turned his head and stared down the Avenue of the Dead. Unlike the pyramids of Egypt, Teotihuacán was situated in a plush valley. Like a mountain pasture, its surrounding landscape was green and lush. As Max started to walk, he couldn't help but wonder how the pyramids had been built and toward what purpose. Yes, there was art and precise workmanship in their architecture, but Max found the idea of functionless design terribly difficult to accept. The same was true of Egypt's pyramids. Were they simply tombs for dead rulers, or was there more to it than that?

In spite of its age, Teotihuacán felt modern in its layout. There was a clear artistry and flow that existed in the organization of its roads and structures. Max knew from what he read that many areas of the complex had been uncovered from total oblivion under layers of vegetation and restored.

Before continuing down the calzada, Max stopped to wander around Quetzalcoatl's palace. A courtyard in the center of the structure was open to the skies. According to the brochure, it was one of the only remaining buildings with an original roofline. Pale pink frescoes were painted throughout and Max figured they had at one time been rich shades of red.

Flipping through his travel brochure, Max stumbled on a passage that caught his eye. *The builders of Teotihuacán were extraordinarily skilled at tracking the passage of time and predicting astronomical events.* Max read the sentence over and over. The confirmed uses of the Antikythera Mechanism were also about tracking time and astronomical events. A chill ran up his spine as he considered a possible connection.

He moved on, carefully examining the architecture, taking snapshots of any features he found interesting. Satisfied with his tour of the temple, Max returned to the Avenue of the Dead, where many local vendors and artisans were desperately pushing sales of their merchandise. Several called out to him, but he kept walking. It became clear to him why the Avenue of the Dead had its name. A series of stone structures resembled tombs along its entire length.

Max strolled along, speculating on the vanished culture and society responsible for Teotihuacán's construction. Why and how had they disappeared without a trace?

Nearly two hours later, Max arrived at the other side of the calzada, where he stood gazing up at the Pyramid of the Moon. On his right, the Pyramid of the Sun loomed. The weather was tolerable, but he had been walking a while. He pulled out the water bottle Elízar had given him and drank. Max was amazed that he didn't feel hunger since he hadn't eaten all day. He took another sip of the water, then returned it to his bag.

Although the Pyramid of the Sun appeared more than twice the size of the Pyramid of the Moon, they were both equal in height. Max knew he would climb one, if not both, of them. Somehow, the Pyramid of the Moon seemed more elegant in stature. Max gazed at it, sizing it up. With his mind made up, he took to the steps and began to climb.

More than halfway to the top, he noticed the first monarch butterfly. Like a painter's palate, beautiful shades of oranges, yellows and blacks shone like a kaleidoscope of wings. The butterfly drifted along like a feather, delicately floating on the wind. As Max continued up the steps, he noticed a myriad of other monarchs along the way. For some reason, they were congregating around the pyramid's summit.

Minutes later, he arrived at the top and was privy to a spectacular view of the complex. From the apex, he could see details in the Pyramid of the Sun's architecture that were invisible from a distance. From other angles, and certainly from afar, it looked more like a mountain. But now, its levels were infinitely more defined.

From above, the number of monarch butterflies with him on the pyramid was in the hundreds if not the thousands. Some were grouping in twos and threes and tumbling through the air. Max pulled out his camera to photograph them along with the spectacular view.

After he'd taken a dozen snapshots, he scanned through the photos until he stumbled onto the one of himself at the bottom of the Money Pit. Max stared at the shot that had been captured just minutes before he nearly drowned. It was eerie to think that it could have been the last photograph of him ever taken.

Suddenly, he felt lightheaded. Probably his blood sugar was dropping coupled with a reaction to the region's high altitude. His hunger was now at a crescendo. Max retrieved his phone and called Elízar for a ride back to the hotel. Perhaps there would be news of his initiation, which would hopefully involve food. The phone rang several times before Elízar picked up.

"Hola."

"Elízar, it's Maximilian Battenberg."

"Señor Battenberg, cómo estas? You enjoying the pyramids?"

Max was almost speechless as he looked over the complex. "It's unbelievable, Elízar. Tell me you've been here."

"Of course, Señor. Look to the Calzada de los Muertos."

At first, Max didn't understand. Elízar had requested that he look to the Avenue of the Dead. Finally, he gazed down at the runway-like path. He saw someone waving in the center of it. Although he appeared tiny, he could see it was Elízar. He was waving with the hand carrying his cell phone. In his other hand, there was a case.

"Elízar, is that you?"

"Si, Señor. Estoy aquí."

As Max turned his focus to Elízar, he realized it wasn't just any bag he was carrying. It was the case Demetrius had given him. The one in which there were five bars of gold. A sinking feeling overcame him.

"Are you here to pick me up?"

Max could hear Elízar breathing into the phone, but he didn't answer. Down on the avenue, he was simply shaking his head no. After a brief pause, Elízar finally spoke, but now his voice was serious.

"It is time, Señor Battenberg."

While visiting the complex, Max had been in his own world. But at some point, the crowd of tourists had thinned. Vendors were beginning to pack up their knick-knacks to return home. Max rarely suffered from nerves, but his stomach was jittery now, as if the monarch butterflies had instantly congregated there.

"You want me to come down?"

"No, Señor. Stay there. I will come to you."

Elízar ended the call, placed his cell phone in his pocket and then bent over again to pick up the heavy case of gold. He looked around to see who was watching. Satisfied, he grabbed the case and began walking toward the Pyramid of the Moon.

Max could tell Elízar was trying to appear inconspicuous, but this was difficult while managing a case that weighed well over a hundred pounds. Elízar wasn't terribly old, but too much food, drink and smoke had left him in mediocre shape. When he reached the base of the pyramid, he accosted a virile-looking vendor. Max noticed a brief conversation followed by an exchange of cash.

Finally, the young man took the case from Elízar and began lugging it up the pyramid, followed by Elízar. He was strong, but he still needed to stop periodically to catch his breath. After each respite, he and Elízar would resume climbing until they eventually ascended the final steps, soaked in sweat and breathing as if they'd just run a marathon.

"Señor Battenberg, qué tal?" Elízar was gasping for air. "I am slow but I need the exercise." Elízar jiggled his belly, saying, "I have to get rid of this," and then pointing toward the young vendor, "This muchacho was kind enough to assist with the case."

Max nodded. "Hola, buenas tardes."

The man nodded as Elízar fished out his wallet and removed several additional bills. He tipped the vendor for his services. "Muchas gracias, señor."

The vendor looked to be in shape but he was sweating as much as Elízar. He pocketed the money, mumbling "Buenas noches" under his breath. Then he turned and descended back to the calzada.

Max gazed upon the Avenue of the Dead. It was practically clear of vendors and artisans, as the majority had already packed up to return home. He stared Elízar in the face. "So, now what?"

"Now, we wait." Elízar took a seat at the top of the pyramid. The sun was hovering low in the sky. "It's so beautiful here. I wish I could come more often."

"No one said anything about the butterflies."

Elízar smiled as two monarchs tumbled by. "They are mating, Señor Battenberg. What more romantic place could you find?"

Unable to disagree, Max stared down at the briefcase full of gold. "What's supposed to happen with the case, my man? You have any idea?"

A jovial smile crossed Elízar's face as he watched a large monarch floating by. "Patience, Señor. In just minutes you will know."

A chill ran down Max's spine. Elízar's words immediately reminded him of what Indigo and his father had said: *all will be revealed.*

Max and Elízar chatted about nothing until sunset came. If the steps up the pyramid had been difficult in daylight, they would be extremely problematic at night. He turned to Elízar, concerned. "We're not staying the night, are we?"

Elízar pointed toward the moon. "Full moon tonight, Señor."

Max followed Elízar's gaze. Even though it wasn't quite dark, the moon was glowing bright and full above the hills. Elízar turned to face the larger Pyramid of the Sun. In direct alignment behind it, the lower edge of the sun was just dipping beneath the horizon.

"Vamanos ahora." The plump man jumped to action, pulling a round lens about six inches in diameter from his jacket. He hurried to the topmost point of the pyramid, where a tiny, nearly impercep- tible groove was etched in the center. It almost looked like damage or a flaw in the stone. Elízar placed the lens in the groove, where it fit perfectly. He stared back and forth from the setting sun to the placement of the lens. "Bueno. Está bien."

Max watched in awe. On his left the moon, shining like an enor- mous omen in the sky, seemed to be rising from behind the Pyramid of the Moon. At the same time, directly to his right, the sun, in bril- liant colors like the wings of the butterflies, was disappearing in alignment with the Pyramid of the Sun. Like a strange waltz, the pyramids were perfectly aligning in a dance with the cosmos.

As the sun took its bow beneath the horizon, a beam of light shot from the apex of the Pyramid of the Sun and struck the lens that Elízar had placed on the roof of the Pyramid of the Moon. The lens lit up for a brief moment, just a few seconds really.

To Max's astonishment, he felt the entire pyramid begin to vibrate ever so slightly. It was as if Elízar had used the lens to bring to life some kind of engine within the structure. The subtle rumble unnerved Max.

"What is that?" He tried to steady himself, figuring he was experiencing an earthquake tremor.

After a moment, the vibration became a rhythmic hum, hitting different pitches until it reached a solid sound. The entire process felt like the rough start of a car that was now running smoothly.

Before Max's eyes, a circular portal snapped open like a camera aperture in the pyramid's roof. Aside from the small groove containing the crystal, no visible deviation had been apparent in the large stone, but a doorway had appeared nonetheless.

Max was dumbfounded. "You're shitting me!" He gazed into the doorway to witness a spiral staircase descending into the depths of the pyramid.

Elízar gestured him inside. "Hurry, Señor, it is important no one see us."

Elízar looked down to see the last vendors packing their things, but they were oblivious to Max and Elízar at the top of the pyramid. He grabbed the lens from the apex while Max crossed to the opening. He dipped his foot inside as if he were testing the waters.

"Hurry, Señor, you wouldn't want to be halfway when it closes."

"That case is heavy, Elízar, hand it to me."

"Don't worry, Señor. I will carry it. Please go."

Max stepped onto the first step, then quickly descended into the stairwell. Elízar followed, lugging the large case of gold. Air rushed into the pyramid as if a large vacuum were sucking it inside. Seconds afterward, the vibration slowed to a halt and the portal slammed shut, plunging them into darkness. The strong draft immediately ceased.

Elízar fumbled in the darkness. "Just one minute, Señor." Although it seemed an eternity, it was only a few seconds before he found what he was looking for. He had managed to find a groove similar to the one in the roof of the pyramid. When he placed the crystal inside it, a warm light began emanating from it into the chamber.

Max gazed down the stairwell and noticed similar lenses beginning to glow. Within seconds, the entire passageway was brightly illuminated.

Elízar turned to Max with a large smile on his face. "Now, Señor, we can go."

CHAPTER 21

*J*ust an hour before, Max had been a mere tourist, strolling the Avenue of the Dead, admiring Teotihuacán with its breathtaking temples and pyramids. Now, amazingly, he was inside the Pyramid of the Moon.

"Elízar, how did you do that? And why the hell are we in here?"

"Just wait, Señor, you will see."

Elízar began descending the stairwell into the pyramid. Max followed, terribly curious about their destination and in awe of what they were doing. The doorway's closure had not only left them in darkness, but, with the rush of fresh air arrested, the atmosphere in the pyramid was now heavy and stale.

Max didn't want to admit it, but he was nervous. He gazed down the spiral staircase. Like a chain of DNA, it descended deeper and deeper into the pyramid's belly. Teotihuacán was not only a diversion but was also the location of his initiation. When he thought of what might transpire, it was the worst-case scenarios that ran through his head. He envisioned the indignities of hazing and wondered if he might be beaten, branded or both.

Suddenly, he and Elízar were in a large chamber. At their arrival, strategically placed lenses began to glow, illuminating the room. Throughout the chamber, ornately decorated columns ran from floor to ceiling. As the crystals shone brighter, Max took note of colorful hieroglyphic scenes painted across the walls in a huge kind of story-board. Untouched by the sun's powerful rays, the images depicted were in rich hues, as if they had just been painted.

Across the chamber Max spotted a series of shelves. Each was heavily laden with artifacts, including jewelry, pottery, artisanal pieces and ceremonial masks.

Elízar, looking excited, urged Max toward one of the displays. "Hurry, Señor, they will be waiting for you."

As the heir to one of America's wealthiest families, Max had been made witness to many amazing things. None paralleled what he was currently seeing. He marveled at the display of art. "It's like a museum in here."

Elízar heaved the briefcase full of gold, carrying it across the room. He set it down before a unit of shelves against the wall. On the top shelf, there were a series of masks. "You need to choose a mask, Señor. You must wear it."

Max couldn't believe what he was hearing. The masks had to be ancient. One stood out to him. It appeared a simple mask, but when he looked closely, there was a great deal of detail in it. It was the head of a jaguar with warriors carved into the sides. The jaguar's fangs were bared. Max pointed to it. "This one."

"Take it, Señor. Place it over your face."

Max gingerly picked up the mask. A strap of leather was attached to its sides. He placed the mask over his face and secured it with the leather strap.

"Perfect, Señor. Now, if you would just remove your clothes."

Max was certain he misunderstood. "Excuse me?"

"Later you will understand, Señor. Please, remove your clothes."

"All of them?"

Elízar looked embarrassed to be asking. "I am afraid so."

Fear of the unknown stirred in Max. Hesitantly, he began to disrobe, first removing his shoes, pants and shirt. Elízar carefully folded each garment and placed them on the shelf where the jaguar mask had been. A deep growl rumbled in Max's stomach as he removed his socks and underwear. When Elízar refrained from taking these, Max placed the undergarments on the shelf. He felt silly standing there naked with a mask over his face.

Seemingly satisfied, Elízar produced a large burgundy cape adorned with feathers and tiny jewels. Max immediately knew he had seen artistic depictions of it in the hieroglyphs of Quetzalcoatl's temple. Elízar covered Max with the cape, evaluating him visually to be sure he was prepared. With a smile, the plump man nodded to acknowledge Max's readiness.

"Now what?" Max asked, the cold floor making him shiver with a chill.

"Now, you join the others." Elízar lifted the case, straining from its weight. "You must take this, Señor, and descend alone to the next level. From here, I can no longer assist."

"Do you know if my father's here?"

Elízar shook his head. "They wear masks for a reason, Señor. No one can know who is here. The others will be hidden from you. It is best this way, no?"

For weeks, Max had been full of questions. Questions for his father, questions for Indigo and for Dr. Miklos. There were even questions for Elízar. Now, Max feared the answers were about to begin.

With a deep breath, he took the heavy case from Elízar. "Okay. I guess I'm going in."

Elízar led Max across the chamber to a long ramp that descended into darkness. He pulled another lens from the inside of his jacket and found a groove in which to place it. The corridor slowly illuminated. "You must follow the ramp, Señor. You will see the way."

Max followed instructions and descended the ramp alone. Every few feet, there was a crystal glowing to illuminate the way. The interior of the pyramid was silent and crypt-like, allowing Max to hear his own footsteps and the growling of his stomach.

After several circuitous passageways, he finally reached another large chamber carved from the bedrock beneath the pyramid. There were no crystal light sources in this room. Instead large candles flickered, barely lit. Max imagined it was because there was very little oxygen in the chamber. Suddenly, he felt a draft of fresh air. Somehow, it was being piped in. The tiny flames sprung to life, doubling in size as they gulped at the air.

In spite of the candlelight, the corners of the room were obscured by darkness. Max could see people strategically placed throughout the stone chamber. In the center of the floor, a structure of copper piping had been assembled in the skeletal shape of a pyramid. About ten feet in front of the copper pyramid, there was a stone altar with a large crucible on top of it.

A man wearing a beautifully carved eagle mask approached and instructed Max, "Come this way." He gestured toward the altar, his arm extending out from beneath a large black cape.

Max swore it was his father's voice. In a whisper, he questioned, "Dad?"

The masked man gave no reply but led Max to the altar. "Kneel."

Max set the case on the ground before kneeling on the cold stone floor. He couldn't tell exactly how many people were in the chamber, but he estimated it to be between twenty and thirty. Several attendees stepped from the shadows and approached the area behind Max.

The man in the eagle mask strode around the altar. It was clear he was going to preside over the initiation. He began in a language Max couldn't identify. "Vagyunk ma itt össze, hogy üdvözöljük az új mellett sorainkban."

The strange tongue sounded like nothing Max had ever heard. The masked man continued for several minutes as participants in the rear repeatedly stood and kneeled in a ritual reminiscent of a Catholic mass.

The leader stepped around the altar and stood in front of Max. He had large gold rings on both thumbs with talon-like claws that snaked around his fingernails. Reaching out, he grabbed hold of Max's wrists and dug the claws into the palms of Max's hands. Max gasped as blood oozed from the puncture wounds.

The leader pulled Max to his feet and dragged him to the altar. He positioned Max's hands over the crucible so blood could drip into it from the incisions. Three red drops pooled inside.

Seconds later, two areas on the altar began to glow. As they grew brighter, Max could see they were indentations in the shape of hand-prints. The man in the eagle mask pulled Max nearer and neatly positioned Max's hands in the indentations. The stone table vibrated ever so slightly as it came to life. Within seconds, Max felt warmth emanating from the stone crucible, soothing the pain in his hands.

The man behind the eagle mask spoke, gesturing at the case of gold. "Remove the gold and place it in the crucible."

The more the man spoke, the more Max doubted he was Demetrius. There was something reminiscent of his father's voice, but the quality of speech was gravelly and slightly modulated. The room was now brightly lit, since the crucible had begun glowing red-hot and was actually turning white with heat.

The cuts in Max's hands had stopped bleeding, but they stung nonetheless when he tried to lift the case. He lugged it to the altar and opened it. The man in the eagle mask nodded as Max removed the first few bars of gold.

"Place them inside."

The man looked to be of a similar height to Demetrius, but his cape covered and obscured his true proportions.

Max approached with a bar of gold in each hand. He placed the first inside the crucible. The bar immediately began to buckle from the heat. By the time he placed the second bar inside, the first had begun to liquefy. Max could feel hair singeing on his arms and hurried to put in the other bars, watching in amazement as they liquefied. He noticed the gold was boiling as he dropped in the final bar. The eagle-masked leader came around the altar as if he were some kind of minister. "Kneel," he ordered. Then he placed his own hands against the table in a similar position to where Max's hands had just been.

Max did as asked and kneeled before the altar. Together with the eagle-masked man, the entire room began to chant. They spoke in the strange language Max didn't understand. "Elfogadja ezt kínálja..."

The crucible was like a fireball atop the table. The stone chamber, which had been cool and damp, was now brightly lit and hot like a sauna. Sweat broke out on Max's skin and trickled down his body. All of a sudden, there was a bright flash of light as if a hundred flash bulbs had simultaneously ignited. The container of liquid gold immediately began to cool, its color turning from bright white to shades of yellows and oranges. As it released heat, its glow completely dissipated until the crucible looked once again like granite.

Max watched in horror as a woman in a bear mask stepped from the crowd carrying a naked baby boy. He couldn't have been more than a few days old. The infant's arms and legs flailed as it hollered, gazing up at the bear mask. Visions of brutal sacrifices like the ones described in the Temple of Quetzalcoatl immediately ran through Max's head.

This is not what I want. Max considered trying to stop the ceremony if they actually tried to harm the child.

Like an offering, the woman lifted the screaming newborn high above her head as she continued in the strange language. "Ezzel a szertartás hagyományait folytatja".

For a second Max thought she was going to toss the infant into the crucible. He wondered if the baby would melt as the gold had, or would he burst into flames and fill the room with the smell of burning flesh? Max sighed with relief when she placed the child on top of the altar beside the crucible.

The priestess turned to Max and spoke, "Készülj fel a legrosszabbra," leaving him dumbfounded by the strange, unintelligible language.

How could she think I'd understand?

"A tudás fája kb kell szállítani." She rattled off several more phrases, then pulled Max to his feet. She detached the cape Elízar had provided and threw the plush garment to the floor.

Max stood naked and vulnerable before the crowd, but he had to admit he felt cooler without the heavy garment.

The bear-masked woman, pointing, urged him to enter the copper-framed pyramid. He did as instructed and, not being able to stand upright, sat cross-legged inside.

The man in the eagle mask removed a large crystalline chalice and a clear carafe from beneath the altar. Max watched him scoop a glistening white powder from the crucible and spoon it into the chalice. Somehow, the intense heat had vaporized the gold, transforming it into powder. With the gold powder now in the chalice, the man then poured in liquid from the carafe. He stirred the strange concoction. The final product was a slimy, white gelatinous liquid. Tiny flecks shone like miniature diamonds in the gooey suspension.

The woman in the bear mask took the liquid-filled cup from the eagle-masked man. Together they approached Max. The man reached into the pyramid and removed Max's mask, leaving him completely exposed. The woman handed Max the strange elixir.

Max gazed at the chalice, disgusted by its contents. He knew one ingredient was gold powder, but what else had been added? As he stared at the container, his stomach turned. The strange concoction resembled, at best, a large cup of semen. It was hardly what he desired after a day's fast.

The woman barked a command in the strange language. She reached for the chalice and shoved it in Max's face. Millions of insane, crazy thoughts ran through his head. For one, he found himself trying to calculate just how expensive the concoction was. Five bars of gold didn't come cheap. Then he thought of his father's words and of Indigo's prophecies. He even thought about Brigitte and wondered why he had felt the need to create Ian.

The woman struck Max on the shoulder. She wasn't large but there was power in her blow. Max wanted to throw the drink in her face, but decided against it. Anxious to get it over, he raised the crystal chalice and began downing its contents. It wasn't at all what he expected. While there was a slight sliminess to it, it wasn't nearly as repulsive as it appeared. In fact, it was tasteless and strangely light. Like a smooth alcohol, it warmed his throat and stomach.

Then it happened. A shiver ran through Max's body as blood

began rushing to his brain. He felt dizzy as pressure built in his temples. Then violence hit him. The sensation was like being struck in the head with a baseball bat or an iron cast skillet. Max had the sense of falling as if he'd truly been knocked out. Then euphoria set in. Suddenly, he felt light and warm.

As he came to and looked around, he became conscious of participants in the room sitting in a triangular configuration, with the widest row of attendees at the rear of the chamber. Max was acutely aware of everything being in great detail. The masks were shimmering in brilliant colored design and, for the most part, everyone was covered in long flowing capes or gowns of beautiful fabrics.

Staring about the room, Max saw something startling. Someone else was seated in the copper pyramid. The sight immediately disoriented him. He didn't remember stepping out of the peculiar metallic construction. So who had traded places with him? Max stooped down to see, but it was his own face staring back at him.

What the fuck? How is this possible? It was as if he left his physical body and was now looking back at himself. He realized that he must be hallucinating.

To make things more confusing, the bear-masked woman and the eagle-masked man began to speak in the strange language again. "Mint azt, úgy lesz..."

Somehow, in some inexplicable way, Max now understood what they were saying. The words were bizarre and foreign, but they held meaning at the same time. When the woman in the bear mask continued, there was a softer quality to her voice.

"...the time has come. Prepare yourself, for the truths of our legacy are about to be revealed."

Without warning, a 3-D holographic rendering of the solar system filled the room. All nine planets, perfectly depicted, rotated with precision around the large, blinding sun. Awe-struck, Max watched the scene as a gargantuan red planet approached. Twenty times as large and many shades deeper than the red of Mars, the strange burgundy-colored body completed its rotation into view.

Max stared around the room, then heard his own voice speaking the strange tongue. "What is this?"

The masked woman looked from Max to the leader. "It has almost taken effect." Turning to Max, she continued while gesturing toward the red planet. "Behold the ancestral cradle—Nibiru."

Max spoke again, but had the distinct sense of being in two places at once. His voice echoed as if resonating from his physical body still seated in the copper pyramid. At the same time, he perceived himself floating weightless in the center of the room. With an astral view of the chamber, Max observed his own body and the ceremony going on around him.

Inside the copper pyramid, tiny lights began to emanate from different points along the center of his spine. First, an indigo light appeared between his eyebrows. And then a purple light engulfed his crown. In the center of his chest, a green light came to life. And below that, a yellow and then an orange and red light appeared consecutively. It was as if miniature, colored light bulbs had been placed along his spine and were now being illuminated inside of him.

As he looked around the room, similar lights began appearing on other participants, but they varied in shade and intensity. When he looked upward, he could see clear through the rock to the upper chamber where Elízar waited. Amazingly, he noted that on Elízar, the lights were stifled and dull, flickering at times.

At the front of the room, the opposite was occurring. The brightest of all the lights radiated from the spine of the tiny baby on top of the altar. In amazement, Max approached the infant and a shiver ran up his back. He suddenly felt overrun with emotion.

Visions raced through his mind as if he were being shown hundreds of movies at once. At the same time, while he felt himself floating above the chamber, the sensation of spinning struck him. Everything around Max, sights and sounds, became a blur as if he were caught in a vortex of time and space. The experience felt like the annihilation of his senses, and then there was stillness.

Max now found himself floating in a void of total darkness, perceiving utter and complete nothingness. The idea that he no longer existed crept into his mind, that he was dead — giving rise to a panic that immediately subsided into peacefulness and harmony.

In that instant, the ceremony in the Pyramid of the Moon fled his consciousness and there was just Max becoming one with the universe. All of Max's hopes and fears escaped into the void, releasing him of all animosities. Aware of the tranquility, Max savored the moment.

In a flash of blinding light, now love engulfed him as color and sound. For Max, it felt like the most beautiful note he had ever heard being played continuously as it shimmered in a colorful green palette. The green hues seemed an infinite pasture but then, just as if a piano key had been struck, the tones and colors changed. A kaleidoscope of oranges and reds wrapped around him, and the vibration of the note heated his soul. Max knew he was feeling passion in its purest form. A sense of bliss settled over him.

A concerto of color and sound played all about him as Max became aware of his own body in flight, soaring as the eagle must soar, passing in and out of red-hued clouds. Max perceived he had control of his flight, rising or descending with only a thought to do so. With no knowledge of his position in time or space, he felt drawn to something or someone below.

With simple intention, he dove through crimson clouds until the enormous red planet came into view. Max quickly descended, viewing the terrain. Built solidly into a huge circular crater was a massive complex of pyramids, roadways, obelisks and temples. From high above, the city's symmetry was strikingly artistic. Max banked to the left to witness a pyramid's construction in progress.

A huge airship hovered above the construction site. Max marveled at its size, like no craft he'd ever seen. In some ways, it resembled a blimp, but it was sleeker and more aerodynamic. Toward the rear of the craft were three sets of fins. Whatever was propelling the ship, it floated and maneuvered effortlessly.

Suspended on cables beneath the enormous craft were huge perfectly carved blocks of stone. One by one, they were being lowered to workers who maneuvered them into place to form the base of a pyramid.

Max crossed over the construction toward a magnificent palace. Just as his intention had directed his flight, he found himself questioning, *What is this I'm seeing?* He became acutely aware of someone or something on the ground below.

A musical note played loud and shrill and Max recoiled from it. Shades of black swirled about like negative space and Max felt anger, envy and spite. The colorful emotional tonalities engulfed him in concert. Max attempted shrugging them off but they were too intense, pulling him in as a black hole draws in everything about it.

Like lightning to a copper rod, Max felt his essence merging with the source of turmoil below. The process was awkward and uncomfortable, like a square peg being jammed into a triangular hole. Just as he had controlled his flight, Max thought of freeing himself from this essence that was not his own. But his efforts were not fruitful.

Slowly, Max relented, comprehending that his desire to understand was stronger than his discomfort. With intense clarity and purpose, he merged with the source of rage.

CHAPTER 22

*F*urious, Enlil stormed from his chambers and ran out onto the huge veranda just outside his quarters. He stared across the ocean, allowing a gentle breeze to caress his cheeks and soothe his flushed skin. He could feel moisture in the air from the onshore flow blowing in across the water.

The ocean, vast and expansive, rendered the expression "as far as vision discerns" more than inadequate, especially since Nibiru was a planet that was nearly eleven times larger than Earth.

Enlil was quite magnificent with flawless, mocha skin and fine, delicately chiseled features. He stood a full seven feet tall, but his proportions were elegant and well formed. Gazing across to the horizon, he breathed in the outdoor air, trying to calm himself.

The skies were tinged with shades of red and burnt orange that lent themselves to dusk even though no such thing existed on Nibiru. So distant from the sun, the humongous tenth planet of the solar system should likely never have supported life. But a strange set of circumstances had dictated otherwise.

As a young child, Enlil had been educated about the source of Nibiru's power. Deep within its core, the planet had powerful, life-sustaining energy. Yes, it had taken billions of years, but Nibiru's radiant core had eventually cooled to temperatures compatible with life. At the same time, a symphony of well-placed volcanoes had erupted, spewing necessary gases into the air: sulfur, nitrogen, oxygen and carbon dioxide. The curious circumstances had allowed an atmosphere to develop even in the absence of a nearby sun.

But it wasn't an abundant existence. Enlil knew that well. Nibiru's extreme distance from the sun, the giver of life, had predestined that survival on the planet would be difficult. The only resources that had ever been plentiful were land and water. But millions of years had afforded Nibirians the opportunity to tame their environment. Versed in science and technology, the inhabitants of this planet, the Anunnaki, had forged a way to survive.

Finally calmed from his anger, Enlil stepped away from the ledge and crossed past his chambers to the other side of the veranda. The vantage point allowed a magnificent view of the Capitol City. What looked like a large, cobblestoned runway ran for miles and miles, flanked on each side by rows of huge sphinxes that majestically faced one another. The view, while reminiscent of ancient Egypt in its heyday, was infinitely more glorious.

At the end of the expansive runway, a mammoth obelisk shot into the sky like a light tower to the monstrous ocean whose waves continued out indefinitely.

Enlil turned to witness the huge airship hovering above. Beneath it, workers were helping to lower enormous stones into the base of a gargantuan pyramid structure. Nibiru's latest construction had been commissioned by Alalu, their recently deposed ruler. Enlil knew Alalu would never see the pyramid's completion, as he had literally been chased from the post of supreme leader. The success-ful coup was a plan that he himself had devised.

Enlil's mother, Ki, nearly as tall as he at six-five, stepped onto the veranda to watch her son. She hardly looked a day older than Enlil. Just as Nibiru's atmosphere had found a different set of laws to sustain life, the passage of time there also obeyed a different set of rules from those that existed on Earth.

The disparity between time's passage on Earth and its passage on Nibiru couldn't be quantified by an exact equation, although crude approximations had been made. One Earth year, or 365 days, corresponded to a single revolution of planet Earth around the sun. 3,600 Earth years were needed in order for Nibiru to complete one elliptical orbit around the same sun. As time went, Nibirians could survive thousands of Earth years without even seeming to age.

While Enlil's mother had only been the messenger, she was well aware that her news had placed Enlil in a terrible state. One of the planet's most important expeditions was about to occur and his older half brother had been chosen over him for the journey. The more intently he searched for calm, Enlil couldn't help but bristle with rage.

His father's recent coup to overthrow Alalu had, of course, turned Nibiru on its side, but that was the least of anyone's worries. Considering the frightful circumstances of Nibiru's dying atmo-sphere, the more important question was whether anyone at all would survive on the red planet.

After billions of years, Nibiru's life-sustaining core had cooled and its atmosphere, the air they breathed, was slowly escaping into space. The sparkling red beacon that Nibiru had always been was now dimming. In his desperation, the sitting leader Alalu had ordered several nuclear detonations in surrounding volcanoes, hoping to revitalize the planet's core. So far nothing had proven useful in reversing the environment's deterioration.

Ever the opportunist, Enlil had seen an opening. For many millennia, Alalu of the Ne'fil clan had ruled with an iron fist. But Enlil's father, Anu, was extremely well placed politically. He could conceivably seize the moment to depose the ruler whose ineffective efforts had failed to restore their atmosphere. It was Enlil who planted the idea of a coup in his father's head. It was Enlil who reassured his father of the people's support. Fear over the future had crept into the public psyche and something drastic had to be done.

One morning, while lying in bed, Enlil had devised a plan to seize Nibiru's throne. Over the next weeks, he had convinced his father, Anu, that a rebellion should be launched. At the very least, people would take solace in the idea of something proactive being done to preserve the air they breathed. Of course, Anu would then be tasked with finding a solution to an imminent environmental disaster. If he failed, however, no one would be around to protest.

After he agreed to the plan, it took Anu three days to solidify it. On the fourth day, he gathered his supporters and successfully deposed Alalu. That very day, Enlil and Ki had hurried to the royal palace to take up residence. In fact, it was from one of the royal verandas that Enlil was now enjoying the view.

Now, only months later, they all feared for their stability. After being dethroned, Alalu had commandeered one of the fleet's fastest and most powerful warships. Fearing for his life, he had fled to the third planet orbiting the sun. From the enormous distance, the deposed ruler had relayed a message that could change the fate of all. Alalu had supposedly discovered massive deposits of Number 79 on the periodic table. Au, or, as it's more commonly known — gold.

Nibiru's most elite scientists knew there were properties contained in the precious metal that were crucial to their atmosphere's restoration. Likewise, Enlil also understood that if he and his mother were to remain in the palace, Anu would have to proceed carefully with regard to this new development. If gold was obtainable on Earth, it could change the playing field completely.

As far as Enlil was concerned, he had proven himself of value.

After all, it was he who had assisted in organizing the royal coup. When he spotted his mother on the veranda, Enlil turned away.

"Enlil, you must be patient." Ki's voice was soft and maternal.

"I'm sick of being patient, mother. If it weren't for me, none of us would even be in this palace."

Ki placed a tender hand on her son's shoulder. "This is true, deposing Alalu was your idea. But still you must respect your father. Allow him to choose as he sees fit."

"What took you so long anyway?"

Ki was struck by Enlil's question almost as if he had punched her in the gut. Because of Anu's status, he had been entitled to and had ultimately taken two wives. As his first, it had been Ki's duty to provide him an heir, but she hadn't done so in a timely manner. Her intention had been to soften her son's anger but the opposite was occurring.

Enlil felt his face flushing as blood surged in his veins. "You are the first wife, mother. Which makes me the first heir. To send Enki is insulting to us both."

"Calm yourself, Enlil. You'll make yourself ill. Your brother — "

"Half brother," Enlil corrected. "You realize because he's older that he considers himself the first heir? Which is preposterous!"

"It is true, Antu provided an heir before I did..." Ki's words trailed off.

Enlil knew the topic pushed her buttons, but he was too angry for restraint. "You are the first wife. In the hierarchy of things that makes me the first heir. Why is this so difficult to understand?"

Losing patience, Ki grabbed Enlil tightly by the arm. "Your father values you more than you know. You must be patient. Your time of greatness grows near."

Enlil stared into his mother's eyes, wondering if there was any truth in her words. Suddenly, the hairs stood on his arms and neck as electricity trickled through the air. Enlil immediately understood why. He looked at his mother, completely aware that she also understood. The familiar phenomenon related directly to the upsetting news she had just delivered about Enki and the expedition.

Enlil rushed around to the other side of the veranda to observe the runway flanked by sphinxes. An obelisk-shaped craft, slightly larger than a Learjet, was floating down the path. It looked like brushed gun metal with windows on each side. As it came closer, Enlil realized it must be his half-brother, Enki, piloting one of the fleet's transports.

He's on his way to meet Alalu to confirm if the stories of gold are true.

If the small, blue planet indeed had supplies of the precious ore, it would be a monumental find. Enlil desired a role in the affair, but his half-brother had been chosen instead.

As the transport's ionic technology was charging, the surrounding air felt awakened and revitalized. Invisible sparks of energy crackled about them as the ship rose higher into the sky.

Enlil was aware of his brother's antics. Enki had purposely maneuvered the ship in order to be seen. His point had been made. As first born, it was likely Anu did consider him the first heir. A combination of anger and resentment flushed Enlil's cheeks.

As the transport drifted nearer, Enlil was certain he could see Enki smiling from the cockpit. The craft was whisper-quiet without flames or rocket propulsion. Then, in the blink of an eye, it vanished, literally slingshotting through time and space.

Nibiru, in its 3,600-year path, had rotated into the cluster of nine planets surrounding the sun. As such, it was as near to Earth as it ever would be. Enki's trip there would be only a matter of hours, so Nibirians would soon know if the tiny planet contained gold, and thus, if their atmosphere could be saved.

CHAPTER 23

Suddenly, Max felt liberated as if sprung from a cage. He rejoiced as Enlil's anger and hostility shed from his being like the skin from a snake. Then, an extreme violence rocked his body as if he had been slammed against the ground. Recovering from the shock, he gulped in air, coughing to catch his breath. He was once again aware of himself in the copper pyramid. Max felt numb and weighed down compared to the lightness he had felt only a few moments before.

The woman in the bear mask reached for him and pulled him to his feet. Max stepped from the copper pyramid and stared around the room. The strange glowing lights he had witnessed on the spines of everyone were now gone.

Max was wobbly on his feet as the woman helped him move toward the altar. Regaining his bearings, he took note of his body covered in sweat. The masked man and woman covered his nakedness with the large cape and returned the jaguar mask to his head. They continued in the strange language, but Max found he could still understand it.

"What are we speaking?"

"The ancestral tongue," the man in the eagle mask responded.

"And how am I able to speak it?"

The woman in the bear mask raised a finger to the lips of her disguise to shush Max. When he fell silent, she turned and picked up the baby, who had been very quiet all this time and continued so. Perhaps it was asleep. But once again, Max feared they would ask him to participate in some weird ritual sacrifice. The woman approached with the child, lifting it above her head. She continued in the strange tongue.

"Herein lies the new generation, which we dedicate to the service of our people." Lowering the infant, she turned to Max. "Do you vow to honor the sacred system given to us by our forefathers and by their fathers before them?"

Max looked around, unsure of his answer. The man in the eagle mask nodded, urging him to continue.

"I do."

The priestess of the ceremony continued, "As it always has been, so shall it come to pass that a new generation protects and serves the interests of our kind. From this day, do you, Maximilian Battenberg, vow with your life to hold in confidence the sacred legacies that have been passed down for more than a hundred millennia?"

Max looked again to the man in the eagle mask, who gently nodded until Max answered, "I do."

Like a baton in a relay race, the woman passed the child into Max's arms. "Entrusted to you is this new generation and its descendants. In your responsibility rests its management, nurturing and care. As it always has been, so shall it come to pass."

Max was pleased when the woman took the child from him and passed it to someone in the crowd. She circled back and took Max's hands, holding them together as if in prayer. To close, the entire room began chanting in the strange language. Max thought of the hymns that were sung at the end of church mass. The initiation, it seemed, was winding down. As the attendees broke formation, people mobilized about the room.

Max whispered questions to the masked woman, "What is it you gave me? And how am I speaking this language?" Even though he couldn't see her face, Max felt the woman was smiling behind her mask.

"Gold, when vaporized, transforms into something infinitely more precious. The sacred elixir activated something in you, which has lain dormant until now. You, my friend, have tasted from the Tree of Knowledge."

Max remained perplexed and mumbled, "I was hallucinating. I had to be."

The woman leaned closer and spoke in a throaty voice, but the words were English this time. "No one can know what you saw. You must hold it secret. The stability of our traditions depends on it."

The room was spinning, but no longer because of the powder Max had been given. He was simply overloaded with information. The woman grabbed him firmly by the arm. "You will learn the ways and you will abide by them. A hundred millennia we've existed and a thousand more we will endure."

Max recoiled, his arm smarting from the strength of her grip. An eerie connection occurred to him as he remembered Indigo's words: *when you've learned what you don't know, come back and tell me who should be ashamed.*

Max trembled at the thought. It was as Indigo predicted: She had said the cycle of control was diminishing, *and then your kind will retreat into nothingness.* Those had been her exact words. But what did it all mean? The psychic had screamed at Brigitte, telling her she had no idea what she was dealing with and that Max had deceived her. She had warned, *He is neither who nor what you think he is.* And now, Max was unsure himself what that might be.

As hard as he tried, he couldn't slow his head from spinning. Maybe it was the white powder of gold still working on his brain, or maybe it was lack of sustenance. Everything was beginning to blur.

People were now circulating about the room. The frenzy lasted only a few minutes and then Max watched a mass exodus. During the commotion, he approached the crucible atop the altar, taking his advantage to retrieve some of the white powder from inside. He carefully secreted the powder in a fold of his cape that was tightly clutched in his hand.

No one said another word to him as the chamber emptied of its masquerading participants. Not knowing what else to do, Max made his way to the ramp and ascended to the original room where Elízar was waiting. The Battenberg representative for Mexico City jumped to his feet.

"How are you, Señor? Was everything fine?"

Still too stunned to respond, Max stared blankly at Elízar and nodded. It wasn't the first time Elízar had witnessed the astonished expression. He retrieved Max's folded clothes before attempting to remove the cape.

"Wait, Elízar, just give me a minute."

"Of course, Señor, lo siento." Elízar half bowed and half nodded. He placed the garments beside Max, then stepped away into the corner of the room.

Max leaned against the wall and slid down it into a seated position. His fist was still tightly clenched around the cape, encapsulating the white powder.

Placing the cape on the floor, he removed his water bottle from the daypack and sprinkled the gold powder inside. He returned the bottle to his bag, dusted off the cape and dressed. Within what seemed minutes, he and Elízar were in a car speeding back to his hotel in Mexico City.

Max couldn't quite remember how they had left the pyramid. Had they exited and descended the steps, or was there another secret passage that no one knew about? In the end it didn't matter. Given everything that had transpired in the ceremony, he didn't have the confidence to trust his own memories.

During the return trip to the hotel, he and Elízar spoke very little. Instead, Max stared through the window, unable to adequately process anything running through his mind. *What did they do to me? I must have dreamt the whole thing. Or hallucinated it.*

Rather than accept the experiences of his initiation, Max began telling himself the story he needed to believe in order to dismiss the impossible from his thoughts.

Psychedelics... The whole thing was some elaborate drug trip.

Max continued staring through the window. Outside, there were people, houses and cars passing by. *This is reality. This is reality. This is reality.*

By the time they reached the hotel, Elízar was behaving matter of fact and upbeat, as if nothing out of the ordinary had happened.

"Okay, Señor Battenberg? I hope you enjoyed your visit to Teotihuacán."

"Yeah. Thank you, Elízar." Max thought of asking questions, but he had no idea how much Elízar even knew. He had also vowed with his life to keep everything secret.

"How much longer will you stay in Mexico City?" Elízar asked.

"I think I'm finished. Is there anything I need to hang around for?"

Elízar shook his head. "No, Señor, I believe you are done."

"Then probably, I'll be on a plane back to Chicago first thing in the morning."

"Very well, Señor Battenberg. It was my pleasure to host you here in Mexico."

Max smiled and nodded at Elízar with genuine appreciation, but given his experiences, the exchange of pleasantries was utterly surreal to the point of being absurd.

"Good night, Elízar. If ever you're in Chicago, you let us know."

"Of course, Señor Battenberg, claro qué si."

The two men shook hands and Max returned to his hotel room. He locked and bolted the door, then collapsed on the bed. Staring at the ceiling, he re-ran the events of the pyramid through his head.

Impossible. If the strange powder was a hallucinogen, it still didn't explain the opening of the doorway in the pyramid. *I hadn't had the drink yet. Did I also imagine that?*

With a deep sigh, he thought of the gold bars and of the strange liquid he had been given. This moment of stillness made him aware of the concoction's continued effects. He still felt lightheaded, but the feeling was different from drugs or alcohol. He also felt a strange vibration through his body. *The elixir is still in effect.*

He crossed into the bathroom and splashed water on his face. Max studied his reflection, befuddled and exhilarated at the same time. *Why was I able to speak a language I don't know?*

The initiation was designed to show he belonged to an elite group, but truthfully, this wasn't new information. As a Battenberg he already belonged to an exclusive group. *But an alien planet?* Max desperately needed clarification. *My dad will know. I have to speak with him.*

Max grabbed his phone to call. Prior to the Hades alert, Demetrius had given him a special number for urgent occasions. This certainly qualified. The phone rang a half dozen times, but Demetrius ironically didn't answer. Voice mail kicked in and a computerized female voice delivered the outgoing message. Max waited for the beep.

"Dad, it's me. I'm still in Mexico, but I wanted to talk. Call me when you get this message."

Max ended the call, then sat on the edge of the bed for nearly forty minutes before he remembered he hadn't eaten in days. *How is time passing so fast?* Everything felt accelerated, which left Max feeling anxious and uncomfortable. Jumping across the bed, he scooped up the hotel menu from the nightstand and quickly thumbed through it. The photographs alone of beautifully presented food caused his mouth to water. Max quickly snatched the phone off its cradle and dialed room service.

"Hi, the kitchen's still open, right? Great, I'd like to order..." Max proceeded to order more than he could ever hope to eat. He asked for a sirloin burger with grilled onions, grilled mushrooms, Swiss cheese, bacon and avocado. He also ordered sweet potato fries, shrimp tacos and tortilla soup. When he was done, he hung up, unsure if he could stand the predicted wait of twenty minutes. Within seconds, memories of his initiation came flooding back.

I don't want to overthink this. It's not the time to overthink this...

Max grabbed his phone and rang both Brigitte and Chandler, but neither answered. He also got voice mail when he tried his friend Ted. *I can't sit here like this.*

Rather than wait quietly, he showered before changing into fresh clothes. Afterward Max grabbed his phone to verify whether Demetrius, or anyone, had called back. There were no missed calls. Given he had called an emergency number, it annoyed him that Demetrius hadn't checked to see if he was okay. In the morning he would return to Chicago. There, his father could fill in the blanks about everything going on.

A knock at the door thrilled Max. He was finally going to have his feast. He prayed that the food would clear his mind and get rid of the strange vibrations he was still experiencing. Max whisked open the door to find a young man carrying a large tray.

"Good evening, Señor."

Max stepped aside and the food porter entered. He placed the tray on the table and lifted the first lid. "Sirloin burger, sweet potato fries..."

The aroma of food engulfed Max, and he could feel his stomach grumbling in protest of the fast. The porter replaced the lid and lifted another from a smaller plate.

"Shrimp tacos and you also had tortilla soup."

"Yes." Max could hardly contain himself. He filled in a generous tip on the bill and signed it before escorting the porter from the room. Without hesitation, Max plopped down before the TV and set the tray beside him. He lifted each lid again, amused by how happy he was at the sight of a simple burger and fries.

As Max bit into the burger, his mouth seemingly exploded with both flavor and joy. He knew he should eat slowly, but he couldn't help himself as he shoveled fries into his mouth between each bite of the burger. Still chewing, Max crossed to the mini bar and removed two bottles of beer. He popped open the first one and used it to chase down his food.

Twenty minutes later, he was sprawled across the bed, hovering in a peculiar zone between satisfaction and nausea. At the same time, the room service tray was piled high with the wreckage of empty containers. Max had to admit he did feel better, even if the strange tremors were persisting.

After a long while, he rose from the bed. There would be little chance of him sleeping and no one was returning his calls. He crossed to his suitcase, fished a Ziploc bag from his toiletry sack and placed the plastic water bottle with the white powder of gold inside. Max sealed the bag and placed it next to his passport in the hotel safe. After a quick glance, he picked up the passport and slid out the photograph of him with his mother and brother. Max gazed at his mother's face.

"You too. Would you have told me this if you were still here?" He waited, but there was no answer.

Max put the passport and photo back in the safe and locked it. Satisfied, he crossed to the door, where he hesitated. On impulse he removed the necklace with the tiny, dangling microchip. *Tonight I will travel alone.* He returned to the safe and placed the minuscule GPS inside. Even as he felt the vibrations continue, Max disappeared through the door for one last night in Mexico City.

CHAPTER 24

*T*he woman in the bear mask had called it the sacred elixir or the Tree of Knowledge. *Is that what they were referring to in the Bible?*

Max had not yet completely shaken the strange concoction's effects. Tingling sensations roamed up and down the surface of his skin and somehow he felt more alive, with his senses turned full throttle.

After leaving his room, he followed a long corridor to another wing of the hotel, and from there he descended a stairwell to the hotel pool. After scanning the mostly deserted grounds, Max made his way to the street and hailed a cab.

The driver pulled away from the curb before inquiring, "A donde vas, amigo?" With a glance in the rearview mirror, he rephrased his question. "Where to, my friend?"

Max hesitated, in need of a cocktail but unsure where to get one. "You tell me, jefe. If you weren't working tonight where would you go?"

"Oh, I don't know, Señor." Max could see the driver was blushing. "I have family. I work all the time."

"What's your name?"

"Rudolfo," the driver replied.

"Rudolfo, I'm Max. Tonight's my last night in Mexico. Quiero ver la ciudad crudo cómo todo la gente qué vive aqui."

Rudolfo continued smiling. "Your Spanish is very good, Señor."

"I went to the pyramids today. You been there, Rudolfo? To Teotihuacán?"

"Si, is very magical, Teotihuacán. People make pilgrimage there. But the Teotihuacános, they disappear. No one knows where they go. Just gone." Rudolfo continued eyeing Max in the rearview mirror.

"Where do you think they went?"

"Ah, señor, yo no se. Teotihuacán en Nahautl se dice Ciudad de los Dioses. The Aztecs called it the City of the Gods. If this is true, perhaps they return to the heavens."

Max glanced at his watch and was in disbelief of the time. When he and Elízar returned to the hotel, it was 8 p.m. Now, it was past midnight. He couldn't shake the feeling that he was losing time. Struggling to stay focused, he concentrated on Rudolfo.

"Yeah. That's an interesting point of view, Rudolfo." Part of Max wanted to break down and reveal what he had seen only hours before in the Pyramid of the Moon.

"Here, many believe this, Señor. The archeologists, more than fifty years they look to find where the Teotihuacános go. They find nothing, Señor. Nada." Rudolfo was smiling at the idea. "Is funny, no?"

"Rudolfo, escúchame uno momento."

"Yes, señor."

"How about I hire you tonight? The whole night you drive and we hang out. It'll sort of be like a night off."

"Oh, Señor, I don't know."

"Name your price. I'm not interested in any tourist traps. I just want to see Mexico City." Max could see in the rearview mirror that Rudolfo was still smiling. There was a warm friendliness about him. "Five hundred American, Rudolfo. Is that enough for the night?"

"Oh, Señor," Rudolfo laughed. "If you are serious, this is very generous."

From the back seat, Max counted out two hundred in cash. "I tell you what, I'll give you two now and three at the end of the night. How's that?" He handed Rudolfo the bills.

"Very good, Señor." Rudolfo took the cash and slipped it in his shirt pocket.

"Perfect. Take me wherever you like. As long as I can get some alcohol—beer, tequila, it doesn't matter what."

Rudolfo smiled as he glanced at Max's reflection in the rearview mirror. "Very well, Señor. We go somewhere nice."

Max felt secure with this stranger as his guide, and they chatted for the next fifteen minutes on their way across town. Max stared through the window and was pleasantly surprised by the view.

"Looks like Spain, Rudolfo."

"Si, si. The area is La Colonia Roma, one of Mexico City's most traditional neighborhoods. We will drink here. It's okay, Señor?"

"Totally your call, my friend. Looks great to me."

"The neighborhood of Roma is where the Spanish aristocrats settled when they first arrived in Mexico."

Max looked around and noticed an array of spectacular multi-level mansions lining the streets. The architecture was largely Porfirian with a mixture of French, Roman, Gothic and Moorish elements. Much of it appeared like the streets of Madrid, although the landscape had morphed quite a bit in the last decades. A collection of taller, more modern offices and apartment buildings peppered the area, slowly replacing buildings that had crumbled either from age or from the 1985 earthquake.

Rudolfo parked the taxi, then led Max across the street toward a beautiful majestic building. The structure, which could have been a large chateau when it was built, appeared to have been converted into commercial spaces with offices and storefronts. Max was expecting some semblance of a crowd, but the streets looked semi-deserted.

"You sure this is good, Rudolfo? It's like a ghost town." Although Max had decided to trust Rudolfo, Roma's deserted streets led to thoughts of the Hades alert and the bizarre attacker who had accosted them in New Orleans. Without thinking, he reached up and stroked the thin scar across his face.

"Amigo, you say you want the real Mexico City. I show you one of the best discotecas. No es turístico aquí."

Rudolfo led Max into the building's interior courtyard, where several couples were smoking and chatting. Max felt a sense of relief when he spotted the small crowd. The inner square consisted of a half dozen boutiques that were all closed at the late hour.

Max followed Rudolfo's lead until he noticed graffiti on a large column. Spray painted in black was a man's head with the word "RIZICK" elongating from his lips as if it were being blown in a large gob of chewing gum. At first Max didn't recognize whose head the image depicted, but then he realized as they approached. It was Italy's former prime minister, Silvio Berlusconi.

He had seen similar graffiti in Chicago outside of the club where his father had him abducted. "RIZICK" had also been painted there, but it was George W. Bush's face that was portrayed.

"Rudolfo? What does this Rizick thing mean, do you know?"

Rudolfo looked at the tag and shrugged. "Yo no sé, Señor. I have no idea."

Moving along, he and Max descended a stairwell. Wherever they were going was beneath the building. Max never saw any signage, but he suddenly heard music playing. Half a dozen people were standing in a foyer hovering around a large, ornate wooden door.

"When I have dinero, Señor, and the time, this is where I come."

Rudolfo pulled open the large, embellished door and they stepped into a dark, smoky bar that was much larger than it looked from outside. Directly to the right were a series of leather booths. Most were full with parties of four or six, eating and drinking. Directly in front of them, three steps led up to a long bar.

"You hungry, Rudolfo? You want a drink?"

"I am driving, Señor."

"Come on, one drink won't kill you."

Max pulled Rudolfo to the bar and ordered four tequila shots. He looked around, evaluating the venue of Rudolfo's choosing. The wood surface of the counter was faded and missing varnish. Years of traffic had dulled the red carpet. The area where Max stood was worn and threadbare.

The bartender, a portly woman in her forties with short, curly hair, slammed four tequila shots on the bar before them. Max paid, then held up his glass to toast Rudolfo.

"To Mexico City and Teotihuacán."

The minute they finished their first round, a woman approached and began speaking to Rudolfo in Spanish. Max wasn't sure why, but a rush of emotion overcame him. For no apparent reason, he felt conflicted and torn.

He shifted his attention back to Rudolfo. The cab driver's conversation with the woman was growing heated. Sensing her to be more than a friend to his companion, Max picked up his remaining shot and excused himself. With each step away from Rudolfo the feelings of turmoil dissipated and eventually faded away.

Max downed the second shot as he wandered down a long corridor toward the thumping sounds of music. On some level, he felt foolish being out immediately following his initiation. But he was desperate to replace the unsettled sensations of the pyramid with a good old-fashioned buzz. For Max, being intoxicated was familiar territory. *Finally, the tequila's kicking in.* But the alcohol did too little to lessen the elixir's lingering effects.

Max reached the end of the hall and crossed through a set of double doors into a darker and smokier wing. As the doors swung shut behind him, he was on the dance floor.

A track was playing that was catchy and tribal in nature. Extreme bass thumped, causing his skin to tingle with every beat. While Rudolfo's choice of club wasn't a true dive bar, it was only steps away in terms of ambiance. Max scanned the room, pleased by what he saw. An attractive, trendy crowd undulated to the beat like several hundred blades of grass wafting back and forth in the wind.

Another drink should shake this feeling. At the bar, Max ordered a third tequila shot. Before he received it, a wave of joyful exuberance washed over him. Caught completely off guard, he laughed. *What's going on with me?*

Max turned to his left and noticed a group of three friends. They were sipping on beers and chuckling at something. One man, younger than Max, was practically bowled over with deep, roaring laughter. Max found his guffaws infectious and was immediately overcome with unbridled laughter of his own, as if his worries had all washed away. *The tequila's finally working.*

When his third shot arrived, Max sucked it down and crossed toward the dance floor. With every step away from the bar the light-hearted feeling diminished. *Shit. The elixir's still with me.*

Max at least drew comfort that the earlier feelings of conflict hadn't returned. Shaking off the collection of confusing emotions, he suddenly became aware of a new rhythmic beat playing in the background. As a new song began he stepped onto the dance floor and swayed in the crowd, slowly losing himself to the track. His movements were fluid, sensual, even seductive. Although he hadn't yet realized it, he was quick to catch the eye of two couples dancing beside him.

At first glance, the couples seemed ordinary — two men each dancing with women. But Max soon noticed something unusual. It seemed the two girls had paused to speak with one another when in actuality the partnering had switched. Now, the two women were dancing together in a provocative manner. When he looked at the men they were doing the same, seductively rubbing and sliding their bodies against one another.

After a brief show, the partners switched again—two men, each dancing with a woman. Max turned away, deciding to ignore the spectacle. Neither couple was particularly attractive, but, in some way, Max felt titillated nonetheless. He imagined, beneath brighter lights, that they might all be quite homely.

The couples drew closer and Max's eroticized feelings further intensified. *I need to have sex*, he thought. He couldn't determine why, but his body felt as if he'd just been slipped a hit of ecstasy. While he hadn't used the drug in years, he had experimented during college. Suddenly, Max found he wanted to touch and be touched. He tried pushing the thoughts from his head when it finally occurred to him: *What if this isn't me? What if these aren't my feelings?* As strange as it seemed, Max appeared to be channeling other people's emotions.

Only ten minutes earlier, he'd been filled with turmoil in the presence of Rudolfo and the woman. At the bar, he felt elation, for no apparent reason except for the strangers who had been laughing beside him. Now, surrounded by the two couples on the dance floor, he was feeling aroused.

While Max didn't know it, Rudolfo had run into his mistress and was conflicted about the affair. The sensation of havoc that appeared to be his own had arisen from Rudolfo's guilt. Indeed, the elation he felt had belonged to the laughing threesome at the bar. Now, Max was beside two unappealing couples who had all dropped ecstasy. Like a sponge, he was unwillingly absorbing their sense of excitement.

But how? The elixir. It has to be.

Max felt betrayed by his own body. He had, on occasion, been turned on by attractive people he ended up finding unlikable. But he had never been drawn to people he found visually unappealing. He watched the couples as they continued swapping partners. No matter how they paired, their dancing was provocative and erotic.

The couples inched their way closer to him, intrigued by the lone and handsome stranger. The less homely of the two girls leaned in and yelled over the music.

"Hola guapo, cómo te va?"

Max didn't acknowledge her and simply carried on dancing.

"You speak Spanish?" she continued.

He smiled, unsure if he wanted to engage. "Un poquito. But I see you speak English."

The woman was flirtatious, but not in a way that was sexy or enticing. "Just a little también." Although uninvited, the girl approached and began to dance with Max. She came in close. "I'm Graciela. These are my friends Eulayia, Hugo and Gustavo."

A profound sensuality overwhelmed Max as he shook everyone's hands. "Nice to meet you. My name's Ian."

Graciela leaned in so close that her lips gently brushed Max's cheek. "Nice to meet you, Ian."

A feeling of bliss overcame Max. The sensation of a dozen feathers tickling him exploded in the area where Graciela's lips had touched his skin. Slowly, his buzz was transitioning to intoxication, but it still hadn't overpowered the effects of the initiation's white powder of gold.

The couples artfully inched into position, surrounding Max as wolves do their prey. At the same time, the DJ eased into a powerfully rhythmic song. Graciela and Eulayia screamed with joy.

The women pulled Max and their boyfriends deeper onto the dance floor. This time, Max was included in the rotation. At times, he would find himself dancing with either Graciela, Eulayia or both. At other times, he would find himself surrounded by Hugo and Gustavo. In the end, it didn't matter who approached, every move was filled with sexual tension.

At one point, Gustavo put a hand around Max and pulled him close, so they were slow dancing face-to-face. "What brings you to Mexico City?" Gustavo asked.

Max slurred his words as he answered, "Part business, part pleasure."

This time, Gustavo did as Graciela had done only minutes before. His lips caressed Max's ear as he questioned, "What about tonight? Business or pleasure?"

Before Max could respond, Eulayia came up and grabbed him from behind. She wrapped her arms tightly around Max's belly, pulling him close until they were spooning on the dance floor.

"What're you guys talking about? Qué dices, Gustavo?"

Gustavo and Eulayia began a conversation with Max sandwiched between them. Before Max knew it, the couple was kissing, their faces pressed very warmly against his. He could smell their scents and hear their lips and tongues moving. Max closed his eyes and felt Gustavo's arousal pressing against his leg. Eulayia began to grope whatever she could, leaving Max unsure if her hands were hunting for him or for Gustavo. She found them both.

Sexually charged energy coursed through Max's veins, overpowering any sense of reason. He wanted to break away from the couples but could not. Suddenly, hands were unfastening his belt and pants. Max didn't fight. In his obliviousness, he hardly noticed a photographer snapping shots from across the room. The igniting flash bulbs were easily camouflaged by the club's strobe lights.

In an abrupt move, someone grabbed his arm and tugged him from the sandwich that was Gustavo and Eulayia.

"Max! Out again I see."

It took a moment for Max to snap out of it. When he looked up, he saw Amalia Salazar staring back at him. "Oh, hi." He didn't remember her name.

The foursome's lure lost its potency as Amalia pulled Max further away.

Amalia's brother, Jorge, was at her side. He smiled at Max, nodding in the direction of the two couples. "I see you're enjoying the city."

Eulayia and Graciela were visibly perturbed that Amalia had barged in on their affair. They were even more perplexed that she had used the name Max. Eulayia tossed her long, black curls over her shoulder and stared.

"Max? I thought your name was Ian."

Max thought of explaining but was too indifferent to bother.

Amalia smiled at the two couples, addressing them out of respect. "Buenas noches. Me llamo Amalia."

The couples offered smiles, but they were hardly genuine. In the end, Amalia had blocked them from their prey.

Amalia leaned in and whispered in Max's ear, pointing across the dance floor. "You see that guy? Paparazzi. And guess who he was photographing a second ago?"

Even through his intoxication, Max only needed a moment to comprehend. He was the son of an influential man. Through the haze he mustered a response, "Oh, shit." He took note that his belt and pants were undone and refastened them.

Amalia stared across the dance floor. "This isn't our nicest club, but it is trendy. Usually, there is a paparazzo or two hanging about."

Max sighed, trying to regroup in the center of the dance floor. As the DJ transitioned to a new song, the racy couples lost interest and departed. Max glanced their way as they faded into the crowd. He was sobering. He closed his eyes as mental acuity seeped back into the crevices of his mind.

Am I channeling still?

He looked at Amalia, wondering if the clarity he felt was hers or his own. Either way, he had enough wits to realize he had just been rescued from an extremely compromising situation.

Max held no delusions as to why he had ventured out on the very night of his initiation. Some vestige of him longed for a return to the easy life of a billionaire's son: the life he had prior to Indigo and the Antikythera Device, before the New Orleans attack, the latest Hades alert or his initiation. He yearned for the effortless simplicity he had enjoyed only days before. But Max knew perfectly well that things would never be the same.

CHAPTER 25

When Max returned to Chicago, he was in a complete daze and stinking of alcohol. The stench of tequila seeped from his pores like steam rising from the nooks of burning asphalt. The last thing he remembered was Amalia taking him aside on the dance floor. What remained of the previous night he could barely piece together, including his mode of return to the hotel. If Rudolfo, the cab driver, had driven him, Max couldn't recall. Rather conveniently, he had also forgotten the paparazzo incident on the dance floor, at least for now.

From the cozy comfort of his own bed, Max gazed upon the morning light in the Japanese garden of his atrium. For over an hour, he had been staring in a complete haze, playing and replaying in his head the same scenarios from his initiation. The more he sobered, he could hear the strange yet familiar language echoing in his brain. In his mind's eye, the imagery of Nibiru's pyramids and spacecraft remained incredibly vivid. The faces of Demetrius and Indigo appeared intermittently like ghosts, screaming that all would be revealed.

Max sorted through the memories, but he needed affirmation. He suddenly needed Demetrius to explain exactly what had happened, if indeed those things had occurred. He grabbed the phone and speed dialed the emergency number for Demetrius, only to have voice mail kick in as before. In exasperation, he ended the call and dialed a new number. A pleasant female voice picked up on the other end.

"Battenberg Industries."

"It's Max Battenberg. Is my father available?"

There was a brief pause before the female voice continued, "Hello, Mr. Battenberg. Let me see if I can get him."

Music immediately played into the phone. After several minutes, the receptionist came back on line.

"I'm sorry, Mr. Battenberg, your father is unavailable."

Max was losing patience. How could Demetrius still not make himself available? "Let him know I need to speak with him as soon as possible."

"Certainly, sir. Is there a particular number — oh, one moment,

Mr. Battenberg."

Hold music continued briefly. Max anticipated that Demetrius was about to pick up, but it was Otto who came on the line.

"Max! How the hell are you? I heard it was you on the wire."

"Hi, Otto." Max couldn't hide his disappointment that it was not his father.

"Great news, buddy. We got it. The golden dial has been authenticated. We have officially completed the Anti-k Device."

"You're kidding." Max was excited, but he felt unable to fully express it with so much else bouncing around in his brain. "Otto, that's amazing."

"It's big news, Max. But we have to sit on it a while."

"All right... When can I have it assembled?"

"The minute I get Miklos back here. We're in the process of importing him now."

"This is fantastic news, Otto, something I really needed." Max tried hard to archive this new information as he fingered the tiny pendant with the GPS microchip inside. Before leaving Mexico City, he had replaced the intricate technology around his neck. "Where's my dad, by the way? I need to speak with him."

"Get in line, pal. The old man's in meetings all day. Then he's off to Istanbul."

"Can you tell him it's urgent I speak with him? He knows what it's about. We were on Hades when I left. Now, I can't even get him on the phone."

Otto sighed. "Just follow protocol, Max. There's nothing to worry about."

"When can I get the dial? I'd like to have it back."

"You back in town?"

"Yeah. Got in this morning."

"Give me a day or two. We should have Miklos by then."

Max thanked Otto before hanging up. He welcomed news of the Anti-k Device, but his disappointment in Demetrius placed a damper on his enthusiasm. It wasn't just that Demetrius wasn't returning his calls; there were years of missed ballgames, recitals and other important occasions, and it had taken a toll.

Now, I can add my initiation to the list.

Each time Demetrius failed as a father, Max found himself long-ing for the love of his mother, Fiona. Sadly, there were occasions where he couldn't remember her face. But his memories were of a kind and gentle woman. Max felt soothed by these thoughts, but the ringing of his phone quickly jolted him back to reality. He grabbed the smart device, thinking it might be Demetrius, but the name Ted Sanderson was flashing across the screen. It had been more than a week since he'd last checked in with Ted, who was more or less recov-ered from the Mardi Gras attack. Max clicked on the talk button.

"Hey."

Ted seemed giddy as he began. "Dude, are you still in Mexico City?"

The question surprised Max since, in theory, no one knew where he'd been. "How'd you know where I was?"

"There're pictures of you all over the web, chief. News stations are running a story now."

Max faltered, but guessed the worst. The blood rushed to his cheeks. "Dude, what are you talking about?"

"Who's that chick? Brigitte's way hotter, dude."

Max's heart sank as the memories surfaced — Amalia's rescue from the two couples. "Fuck." A sigh of exasperation escaped his lips. "What're the photos?"

"Turn on channel four and see for yourself. You and that chick are gettin' kinda freaky in some club. Dude, is Brigitte with you?"

Max clicked on his television and surfed to the channel. "No. Actually, I'm back in town." Max caught a glimpse of himself with Eulayia and Gustavo. *Fuck. Fuck.* There was no denying it; his life had just grown infinitely more complicated. This type of breaking news would no doubt damage his relationship with Brigitte.

The TV announcer continued, "Last night, in one of Mexico City's popular night clubs, Maximilian Battenberg, son of billionaire Demetrius Battenberg, was spotted partying with Mexican fashion model Eulayia Sanchez."

"Fashion model!" Max threw his remote control to the ground, smashing it to pieces. "I'm guessing Brigitte's on the phone right now, having this exact conversation with someone."

"Dude, you better call Tiffany's. You're gonna need jewelry for this."

Max's phone beeped as another call came in. "Oh shit, that's probably her now." He glanced and saw the name Chandler flashing on the screen. "Ted, I have to take this. Are you okay, dude?"

"Yeah, I'm cool. Still getting used to these scars but then again, you know how that is."

"I have to get this call, but we'll talk later, okay?"

Max switched to the other line to hear much of the same report, only Chandler wasn't getting quite as much pleasure from it. To his dismay, Chandler informed him there were other stations covering the story.

"Fuck!" Max yelled out. "This is bullshit. People weren't even supposed to know I was down there."

"Don't worry about it," Chandler assured, "I've already put a call in to legal. We'll file an injunction and get the pics removed."

"No offense to our people, but Battenberg Industries will be quicker to get the stuff down. What I'd like you to do is run defense. Let's get something juicy up on the Badem websites — anything that'll draw attention away from this." The phone chirped and Max saw that it was Brigitte beeping in. "Chandler, Bridge is on the other line. I need to talk to her, but I'll call you later. Are we good?"

"Yeah, we'll run interference. It's no problem."

"Okay, thanks." Chandler's call dropped and Max stared at Brigitte's name and picture flashing across the screen. Without a plan to explain the discotheque photos, he pressed ignore and sent the call to voice mail. Seconds later, a text message appeared on his screen. 'CALL ME WE NEED TO TALK!'

Max read the message repeatedly, but he wasn't ready to speak with Brigitte. Not yet. He tried the number for Demetrius once more, but the assistant was still unable to get him on the line. Max couldn't be more irritated. The truth was, he didn't have the energy for any of this. With his father's assistant still on the line, he made a simple request. "Could you please have the Mexico City photos removed?"

Even without an injunction, Battenberg Industries absolutely had the power to make such things disappear. Website photos would be no problem to eradicate, but the damage had already been done.

Demetrius' assistant replied, "It's already being handled, Mr. Battenberg. The photos should be down within the hour."

"Thank you."

Max hung up, satisfied that the debacle would be resolved by day's end. But there was still the business of dealing with Brigitte and an urgent need to contact his father. Max paused with an idea. He reached across to his nightstand and rummaged through the top drawer. Unable to locate what he desired, he retrieved his phone to call LC. After a few rings, Cora answered.

"Good morning, sir, how are you?"

"Sorry to bother you, LC, but things aren't going so well today."

"I'm sorry to hear that, sir. Is there anything I can do to help?"

"Actually, yes. I was wondering if you could help me find something."

"Of course, sir. What is it?"

"There are a couple of business cards I got a few weeks back— "

"It's so uncanny how much you and your mom are alike when it comes to filing things away."

"Oh, really."

"She was notorious about misplacing things, especially her journal. Half the time she couldn't even remember what house she left things in. Matter of fact, I don't think she ever found that thing."

"My mom kept journals?"

"She had a few she filled up. I remember her looking for one the summer before the accident. We spent weeks trying to locate it." Cora chuckled. "One of us even had to trot around the globe looking in all the residences."

Without any serious lasting memories of his mother, Max felt his curiosity piqued. But there wasn't time. Not now. "One of these days, you'll have to tell me about it, LC. But right now I need that card."

"Of course, sir. Under the latest system, any cards you leave around have been scanned and can be accessed from your desktop or your phone."

"Oh, great. I forgot about that. Thanks, LC. I'll talk to you later."

"You take care, sir."

After hanging up, Max scrolled through his phone until he found Indigo's card. He felt conflicted about calling her, but he hoped Indigo might have answers, even if they were just to questions she herself had posed. The bizarre psychic had predicted many things, some of which seemed to be occurring. Since Demetrius wasn't talking, maybe she could help to resolve some of his confusion.

Max dialed the number. After several rings, Indigo answered.

"Hello." Her voice was raspy, yet relaxed.

Unsure of what to say, Max faltered. He could hear her breathing lightly on the other end. She seemed patient, in no hurry to hang up, although he said nothing at all. When the psychic finally spoke, her voice was smug and resolute.

"Do you believe me now?"

Max stared at the phone, incredulous. Her question insinuated that she knew exactly who was on the line. In shock, he ended the call. He had never before believed in psychics, but so far, Indigo's predictions had been spot on. Beyond a doubt now, the initiation at Teotihuacán had proven he did belong to something larger, something he hardly understood and didn't want to believe. Indigo was just one item on a long and growing list of inexplicables.

One by one, puzzle pieces were coming together, but they made Max's head throb when he tried arranging them in a coherent picture. Without his father's input, he didn't believe he could even trust his own memories.

So, resolved instead to deal with issues he could handle, Max jumped in his car and headed toward Brigitte's. *I'll speak with her in person*, he thought. Given the circumstances, this seemed the best solution.

Brigitte answered her door, but didn't step aside for Max to enter. She offered no hellos, no how-are-yous, she simply stared at Max.

"Bridge, I am so sorry. But before you get all bent out of shape, I want you to know nothing happened."

Brigitte stood firm and unbudging, barring entrance to her home. "There are photos of you all over the net and I didn't even know you were back."

Max paused before answering, "I got back this morning."

"Great. Photos of you with that woman—and some man. But you couldn't even call to say you were back in town. How's any of that supposed to make me feel?"

"Bridge, a lot of shit went down in Mexico. Was me cheating one of them? No. I got drunk and that couple took an interest on the dance floor. That photo, all it shows is them trying to take advantage, which people often do. Even in New Orleans they did, and sometimes it was with you. The only difference is, we were together."

Finally relenting, Brigitte stepped aside, allowing Max to enter. "For all I know, they could've been working with that photographer. You know how paparazzi are."

Max could sense Brigitte's outrage deflating. There were more than a few false stories planted about them when they first began dating. Hearing his explanation at least made her wonder.

"It's all shit, Max. It's fucking embarrassing. People I don't even like are calling to ask what's going on."

"Because they're miserable, Brigitte. I fucked up, I admit that. I got drunk, I wasn't in control, I was alone."

Brigitte's voice was calm when she spoke. "You know what I couldn't help thinking when I heard this? About all that stuff that woman said at Mardi Gras."

Max thought he had begun to diffuse the situation. Instead there was tension creeping back into the conversation. "That's not fair, Brigitte."

Brigitte was glib. "She said you'd hurt people, Max, including Ted and me."

The words struck at Max.

"You could say that about anyone. At some point it'll be true. And no one feels worse about what happened to Ted than I do." Max knew his argument was weak. To make things worse, he knew Indigo had been right on almost all accounts. More than likely, he would hurt Brigitte. He had just hoped the time wouldn't come so soon. He approached and wrapped his arms around her. "Please don't be mad. Nothing happened with those people. Do you really think I'd jeopardize what we have for them? Did you see them?"

Although rigid at first, Brigitte's posture softened. "I saw them all right. I thought, what the fuck is he doing?"

Bingo, Max thought. He had opened the door, maneuvering the situation with smiles, kisses and cuddles. "I'm really sorry, okay? What we have is too important to me. Do you believe that?"

Not completely freed of her anger, Brigitte punched Max in the arm. "I don't know."

"Well, I am. I'm sorry." Max delivered the words with sincerity.

"Okay." Brigitte looked down, blushing ever so slightly. Somehow, she was still embarrassed by the situation. "I suppose I forgive you."

Max gazed at Brigitte with a half smile and puppy dog eyes. The technique was foolproof and always made her melt. "You want to go for a ride? We can get takeout from that deli you like and bring it back here."

"Yeah, I guess. Let me just get my stuff."

In a quick sprint, Brigitte ran to grab her shoes and purse. Minutes later, they were zipping across town to one of Chicago's upscale delicatessens.

CHAPTER 26

*D*uring the drive across town in his Range Rover, Max's phone rang continually. Each time he retrieved it, hopeful that it was his father, but it never was. With growing stubbornness, he resolved not to think any further about Demetrius or his poor paternal instincts. But his anxiety remained. As he drove, Max was unaware that his hands were tightly clenching the steering wheel and that his foot was pressing more heavily than usual upon the accelerator.

Minutes later, he and Brigitte strolled into Les Delices. Upon entering, it was easy to discern that quite a bit of money had been spent designing the establishment. Small black and white checkered tiles created a path to the host's station. Inside, high quality cherry wood had been used throughout in all the furniture and paneling. The restaurant with its open floor plan sprawled for nearly a quarter of the block. Huge windows wrapped around the dining area, providing a view of Chicago's busy streets.

Directly to the right of the host's station, a much smaller area served as a to-go deli. A sizeable, L-shaped display case contained dozens of savory dishes and desserts. The cases were always immaculate, their glass barriers appearing virtually invisible.

Les Delices' best marketing feature stemmed from on-site preparation of everything on their menu. Aromas of various dishes teased anyone passing outside on the sidewalk and enveloped anyone who entered their doors.

As they stepped inside, Max was pleased that the mood between him and Brigitte had shifted back to normal. He took her by the hand and breathed in the wonderful scent of Les Delices' selection. Already, his mouth was watering in anticipation of their meal.

Max didn't see the man at first, since a congregation of taller people was surrounding him. The little person, barely four feet tall, stood directly before the display case. Then he caught Max's eye. Although Max was unaware of it, he was staring at the midget, his mouth agape. *You've gotta fucking be kidding me.*

"Max," Brigitte questioned, "what's wrong?"

Ever since the Money Pit, the little man and the blonde woman had haunted his dreams. Now, it appeared they were visiting his real life. Max scanned the deli for the woman, but he didn't see her anywhere.

The tiny patron had brown hair and large blue eyes. This time, he wasn't in the suit or in white face. Instead he was dressed in jeans and a T-shirt and he appeared to be minding his own business.

Max watched as he chatted and laughed with two taller friends. As hard as he tried, Max couldn't shake the feeling that he was being watched. Certainly, news of the family's Hades alert did little to alleviate a growing paranoia.

Brigitte, noting Max's astonished expression, followed his line of sight. From her point of view, there was nothing out of the ordinary aside from a stocky, compact man. At least a half dozen other patrons were standing along the counter, laboring to make their selection. She had only known Max to raise his voice once before, when he hollered at Indigo in New Orleans. She was astounded when he did it again.

"What the hell are you looking at?"

Brigitte stared wide-eyed, watching Max in an aggressive posture she had never seen before. While she couldn't be sure whom he was addressing, it seemed he was screaming at the very short man standing before the counter.

The little person looked from Max to his two friends, both athletic men maybe in their thirties.

"Yeah, I'm talking to you." Max stepped closer and raised his voice even louder. "How much of this do you fucking think I'm going to take?"

"Max?" Brigitte protested meagerly. There was no one more alarmed by his outburst than she.

"He knows what I'm talking about." Max took another step forward, intimidating the small man. "Keep hanging around and see what happens."

For a moment, there was complete quiet in the deli. But the silence was soon replaced by chattering whispers from the crowd.

Both of the small man's friends turned to him, questioning, "Do you know this guy?"

The small man shook his head. "No."

With that, one of his taller friends raised a hand to prevent Max from advancing any further. "Take it easy, pal."

But Max refused to back down. "You a part of this too? Where's the woman? The blonde."

Worried that things might escalate, Brigitte gently took Max by the arm. "Babe, calm down. Who is that?"

"He was in New Orleans when Ted got attacked. And now he's following me. I'm not going to be bullied."

The little man turned to his companions and shrugged. "He's insane. I've never seen him in my life." Feeling empowered by the presence of his friends, he took a step toward Max. "Get lost, pal."

Max broke from Brigitte and lunged for the man. But his two companions grabbed Max and slammed him against the wall.

"Calm down, dude. What the fuck are you doing?"

The taller of the friends grabbed Max's arm and twisted it behind his back. He felt a sharp pain in his shoulder. When he struggled, the other friend used an elbow to clamp down on Max's neck.

"Let go of him!" Brigitte screamed.

In that instant, the entire scene blurred for Max. He could hear the men and Brigitte screaming, but their voices melted into an indistinguishable mish-mash of sound. Other patrons were reacting as well, but Max was completely unaware.

Almost as if it were happening in real time, Max felt transported to ten years earlier. When he was fourteen, Demetrius had encouraged him to pursue martial arts. Instead of taking instruction in a group, a series of masters had visited at their home. For months, a young Max had studied various techniques, including Jujitsu, ancient Shao Lin Kung Fu and Filipino knife fighting.

In a short period of time, he had grown quite proficient even though the extent of his sparring had been with instructors. Of course, none of them had truly challenged Max in combat for fear of injuring Demetrius Battenberg's only son.

Only days before, Max had suffered a terrible embarrassment. Despite the years of self-defense training, he hadn't been able to avoid being abducted from the men's club. Even worse, he hadn't defended very well against the New Orleans attacker in the spider costume. Yes, his would-be abductors had turned out to be Demetrius' men, but Max lamented how inadequate he had been. He was sure Demetrius felt the same. Now, as he was being restrained once again, vivid memories of more than a year of lessons were resurfacing.

Until now, Brigitte had been certain that she knew Max better than anyone. Never in her wildest dreams did she think him capable of the aggression he was showing. And to her chagrin, he was being strong-armed in a horrible scene of his own creation. She was too frightened to physically intervene. Thinking fast on her feet, she removed her phone to call the police.

"Let go of me." Max demanded, continuing to fight his captors. Ignoring the pain in his arm, he twisted in a release move. He had never officially tried it outside of practice all those years before. But today, Max refused to be overpowered.

To Brigitte's amazement and horror, Max broke away from one of the men. He immediately kicked out, knocking the man to the ground. Using his free arm, he whacked the second man in the temple, then executed an attack move to his gut. The second man promptly crumpled to the floor.

Max glared at the men he had felled like saplings, then he turned to the small man. "You stay away from me. I won't tell you again."

The man had his phone in hand but was trembling too hysterically to use it. He looked around, wondering if anyone else might come to his aid.

Brigitte took a breath, both exhilarated and mortified at the same time. In the lowest voice she could muster, she whispered, "Max, I think we should go."

Max turned to see everyone staring at him as if he were a complete lunatic, which he supposed he was. He grabbed Brigitte by the hand and hurried back to his Range Rover. They hopped inside and quickly slammed their doors. Max started the car and peeled out, his tires screeching as they skirted into the street.

Brigitte hadn't realized it till now, but she was almost hyperventilating. "What the hell was that back there?"

"I never said anything to you because I thought I was imagining it. But that guy's been following me, I'm sure of it."

Brigitte looked at Max, her face full of worry. "Max... are you sure?"

The more distance he placed between himself and the scene at Les Delices, the more Max wondered whether or not he was losing his mind. Perhaps it was a mistake. "Like I said, I saw him several times in New Orleans. He was in Mexico City. Hell, I think he's even been in my house. He's always with this woman." Hearing the words spoken aloud, Max realized how he sounded. "I'm not insane. With everything that happened in New Orleans, I don't know, I have to play a little defense here." Max reached across the center console and took Brigitte's hand. "Why don't we just go back to your place and order takeout?"

Full of trepidation, Brigitte smiled and squeezed Max's hand. "Okay."

Twenty minutes later, she was doing her best to pretend everything was cool, but a zillion questions were running through her mind. *What happened back there?* Deep down, she was completely off kilter. *Is he losing it?* Max's list of inexplicable behaviors seemed to be growing exponentially. There were so many questions, and for the first time in their relationship, Brigitte was afraid to ask them out loud.

Minutes after their return, takeout was delivered from a Thai restaurant around the corner. Brigitte tossed a tablecloth over her living room coffee table and then spread out the numerous Styrofoam containers for them to dine. Resigned to pleasantries, she chimed in.

"When you said you were leaving the other day, I was sure you'd be gone at least a week."

"Yeah, I was too."

"Now that you're back, I guess we can go to Marilyn's party."

"Yay," Max exclaimed with feigned enthusiasm.

Brigitte hesitated. While she may have decided not to inquire any further about his aggressive behavior at the deli, all other questions were free game. "So, can you talk about what happened in Mexico? Aside from that floozy, I mean. What're the famous Battenberg initiations all about?"

Even if Max were allowed, this wasn't a question he could easily answer. "Trust me, you wouldn't believe me if I told you."

Brigitte's eyes grew wide. "Was it like some fraternity hazing thing? Skull and Bones."

Max reached once again for the microchip around his neck and fingered it, paranoid that anything he might say would be heard. "It wasn't even close to anything I imagined. All I could do afterward was get drunk. That's how I ended up at that club."

Brigitte smiled but there was no true levity in her eyes. "Honestly, Max, I thought you had better taste. That woman was a total tramp."

Max laughed. "On the TV, they said she was a model." He pulled her close. "Come here," he said, and kissed her. It was easy to discern Brigitte was still tense from the day's drama. "I wish I could tell you what happened." Deep down Max wanted to share his Mexico experience, but he didn't dare.

Before he could utter another word, his cell phone came to life again, vibrating in his pocket. "I hope that's my dad." He removed the smartphone and the name "Battenberg Industries" was indeed flashing across the screen. Max clicked into the call. "This is Max."

"Mr. Battenberg, it's Rosalee from your father's office."

Max deflated. While it wasn't his father, he had at least gotten someone on the line. As his father's number one assistant, Rosalee was the final gatekeeper to Demetrius.

"Hi, Rosalee, I've been waiting on his call."

"I'm afraid he isn't available just yet. But he's asked me to find out if you're free to meet this Saturday at the penthouse at 3 p.m. That would be three days from now. Is this a possibility?"

"Three days?" Max was stunned at how Demetrius was dragging things out. "Is that the earliest he can meet?"

"That's his earliest opening, I'm afraid."

Dammit. Even over the phone, Max could feel Rosalee's cold and steely demeanor. "Yeah. Okay. Three days from now then."

Rosalee remained steadfast. "Very good, Mr. Battenberg. I will let your father know. Of course, if there are any changes to your schedule, please let us know."

"I'll be sure to do that." The word *bitch* crossed Max's mind, but he held his tongue. "Thank you, Rosalee."

"You're welcome, Mr. Battenberg."

Max was incredulous as he hung up and turned to Brigitte. "My dad is something else. Here's this unique family tradition and he's the only one I can talk to about it, but, as usual, I can't even get him on the phone." Max perceived the slow build of his fury and resentment with the gravity of what he had gone through in Mexico. He felt an urgency to speak with Demetrius, but it appeared there would be no cooperation on his father's end. "He wants to meet in three days."

"Most people wait months to get on your father's calendar. I'm guessing three days is pretty damn good."

"Yeah, whatever." Max was hardly comforted by Brigitte's effort to lighten the mood. Instead he proceeded to do something he had learned at a very young age. He squashed down his anger, tucking it away in some barely accessible place. He had already waited twenty-four years. If he had to, he could survive another three days. "Let's just finish eating."

He stared down at a half dozen open containers still steaming on the coffee table. Sadly, Max had already lost his appetite.

Tomorrow will be better, he thought. *Tomorrow will be better.*

CHAPTER 27

*I*t wasn't that Max had forgotten the Hades alert. A mere fourteen hours earlier, Otto had reminded him to follow proper protocol: he and his relations were to remain at all times in approved "safe" locations. Instead, in an act of defiance, he had agreed to stay the night at Brigitte's. During Hades, her house was considered off the map and completely unsecured.

His decision to stay wasn't made lightly. One night in Mexico City and a fight at Les Delices had damaged their relationship. If he left to abide by procedure, Brigitte was certain to find fault regardless of the circumstances.

All of his mysterious experiences had left him struggling with an unwanted sense of insecurity, and Max felt weak when he was scared. He often rebelled against his fears, refusing to let even the slightest phobia paralyze him. Even if he wanted to leave he couldn't do so now out of pride.

The glue, he thought, *of any strong relationship is lovemaking.* The moment their food settled, Max worked on his seduction. To begin, he took Brigitte's feet and shifted them to his lap so he could gently massage them. He watched as she closed her eyes and exhaled with relief. Slowly, she sank deeper into the couch.

After several minutes, Max switched his position and moved to the floor. On his knees, he massaged the toes of her right foot.

"This toe here, tastier than the best egg roll," he grinned.

Brigitte watched Max maneuver her foot toward his face. He placed the toe in his mouth and sucked it gently. A shiver ran up her spine as he licked his tongue along the top of her foot. He kissed the full length of her lower leg. Brigitte's chest rose and fell as she anticipated his next move.

Max lifted her blouse and pulled it over her head, exposing her bare midriff and bra. He kissed her cleavage and neck, then he kissed her mouth. The night of impassioned lovemaking on Brigitte's couch allowed them both to release more tension than they knew they had. Later, they crossed into her big bedroom where they collapsed, exhausted. In no time they were asleep.

In the middle of the night, Max awoke to an ethereal scene. Brigitte's bedroom, although dark, appeared to glow, everything perfectly illuminated as if through a filter of night vision. He felt alert, but swiftly realized his perceptions were through the cloud of a dream—his recurring dream.

The woman and midget were in the bedroom. Max didn't see them at first, but he knew they were there. From his position in bed, on his right side, he could see Brigitte sleeping quietly. He wanted to rouse her but was paralyzed as before, his body refusing to obey. To his horror, the midget appeared at Brigitte's end of the bed. *No! I warned you.* Max ordered his body to move so he could strike the intruder, but his efforts were fruitless.

The midget reached for Brigitte, but was too small to gain needed leverage. Sensing movement, she bolted up in bed. Upon spotting him, she screamed in horror. The miniature assailant grabbed her in an attempt to subdue.

Struggling, Brigitte leapt to her feet, screaming and fighting, punching and clawing. Max willed himself to wake from the nightmare, but it continued. The midget, while small, was built of thick, sinewy muscle. He wrestled Brigitte back to her spot on the bed as she scratched and hollered, her legs kicking and flailing.

Unable to do more than watch, Max sat completely immobilized, stewing in his own terror. The blonde was instantly at her partner's side, rushing to his aid. The man struggled with Brigitte while the woman removed a tiny, red dot and pressed it against Brigitte's forehead. The reaction was instantaneous: Brigitte relaxed, melting down into the blankets of her bed.

For a moment, the woman and midget paused to share a glance. They carefully repositioned Brigitte in bed. The small man adjusted his clothing, then turned his gaze on Max. He crossed out of Max's view, heading around to the other side of the bed. Max couldn't move but he could feel his body's reaction as the fight-or-flight mechanism kicked in. One last time, he tried to scream but couldn't...

Suddenly, Brigitte was shaking him. "Wake up, babe."

He bolted up, disoriented. Max looked about the room. It was just after dawn and the first rays of sun were creeping above the horizon. He frantically scanned the space that was Brigitte's bedroom.

"You were having a bad dream." Still groggy herself, Brigitte took note of the sweat on Max's brow. "You okay, hon?"

"Yeah. I guess." Max sighed as he settled back down on the pillow. "It was just a dream."

Brigitte reached across to stroke his hair. "A bad one."

He closed his eyes, wondering if anxiety was getting the better of him. "I don't know. It was weird, I was fighting..." Just like Brigitte, he didn't wish to bring up the altercation at Les Delices.

Brigitte frowned at his recount. "Maybe if you stayed over more you wouldn't have nightmares while you're here."

Max wanted to shake the nagging feeling that his dreams were real, but seeing little people everywhere was making this harder to accomplish. To make things worse, the nightmare was becoming more chaotic and violent. Even though he had awakened, Max couldn't quite shake off his body's fight-or-flight mechanism. And more disturbing, it seemed his warnings to the man at Les Delices had been in vain.

Brigitte rolled over, covering her head with a pillow. "We're not falling back to sleep, are we?" Once again, she was trying to make light of circumstances she truly found troubling. While she hoped it may have been silly, Indigo had planted a seed in her brain that Max would hurt her somehow. *Yes, it was a bad dream, but he's hiding something*, she thought.

Max felt unable to give voice to the recurring nightmare that was unsettling him more and more. The first one had occurred the very night of his return from the Money Pit. The second occurrence took place days later at the hotel in Mexico City. Now that he was at Brigitte's, the unusual couple had appeared again. But somehow, he kept awakening as if they were just figments of his imagination.

Brigitte emerged from beneath her pillow and watched Max rubbing the furrowed space between his eyebrows. "That must've been some dream."

"No, not really." Max lied again. But something drew him on. "In it, we were sleeping here," Max hesitated before continuing, "and someone broke in."

"I was in it?"

"Yeah," Max paused, somewhat confounded. "It was the midget again. He attacked you and you were fighting." While he didn't intend to show it, Max's words were tinged with desperation. "But I couldn't move, I couldn't help you."

Brigitte listened, trying to make sense of the dream. "So, that little guy from Les Delices broke in here?"

"I know it sounds crazy, but his face is always covered in white makeup."

"Max, maybe you should see someone. If you keep having the same bad dream it has to mean something, right?"

"I don't know." After a moment's contemplation, Max continued, his tone tinged now with sarcasm: "Maybe I should see a psychic."

Brigitte broke into laughter while playfully punching at his arm. "Okay, wise guy, I get it."

Max hollered playfully from the sting of Brigitte's blows. He was thrilled that his body was once again responding to sensations and commands. But after the horseplay, he froze, unable to contain his shock.

"What's wrong?" Brigitte questioned.

He pointed to her arms, his brow deeply furrowed with concern. "What happened there?"

Brigitte followed his gaze until she caught sight of the bruises on her skin—handprints.

"He was holding you down, I saw him." Max couldn't help but recoil.

Brigitte stared, appraising the state of her arms. "Was last night that unmemorable?"

Max remained dumbfounded. "Are you saying I did that?"

"Yes, Max, that's what I'm saying. You don't remember sucking my toes and holding me down? It's not like last night was the first time."

Max remained pensive, trying to sort through the details. "They've been at my house, and I'm sure they were here last night. And now they've hurt you!"

"It was a dream, Max. You said it yourself. But we're awake now." Brigitte frowned, evaluating Max as he smiled in the most unconvincing manner.

He carried on stroking the marks on her arms. "Yeah, I guess you're right..." Then his cell phone vibrated, alerting the arrival of a text message from Otto. Max quickly read its content and his face brightened.

"What is it?" Brigitte questioned.

"I need to get going. I have to meet Otto." Max hopped from the bed to gather his clothes from the other room. "Turns out that dial from the Money Pit is exactly what I was looking for."

"You're kidding. That's great news. How come you didn't say anything?"

Max shrugged, pulling on his pants. "I meant to. Just got caught up, I guess. With all the other stuff going on, it just didn't seem like the right time." Within seconds, Max was dressed and ready to go. He offered Brigitte a goodbye kiss. "I'll see you tonight."

"Yeah, sure." Brigitte was unconsciously rubbing the bruise on her left arm. "Call me later."

"I will." Grabbing his keys from the nightstand, Max disappeared through the door into the pale light of dawn. At long last, he was about to discover exactly what the Antikythera Mechanism had to offer.

CHAPTER 28

*I*n a pit stop, Max swung by his house to shower and change clothes. Excitement over the Antikythera artifact had switched his spirits into much higher gear. For the first time in days, he didn't have Demetrius in the forefront of his mind.

He arrived at Battenberg Industries in the early morning and was directed to a private observation deck near the roof of the Spire. Max boarded the private elevator that shot him like a bullet toward the hundred and fortieth floor. The moment he stepped onto the observation deck, a powerful wind, the kind that jostles airliners, whipped through his hair and clothes.

"Max! Over here!" Otto screamed from the six-foot glass barrier at the edge of the deck.

Oskar Miklos, the Greek doctor whom Max had met at the Children's Museum, was at Otto's side. The Plexiglas box that contained the mechanism sat beside them on the concrete.

Max, smiling ear-to-ear, crossed the deck and was surprised to find a cessation to the wind. He quickly realized it was the clear barrier wall blocking the gusts. The day was gorgeous and clear, and the early sun warmed his skin.

"Otto, Doctor Miklos, how are you?" Max shook their hands.

Doctor Miklos was nothing like he had been at their first meeting. Today, he was smiling and jovial. "Monsieur Battenberg, I had no idea the last time we spoke that you would be the one to complete the mechanism."

Max bristled with pride at the compliment. "It's a good thing you directed us to the Money Pit. That was a crazy day, is all I can tell you."

"Certainly, Mr. Khrzinsky filled me in on the lengths you went to in recovering the final element."

The thought of almost drowning in the Money Pit sent a shiver up Max's spine. He shook off the feeling and continued, "The bigger question is, can you make it operational? We'd all like to know what this thing can do."

Doctor Miklos spit out a laugh. "This I cannot promise, Monsieur

Battenberg, but I shall do my best."

Otto was smiling at Max. "You ready, kiddo?"

Max, nearly shaking with anticipation, couldn't recall the last time he had been so giddy. "Yeah, let's do it."

Otto reached into a large canvas saddlebag and produced the ornate leather box from the Money Pit. "Here it is." He handed it to Miklos.

The Greek doctor took the box, his hands trembling ever so slightly. "I never thought I'd live to see this." Miklos flipped open the lid and gazed at the dial. It was sparkling in the sunlight. "The missing component." Without removing the dial, Miklos handed the case to Max, then fumbled to open the Plexiglas box that housed the larger mechanism.

"Careful, doctor," Max warned, nervous that the good doctor might damage the device in his excitement.

After removing the device, Miklos closed the Plexiglas box and placed the ancient artifact on top. "Keep in mind, my thoughts on Antikythera are purely theoretical." Miklos reached for the dial and gingerly removed it from its case. For a long moment, he was silent, reveling in admiration of the artistic archeological find. "It must be calibrated, much as the astrolabe is configured." Miklos lifted the dial up to the sky, paying close attention to several tiny, nearly imperceptible holes. Pin-sized beams of light shone through the dial, casting a magical pattern across Miklos' face.

Max and Otto shared a glance while watching the doctor work. Miklos pivoted his body to reposition himself, trying to catch a specific direction in the sky.

The dial, constructed of several thin gold plates, had movable parts. Miklos began shifting them, causing the pinpoints of light to dance across his face.

"The trick is to find our current astronomical as well as astrological position." Miklos turned to Max and Otto. "Once this information is fed to the device, I believe it can be activated."

For another twenty minutes, Miklos faced the sun, repeatedly fidgeting with the dial and affixing it to the larger assembly. At no point did the device ever create any visible effect outside of its clock-like moving parts when Miklos attempted to wind its gears.

Max turned to Miklos, losing patience. "Do you have any idea what it's supposed to do?"

"Monsieur, as I mentioned in New York, it is presumed capable of unlocking cosmic knowing."

It was clear Otto was also losing patience. "But what does that mean? For all we know it could be working, we just don't know what we're looking for."

"Messieurs, as I've already stated, this is all theoretical. I must study the device further. I will need more time. Perhaps another week..."

Max immediately interrupted. "All due respect, doctor, but I'm not prepared to part company with the device just yet. If you need time, arrangements can be made, but it'll have to be here on the premises or in some other Battenberg facility."

Miklos tried but couldn't hide his disappointment. "Of course, Monsieur Battenberg. I have flown such a long distance for this reason."

Max turned to his father's friend and right-hand man. "Otto, you can arrange that, right?"

"Of course."

"Great. By the way, do you have any idea if my dad's available later today?"

It didn't take an expert to sense Otto's irritation at Max's question. After all, he was hardly one of Demetrius' assistants. "I'm fairly certain he's on a plane. But Rosalee would know a bit better the specifics of his schedule."

"So," Doctor Miklos questioned, "when will I be able to study the device?"

Under normal circumstances, Max would have invited the doctor back the following day, especially since they had just summoned him all the way from Greece. But he knew he couldn't sit by idly while Miklos figured things out. Already he was being asked to wait for Demetrius to answer questions about his initiation and the ramifications of what it meant to be a Battenberg.

He turned to Miklos. "We appreciate you flying all this way on such short notice. If you could just sit tight a few days, we'll arrange it." Again, Max caught a glimpse of the Miklos he had met in New York.

"Very well, Monsieur." A fire — an anger — burned behind the

Greek doctor's eyes. "I will wait most patiently for your call."

Otto, who was impressed to see Max handling the doctor in such a firm manner, extended his hand. "Thank you, Doctor. We'll be in touch."

Drawing in a deep breath, Miklos stared at the device sitting on top of the Plexiglas box.

Max smiled. "Don't worry, we'll take good care of it."

Otto placed a hand on the doctor's shoulder. "I'll see you out."

"Very well," Miklos responded as he and Otto headed toward the building.

Max watched them re-enter the Spire, then gingerly returned the device to its Plexiglas housing. Turning back to the glass barrier wall, he looked out across Lake Michigan and its still waters. The Anti-k Mechanism was officially in his possession. For the first time in a long while, Max knew perfectly well what he needed to do.

CHAPTER 29

Getting a plane wasn't easy. His father's alert system, also called the Hades protocol, had strict guidelines that were to be followed to the tee. Max knew very well adherence to its rules banned travel of any kind. In addition, there was the problem of the Anti-k Mechanism, which was considered too valuable for casual transport.

At the same time, Max was aware of the simple fact that while the Battenbergs often made the rules, they were rarely faithful to them. *Rules,* Demetrius had once said, *are for the masses.*

In the end, Max had needed to pull more than a few strings to secure a private Battenberg jet. The feat had required a few hours in Otto's office, but it had been done.

Only moments after the itinerary had been set, a black Dodge Durango with midnight-tinted windows arrived to shuttle him and the Greek artifact to Chicago's O'Hare Airport. There, he boarded the private Learjet for the two-hour-and-fifteen-minute flight to New Orleans.

As soon as he stepped from the plane, Max immediately noticed Louisiana's warmer climate. He descended the steps to the tarmac and watched as the Plexiglas box, now encased in a black leather carrier, was loaded into another large, jet-black SUV. Within minutes they were on the move, heading across town toward a storefront with a neon sign above it that read, "Indigo Blue, Psychic, Reader Of Tarot."

Even though he had gone to great lengths to organize the trip, Max remained in quiet disbelief of his decision to return to New Orleans. In an odd way, he was on both sides of his own fence. It had been seven weeks since his last visit. He stared through the window as they traversed a series of run-down districts. With the festivities of Mardi Gras over and done with, the streets were considerably calmer and less crowded.

Twenty minutes later, they entered Indigo's neighborhood. The once incredibly vivacious block now seemed run-of-the-mill. Heaps of parade garbage had been removed, but Max could see that the area was economically depressed. So much of New Orleans had never recovered from the havoc and devastation of Hurricane Katrina.

As the driver brought the car to a halt, Max felt his nerves on edge. Suddenly, he was unsure if he could actually enter Indigo's abode. It all seemed so ridiculous, but he had come too far to back out now. Max stepped from the car and removed the Plexiglas case. Looking around, he took a deep breath, then crossed and entered the building.

The moment Indigo's front door swung shut behind him, he noticed the same effect that had occurred on his first visit. It felt as if he had entered another dimension where both time and velocity had slowed. There was calm within the walls of her sanctuary. Max looked around nervously. He was skeptical, but deep down, he wanted answers.

I can't believe I'm doing this. As he pondered whether to stay or leave, Indigo strode into the room, laughing and chatting with a pretty African American girl.

The psychic froze upon spotting Max with the large leather box. The action didn't go unnoticed by Indigo's client, who immediately looked on alert. To cover, the psychic gently grabbed the girl's hand.

"You have any other problems, you call me."

The girl smiled. It was clear she could feel the tension in the room. "Thanks, Indigo." She gathered her things, glancing curiously at Max. Turning to Indigo, she continued, "As usual, you've been a great help." Indigo's client hurried out into the street.

The front door swung shut and Indigo turned calmly to Max. "I figured you'd return."

He smiled, offering a meager attempt at levity. "I guess that's the hazard of being a psychic."

Indigo didn't laugh. Just as before, she was wearing heavy makeup. Clothed in a tight, red and black paisley pantsuit, she sported black leather boots that rose to her knees. A red, jeweled veil was flipped to the back of her head. She lifted it and brought it forward to cover her face.

Max watched her quizzically, imagining her as the star in some music video. He still couldn't figure out her gender, but in her own way, she was quite beautiful.

She turned and headed toward the back room, pausing in the doorway. "You coming, darling, or what?"

Max lifted the black leather case by the handle and crossed to the door.

Indigo stopped him, holding out her hand. "I need your phone."

He recognized how extremely smart this was of her, and handed it over. Indigo crossed to a metal cabinet with a boom box on top of it. She removed a brown sack from the top drawer. She wrapped the phone in a wrinkled piece of tinfoil, slipped it in the sack, then returned it to the top drawer and closed it. Finally, she turned on the boom box. Blues music bounced into the room. The clairvoyant cranked up the volume.

"Come. Follow me." She turned and led Max to the consultation room.

Indigo plopped down at the table, gesturing for Max to sit across from her. He took a seat uneasily.

"So, cheri," Indigo began, "what brings you here today?" There was a smug look on her face. Max could tell it was her way of saying I told you so. "Have you learned a bit of what I spoke?"

Although it was difficult, Max had to admit, "Yes. Quite a bit in fact. More than I bargained for." Max motioned toward the Plexiglas box at his side. "I have the device you spoke of."

Somewhat incredulous, Indigo gazed at Max through her veil. "I see."

"That's what you asked me to get, isn't it?"

Squinting her eyes at Max, she continued, "Completion of the device was considered unachievable. But I see this is no longer true. What is it you wish to know, Monsieur Battenberg?"

Before he could answer, Indigo reached across the table and clasped his hands in her own. Max's palms were sweaty, but she didn't seem deterred. For a brief moment, he locked eyes with the seer.

"There's so much I need to know, including how to activate the device."

Still clasping his hands, Indigo pressed her eyes shut. After what seemed an eternity, she spoke. "I see nature's beasts... the bison and the deer... the elk... all in a cave."

Max watched Indigo closely, but she held her eyes shut as she continued.

"Predators and prey. The jaguar and the bear... the eagle's eye... but wait..." Indigo opened her eyes. "They are not animals at all.

There is fire glowing brightly."

Max watched as beads of sweat formed on Indigo's brow. Then he mumbled, "My initiation."

Indigo didn't seem to hear as perspiration ran down the sides of her face. "It's some type of chamber. Not animals but masks." She released Max and drew back her hands. Removing a handkerchief she reached beneath the veil and dabbed delicately at the sweat on her face. "Quite a strange ritual this is."

Something in Max questioned whether Demetrius had hired Indigo as a test, and he felt a fear start up. If she had heard him acknowledge his initiation, a crew might jump out with cameras and microphones and tell him he had just been duped into revealing the family's most prized secret.

Max stammered, unsure exactly where to start. "A few weeks ago, you said it didn't matter who my father was, it was more what he was. What did you mean by that?"

"But, Monsieur, you know the answer to this question. You have seen it."

Max shook his head, unable to grasp the things he'd seen in the pyramid. "I need you to say it. What I saw — I don't know anymore what I saw."

Indigo smiled, removing a cigarette from a pack inside her jumpsuit. "Your mind won't let you believe. This, I understand." She gently lifted the veil from her face and flipped it to the back of her head. She lit and dragged on the cigarette before blowing out a large plume of smoke. "The Anunnaki. Over a thousand generations have passed since their arrival. In their eyes, we were primitive, savage even. They were so convinced of their own superiority. Technologically, I suppose they were right. But spiritually, no one is more bankrupt." Indigo glared accusatorily at Max. "At the start, their goal was to extract resources. But this changed. Just as it is about to again."

"Why does everyone insist on speaking in riddles? I came to you for help."

"It is the end of an age, mon cher. From Pisces to Aquarius to be exact."

"Look," Max was becoming more and more convinced he'd made a mistake by returning to New Orleans. "You should know I've never followed astrology. I can't— "

"Each year, thousands of you flock here for Mardi Gras, and not one among you has even the slightest clue to its origins. The fanciest education money can buy and yet there's so little you actually understand." Indigo took another drag and exhaled a cloud of smoke. "Had any of you cared to investigate Mardi Gras' significance, there wouldn't be nearly the interest in drunkenness and debauchery. Still, year after year, you arrive focused on the destruction of N'awlins, our fine city. Even worse, you work on your own destruction."

Suddenly, Max felt ridiculous. He had flown to Louisiana to sit with an individual who was insulting and whose gender he could barely determine. "Maybe coming here was a mistake."

Indigo spit out a hearty laugh. "You believed this true of your first visit and yet here you sit today." When she continued she dragged out her words, giving them particular emphasis. "Something is coming, mon cher. Instead of drinking and screwing perhaps you should get prepared."

"It was stupid of me to think you could help." Max reached for the Antikythera Device, but Indigo continued.

"Just as blood circulates through your veins, so do the stars and planets rotate in the heavens. There are cycles in the cosmos, mon cher, similar to the ones contained in our own bodies. It is all part of a larger design."

At the very best, Max remained skeptical of Indigo's words. "How do you fit in to these cycles?"

"But this isn't for you to know, mon cher. The question for you is how do *you* fit in? So many teachings have been lost, even the ones right before our eyes." Indigo stood and retrieved a calendar from the wall. She placed it on the table before Max. "Have you any idea how they select the dates of Mardi Gras or Easter?"

Max hesitated, unaware of the correct answer.

"They are determined in the skies, mon cher." Indigo's eyes grew large. "This is part of the design."

Max knew the actual date of Easter varied, sometimes landing in March and other times in April. But Indigo was correct that he didn't have a clue how the dates were determined.

She opened the calendar and quickly found March 21, the first day of spring. She continued scanning forward, day by day, and then flipped to April. After perusing, she found what she was seeking. "Voila! The first full moon of spring." Indigo pointed to the day, which featured a solid white circle beside it. "Advance forward to the following Sunday." She slid her finger across the calendar until it landed on Sunday. "There you will find Easter following the first full moon of spring."

With his own eyes Max read the word 'Easter' next to Indigo's finger.

"Forty days before, you will find Ash Wednesday." Indigo flipped back to February and pointed out Ash Wednesday on the grid. "One day before this is Fat Tuesday, or as the French call it, Mardi Gras: when you came to my store. Perhaps this too was celestial in nature."

Max studied Indigo's face, somewhat stunned by her simple explanation. Only a few days had passed since his initiation in the Pyramid of the Moon. Now, he was being told that Easter and Mardi Gras were both determined by the position of the moon.

"We find ourselves in a very important year, Monsieur. As you might know, we are nearing a planetary alignment. Energies are building as the era of Pisces transitions to Aquarius. Signs of this are everywhere if only we choose to look. Earthquakes, tsunamis, volcanoes. Hurricanes and global financial collapse. Only through such events will universal forces be alleviated."

"I can't really argue with anything you're saying. But it still doesn't mean I believe in it."

Indigo smiled. "These are the old energies enveloping you — the confusion of Pisces — two fish swimming in opposite directions. The Maya predicted this as the Great Forgetting." Indigo narrowed her eyes at Max. "As so many of you have aptly demonstrated, it is because of families like yours that the masses remain disconnected. They have lost sight of what is truly important."

Max didn't know why, but Indigo's words resonated as truth in his ears. After just five minutes, he found himself wishing for an off switch that could silence her voice. But the strange, androgynous woman droned on, delivering poignant knowledge from a little shabby room.

CHAPTER 30

*F*or nearly twenty minutes, Max sat across the table listening, but not fully comprehending. He was on overload, and Indigo, although impassioned, droned on like a preacher with a sermon.

"Humanity is at an important crossroads, for the Age of Pisces is ending. The time has come for the fish to leave their water. Like everyone, you are in the throes of discovering exactly what that means for you." Indigo thumped her cigarette above the ashtray and released a large segment of ash inside. "Just as the Maya predicted, the end of the Great Forgetting is near. To fulfill her duty, Aquarius or the Bearer of the Gourd will pour out the gourd's contents, unleashing onto the ground the very water in which the fish of Pisces swim. Those who are more sensitive can feel this transition occurring. It vibrates deeply within us like energy, permeating flesh, skin and bones. For many, the sensation feels like agitation, just like you and so many others are experiencing. This is the fish out of water."

Max was more focused now and sat as if nailed to his chair. With a puff of smoke, Indigo carried on with her story.

"It is because of the Great Forgetting that so few remember the origins of Mardi Gras. Indeed, they trace back to the golden years of Egypt. More than seven thousand years have passed since they perfected their calendar. With 360 days and five additional ones that were considered to be 'time outside of time.' During those five days, time itself was deemed to have stopped: A well-deserved break that allowed the ancients to celebrate with feasts and music quite similar to the ceremonies we see at Mardi Gras." Indigo's voice grew softer and was tinged with disappointment. "Only today, the festivities have eroded into beads, cocktail glasses and T-shirts. Its true origins have been wiped from public consciousness... I presume you are Catholic, Monsieur Battenberg."

Max stared at Indigo and nodded. Without skipping a beat, she continued bombarding him with information.

"These final days before Mardi Gras are very much like time outside of time. It is the last opportunity for indulgence before Lent arrives."

"Forty days of sacrifice."

"Voila, Monsieur. To end time outside of time meant a return to business and hard work. This is why they celebrated. It was the last opportunity before the hardship began. For Christians, Lent is the same thing. Getting back to business with a sacrifice of something you truly desire."

Max seemed in a daze as he practically finished Indigo's sentence. "All the way up until the final Sunday of Easter."

Indigo nodded in agreement. Max simply stared at her, completely daunted by her wisdom.

"How is it you know all of this?"

She took another drag from her cigarette. Max noticed her hand trembling ever so slightly. She was covering well, but it was clear he made her nervous. Exhaling smoke from the cigarette seemed to relax her.

"So much I have seen in the Akasha."

Max was unfamiliar with the word. "The what?"

"The Akashic Record. A spiritual library of sorts. Contained within its walls is the history of anything and everything that has ever occurred. From every star's formation to every blade of grass that has ever grown."

"I'm afraid to ask how that even works."

Indigo snickered at the comment. "It exists in the ether, mon cher. We all have access when we open ourselves up to it." She fixed Max in her gaze. "Do you meditate, Monsieur Battenberg?"

Max refrained from answering, unsure if Indigo had even expected a response. He was trying to wrap his head around things, but getting used to the idea of all things paranormal would still take time.

"To view the Akasha requires calm. And utter concentration. Its form, how it appears, depends entirely on the person accessing it."

Max took his own opportunity to chuckle. "So, it isn't real. It's something for psychics." Max couldn't hide his sarcasm when pronouncing the last word.

"Au contraire, Monsieur. While it may not exist in this plane, the Akasha is quite real."

"All right," Max's voice was tinged with skepticism, "I can't believe I'm going to ask this, but these Anunnaki—you believe my family is descended from them?"

"Of this I have no doubt," Indigo barked. "Your aura stinks of them. With very few exceptions, we are all their creation, but you, mon cher," with one eyebrow raised, Indigo glared, "let's just say some of us contain more of their DNA than others. Even today, you struggle to keep the line of blue bloods pure."

"In the ceremony you saw... with the animals, I could speak a strange language. I have no idea how."

"No one can know all the magic you possess. You that hide behind so many names — the Anunnaki... the Nephilim. Nibirians."

Max pondered Indigo's words, searching for meaning, but mostly, he could not comprehend.

She took a final drag from her cigarette. "The force of true spirit is limitless and all conquering." After blowing out a cloud of smoke, she smashed the butt in an ashtray. "But it can be crushed. When the spirit is broken, the most powerful of men become child-like and controllable. Open to coercion. Voilà les choses, mon cher. La domination est comme ça. Your kind have accomplished this again and again. And not just here on Earth. Through trickery and tomfoolery, you have lowered the veil deeply over our eyes." Indigo carefully removed the red veil from the back of her head and lowered it dramatically over her face. "As long as the veil is in place, so will humanity be enslaved."

Max continued to listen as Indigo grew angrier and more animated.

"Look around you, Monsieur. Have you not noticed that the majority of us are in servitude to an intricately organized system — slaves, handing over our most precious resource? Not gold or diamonds, mon cher: I speak of our own free will."

"If, like you say, we're all descended from them... why are you singling me out?"

Indigo laughed out loud. "You, mon cher, hail from the Anunnaki supreme. Your family sits at the very top of their pyramid of oppression. You are the one percent, entrusted with the keys to the chateau. I've asked before, from where do you think your family gains its riches?"

Max was beginning to feel apprehensive. While Indigo's words were difficult to accept, he somehow knew them to be true.

"Even now, a dark cloud swirls about your aura."

Max found the idea peculiar. "Are you saying you can see my

aura?"

"Of course, mon cher. This is what I do. But you mustn't despair. Even in your darkness, I see a light. The question is, will you ignite it?"

Max wasn't sure why, but he was beginning to relax. "How does this veil thing work?"

Indigo cracked a smile, raising her veil to sip from a glass of water. When she finished, she abruptly slammed the glass on the table, startling Max. "The veil is what gets your attention, Monsieur. Did I get yours?"

Recovering, Max settled back in his seat and shrugged at the obvious. "Yes, of course."

"Welcome to the function of the veil. It is what you see instead of the truth. When distracted, you lose focus. The important things, while still there, fade into the background. Consider dirt being thrown in the spiritual eye, soiling it, corrupting it. The truth of universal laws has been replaced with religions that rationalize and justify the Anunnaki system of control. Today, your average man has little or no idea what he truly believes." Indigo was growing more impassioned as she continued. "Is there a God or no God? A Heaven or a Hell? Should we look out for one another or just for ourselves? And while we thrash about like fish trapped on dry land, you and families like yours exploit us all, extracting wealth with complete disregard for balance or equality."

"I'm sorry, but I can't believe..." Max floundered, unable to finish his sentence.

"What? You can't believe that the iniquities of the world turn out to be by design? Please, Monsieur, these things are very much the tip of the iceberg. As I stated in your last visit, all shall be revealed to you. Before this year's end, in fact."

Uneasy, Max forced a smile. "Not sure if I should be excited or worried about that."

"Be worried, Monsieur. You should be very worried. I sense good in you, but there are limits to your abilities — that you might be prepared to handle what will come your way."

Max recalled the mind-boggling events of the last weeks. But now Indigo was supporting everything he wasn't quite ready to believe. He gazed at the Plexiglas box on the floor.

"What about this? You suggested I get it, but no one knows how to operate it."

Indigo was smiling when she stood, her voice filled with cocky petulance. "No one, monsieur?" She came around the table and stood beside him. "Show it to me."

Max stood and unzipped the device's leather carrying case. He pulled the Plexiglas box free and set it on Indigo's table. "So, you know how it works?"

Indigo didn't speak but her chest was rising and falling as if she'd lost her breath. She turned to him, all smiles. "This task was a test, Monsieur. To see what you're made of. I believe there is hope. Maybe you will ignite the light after all."

Stunned by Indigo's words, Max deflated like a popped balloon. "I almost died getting this thing and you're saying it was a test?"

"Recovery of the device was not written. Not by you or anyone. Your intentions are powerful." Indigo studied Max's face. "This is good."

"An expert on this thing says it can unlock cosmic knowing. I don't even know what that means."

"In order to activate the device you must first pose a question."

Indigo crossed to a shelf and removed a sharp stickpin from an apple shaped cushion. She returned to the table and took ahold of Max's index finger. She jammed the pin into it. Max jumped in spite of himself. A large drop of blood pooled at his fingertip. He moved to suck the blood, but Indigo grabbed his wrist, immobilizing him.

"A question, Monsieur, with strong and pure intention to know its answer."

Max thought as hard as he could given that his hand was being held down. Indigo guided his finger to the golden dial from the Money Pit. She pressed the drop of blood into the center of it. With the amount of detail on the device, no one, including Doctor Miklos, had noticed the small, perfectly round indentation in the artifact. The receptacle was now full of Max's blood.

He gazed quizzically at the tiny area on the dial. The procedure evoked memories from his initiation when the eagle-masked man had drawn blood from his palms.

The intensity of Indigo's stare burned through the veil and through Max. "Our DNA is nothing more than a physical manifestation of spirit. Your blood and the artifact, they are simply keys to unlock the device. Your birthday, Monsieur, what is it?"

"December fourteenth."

Indigo busied herself, adjusting the movable plates of the dial.

"You must also input the year."

Max hesitated, then leaned over the device to adjust the year of his birth. With a smile, Indigo confirmed that the Anti-k Mechanism was properly set. She stared at Max.

"Your question, Monsieur? Have you prepared it?"

With a simple nod, he replied, "Yes."

He was watching, but didn't quite catch what Indigo did to trigger the device. Its gears cranked into action as the Antikythera Mechanism came to life. For a moment, Max had the sense of watching a clock. The gears ticked and turned, and then it happened.

Max and Indigo both felt electricity flowing through the room. Without warning, items on the table floated weightless into the air. Indigo's keys, the ashtray and the cigarette she'd mashed out only minutes before floated as if the shop were a rocket that had just broken through orbit into the gravity-free reaches of outer space.

Max didn't so much see as hear the machine's gears accelerating, ticking faster and faster. The zone of weightlessness was growing as more and more things floated into the air. In a flash of light the room transformed, everything in it represented as a trillion points of light.

Max stood transfixed. Indigo, the table, the books, the shelves and walls all appeared as tiny, fragmented dots of light. The amalgamation of glowing pinpoints took shape as if he were seeing the atoms themselves. Suddenly, everything seemed transparent.

With perfect clarity, Max saw everything in the room. At the same time, he could see beyond the walls as cars, trees, birds and pedestrians appeared, each a shining beacon of luminescent energy. The scene was beautiful until the room began to spin, the lights blurring together into a hodgepodge of complete disorientation. Max felt nausea overtaking him as the sound of a thousand Niagara Falls roared in his ears.

What had seemed beautiful at first was now unbearable. He wanted it to stop, but he was no longer aware of Indigo or even of himself in the room. Just when the stimulation seemed too great to bear, he remembered Indigo's words. A question, she had said. *Your intention to know its answer must be strong and pure.*

Remembering what he'd seen during his initiation, Max gathered his thoughts and concentrated on a single question. *What happened next with the brothers back on Nibiru?*

CHAPTER 31

*E*nki knew his half brother was angry, but the truth was that he didn't care. Their father, Anu, in a grab for power, had successfully deposed the sitting government. Nibiru's previous leader, Alalu, had fled the planet, and everyone in Anu's clan had profited. In a matter of weeks, they had each received apartments in different wings of the royal palace.

Because she was Anu's first wife, Ki and her son Enlil, Enki's half brother, had been given slightly superior quarters: a better apartment in a better location with a better view. According to Nibiru custom, Enki and his mother, Antu, who was Anu's second wife, were considered subordinate under hierarchical law.

But Enki never complained. The living arrangements were of little consequence, especially since he was their father's favorite. His stoic disposition in matters of political importance had earned his father's favor, he suspected. It also didn't hurt that he was Anu's firstborn child.

Enlil, on the other hand, was a constant complainer. Enlil's grumblings often helped him in the acquisition of things he desired, but it was aggravating and annoying. Anu would never admit to it, but Enki knew their father didn't fully respect the younger son. Enki truly believed Enlil had made it his mission to dog his every move, complaining about the inequalities that life had offered him.

Contrary to Enlil's belief, Enki was indeed Anu's number one heir. Yes, Ki was the first wife, superior to Antu in status, but she had nevertheless failed in her duties. She had been given ample opportunities to provide Anu a son, but her efforts had been unsuccessful. It was much later that his mother, Antu, had entered the picture and within months, Enki had been conceived.

Yes, the younger Enlil had a better view from his apartment. It was in fact the perfect vantage point for the annoying sibling to witness their relative true standing in their father's heart and mind. On the day of travel, Enki purposely maneuvered his ship over Enlil's deck at the royal palace. He even spotted Enlil and Ki on the veranda, so he knew they understood his point.

The entire stunt was Enki's way of saying, *Take that!* Only then did he engage the zero point energy drive, shooting off through time and space toward the third planet, Earth. He loved to fly, and gloated that he had been chosen over Enlil to make the journey. With the drive engaged, the craft had begun using the very atoms of air to slingshot itself toward Earth. Finally, away from Nibiru, he would be free of Enlil and his unyielding resentment.

For Enki, space travel was like meditation. Nestled within the cockpit, he gazed through the glass, watching as time and space sped by. Already he could feel himself relaxing, and within minutes he completely forgot about his younger half-sibling. He was on a mission after all, and there were more important things to consider.

Enlil may have been angry, but there was no comparing his state of mind to that of Alalu's. The deposed leader had been banished from the palace and chased from his position as supreme ruler. Within days, Alalu's life and stature had crumbled into ruin. In defense, he had stolen weapons, and more importantly, he had taken the stone tablets referred to as the Table of Destiny. Renowned for their powerful predictive powers, the tablets had always been in the hands of the supreme ruler. Although Anu had taken power, he was greatly disadvantaged without these stones. The fugitive Alalu had to be pursued in order to reclaim the powerful weapons, but more importantly, to recover the Table of Destiny.

In addition, the fallen monarch had declared that gold was in ample supply on the small blue planet. The ore was something Nibiru desperately needed. Anu needed an emissary he could absolutely trust to confirm Alalu's claims. In a power play of his own, Enki had volunteered for the mission.

Even before his arrival on Earth, it was clear to Enki that Alalu's assertions of gold were true. With the Table of Destiny in his possession, Alalu would certainly know exactly where the precious resource existed. But there was still a need for caution since the fallen leader had usurped a powerful stockade of weapons.

Enki's reconnaissance ship, while one of the fleet's fastest, had little to no weaponry with the exception of simple photon blasters.

The vessel's propulsion system utilized simple atoms, polarizing them to create momentum. Negative charges at the front of the craft formed a black hole effect that pulled the ship forward. At the same time, positive ions accumulated at the craft's rear to generate opposing force. In essence, the ship was simultaneously being pushed and pulled through space. At every step, acceleration continued, catapulting Enki faster and faster toward Earth.

When necessary, the ship easily exceeded light speed, an aspect Enki adored about flying. At the precise moment the light barrier was broken, the universe looked different. If only for an instant, both time and space felt frozen in a snapshot. Enki loved to gaze through the cockpit glass and witness light's progression as if luminescent molecules were jogging along outside of the ship.

He had been in flight only a few hours, but already Earth was only minutes away. Enki disengaged the ship's propulsion just outside the asteroid belt. At such high speeds, he couldn't risk even the tiniest chance of a collision. As always, the initial process of deceleration was unsettling.

As history was told, millions of years before Enki's and Enlil's birth, their planet, Nibiru, had rotated directly into the path of another huge celestial body, Tiamat. The collision smashed Tiamat, effectively breaking it in two. Over time, the remnants evolved into what is now known as the Earth and its moon. The asteroid belt had formed of Tiamat's residual fragments and collateral debris.

Nibirians were quite proud of Nibiru's "victory" over Tiamat. In their hearts and minds, they believed they were conquerors just like their planet. They were the victors over their own poor eco-system, learning not only to survive but also to flourish. In their estimation, the universe had become an extension of their planet, something to be conquered and controlled.

But the Nibirians had been wrong. It wasn't immediately apparent, but Nibiru had suffered damage. Among their wisest, most scientific minds, it was believed that Tiamat, in her final breath, had struck at Nibiru's atmosphere. The fatal blow, it turned out, would be accompanied by the planet's slow and painful demise.

As he entered the asteroid belt, Enki powered up the ship's photon blasters. If he maneuvered well, he wouldn't need them, but this was rarely feasible. When asteroids were unavoidable, the ship's weapons could easily create a conduit for its safe passage. Enki began firing, obliterating anything in his path. The entire process took longer than anticipated, but Enki was skilled and made it through unscathed.

Within minutes, he burned through Earth's atmosphere. From the ground, his ship likely resembled a fiery dagger slicing through the sky. As he leveled off, the flames settled and the ship cooled, affording Enki a magnificent view of Tiamat's remains. Just like Nibiru, Earth had vast oceans covering the land. But it was disparate in every other way. While Nibiru was scarce of provisions, Earth's resources were abundant and varied, with its continents of lush vegetation, mountain ranges, deserts and ice.

As a radiant planet, Nibiru thrived off energy from its own core. On Earth, its sun was the giver of life. Enki found it strange that a planet could survive on another body's energy, the power of a star.

He glanced at the ship's instruments to be sure he was on course to Alalu's coordinates. The lower he flew, the more he could see of Earth's landscape. He traversed miles of green pastures and forest until he reached an ocean. Then he spotted it on the shore: Alalu's ship. It was like a huge beached whale dug into the sand, with waves splashing against its hull.

Enki set his ship down on the sandy beach away from the water. Only then did he notice extensive damage on the stolen warship. He immediately surmised what had occurred: Alalu hadn't properly navigated the asteroid belt, but had nevertheless managed to land just off shore and maneuvered the ship onto the beach.

Enki exited his craft and took a deep breath of Earth's atmosphere. This made him immediately aware in a new and vital way of his own planet's atmospheric predicament. Breathing Earth's air was like sipping cream while the atmosphere of Nibiru resembled skim milk. Enki could feel the sun's warmth washing over his skin. With the waves gently lapping ashore, Enki reveled in his victory over Enlil. He was officially the first son to leave Nibiru. In fact, he was the first son, period.

In less than five minutes, Enki knew also that Earth would be his. Enlil and Ki had successfully claimed the plushest of apartments in the royal palace. As far as he was concerned, they could have them. If gold was here, Enki would build a larger, more magnificent palace, and he would oversee procurement of the gold himself.

Alalu had not presented himself. Proceeding with caution, Enki entered the warship to confirm if the fallen leader was on board. The enormous warship had a deck rather than a cockpit. The spacious navigation room was filled with instrument panels and a large panoramic window that wrapped around its front in a U-shape. It made sense that the craft was damaged, as it would have been impossible for Alalu to properly pilot it on his own.

Enki crossed to the control panel and, because he had been trained to use a warship, pulled up several screens showing different parts of the ship. From all signs, the deposed ruler had abandoned it. He quickly took advantage and rummaged through a series of weapons caches in search of the stolen tools of war or of the Table of Destiny. The seer stones were nowhere to be found, but Enki froze upon opening the final compartment. Sitting before him were two of Nibiru's most powerful devices. Technically, neither was a weapon, but the Atu-waa and the Ark, when used improperly, were capable of immense devastation.

Their sheer power was quite ironic given how gorgeous they were. The Ark was housed in a beautiful, rectangular golden box adorned with the hieroglyphs of Nibirian society. On each side were sphinxes, pyramids, obelisks and what appeared to be mythical creatures like Earth's centaur and griffin. A pair of intricately carved wings served as handles on top of a large golden lid. Somehow, it was poetic that the device was housed in a box made of gold.

Then there was the Atu-waa, crystalline and glowing. Not even the oldest of Nibiru knew of its precise origins. This other stolen device was nearly a foot tall and had the shape and detail of a perfect pyramid. Its soft light illuminated Enki's face as he stared at it.

With no time to waste, he removed both devices and placed them in his own ship. Within minutes of getting them on board, Enki was airborne, flying across the water. If Alalu returned, there was no doubt he would shoot Enki down. He considered engaging the zero point engine, but such a move would catapult him into orbit. Instead Enki flew low, taking in the gorgeous view that was Earth. Patches of clouds hovered low to the ground and Enki weaved in and out of them.

Once he had put adequate distance between himself and Alalu's ship, he scanned the terrain for an area to land and hide the devices. To his amazement, there was movement on the ground. Enki circled lower to get a better look. It appeared there were humanoids chasing a large wooly beast, a mammoth in fact. The small apelike creatures, dark and hairy, ran behind the behemoth, screaming and waving spears. Before his eyes, the large prey plunged into an open pit that was camouflaged with dirt and tree branches.

Enki was impressed. The primitive beings had trapped the beast.

The strategy had been sound and particularly useful since Enki had distracted them with his flyover. Several of the hunters had now abandoned their pursuit and were staring up and pointing at Enki's ship. Ironically, Anu's eldest son was just as mesmerized by them in turn.

With a large smile, he navigated west, flying over the hunting party and off into their horizon. He had already traversed a thousand miles when he spotted a mountaintop. He circled a few times to make sure it was abandoned, then touched down on an open plateau. With a sense of urgency, Enki proceeded to bury the things Alalu had stolen. But there was still business to be handled. First, he needed to determine whether or not Alalu's assertion of gold was true. But he would also have to move quickly in order to find the Table of Destiny.

CHAPTER 32

*E*nlil could think of nothing worse. Alalu's declaration of gold had been true. The precious ore was not only present on Earth, it was abundant. And his older half-brother, Enki, had been put in charge of its retrieval and transport to Nibiru. Alas, if the atmosphere were to be saved, Enki would take credit while he sat passively in the palace. No one, not even his mother, understood how this made him feel. It was preposterous that four Earth centuries had already passed and he had still not been invited to a more proactive role.

Enlil had always known he was destined for greatness. This is why he had suggested overthrowing Alalu in the first place. Now, even the deposed king had a stronger, more integral role than he in the operation to save Nibiru's atmosphere. To placate the fallen despot, his father had offered Alalu an outpost on the other red planet called Mars. Once extracted from Earth, the gold was being delivered there to await the final leg of its journey to Nibiru.

To Enlil's disgust, his half-brother and Alalu had both been permitted to commission temples and palaces on Earth and Mars respectively. All of it made him look bad. In the eyes of his people, he would certainly be seen as lazy and ineffective. Powerful rulers had to act swiftly and with determination. Anu had offered little or no opportunities for Enlil to do so, until now.

For hours, Enlil had been waiting in his father's reception chamber. A warm breeze blew in off the large balcony, which wrapped around the leader's royal quarters. Every apartment in the palace was constructed of finely chiseled stone, with each brick heavily laden with artisanal designs. Some were patterned with circles or lines while others featured hieroglyphic displays. The stone's natural beige color created a needed calming effect in the minimalist room.

Strategically placed about the chamber were rich woodcarvings and delicate sculptures. Each sat atop stone pedestals on the finely polished marble floors. The sparse decor should have led to a sterile and cold environment, but this was hardly the case. The choice of objets d'art and their placement, instead, led to an ambiance that was warm and artistic, even beautiful.

Finally, Anu, Nibiru's newest ruler, swept into the room. He was of the best and strongest stock that Nibiru had to offer. Taller than both of his sons, he towered as if he himself had been sculpted from stone. His features, hard and masculine, were at the same time symmetrical and precise. A full head of curly brown hair was tamed into a single column by a tight wrapping of gold thread. The bound tresses sunk down his back and landed just between his shoulder blades. Whenever he entered a room, his stature commanded respect.

Enlil bowed in a display of submission, not because Anu was his father, but because he was the newest King. "Father, I am honored for your time."

"For many days, your mother has made it known you wish to speak with me."

"Word of the Earth project has come to light. The lack of progress on Enki's part is now common knowledge, a fact that is not well received by the council."

"You imagine you can do better."

"When I suggested the coup against Alalu, it was not to suffer disappointment of any sort. If the failure Enki suffers were a reflection only on our family, this would be bad enough. But we both know it is larger than that. Without the gold, it is all of Nibiru that will succumb along with our failing atmosphere."

Bristling with rage, Anu swept a large sculpture of a Nibirian cat from its base. The object exploded into pieces as it struck the marble floor. "Words of sacrilege you speak."

Enlil barely flinched at his father's outburst. The older Enki may have resembled Anu more in looks and size, but Enlil had inherited every bit of his courage and some of his rage. It was Enlil's determination that made him confident of a successful coup against Alalu and his regime.

Anu continued, "Just like our glorious Nibiru, we have always been and will forever be conquerors. It is our birthright. It is our destiny. For this alone we were created. We, my son, are the usurpers of the universe."

Enlil finally had his opening. He always knew he would. Enki had built himself up too large in their father's eyes. Earth's mining operations were grossly behind, and there were other aspects of his half-brother's tactics that were failing. From all accounts, work on the small blue planet was difficult and backbreaking. While the outpost was abundant in resources, getting to them was laborious.

To make things worse, Enki was too soft and easygoing and didn't know how to handle Nibiru's workforce — the Igigi.

"Father, with your permission, of course, I should like to travel at once to Earth to oversee Enki's progress. To ensure that the gold arrives here in a timely manner."

A sly grin appeared on Anu's lips. "I am in agreement with such a plan. You shall assemble a team and take immediate transport to Earth. While there, you shall ensure adequate supplies of the ore. Yes, this is correct. So shall it be."

Brimming with satisfaction, Enlil bowed once more. "Thank you, father. I promise I shall not disappoint."

Enlil turned, preparing to leave the room, but Anu reached out and laid a firm hand on his son's shoulder.

"Yes, father."

With a dismissive gesture at the shattered statue, Anu continued, "First, clean this mess."

What was once Enlil's satisfaction quickly turned to rage for him in turn. But he choked it down and forced his most convincing smile. "Of course father."

As Enlil stooped to pick up the pieces, the hulking form that was Anu turned and exited the chamber.

It was done in record time, it seemed. His crew already assembled, Enlil watched as his space cruiser was loaded with weapons and supplies. Ki, the proud mother, kissed her son as he prepared to board the transport.

"Stay alert, my son. On the small, blue planet there is no one to look after you."

"Don't worry, mother. The truth is, it is they who should look out for me."

Mother and son hugged before Enlil traveled up the ramp and disappeared into the ship. Within minutes the hair stood on Ki's neck and arms, at which point the craft floated into the air and vanished, slingshotting through time and space on its journey to Earth. Ki stared into the now empty sky, hopeful that her son would finally find the happiness he sought by proving his worth to his father.

CHAPTER 33

*I*t didn't quite feel like waking from a dream. The exit from the Enki and Enlil story was much more abrupt. Just as in a film, historical details had unfolded in extreme detail. Now, in the mere blink of an eye, Max was staring at Indigo across the table. At the same time, the items floating in the air came crashing down. The keys and ashtray clanged as cigarette ashes exploded into a tiny cloud.

"Wait, is that it?"

"Did you find the answer, Monsieur?"

Max stammered, still too disoriented to answer. With the growing evidence, a part of his brain struggled to grasp what was swiftly becoming real—mediums, astral projections, extra-terrestrials, all of which Max had never before pondered. He couldn't imagine what else there might be to learn. As he regrouped, Max finally answered Indigo's question.

"Only partially. There's more. There has to be more."

Indigo was intense. "Might it be you didn't ask the right question?"

"How long was I gone?"

Indigo seemed puzzled by the inquiry. "Monsieur?"

"I had to be gone at least an hour, right?"

"You never left, Monsieur. The device only ran a few seconds."

"Huh?" The revelation perplexed Max. "Maybe that's why it didn't finish."

"Shhh." The psychic quickly lifted her head, looking toward the ceiling. She remained still, as if she were listening for something. "You must go, Monsieur." In a rush, Indigo grabbed her purse from a nearby chair and rummaged through it. After plopping lipstick, sunglasses and a hairband on the table, she finally removed a business card. Indigo scribbled on the back of it, then handed it to Max. "This number, you must remember. Promise me you will memorize it."

Max took the card and stared at the number scrawled on the back —7129. "Seven-one-two-nine."

"Consider it your lucky number, Monsieur. In the coming months you will need balance." Indigo looked at Max, captivating him in her gaze. "The number will help."

Once again, Max was reticent. "Okay." He flipped over the card. It was old and tattered and had likely lived months in Indigo's purse. On the flipside, in block letters, were the words "Sandra's Hairweaves." Beneath the name was a badly drawn depiction of an African American woman with long flowing hair.

Indigo grabbed hold of Max's hand. Her grip was tight and forceful. "It's important you remember the number. You must look everywhere for it, in all aspects of your life. And remember to meditate, Monsieur."

Things were moving too fast for Max. "But I don't, I don't even know..."

"Then you must learn. To meditate is the antithesis of the veil." Indigo stared into Max's eyes before insisting, "The number, have you memorized it?"

Max stared back at Indigo. The intensity of her stare unsettled him, but still he was unable to look away. Finally, he glanced at the card before speaking it aloud again: "Seven-one-two-nine."

With a frown, Indigo came around the table. "You must leave now, Monsieur." She gently touched a finger to the microchip around his neck. "You've lingered too long. It's no longer safe for us to speak."

"But I need you to show me how you activated the device."

Without answering, Indigo nudged Max, urging him to pack up the Antikythera Mechanism. "Our meeting is done, Monsieur. You must go." She watched Max gather up the device before hurrying him to the cabinet in the other room. "Stay always alert, Monsieur Battenberg. For you, there are very few safe places. So many are the Anunnaki oppressors that you must be wary even in your own home. It is of the utmost importance that you remain vigilant." Disdain painted Indigo's words as a deep sadness overcame her. "You amass riches beyond compare, then lead lives in perpetual jeopardy. Sadly for some, even too much is not enough. Now, Monsieur, you must go."

Before Max could respond or question, Indigo turned off the boom box and retrieved his phone. She returned it and shoved Max through the door out into the street. Before he could properly say good-bye, Indigo clanged the door shut. Once again, he was off kilter at the front of her building, this time clutching the leather case that contained the Antikythera Mechanism.

A long moment passed before he even noticed there was traffic on the street. It was rush hour. Horns were honking and people were yelling. Max still didn't know how, but Indigo's small shop was a sanctuary. Somehow, she had created calm by blocking out the pandemonium of everyday life in a big city.

Gathering his wits, he hurried to the waiting SUV and entered with the Antikythera Mechanism in tow. In the last hour, he had been asked to digest a lot: the Akasha, the concept of the veil, the Anunnaki and some peculiar talk of the number 7129. Slowly, the usual reality crept back in, or whatever Max could still venture to consider reality.

Another long moment passed as he sat staring into the street. The visit with Indigo had left him in a daze. As his focus returned, Max became aware of the driver awaiting instructions. With a false smile and feigned composure, he gave them. "Let's go."

The SUV roared to life and pulled away from the curb. For safety, they used a different route for the airport return. Within minutes, a spectacular view of the ocean appeared. Under normal circumstances, Max would have appreciated the beauty of such a setting. Today, he hardly noticed.

The driver accelerated, switching into the fast lane, at which point a deep nausea overcame Max. He cracked the window, hoping a breeze would refresh him. It didn't. Sweat broke out on his brow and he became convinced he would vomit.

"Driver, I need you to pull over." Flustered, he drew in a deep breath. "Please."

The chauffeur could tell Max wasn't well and pulled out of traffic at the first opportunity. Max bolted from the car, frantic to regain his bearings. He didn't know the nature of his malaise, but was pleased to find it quickly subsiding. Just a few yards away, cars were racing up and down the highway. Max looked toward the coast and, for the first time, noticed the gorgeous view of the sun setting over the Gulf of Mexico.

Max flashed a thumbs-up to the driver, then darted into traffic, successfully crossing all four lanes of the road. He could hear the driver's protests, but simply turned and yelled, "I'll be right back." He wasn't sure if the chauffeur heard, but he knew he would wait nonetheless.

Max stepped onto a strip of sand so narrow it could hardly be called a beach. He tore off his shoes, then stepped toward the water to gaze across the ocean. Waves rhythmically washed ashore, creating a perfect sense of calm. As the sun slipped beneath the horizon, the sky further transformed into brilliant shades of orange and red.

Max inhaled the ocean breeze, reveling in the moment. He had returned to New Orleans for information. Arguably, he had gotten what he asked for. The androgynous medium he had fought with only weeks before had predicted or perhaps warned that all would be revealed. Max marveled at the concept of having even more to learn when, already, he was overwhelmed by his newfound knowledge.

The phone in his pocket vibrated, jarring him from his reverie. He removed it to discover three missed calls. One was from Brigitte, another from Chandler and, shockingly, there was a call from Gary Richards. Max knew Gary was now living in Washington, DC, but they hadn't spoken in more than a year. He wondered what the old acquaintance might want. Somehow, deep down, he feared it wouldn't be long before he found out.

CHAPTER 34

$\mathcal{T}$he same night, Max quietly returned to Chicago under his security detail's watchful eye. For the most part, no one even knew of his day trip to New Orleans. Once at home, he carefully locked the door and rearmed his alarm system before falling back against the wall. In the midst of a Hades alert, both he and the mystical device were safe.

Max contemplated how bizarre and unpredictable his life had become. At Mardi Gras, his first experience with Indigo had been incredibly unpleasant. But the latest visit had calmed him. It was hardly the easygoing feeling he had had before his initiation, but at least he didn't feel like jumping out of his skin.

In just two months, he had completed five trips. Each journey, in its own way, had transformed him. The evolution, while small at the start, had already proved extremely significant.

The mysteries of his life were beginning to unfold, and Max now found the psychic's original unflattering assessment of him that much harder to ignore. He held little doubt about his shortcomings. He lied, and sometimes he cheated. It was this side of him that gave rise to Ian, who might prevent his ever having to see or acknowledge his faults. Then came Indigo's accusations like a shining beacon, illuminating the very corner of darkness that Max wished to hide. Because of her, he had made a second trip to New York and then a third to the Money Pit where he had nearly lost his life.

It seemed foolish risking so much for a device he knew nothing about. Yes, Indigo had angered and insulted him, but there was something in her predictions that piqued his interest. If there hadn't been he would never have sought the Anti-k artifact whose technology was somehow out of order historically.

And Max didn't regret the decision. The artifact's recovery, in reality, filled him with pride. The find had not yet been released to the media, but Max knew it would go down in the history books. Finally, he had accomplished something of note, outside of simply being born a Battenberg.

Then there was his fourth trip: the initiation. The things he saw in Mexico City had been the most impactful until his denial settled in. As it turned out, the events of Teotihuacán simply seemed too incredible to accept.

Now, returning from his fifth and latest trip, Max was undeniably changed. Added together, the increments of growth from each journey were infinitely larger than the sum of their parts. Max felt his legacy crashing down on him like a ton of gold bullion.

He stared at the leather case as if a wild animal were inside, waiting to burst free. The mystical contraption whose origins were unknown both scared and mesmerized him. He wondered what else it could reveal, but didn't dare activate it on his own.

Instead, he marched up his steps into his closet, where he pressed an open palm against the surface of his large, full-length mirror. After a moment, a digital keypad appeared embedded beneath the glass. He quickly entered a code that caused the mirror to swing open. Camouflaged behind it was a five-inch-thick metal door.

Max stepped into his home's control center, a perfectly encapsulated vault. Unlike the rest of the house, which was painted white, the "panic room" was the color of rusty clay. A large control panel covered the left wall. A motherboard of security measures armed the house with a series of closed circuit monitors displaying key strategic locations.

Three additional doors within the control center led to a modern full bathroom, a pantry of food stocks and a small sleeping chamber or makeshift bedroom.

Max heaved the large Plexiglas box onto a shelf to the right. Beside it, he spotted the used water bottle from Mexico City. He had almost forgotten the white powder of gold salvaged from his initiation. The mysterious powder, still in water, had turned to sludge at the bottom of the container. Max wondered what might be discovered if he ever decided to use the device and the white powder of gold together.

He opened the bottle, dipped his pinky finger inside and scooped out a bit of the mixture. He smelled and then tasted it. The rush was immediate, not unlike cocaine. Everything around him, both sights and sounds, became more vivid, as if the world had slowed and left him operating at normal speed. *Oh, God, this is trippy.*

The ring of his land line blared through his house speakers, causing Max to jump. From his altered perspective, the sound reverberated like concert speakers at full blast. The sound was deafening, but Max continued staring about the room, distracted by details he normally didn't see.

A desert of tiny dust particles danced across the floors as well as on top of furniture and counter tops. Max turned to the light fixture embedded in the ceiling. In some ways it resembled a sprinkler shooting a fine mist of light across the room. Max held out his hand and watched light accumulating in his palm. After a moment, it seemingly spilled over and dissipated into the room.

Like a giant gong, the blare of the house phone vibrated again in his ears. Finally, he crossed to the control panel at the room's entrance. He clicked on the phone, but was too distracted by the many visual cues to speak.

After an awkward pause, Brigitte's voice bounced into the room. "Hello? Max?"

He immediately recognized Brigitte's voice, which sounded more like music than usual. "Hi," he answered with a sense of peacefulness and calm.

"What happened? I called you earlier."

She had spoken only six words, but Max could tell she was agitated. She had called hours before while he was still in New Orleans, but he hadn't yet returned the favor. Max tried shaking off the effects of the gold dust.

"Sorry, babe. Otto and I got caught up. Working on the device." Max wasn't slurring his speech, but his words were slower and more punctuated than usual. "Still haven't gotten it to work." He figured it was only a half lie. He had worked on making the Anti-k Device operational, after all, even if it hadn't been with Otto.

Max felt guilty about all his recent behavior. He could tell Brigitte was reaching out for attention, but he had been unable to provide even small increments of his time. He wanted to share details of his experience in Teotihuacán, but he knew that was forbidden. In fact, Max was convinced such a thing might endanger Brigitte, so he resisted any temptation. The truth was, there was so much he didn't understand. How could he possibly explain it to someone else?

For a long while, there was silence on Brigitte's end. Then she continued, "I'm not sure what's going on with you, but we should probably talk in person."

Max was struggling for patience as he waited on Demetrius, but his aggravation with his father seemed to be growing exponentially.

Unfortunately, his ballooning anxiety was now beginning to affect other people, and he and Brigitte both knew there was a wedge slowly being driven between them.

Ever since his return from Mexico, Brigitte's demeanor had been one of dissatisfaction. But Max felt trapped in his options for either damage control or clarity. He couldn't tell her the truth, so he made up excuse after lame excuse. Suddenly, Max felt he could appease Brigitte. Sounding more like his old self, he continued, "I know I've been out of it lately, and I agree we should talk."

"Great. Why don't we have dinner? I can be ready—"

"I know you're going to be mad, but I won't be any good tonight. Remember I'm meeting my dad tomorrow. Can we do it after? Hopefully, it won't be too late."

"Or we can do breakfast."

"No, no, I'll be too distracted and you should have my full attention."

Brigitte paused before continuing, "Okay. Yeah, why not?"

She made an attempt at sounding light and easy, but Max knew it was a ruse. She was unhappy and rightfully so.

"I'll see you tomorrow then."

"There's nothing wrong, Bridge, I'm just going through some shit right now. It won't be forever, okay?" At least Max hoped it wouldn't be.

"Okay. Let's talk tomorrow. You can tell me about it then."

Max hung up, confident that he was gaining better control of the situation with Brigitte. After only a few minutes, the effects of the taste of elixir began to wane. As he settled down, he could feel his body's desire for rest. For the first time in a long while he relented, stopping only to wash his face and brush his teeth.

But first, for several minutes he stood before his bathroom mirror studying the contours of his face. He didn't quite know from where it came, but he felt the urge to do something he had never done, something that made no sense at all. Reaching down, he pulled open a toiletry drawer and removed a jar of petroleum jelly. Max dipped his finger inside and scooped up a small glob of the waxy substance with his fingertip. He spread a thin film of it on his forehead between his eyebrows. His skin glistened as light reflected more brightly in the affected area. Satisfied, he flipped off the light and returned to bed.

As he drifted from consciousness, he thought of the next day's rendezvous, one with Demetrius and the other with Brigitte. Max prayed the meetings would clear the confusion from both his and Brigitte's heads. Shortly thereafter, he was fast asleep.

CHAPTER 35

*T*he noises weren't very loud, but Max nevertheless became aware of them. Someone was in his closet. He had awakened on his side, facing away from the closet door, but he could hear someone rustling through his things.

It was 3:06 a.m. from the digital clock shining across his face with its turquoise illumination. He remembered he had armed the security system, so who could be in his home? A deep-rooted fear arose in his chest as he noticed shadows dancing across his wall. The only thing that would cast such imagery was the reflection of the mirror that camouflaged his hidden panic room.

Max knew this meant someone was in his secret chamber. But who could have infiltrated the best security system money could buy? He wanted to turn, to shift his body for a better look, but once again he felt paralyzed. Max closed his eyes. If he was dreaming, he wanted it to be over. When he opened his eyes, the midget was standing before him, his face covered in white makeup. Max drew in his breath, completely startled once again by this intruder.

The small man pushed a cylindrical device against Max's arm. A pinprick stung him but the pain quickly subsided. The mime-faced man stowed the device in a tool belt about his waist. His sinewy hands were barely larger than a child's, but he placed them on Max and rolled him onto his back. The man was small but Max could feel his power as he repositioned him.

Through the corner of his eye, Max caught sight of the woman in his closet. She had the Anti-k Device resting on top of his sweater table. In a flash, Max saw shirts and perfectly folded sweaters levitating into the air. She had activated the device. Before he could see any further, the midget stepped in his line of sight.

In routine fashion, Max watched the sinewy man remove a tiny red sticker and place it on the forehead of his immobilized body. Instinctually, Max closed his eyes, but not because he had drifted off to sleep. This time he still believed he was conscious.

For several minutes, he heard tinkering in his closet until a whoosh of air crossed over him. Max knew the fortified door to his control room had just been closed.

What happened next was a blur. Max was unsure if he had fallen back to sleep or if the entire episode had once again been his imagination. But the next moment, he awoke to the sun shining through his large picture window. Disoriented, he turned to see the closet door securely fastened. He arose from his sheets and crossed to pull open the closet door. Everything was in perfect order. His sweaters were neatly folded and the mirrored facade door was firmly in place.

Max stepped into his bathroom and gazed in the mirror. The skin between his eyebrows appeared reddish and inflamed. *Or is it?* Max licked his index finger and gently wiped at the area, immediately lifting away what was ultimately a rosy smudge. He thought of the red stickers that were affixed to him in each dream. By using petroleum jelly, he had formed some semblance of a barrier.

At nearly a run, he returned to the closet, placing his hand against the mirrored glass. After a brief pause, the digital keypad appeared. Max fumbled the code at first, failing to open the door. With a deep exhale, he input the correct code and rushed inside the control room. The Plexiglas box was where he had left it. Max pulled it from the shelf, racing to remove the cover. The Antikythera Mechanism was still inside with the dial from the Money Pit intact.

His mind spun, making it impossible for him to put the puzzle pieces together. No one appeared to have been in his home, but Max knew what he had seen. He stepped to the control panel and began viewing his surveillance tapes. *I won't find anything, I know.*

If the man and woman were real, they were too sophisticated to have left any clues. Had he not used the petroleum jelly, Max suspected he wouldn't have discovered the red residue.

He remembered seeing 3:06 a.m. and rewound the footage to an hour before. From there, he carefully reviewed until he saw himself asleep on his back at precisely 3:06. If his memories were for real, Max distinctly recalled awaking on his side. He distinctly remembered seeing 3:06 just before the midget rolled him onto his back. Max continued fast forwarding, but didn't find anything unusual.

He sat staring at his monitors, unsure how to proceed. In a matter of hours he would meet with Demetrius. Should he report his suspicions to the Battenberg security team? Part of him still wondered if the dreams were a strange hallucination. *Or perhaps it's the white powder. I did taste it last night.*

In some ways, the existence of the mysterious couple seemed

to have been triggered by his near-death experience in the Money Pit. The first occurrence, after all, had taken place that same night. *If they wanted the device, why didn't they take it?*

The psychic had warned he wouldn't be safe in his own home. If the episodes were real, it seemed her predictions were once again proving true. The more he thought of the bizarre predicament, the more knots of tension built in his neck and shoulders. Max had always considered his house a safe haven, but his sanctuary was being breached, if only in his dreams. He knew he would have to tell Demetrius in their meeting later that day.

The idea of strangers breaking into his home left Max feeling soiled and violated. It was the first time he had felt stressed in the confines of his own personal space. He prayed a workout would help him unwind, something he desperately needed. When he met with his father later that day, he needed to be as relaxed as possible.

Max rushed to shower, then changed into a pair of sweats. He grabbed his keys from the shelf when he saw it: the business card Indigo had given him. He picked it up and saw the crude drawing of the African American woman. On the flip side, Indigo's scribbled 7129 was flowery like calligraphy, but the numbers were deeply etched in the card's surface as if Indigo had carved them there.

Max tapped the card a few times, wondering what significance 7129 could possibly hold. He glanced at the clock affixed to the wall; it was just after 11 a.m. In less than five hours, he would meet with Demetrius to discuss his initiation and the incredible things that had occurred in the Pyramid of the Moon.

CHAPTER 36

$\mathcal{M}$ax drove across town to one of his preferred sports clubs, a joint called Equilibrium. It was ironic; he hadn't chosen the spot for its name, even if balance is what he was seeking in the turmoil that had become his life. He had chosen Equilibrium because it was the least frequented club. Its decreased foot traffic was of course due to exorbitant membership costs.

The privately owned club was more of a spa than a gym, with services that included skin care, massage, hair and nails. It also boasted a full-service restaurant of organic and probiotic foods. Most patrons of Equilibrium were members by referral, making it by far one of Chicago's most exclusive gyms.

At other venues, a workout for Max was one part socializing and one part exercise. But today, he was in no mood to chat. After he parked, he grabbed his gym bag from the Range Rover's hatch and headed to the entrance. In years of frequenting the location, he had scarcely noticed the building across the street. But this day, it caught his eye and Max stared in utter disbelief.

Across from his gym was a large white brick building. The rectangular art deco structure was nearly a hundred years old, but its design still felt classic. The address on the wall, affixed in bold black numbers, was 7129. Max could hardly believe his eyes. Indigo had asked that he look for the number, and here it was in front of him.

Max wasn't sure how long he stood staring across the street. The building at 7129 was a yoga studio called the Golden Arch. In the dozens of visits he'd made to Equilibrium he had never noticed it. A large gold sculpture of a woman, bending over backwards, framed the entryway in the yogic bridge pose.

Just once, Max had participated in a yoga class at another gym where he belonged. He wasn't particularly thrilled by what he perceived to be simple stretching with a touchy-feely approach. Max took a step closer to the Golden Arch. 7129. What did the number mean? Was it a harbinger of doom or a good luck omen?

After a brief deliberation, Max stepped off the curb and traversed the street toward the large white building. The instant he stepped onto the sidewalk, a surge of calm washed over him like a giant wave that had crashed ashore. Max froze in his tracks, somehow unsettled by such an intense and sudden feeling of tranquility. Could it be he had misjudged the touchy-feely practice of balance and stretching? Had Indigo given him the number to practice yoga?

As he approached the large double glass doors, he hardly noticed a homeless man sitting propped against the building. The man had long hair and a kinky beard the color of sand. Or it could have been gray, Max wasn't sure which. Deep wrinkles creased his leathery skin, and the man's legs were wrapped in a filthy, red plaid blanket. For a moment, Max thought he even saw a large insect sprinting across the woolen coverlet.

Max cringed, not wanting to get too close to the vagabond. At first glance, he believed he was Caucasian, mostly because of the sandy beard. It was difficult to tell if his brown tinge was from pigment or filth. As he attempted to cross in front of the man, Max awaited the pandering requests he had grown so accustomed to hearing from street beggars — *Spare change? Can you help a guy out?* But there was silence.

Max finally locked his eyes on the man's face, which he had strategically avoided. His eyes were closed and his face was in a peaceful expression like a mask. His back was pressed firmly against the white wall. Beneath the blanket, his legs were crossed in lotus position. Now Max understood. The same wave of tranquility that had enveloped him had also captured this man. 7129, it appeared, was in effect.

Max removed his wallet and fished a twenty-dollar bill from inside. Gingerly, being careful not to touch anything, he leaned over and dropped the bill in a plastic fast food cup at the man's side. Had the man asked, Max probably would have given nothing, but there was something poetic about the scene.

The sense of calm Max felt was intoxicating. Part of him wanted to take a seat beside the man where he, too, could close his eyes and ponder the many things bouncing around in his head. Instead he crossed to the entrance of the Golden Arch. Max stared at a large poster attached to the window, a rendition of Leonardo Da Vinci's sketch of the Vitruvian Man. The large drawing illustrated the male nude form, arms and legs outstretched and neatly tucked inside of a perfect geometric circle.

Along the spinal pathway of this figure were a series of seven different colors, each illustrated as a rendition of light. The first, depicted in the groin area at the base of the spine, was a bright splash of red. Rising from there in sequential order were the colors orange, just above the groin; yellow in the belly; green beside the heart; blue below the Adam's apple at the throat; indigo between the eyebrows and finally purple at the crown.

Max immediately recognized the drawing as a portrayal of what he had seen in the Pyramid of the Moon. He had witnessed lights shining along the spines of every participant at his initiation. The brightest of them all had shone on the small baby that the woman placed on the altar. At the time, he hardly understood what he was seeing, but here it was depicted in the window of building 7129.

Near the bottom of the poster was the title, "Seven Power Centers of the Kundalini System." Whether he liked it or not, more puzzle pieces were falling into place. The obscure number Indigo had challenged him to find, it seemed, was already providing him with a modicum of stress relief. The calm he experienced upon approaching the building, however, was slowly beginning to ebb.

Max noticed a class schedule with five sessions for Kundalini yoga. One of them was just ending. He slipped in through the glass doors and made his way to the front desk.

A girl younger than Max, with freckles and curly red hair, smiled with toothy enthusiasm from behind the counter. "Good morning."

Max forced a smile. "Hi. I just noticed the Kundalini poster in the window."

"Uh-huh."

"I don't know much about yoga. I was just wondering —"

"You totally came to the right place," the girl interrupted. "Hatha is probably the most popular yoga method. It's all about stretching, balance, concentration, breathing..."

Max could not help but feel it was too early for such a bubbly disposition, especially since he still harbored the notion that his home and person had both been violated during the night. But the girl droned on nonetheless.

"The word 'Hatha' is actually a combination of the words 'Ha' and 'Tha.' Which means the sun and the moon because Hatha's all about opposites."

A look of disbelief washed over Max's face. "Excuse me? 'Ha' means the sun?"

The girl nodded. "And 'Tha' the moon. You totally got it." Full of smiles, she continued, "Hatha's all about purification of the mind and body, whereas Kundalini is more about breathing and finding the spiritual center."

Max found it ironic that Kundalini was all about breathing, particularly since the girl barely took a breath through her explanation.

"And there's always Bikram yoga, which we don't have here. Bikram's the same exact routine each time but the classes are conducted in a sauna-like environment so you're sweating out all those nasty toxins."

"The poster on the door talked about power centers."

"Oh, totally. Those are the chakras, these really cool energy centers along the spine. Through breathing, meditation, concentration, they're like totally energized. Are you artistic at all?"

Max hesitated. "Oh, I don't know."

"For an artist, Kundalini's like so exciting because the chakras are these really intense portals for channeling artistic inspiration. It's like totally manifesting your spiritual side in a physical way."

"Do you take these classes?"

The young girl's eyes looked as if they were about to burst from her head. "Oh my God, I totally took one this morning before I came on shift. You sure you don't want to sign up? The next Hatha's in fifteen and there's a Kundalini this afternoon."

It had been Max's intention to work out across the street and maybe to have a massage. But Indigo's number had derailed him. "Does Hatha really mean the sun and the moon?"

"Totally."

Max thought of the synchronicities he was continuing to find. Teotihuacán's Pyramids of the Sun and the Moon, the moon as an integral factor in determining the dates of Easter and Lent. Now, yoga somehow involved the sun and the moon.

"Why do you suppose it's called that?"

"It's all about the Ying and the Yang. You know that circular symbol that's half black and half white with a squiggly line through the center? We're all constantly searching for balance between masculine and feminine energies. One way to look at it is, the black is night and the white is day, therefore the sun and the moon."

The young woman made it all sound so simple in her hundred-mile-per-hour delivery.

"Maybe I will. Do a class I mean."

"You totally should. The next session's our community class so it's half price. It's like a total bargain at nine dollars."

Max hated to admit it, but the girl's enthusiasm was infectious. He pulled a ten-dollar note from his wallet and paid for the session. "Thanks for you help."

"It's so not a problem. You should be stoked, it's Arthur's class. You're so gonna love it. Just swing on down to Studio B and don't forget to remove your shoes."

The young girl smiled and winked as Max turned and proceeded down the hall to Studio B, where he would follow his first true class of Hatha yoga.

Arthur's community class was quite full, which made Max wonder if it was the instructor's popularity or the half-price session that drew the crowd. Working-class patrons were either on extended breaks or had simply stolen away to labor instead at releasing their tensions. Max slipped off his shoes and placed them in his bag before stowing it in the corner. He pulled a yoga mat from a large pile stacked against the wall.

Across the room, a huge window looked out on a large patio at the back of the building. Max marched to an open space, laid down his mat and waited.

When Arthur Pesendian entered, Max was surprised by his size. Barely over five and a half feet, Arthur was compact in stature and frame. His dark hair was stylishly cropped and combed toward the back to accentuate a pleasing face. He said hello to the class, then removed his shirt to reveal a lean and muscular body. The symbol for Aries was cleanly tattooed on his right arm.

While he was small, Arthur's voice was assertive and calming. He lit incense and put a new-age CD in the player before starting the session. Max expected nothing more than the simple stretching he had experienced months before at his gym, but Arthur's class was intensely more strenuous.

Within minutes, he was sweating and out of breath. Each new posture brought an increasing awareness of his body and the tightness or looseness of his muscles. To his amazement, he panted, struggling to breathe. Max thought of the ginger girl's explanation and found it to be spot on: *Breathing, balance, purification.*

By the end of the class Max was completely renewed. In many ways, he likened the feeling to that after a massage. Through the intricate postures and stretches of Hatha yoga, a great deal of tension had simply been pulled from his body. Once again, Indigo was right. On the day of his meeting with Demetrius, the number 7129 had served him well.

A moment later, he exited the building, dismayed to see the homeless man still seated against the wall. Earlier, the vagrant had appeared to be sleeping. Now, he was wide-eyed and alert with the red plaid blanket draped about his shoulders. The man turned and watched as Max let the door swing shut behind him. Having just left the class, Max was in a zone of strength and tranquility. It was a state he didn't wish to disturb through some unpleasant altercation.

Max took his first step toward the car when the vagrant stood. Max was stunned by his physique. While seated, the man appeared insignificant, as if life on the street had shriveled his body. Now on his feet, Max could see that he was quite virile. He was taller than Max's estimation and his frame was solid and strong like that of a football player. A stiff breeze tousled the soiled blanket that wafted around his neck like a cape.

Max caught the man's gaze and was mesmerized for a brief moment. Although unkempt, the stranger had eyes that were intense, hypnotic even. For a moment, Max felt naked, as if the man were peering into his soul. Something about him intimidated Max. Figuring that he might be a drug addict, he felt the need to cross the street, but the traffic prevented such a detour.

The down-on-his-luck gentleman tightened his stare on Max, his eyes glistening with strength and wisdom. Max poised himself to be panhandled or for some other form of verbal assault. Instead, the man clasped his hands together and bowed his head with gratitude. As he lifted his head, he delivered a single, melodic word: "Namasté."

The interaction wasn't at all what Max expected. "Excuse me."

"The gift you left earlier was very kind."

Max was surprised by the man's soft-spoken and agreeable voice. "I didn't realize you saw that." He was certain the bum had been asleep or drunk when he dropped the twenty-dollar note in his cup. Max remembered that an insect had even dashed across his blanket, but the man had barely stirred.

The panhandler didn't respond, but his expression of satisfaction eventually made Max smile.

"You have a good day," Max offered as he stepped into the street to cross toward his gym. He couldn't help but wonder about the homeless man's story. How did someone with such a commanding presence end up on the streets? He turned to see the homeless man returning to his spot against the wall. The man nodded as he carefully draped the red plaid blanket across his legs.

Max smiled back, then quickly checked the time. In just a few hours, he and his father would meet. In most cases, he would have doubled back home to shower and change. But the idea that his house had been intruded upon hadn't settled in his mind. With a change of clothes in his bag, he entered his gym. There, he would shower and change before making his way to Battenberg Industries for the long-awaited meeting with his father.

$\mathcal{M}$ax retrieved his Range Rover from the gym parking lot and quickly allowed his exchange with the homeless man to fade away. In the car, he scanned his phone for calls he'd missed or ignored over the last days. There were a few, including some from Brigitte, Ted and Chandler. Others had reached out, but Max, for the most part, was dodging them.

People still wanted to discuss photos from the gossip magazines and what had happened in Mexico City. In the grand scheme of events, he found the topic too trivial to rehash. Things were different now in ways that were impossible to deny.

Max definitely wanted to smooth things over with Brigitte and resume some sense of normalcy with his friends, if that was even possible. As a token of peace, he had phoned Brigitte to remind her about the meeting with Demetrius, explaining that he would see her soon thereafter. She seemed pleased, albeit without her normal enthusiasm. Max could feel that she was still a bit off kilter. But he also knew she wanted things back to normal, just as he did.

After speaking with her, he scrolled through other missed calls and hit send when Chandler's name popped up. His VP at Badem Publications answered after a few rings.

"And he raises his head. How're you, man?"

Max was happy to hear Chandler's voice. "Could say I've been better, but I shouldn't complain, right?"

"Let's see, your father's one of the wealthiest men on the planet, you live in one of Chicago's most amazing properties, you can have just about any man or woman you want. Yeah, you probably shouldn't say anything."

"Whatever, dude."

"I figured I'd see you in the office at least once or twice this week. What the hell've you been up to?"

"You have no idea, my friend, no idea..."

"Cryptic these days? We should powwow soon if you keep working from home. It's been a while since I've hobnobbed with the rich and famous."

"Whatevs, dude. I have to meet my father and then I have to holler at Brigitte. If I don't get too tied up, maybe we can do something later on."

"Sounds good. Give me a call."

Max hung up feeling lighter. The reality he knew was changing so rapidly that he was more than happy to experience any vestiges of his old self that were trying to resurface. Maybe there was some way to reconnect with the life he used to have.

With only minutes to spare, he rushed to his father's offices at the Spire. Tension crawled up and down his neck and shoulders as he strolled into reception to announce himself. Even as a Battenberg, he didn't have complete access to his father's penthouse. Very few people did. As aggressive as Max's security was at his condo, Demetrius' penthouse was like a veritable Fort Knox. Access codes were not enough to ascend into the Battenberg lair.

The doorman kindly greeted Max before checking the log to see that he was expected. He then escorted Max into Demetrius' private elevator tower. The doorman inserted a key to switch the elevator on. Max keyed his personal code into the keypad, which allowed him to ride in the elevator alone. Not everyone had this privilege. The doors closed and the elevator moved upward with such force that Max's stomach dropped.

For an average elevator, a hundred-floor journey would have lasted minutes. This was unacceptable to Demetrius. Time was money, and his time was too valuable to be wasted in an elevator. Just as Max became accustomed to the elevator's speed, the doors were opening on the ninety-ninth floor. He exited and was greeted by yet another receptionist with a shaved head and a football player's build. He looked more like a bouncer than someone who answered phones.

All of Demetrius' receptionists doubled as bodyguards, as such security was essential for a man of Demetrius' worth. This was the reason he had very few women working at the penthouse. When women were employed, they were versed in more than a few of the deadly arts.

The muscular receptionist smiled. "Hello, Mr. Battenberg. I see you're right on time."

"Yes. In the extremely unlikely event that my dad can meet on time."

"You're almost in luck. He is here. I'm afraid he's in a meeting, though. You're welcome to wait in the areas you have access to."

"Thank you, I'll do that."

Max strolled to the lounge where guests typically awaited his father. This section of the penthouse felt very much like a modern office. Floor-to-ceiling windows spanned the suite overlooking a spectacular view of Chicago and Lake Michigan. A scattering of clouds cast shadows across the expansive water, creating the pattern of what could be a giant leopardskin. Furnishings in the lounge were modern with many well-crafted pieces of light-colored wood and glass.

Max approached a set of double doors with a keypad to the right of them. He entered his access code, and the doors unlocked with a snapping sound. Max pushed through and entered a very different part of the penthouse. Here, the high-tech windows contained a chemical within them. At the flip of a switch, they could darken and nearly block out the sun. They weren't currently at their darkest setting, but the mood in this section of the suite was softer and less office-like.

On the wall opposite the window, there was a huge glowing aquarium full of exotic fish and an octopus. Once again, some of the most expensive, high-end furniture decorated the room. After watching the fish a while, Max plopped down on one of the couches. He opened a compartment in the arm of the sofa to reveal a control panel hidden inside. Max pushed a few buttons and a large flat screen television descended from the ceiling. Another button darkened the windows to minimize the glare. Max surfed the stations while he waited.

An hour after their scheduled appointment, Demetrius entered to find Max asleep on the couch. He gently nudged his son. When Max opened his eyes, Demetrius' expression was questioning. "So, how was it?"

Max shook himself awake and immediately felt blood rushing to his face. The reaction could easily have been mistaken for blushing but it was the blood of anger and disappointment filling his cheeks. He was certain Demetrius knew exactly what he'd been through. After making him wait for days, he was now treating it all like some kind of joke. "Let's just say I have a lot of questions."

"Come, we mustn't talk here." Demetrius led Max through a

circuitous maze of corridors and doorways. For Demetrius, the security measures were effortless, since a tiny access chip was implanted somewhere on his body. As such, it was unnecessary for him to key in the codes required to circulate through the building.

Finally, they arrived in a plush lounge, and Max knew precisely why his father had chosen it. The area, which was a part of Battenberg Industries' Research and Development Division, provided the utmost privacy with cutting edge technology that could jam intelligence devices of any kind. In essence, the room was impenetrable to even the most sophisticated spy.

Demetrius gestured for Max to sit on the couch and took a seat beside him. "Welcome. How does it feel being a fully initiated member of the Battenberg clan?"

Max smiled politely, but he felt Demetrius was making light of something monumental. "I assume you know what I went through down there."

"Of course. All of us who are over twenty-five have gone through the same thing."

Max ran a hand through his hair. "Okay. Let me see, where do I start? The more I think about all this, the crazier it seems. But let's go out on a limb and say any of it's believable. Why have you kept it secret all this time?"

Demetrius was stone-faced. "I'm afraid this is not at my discretion, Max, nor will it be at yours. Even if it had been, I would've done it exactly the same way. The rules of initiation and disclosure were put in place long before us. Many millennia before, in fact."

Max stammered, searching for the right words. "Dad, you sent me to a frickin' pyramid down in Mexico." He took a deep breath, contemplating the conversation. "To discover that I'm, that we're some kind of — "

"Go ahead. Say it. Try it on for size. See how it fits. We, and every Battenberg before us, hail from a tremendously powerful bloodline."

"Aliens, dad? Anunnaki? I'm not sure how *you* reacted, but it's a hell of a lot to swallow."

"Of course, Max. But I knew it would make sense to you. Where do you think your fascination for pyramids comes from?"

Max spit out a laugh. "I can't believe you're making light of this. Didn't you think I'd want to talk about this before now? Like, I don't know, maybe three days ago."

Without a reply, Demetrius crossed to the control panel in his couch. He pressed a button and the darkened windows reverted to near perfect clarity, allowing the sun to blaze into the room. "We are blue bloods, Max. From where do you think this term derives? Our bloodline, the ancestral lineage, traces back to the birth of human civilization. Why exactly? Because it is us who created it. That missing link, Max, is us."

Incredulous, Max stared through the wall of windows. If there were any doubts lingering in his mind, Demetrius was quickly disposing of them.

"Think about it. The answers have been right in front of you all along. Hidden in mythology, embedded in the Bible."

Max dropped his head. "Were you at the initiation? Was that you in the eagle mask?"

"Attendance at the meetings is delicate knowledge. When you're entrusted, that's when the network will become apparent." Demetrius crossed to the glass wall to gaze across the city. "If you haven't already, study the mythologies of Sumer." He turned away from the window to face Max. "That's where this all began. Sumer. Babylonia. Or, as it's known today, Iraq. The idea that oil is what makes that region a hot spot, well, that's just laughable."

Max approached his dad at the window and was overcome by a strange and unexpected feeling. He and his father now shared a secret of enormous magnitude. For years, he had desired a firm bond between them. Now, in some strange way, he had it. Together, the Battenbergs, father and son, gazed out across Chicago as if looking down from another planet. On the ground below, traffic circulated like ants in an ant farm. From this altitude, everything appeared miniaturized, like a child's toys.

When Max spoke, his voice was kinder, stripped of the angry edge. "You mentioned a network. How many of us are there?"

"What they say is true. The best estimates have us at roughly one percent. But people like you and I, Max, our number is about three hundred. Total."

In spite of himself, Max took a deep breath. The conversation was entirely surreal. "And what are we supposed to call ourselves? The Anunnaki."

Demetrius laughed. "Let's just stick with Battenberg for now."

"Why wait till I am almost twenty-five? How come you didn't tell me this before?"

"Because children cannot be expected to guard such a sacred vow. Consider a ten-year-old in that ceremony. Even fifteen. Twenty-five is the earliest and safest age to assimilate this kind of information." Demetrius continued, reciting what he knew as if by rote. "Before modern man even walked the planet, it is our bloodline that possessed its resources. Even when those resources have been modern man himself. For eons, the dynamic was known and accepted. Until the uprisings, that is. Revolts by the masses. Workers struggling for some fleeting equality." When Demetrius spoke his voice was tinged with contempt. "First in France, then in the rest of Europe. It's taken centuries, but other parts of the world have followed."

Max tried to speak, but Demetrius cut him off.

"These days, we require both stealth and secrecy to protect our interests. Centuries ago, a fine-tuned system was developed. Most are hardly aware of its existence. The system has many names. One of them we call democracy, where the masses believe they're making decisions..."

Max felt dizzy. He might as well have been back in the Pyramid of the Moon listening to a strange foreign tongue. Demetrius was forthright, but none of what he said fully registered.

"So, the stories about my great-grandfather emigrating, creating a fortune... none of that is true."

"Maximilian. Hard work does not a blue blood make. Each day I fight to maintain our station, as you will do." Demetrius' eyes glossed over with a weariness Max had never seen before. "To occupy the seat of a Battenberg is to juggle anything and everyone around you. We must always jockey for position. Both your mother and brother fell casualty to this."

What? Max turned to face his father, seeing an even larger crack of vulnerability in Demetrius' steely veneer. "What are you talking about?"

"Think about it, Max. Why do I invest so much in security? Not only here at the Spire, but for you as well. At any given moment we are in danger, not just from the masses who envy our station, but from others like ourselves."

Max stared at his father, incredulous. In many ways, Demetrius' words felt like a punch to the gut. His entire life, Max had been led to believe his mother died in a car accident. Now, Demetrius was indicating something different, that his mother and brother had been casualties of some attempt at usurping Battenberg power.

"So, you're saying the accident..."

Demetrius shook his head. "I'm saying there was no such thing. The biggest threat we suffer is from others like us. Others with a different school of thought about resources and their division."

"Jeez." Max felt a sudden urge to cry. *But I won't. I won't.*

"There have always been and will forever be power plays, which is why people like you and me can never be complacent."

Max was reeling. Stunned, he returned to the couch and sat. "So, Mom and Christian were murdered." His voice choked with emotion.

"There was no accident, Max. There were things I did that made powerful people very unhappy. Your mother and brother were their way of sending a message. So many times I warned her, but she just refused to be boxed in." Demetrius stared at his son. "Probably, that's where you get it from."

For days, Max had hoped Demetrius would illuminate the mystery of so many things he found confounding. Never in his wildest dreams did he expect one of the puzzle pieces to be the assassinations of his mother and brother. Max felt blood rushing to his cheeks and didn't know if it was rage, confusion or both. "Is there anything real that I know?"

"I wanted to share these things, but it is strictly forbidden before initiation. You have no idea how arduous it was to reset the date of yours. And it's only because of what happened to your mother and brother that it was even allowed."

An avalanche of emotion swept over Max as the true cause of his mother and brother's deaths sunk in. He choked it back, struggling to reveal only strength and fortitude in front of his father. Max didn't want to allow him the satisfaction of seeing him vulnerable.

"Is there anything else you want to tell me?"

"Our family has grown very powerful, Max. There are more than a few who aren't pleased about this. But I couldn't bring you into the fold until you were initiated. At any given moment, we could be targets. This is partly why Hades is in effect. I needed you to know this."

She said this. Indigo said this... So many are the Anunnaki oppressors that you must be wary even in your own home. Max ran a hand through his hair. "Anything else?"

"I can answer questions if you have them. But to tell you everything," Demetrius' voice was tinged with concern, "it might be upsetting."

"Do you remember anything about a journal Mom had? I was talking to Cora and she said Mom misplaced one around the time of the accident."

Demetrius shook his head. His interest seemed roused, but he was also perplexed. "I knew your mom kept journals, but I wasn't aware that she lost one."

"Where did she keep them? I'd like to see one."

Demetrius hesitated. "To be honest, I don't know. Perhaps Cora or another one of the staff will have a better idea."

"Okay." Max pondered what he'd heard so far and recognized that his father was probably correct about him hearing too much. He was already overloaded with difficult to digest information. "I suppose I should make an appointment if we're going to talk later?"

With a smile, Demetrius placed a comforting hand on his son's shoulder. "Of course. You should call the minute you're ready."

Max stood and smiled at his father. Deep down he felt an instinct to flee. If only he could escape to the simplicity of believing he was the normal son of a normal man who happened to be a billionaire. "All right, I'll call you then. As soon as I can wrap my head around this."

Demetrius escorted Max into the hall, where he entered an access code for Max's departure. "Through those doors, there's an elevator. It'll take you to the lobby."

There was an urge in Max to embrace Demetrius, but such a move was not the Battenberg way. Instead he forced a smile and passed through the doors. Upon entering the elevator, an intense sadness arose in Max's heart. He pondered this melancholy rising within and wondered if it was simply his innocence lost or the mourning of his murdered mother and brother, or both. With a fleeting glance back at his father, the doors slid shut. As the elevator plummeted downward, it further intensified the sinking feeling Max already had in his stomach.

CHAPTER 38

*D*emetrius' private elevator was the fastest in the building, but it still wasn't fast enough to preclude a panic attack. As each floor whizzed by, Max could feel his lungs seizing up, making it difficult to breathe. The sensation harkened back to the Money Pit expedition when he was drowning beneath the platform of oak logs.

The spacious elevator seemed to be closing in like a fisherman's net woven from threads of claustrophobia. Now in panic mode, he punched the ground floor button repeatedly with his fist. Just when he thought he would pass out, the doors slid open. Max sucked in air, sprinted across the lobby and pushed out into the street through the large glass revolving door.

Fresh atmosphere smacked his face and Max found he could breathe again. He inhaled deeply, gulping at it, completely unaware of the passersby that watched with intrigue and concern. He turned his head to stare skyward, but was unable to see the top of the Spire as it vanished into the clouds.

Demetrius had spoken of rules and tradition, but betrayal is all Max felt. His world, or what he had been told was his world, had forever been shattered. Their position, their origins and the deaths of his mother and brother had all been lies. Despite his father's explanation, Max didn't comprehend why he had been left in the dark for so long.

A part of him wanted to pretend it was all a dream, that he'd never met Indigo or entered Teotihuacán's Pyramid of the Moon. But time was passing and nothing had undone those realities. Each day, it seemed, a new puzzle piece snapped firmly into place and, bit by bit, a new world was materializing before Max's very eyes.

Now he had an understanding of what it truly meant to be a Battenberg. The level of privilege went above and beyond anything he had ever imagined. The Battenbergs had descended not from Austrian royalty but, rather, from an alien race. Nibiru and the Anunnaki were names he had been given at first by a psychic, but now his father had confirmed the same thing.

Max looked around, now aware of people circulating about him. There were men and women rushing to and from work and young kids getting off from school or playing hooky from it. He watched their faces while continuing to catch his breath. As a Battenberg, he already felt separate and apart from the general population. Now, he seemed to understand the true meaning of "alien."

Somehow, it seemed the idea of another planet should be racy and exciting. But Max didn't want to belong to something that endangered his family, especially if that entity had caused the deaths of his mother and brother.

He didn't know how long he stood in front of the Spire, but finally, he re-entered the building to retrieve his car. He had promised Brigitte he would stop by after the meeting with his father. In an unexpected way, he wanted more than ever to see her. He needed an anchor, someone who would keep him stable and grounded. Max realized this would only happen through Brigitte and his friends.

His shiny, black Range Rover roared from the Spire's parking structure as he maneuvered into traffic. Typically, he would have put on satellite radio or his iPod, but this day, he drove in soothing silence.

Twenty minutes later, he pulled into Brigitte's driveway and was greeted by a sparkling Audi SUV. Max slammed on his brakes and skirted to a stop to avoid hitting it. He studied the vehicle but was unable to recognize to whom it might belong. He reversed into a spot on the street and walked up the drive to Brigitte's door.

She and her older brother, Bertrand, were talking on the front stoop. Max immediately noticed that Brigitte was distressed. Even Bertrand seemed out of sorts. When they noticed him heading up the drive, they both stiffened, adjusting their posture. While there were smiles and hellos, Max knew it wasn't a warm welcome. There was something terribly wrong, and Max could tell his already bizarre day was about to take yet another turn.

"Hey, guys." He tried to appear casual.

Bertrand spoke first. "Max, how the hell are ya?"

"I was wondering whose car that was in the drive. How are you, man? Long time no see."

"Been traveling a lot. Technically, Chicago's home base, but I'm never here."

Max climbed the five-step staircase and offered Brigitte a kiss on the lips. "Hey, babe, how are you?"

Brigitte looked down at first and half smiled. Max knew when she was forcing the appearance of levity and ease. She finally lifted her gaze. "We need to talk."

He figured she might be stressed about his behavior of late, but she had provided him space over the last days. He hoped it was because she understood what he needed.

After an awkward silence, Bertrand chimed in, "I gotta use the restroom." He glanced his sister's way. "I'll be inside if you need me." Bertrand turned and disappeared inside.

Max knew he had been distant but not to an extent that would merit the icy reception he was receiving. He fixed Brigitte in his sights. "What's going on, babe?"

Tears welled in her eyes. "Yesterday, I was officially late." Brigitte stared again at the ground before lifting her gaze to face Max. "Two weeks late. After I talked to you this morning—" By now, her lower lip was quivering. Brigitte produced a pregnancy test, handing over the small, white baton as if she were in a relay race. "Max, I'm pregnant."

A feeling of utter disbelief washed over Max. He stared at the plus sign before turning to look over the railing. "Jeez. That's not even close to what I was expecting."

"I'm guessing it was Mardi Gras. We were all drinking and I forgot to take a pill. But I never thought..."

Max took a deep breath, once again trying to digest information that was entirely unanticipated. He thought of the recent catalog of astonishing things that were happening. The relaxed feeling from earlier at the yoga studio that he had been trying to reinstill was now completely obliterated.

Brigitte's normally smooth brow was wrinkled with concern. She stared long and hard at Max before continuing, "This is why I've been stressed these last days. We've barely spoken since Mexico. And when we do, you hardly say anything. I don't know if it's because of your initiation thing... or maybe you really met someone down there, I don't know."

Max grabbed Brigitte in his arms and gave her a big hug. "Will you stop it? I didn't meet anyone. I know that, lately, I've been in my own world." With a deep exhale, he took a step back and continued, "What do you think you want to do?"

Brigitte avoided his stare, unsure of her answer. "I don't know."

"Should we have a child right now?" Max tensed as he looked out toward the street, not wanting to hurt her any more, but worried about himself. *Not in the middle of all this shit.* "Either way, we both know it'd be well looked after. That's not the problem."

Brigitte forced a smile. "Max, the two of us come from families... We can't bring babies into the world like this. And no, this isn't some ploy to trap you. I know you have to think about that."

"Don't be silly. I mean, obviously, there's no quick answer. But I need to know what you're thinking. If it's marriage? Abortion?"

"If we have a baby, don't you think we should marry? And we're gonna have to do it fast if we do."

"Okay," Max searched for other words, but none came.

A chuckle rattled in Brigitte's throat, but it was one of irony and sarcasm. "Okay what, Max? We should keep it and get married okay. Or we should get rid of it okay. I need to know what you think."

"I don't have an answer right now, Brigitte. I've known about this less than five minutes. What is it you want me to say?"

"Try anything, Max. Something. Are you happy? Shocked? Upset? Cause I'm pretty much all of those things."

The greater part of Max's brain was still struggling to process the information from his meeting with Demetrius. *They killed my mom. My brother.* His plate was already full and Brigitte had announced that a baby was on the way. "This is all shit," he muttered without thinking.

The words stabbed at Brigitte like a knife. "Fuck, Max, so much for making a girl feel secure."

Max looked at Brigitte, immediately aware that she had misunderstood his words. "That's not what I meant. I know I'm distracted, but it's not because of you. There's just a lot of shit going on right now and most of it I can't even talk about."

What were supposed to be words of comfort filled Brigitte with an overwhelming sense of incredulity. "I shouldn't have asked you to come over." She crossed to her front door. "I figured it was too soon for you to deal with this."

"Is this a good time to find out you're pregnant? No. Is it insurmountable? Of course not. Individually we have more than enough resources and you know that."

"Can we just talk about this later? Maybe when you've had a

little more time to think." Brigitte softened as she opened her front door. "What about tonight? Are we still on for Marilyn's party?"

Max faltered, in disbelief at Brigitte's request. "You still want to go to that?" He didn't feel at all like attending a party and was perplexed by Brigitte's desire to do so. "I think we both need time to think and digest this."

Brigitte closed her eyes, contemplating Max's response, but then she came alive. "I don't want us behaving like this is the end of the world, it doesn't have to be." It was clear Brigitte was trying to convince herself more than Max. "I still want to go, it's Marilyn's twenty-fifth. If you don't want to..." Brigitte stammered, lost in her own frustration and disappointment.

"All right." With so many things on his mind, Max had no desire to dispute the request. A distraction was well in order for both of them. "Then I guess we're going."

Brigitte came away from the door and leaned in to gently kiss Max. He kissed her back and for a brief moment there was heat between them.

"I'll pick you up tonight, okay?"

Without a word goodbye, she smiled, then turned and strolled back into the house.

Max sighed. He had heard many predictions in the last month, but a baby, his own baby, hadn't been one of them. He skipped down Brigitte's steps into the driveway. Within seconds, Bertrand called out.

"Max, wait up."

He turned and saw Brigitte's brother descending from the porch. There was a smile on his face but his approach was somehow aggressive.

"She's pretty upset, guy."

"Understandably so, Bert. We didn't exactly plan this. At least I don't think we did." Max didn't intend the comment to sound so snarky, but it came out that way nonetheless.

Bertrand started to respond, but caught himself before answering with an equally abrasive reply. "She's a good girl, Max. You know that. I just hope you'll do right by her."

"Absolutely. I'd never do otherwise." But Max knew this wasn't necessarily true.

"It's pretty clear you're a good guy. And someone like you doesn't have to be, not when you can have your pick of girls. But I don't want to see my sister hurt either."

Max listened as Bertrand continued desperately trying to defend his sister's integrity. Bertrand rarely interfered in Brigitte's life, but given the circumstances, he clearly thought an intervention was necessary.

In an effort to mask his irritation, Max forced a smile. "We just need time, Bertrand. You've known about this longer than I have, so excuse me if I haven't figured it out yet. Bridge and I will make it work."

"I hope you're right cause this is big, dude. A baby's no joke."

After a series of forced pleasantries, Max and Bertrand shook hands.

"Tell her I'll call her later." Max continued down the driveway past Bertrand's SUV. Relief overcame him as he pulled away, essentially fleeing in his own vehicle.

Pregnant. Max had always left the responsibility of birth control to his girlfriends, and things were no different with Brigitte. He pondered how in just two months his life had drastically transitioned into the realm of the clandestine and utterly complicated.

In many ways, a child could bring Max and Brigitte closer together. But he had been initiated. There was a huge portion of his life that he would continually need to lie about. The more he processed the new developments, the more he understood exactly why waiting until twenty-five had been important.

On some karmic level, Max knew he was on a roller coaster that was still in motion. These things happening, he felt, were the beginning of something much larger. To his growing dismay, the insight was accompanied by a deep and foreboding sense of dread.

$\mathcal{M}$ax arrived home with a simple desire to retreat and lock himself away forever. He desperately needed things to stop or at least to slow down. He thought of Demetrius' suggestion—something concrete that he could do: "Study the mythologies of Sumer." Settling in the upstairs den, he switched on the large flat screen that doubled as a computer monitor. After activating the web, he spoke aloud into a voice-activated microphone system.

"Search Sumerian mythology."

He stared at the top thirty hits on screen. They were only the start of over two hundred thousand possibilities. Max spoke again. "Page down." The screen shifted down a page. He browsed through several screens on Sumerian deities and cosmology.

"Search Anunnaki." Max continued browsing, amazed by the amount of detail he was finding on a topic that was supposedly secret. On website after website, he read stories that most people considered pure fantasy. Some sites described the Anunnaki as reptilian and depicted them as lizard-like and humanoid. Others categorized them as "shape-shifters" who were capable of camouflaging their reptilian appearance so as to appear human. At first Max smirked at the concept until he realized, *What if it's true?*

As he continued to surf through the mountain of information, Max also found a half dozen sites delving into the philosophies of the Anunnaki. A few words that repeated across multiple sites were "heartless," "tyrannical" and "sociopaths."

Max considered the descriptions Indigo had used during Mardi Gras. While more than a few of the sites were nonsense, he took note of the fact that much of what he read appeared to be true. At some point, the world had known of the Anunnaki's existence, but now, only a select few, those who had been initiated, remembered a truth that over the years had slowly transformed into myth.

According to Sumerian text, the Anunnaki in translation meant, "the heavens from which they came."

Max thought of the strange machine in the Pyramid of the Moon. It was used to vaporize the gold bullion given to him by Demetrius.

He continued to read, fascinated by the details in support of things he scarcely wanted to believe about his initiation. *Enki and Enlil.*

Max considered the experience at Teotihuacán and the visions he had after drinking the strange elixir. Somehow, he had been shown a portion of the story. With Indigo's help, the Antikythera Device had provided another puzzle piece. It was true the bizarre language he spoke must have been the Anunnaki tongue.

For more than an hour, he read through a half dozen sites. Then he stumbled onto the "Lost Book of Enki" by Zecharia Sitchin. The author's name had already appeared several times during his searches.

Sitchin, who was considered one of the world's foremost experts on Sumerian cuneiform, had supposedly deciphered Enki's story on a set of ancient clay tablets. Upon translating them, he had essentially uncovered the Bible's story of Genesis. The only difference lay in the tablets' proposition that it was the Anunnaki who created modern man. *What?*

Incredulous, Max pulled up an online Bible to compare to what he had been reading in the Lost Book of Enki. It was all there in the New Jerusalem Bible. Max read Genesis 1:26: *"and God said, 'let us make man in our own image, in the likeness of ourselves: and let them be masters of the fish of the sea, the birds of heaven, the cattle, all the wild animals and all the creatures that creep along the ground.'"*

Why had plurals been used? *Let us make man in our own image.* In other passages of the Bible, God was more often referred to in the third person singular. He scanned other sections and easily drew parallels to the stories of Sumerian mythology.

He read Genesis 2:15: *"Yahweh God took the man, and settled him in the Garden of Eden to cultivate and take care of it."* In deep thought, Max looked away from the screen and spoke the words aloud, "To cultivate and take care of it. That means to work."

Not wanting to rely on online content, he ran to a bookshelf in his hallway. He found an old Bible that had been in the family for years. As he flipped through it, he confirmed all he had read online. "It's all here." In a state of shock he read further, *"Genesis 6:2: the sons of God, looking at the women, saw how beautiful they were and married as many of them as they chose."*

As a young boy, Max had read this passage, but he had never paid attention to the "sons of God" portion of the text. There it was, stated in black and white on the page. It was the sons of the Anunnaki who had taken human women as wives.

Max slammed the book shut and returned it to his shelf. He felt foolish for blaming Demetrius about secrecy when everything he had ever needed to know was inside a book right in his own house. In fact, anyone could discover the story with just a few clicks on the internet.

A part of Max yearned to run into the streets, yelling the truth to anyone who'd listen. Instead he returned to his den and settled on the couch, pondering the blissful ignorance of the general population to which he had so recently belonged. He contemplated his mother's murder and questioned if Demetrius had made the perpetrators pay. He intended to ask the next time they spoke.

For years, he had envisioned the official story of his mother's demise. In his mind's eye, her small Peugeot had slid off an embankment and rolled down a hill, killing everyone inside. That imagined scene was now more violent as he visualized a large vehicle forcing her and his brother off the road. Max quickly dismissed the imagery from his head, hoping at some point that he would find a new way to navigate in the world emerging around him.

Max returned his sights to the large monitor with all of his internet searches upon it. He was aware that his house was outfitted with the most state-of-the-art equipment from alarms to media systems. At the same time, he understood that surfing the web was inferior to the ancient technology he had sitting on the shelf of his panic room. He could read about things, as he was doing, or he could watch the very same events as if they were unfolding before him.

Max went to his closet, keyed in the access code for his panic room and quickly brought down the box containing the Anti-k Device. A chill ran up his spine as he considered the woman and midget. Was it a strange recurring dream or had they truly infiltrated his security measures? Max realized he couldn't take anything for granted.

He removed the leather cover and pulled the device from the Plexiglas box. If his memory served correctly, the woman in his dream had activated it in his closet. He swept his sweaters to the floor and placed the mechanism on the table. Indigo had shown him how to operate the device, but he needed to remember the steps in order.

He opened a cabinet full of drawers and found several packages of brand new dress shirts. He ripped one open and removed a stickpin that was used to fasten down the collar. Max retrieved a lighter from a drawer and ran the stickpin back and forth over the flame to sanitize it. Satisfied, he nicked his index finger to draw blood. Just as Indigo had shown him, he placed a drop of it in the receptacle of the dial.

Max remembered her entering the day and year of his birth, but he couldn't exactly recollect how she had triggered the device. He studied each button and knob, trying to recall exactly what she had done. He began to lose hope until it came to him: memories of the strange dream-like episode with the woman and the midget.

While his body may have been paralyzed, Max recalled everything he had seen almost as if the woman had intended it. Indigo insisted he have one clear question, but there was so much he wanted to know. He needed answers about the Anunnaki and his true lineage. He also wanted to know the truth of what had happened to his mother and brother. And there were the bizarre dreams. *There's so much.*

Max took a breath and made a decision on where to place his focus. Resolute, he reached across and pressed down upon the dial as Indigo had done just a day before. The machine came to life as it had in New Orleans. Max watched in wondrous amazement as items in his closet drifted from their resting places, floating into the air. In a flash of light the room transformed, everything in it represented as infinite points of light. The room began to spin much as it did the first time, lights blurring together in a kaleidoscope of utter disorientation. An instant later, an explosion of colors obliterated his senses.

$\mathcal{V}$ery simply, Enki adored his assignment. He had happily left Nibiru, and for centuries, the Earth operation had been his. With the enormous distance between Earth and Nibiru, he had enjoyed freedom and independence. It was only in recent years that complaints had been leveled against him. The gold shipments were too few and infrequent, and Nibiru's desperate need to heal its environment had grown only more calamitous. Of course Enki had complete awareness of the delicate situation, but the urgency, because he was on Earth, felt considerably less apparent.

To date, he had operated in complete autonomy, but the Igigi laborers had grown weary of work that was backbreaking at best. At first, they had been instructed to obtain gold at all costs, but soon thereafter Enki had commissioned a palace, two pyramids, nine obelisks and four sphinxes. There was no doubt the gold operation had suffered.

In essence, Enki had fallen short at the most important tasks for which he had been dispatched. While the circumstance was grave, it wasn't without cause. In a relatively short period of time, he had transformed the landscape. The lavish complex, while far away, was a small but precious slice of Nibiru. Enki had wasted no time in choosing its name—Eridu.

Because of the low quantity of Igigi on Earth, rest and relaxation was a rare commodity. The work force toiled long hours year after year with virtually no rotation of workers to replenish it. To quell a growing mutiny, Enki had requested that Anu send as many new Igigi as possible from Nibiru.

Each morning at dawn, he crossed onto the royal veranda of Eridu's palace. His pet project, built entirely of sandstone, was three levels high and built in the shape of a horseshoe. The enormous structure was masculine in design with hard edges and right angles. While it may have been only three stories high, each level had 20-foot ceilings, which made the palace appear gargantuan.

On the outside, artisans had been commissioned to beautify the structure. From high above, the complex looked like a simple rectangle with one of its shorter sides removed. Up close, Eridu was a work of art with intricate designs and pictographs carved into the stone. Its exterior walls were embossed with hieroglyphs and elaborate geometric designs — circles, squiggles and lines.

Beautifully manicured gardens decorated the center courtyard. Eridu's inner sanctum was enclosed by an enormous protective gate that sealed shut the open portion of the horseshoe. A series of symmetrically placed rectangular fountains separated the grounds at the front and rear of the palace. Gargantuan statues, each with Enki's face, were placed throughout the grounds like sentinels.

Contingent upon where he sat on the terrace, Enki could observe either the front or inner courtyard of the mammoth construction. Every morning, he chose a spot from which he could oversee the current ranks of Igigi.

The workers believed he made his presence known to ensure an early start to the mining operation. In reality, Enki loved the sun's warm rays, which he found most beneficial at dawn's early light. Nibiru spent the majority of its thirty-six-hundred-year elliptical orbit out of the sun's reach. Even though Enki had passed much time on Earth, he still found particular beauty in the rising and setting of the sun.

The local star had only recently cleared the horizon and already Enki's skin felt warm. His time on Earth had transformed his complexion from what it had been on Nibiru, and it now glowed a golden brown from repeated mornings on the terrace.

Suddenly, the hair on his arms and neck stood on end. Only a few things could cause this, and Enki already knew which one it was. He jumped to his feet and gazed skyward, shielding his eyes from the sun. The shadow of a huge transport ship darted across the landscape, swiftly approaching the palace.

Because it was one of Nibiru's largest ships, Enki marveled that some relief had finally arrived for his workforce. Long ago, a runway had been fashioned leading straight to the palace gardens. Enki watched as the transport silently drifted down the strip, landing almost at the foot of the palace gate. He rushed from the veranda into the building, skipping down the nearest stairwell into the gardens to welcome the new arrivals.

Upon exiting into the courtyard, Enki traveled down a gravel path until he was at the gate. He gazed at the ship but froze when he saw, standing at the entrance to the fuselage, a face he could barely stand to lay eyes upon. His brother, Enlil, had just exited the craft. Behind him, the new crew of Igigi was following.

Enlil turned and made eye contact with his half brother, but only for a moment. He and the others were too busy staring at the magnificent complex that was Eridu.

Enki burst with pride as he watched the new arrivals taking it all in. For the first time in years, there would be others of superior status who could bear witness to the luxuries he had built.

He gestured toward the guards that they open the gates. As they swung wide, Enlil entered and stared about the grounds. The younger of the brothers had been patient for centuries. Deep down, he and Enki both knew this day would come. Back on Nibiru, on the day of his departure, Enki had piloted his ship over Enlil and his mother, Ki. The ship's propulsion had left their hair standing on end with prickly electricity. Today, Enlil had returned the favor.

Enki crossed to head Enlil off at the palace gate, his neck muscles already tightening with tension. "Why are you here? No one informed me you were coming."

Enlil smiled, gesturing all about the Nibirian compound. "Seems it is you who have forgotten why you're here."

"Your assistance is not required, nor is your presence desired. I must insist on an explanation. Why are you here?"

Enlil smiled with an arrogance that made Enki wish to strike him.

"Well, brother. Had you insisted on larger deliveries of the ore, perhaps I wouldn't be here." Enlil circled back toward the gate to get a better view of Eridu. "Impressive. It would seem the bulk of your efforts have been in the pursuit of comfort, while those of us on Nibiru choke on our failing atmosphere."

"There is no purpose for you here. I will speak with father at once. Trust, when this transport leaves, you will be on it."

Enlil spit out a hearty laugh, making it clear he had other plans. When he spoke, his words were punctuated with venom. "I wouldn't count on that. Your farce of a role as leader here is finished." Enlil gestured at the sphinxes and obelisks of Eridu. "I see quite clearly why our gold is behind schedule. If one of us returns to Nibiru, I guarantee it will be you. I am delighted, however, that you have created such a palace. It will serve me well. I give you my word I will enjoy it."

From the very beginning, circumstances had spelled doom for a relationship of any kind between the brothers. Each felt he was better than the other, and Anu had never made the appropriate distinction for either to know his place. Enki knew this dynamic would never improve, which is why he had requested Earth in the first place. But Enlil had pursued, following him off planet, and he would continue to do so until one of them was dead.

Enlil stared at his silent brother, brimming with contempt. "You know this to be true, which is why you hold your tongue. If you wish to speak with father, why not ask him now?"

Enki's face dropped at his half-brother's suggestion. For more than a few decades he had listened to communications from Nibiru with complaints about the gold. But there were criticisms from every angle both on Nibiru and on Earth. Year after year, the Igigi threatened mutiny due to their poor working conditions.

Enki had purposely hidden failing aspects of his mining operation, fearing the appearance of weakness in his command. It was true the deliveries of gold had been smaller and less frequent. But most Nibirians hardly realized that if he pushed harder, there would be no shipments at all. The Igigi were certain to go on strike.

Enki looked at the smirk on his brother's face, wanting desperately to wipe it off with his fist. As children, they had often battled, and Enki always finished on the winning end of any scuffle. Enki knew that even today, he would destroy his brother in a physical altercation, but the timing wasn't right.

Enki's mind raced as he thought of a plan. One way or another, he would punish Enlil. Soon, Ki's first born would wish he had never come to Earth.

Enlil tried but was unable to stifle his grin. He couldn't have devised a better plan. From the moment he exited the transport, he had Enki's full attention. As expected, Enki had taken a position of authority, but Enlil had artfully put him in his place. The moment he proposed a conversation with their father, Enki had fallen silent.

Enki's heart was pounding. He held no delusions about his present predicament. He turned his attention to the large transport where the newest arrivals of Igigi were still filing off. Enki hadn't noticed at first that they were lining up in formation, a line of men on each side of the exit. The last men to step out unrolled a long, burgundy tapestry like a rug between the ranks of Igigi.

In full royal regalia, Anu stepped to the front of the exit. A chest plate, made of individual strips of wood woven together in a vertical pattern, fit his body like a glove. His mane of hair was twisted into three perfectly cylindrical curls. A large strap of leather was fastened just behind his neck, gathering the curls into a single ponytail. Anu's bushy beard was perfectly braided in ten sections and the bottoms of each were capped with tiny, ornate cups of gold. Boots made of the softest leather that Nibiru produced hugged his feet and shins like a second skin.

The statuesque King of Nibiru descended the ship's ramp. When he stepped onto the burgundy tapestry, the Igigi offered obeisance in unison, all of them going down on one knee. As Enlil had done only an instant before, Anu crossed toward the tapestry's edge and gazed up at the complex of Eridu.

Enki tried reading his father's face, but it was expressionless. Finding his wits, he came out of the gate, approached his father and bowed. "Welcome, father. I hope Eridu is to your liking."

"What you've done is impressive." Anu took in the splendor of Enki's palace. "More lavish than the palace we enjoy at home." Anu's blank expression now read as one of disapproval. "Back on Nibiru, we choke on ailing skies. It is a far cry from the comforts you enjoy here."

Enki tried to ignore his reveling brother but impulsively stole a glance at him. The smirk on Enlil's face was now slightly more pronounced.

"As I mentioned, father, I hope it is to your liking. It is all well and good that you have come with replenishments of Igigi."

Anu looked at his workers as if he had forgotten they were there. "Our journey was long. Show the Igigi their quarters." With those words, Anu stepped off the burgundy tapestry and crossed through the gates of Eridu.

Enki attempted to follow, but Enlil stepped in front of him to block his path. "You must do as father asked and tend to the Igigi."

Enki could feel things falling apart. The brother he fled Nibiru to escape had barely exited the transport, and his fragile operation already seemed to be unraveling. An atomic rage engulfed the eldest brother, and he grabbed Enlil by his flight uniform and yanked him in close. "You have no idea what you're doing. This operation hangs by a string."

Not in the least bit intimidated, Enlil knocked his brother's hands away. "This, my dear brother, is why we are here." Enlil turned to the ranks of Igigi waiting beside the ship. "Now, see to it they are attended to while father and I take in the magnificence of your palace."

It was clear to Enki that trouble had arrived on Earth's blue shores, and its name was Enlil. Enki turned to one of his top Igigi and ordered him to situate the new arrivals. Satisfied that he had fulfilled his father's request, he turned and pushed by Enlil, knocking him off balance. Desperate, he stormed back through the palace gates.

Enlil was not in the least bit bothered by his brother's aggressive posturing. He knew already that Anu was disgruntled by Enki's poor results with the Earth operation. During the journey from Nibiru, he had gloated, playing various scenarios through his head on how he would maneuver to humiliate Enki. But what was actually occurring was better than any plan he had conceived. The transport had barely cooled from entering the atmosphere and already Enki was off kilter.

Enlil inhaled the sweet smell of Earth's atmosphere and gazed around at the majesty of Eridu. Before he was through, it would all be his—Eridu, the illustriousness he sought back home on Nibiru and his father's love.

CHAPTER 41

*I*t seemed to be only the blink of an eye before Max became aware that he was standing alone in his closet. Before he could muster even the slightest move, sweaters and jeans rained down around him, falling back to the ground. Max stared at the garments in fascination and disbelief of what he had seen. During the initiation in Mexico, he had experienced Enlil's rage, seeing things through his eyes. And now he had experienced his satisfaction.

The Anunnaki. Max knew they were real, but he hadn't understood why he had been made witness to the beginnings of their arrival on Earth. Now that it was sinking in, he marveled at the idea of life "off planet." If the Anunnaki existed, there must be other life forms elsewhere.

Stepping over the garments, Max quickly packed the device back up and returned it to the shelf in his control center vault. *Enki and Enlil,* he thought, feuding brothers who couldn't see eye to eye. He wondered about his own brother and the likelihood of them having been good friends had he lived. Or maybe they would have been enemies just like Enki and Enlil.

Max still had questions the device hadn't answered. As he pondered it all, a thought crept into his mind. *She might be pregnant.* Suddenly, his attention came back to the more earthly problem of Brigitte's possible pregnancy. *She's a good girl,* he thought. But the idea still plagued his mind that, somehow, Brigitte may have set him up. *But she wouldn't do that. Or would she?*

While Max stood in his control center, contemplating his predicament with Brigitte, he had no idea that the blonde and her small cohort were approximately five hundred miles away. For more than a few weeks, Max had hoped they were part of his dreams, simple figments of his imagination. But the reality of their existence was, as he feared, absolutely concrete.

Tonight, the couple was in a circular room that was quite extraordinary in a variety of ways. For one, every aspect of the space was precisely round down to the tiniest degree. And it wasn't just the room's shape that was impressive. A large curved picture window gave way to a spectacular sight of the night sky. Its glass offered perfect clarity and gave the illusion that one could step directly out into the darkness to witness the stars for as far as the eye could see. Not a single structure impeded the view.

In many ways, the room felt museum-like. The floor glistened like finely polished concrete and its furnishings, while minimalist, were entirely complementary to the space. Each couch, each chair and every table seemed to fuse artistry with simple functionality. Nothing was too large or small and every aspect of positioning created a perfect flow of energy. In parts of the world, a similar system was called Feng Shui. When done well, it seemed as if God Himself had molded the space to create sheer perfection.

The woman approached the window to gaze into the night. Her silhouette, sleek and elegant just like the furnishings, made her appear as a statue or a piece of artwork that had been exquisitely placed. Moonlight shone upon her silky, blond tresses that cascaded down her shoulders like a waterfall. The fine hair, almost white, seemed to fluoresce against the fabric of her dark pinstripe suit.

In a penguin-like waddle, the midget approached and stood beside the mysterious blonde, staring through the extensive picture window. "He just finished using the device."

The woman remained unmoving, staring into the night. "Good." As she turned to face her colleague, a hint of a smile indicated she was pleased. "All seems to be going as planned."

"Yes," the midget confirmed, moving ever closer to the large window. "Do you think we will need to return?"

The woman's eyes narrowed as she contemplated the idea. "It's too soon to determine." She leaned forward to gaze down upon a perfect view of Planet Earth. From so high in orbit, the spherical planet seemed peaceful and still. After a brief pause, she spoke. "For now, we will stay in position, until further notice."

The small man nodded as they stared down from the deck of their ship. While in orbit, the disc-shaped craft remained perfectly hidden behind one of the most efficient cloaking devices in existence.

Throwing off his anxieties, Max closed the control center vault and turned to the needs of the moment. In the deep fibers of his body, he felt a crucial need to unwind. With only a few hours to spare before the party, he drew a hot bath, poured a glass of red wine, and slipped into the steaming water. The touch of a keypad within arm's reach activated powerful jets in the large Jacuzzi tub. The water stung as it massaged his back and shoulders.

The wine and the bath helped to ease Max's tensions, but neither transported him to the feeling he'd had earlier that day in front of the yoga studio. Max thought of the Hatha yoga session, the sun and the moon, and of the seven Kundalini power centers he saw depicted on the poster. The more he thought about it, he was convinced it was the power centers he had witnessed during his initiation.

The ring of his phone shattered his quiet solitude. He sprang from the water and tapped a button on the keypad that was built into the wall beside the tub. It was Gary Richards on the line.

"Max, how're ya, man?"

Max was hardly enthused about the call, but he made an attempt to sound cordial. "Hey, Gary, what's going on?"

"I'm in Chicago. Just got here in fact. I wanted to check in since I'm only here for a day and a half."

"Oh, yeah." Max eased back down into the water.

For quite some time Gary and Max had been out of contact, but Gary remembered Max well enough to tell something was wrong. "Everything okay, man? You still seeing that girl?"

"Yeah, Brigitte and I are still going strong." Max tried sounding upbeat and optimistic, but he wasn't terribly convincing.

"Good. She's a gorgeous girl and you're a gorgeous guy. So, all's well in Camelot I suppose." After an awkward silence, Gary continued, "What are you up to tonight?"

"One of Bridge's friends is having this party. I thought I could get out of it, but she's insisting we go. It's supposed to be a pretty big bash."

"All right." Gary was perceptive enough to feel the brick wall Max was erecting between them. "I tried you a few days ago, but I didn't get you."

"Yeah, I saw, it's just been crazy the last few days."

"No worries. I'm pretty much in meetings all day tomorrow." For about three years, Gary had been lobbying in Washington, DC for large pharmaceutical companies. "I was hoping to grab a second of your time. If it's not too late, maybe we can meet before I leave."

Max thought for a moment, suddenly aware of his own

inhospitality toward an old friend. *There's no harm if I invite him.* "If you're free tonight, why don't you come to this party? I can text you the address."

"You sure that's cool? I don't want to step on any toes."

"It'll be fine, I'm sure. It's a big quarter of a century birthday bash. Brigitte's friend, Marilyn, is having it at a spot called the Aragon Ballroom."

Max and Gary worked out the details for meeting at Marilyn's party. Right as the call was ending, Chandler beeped in. Before he answered, Max had already made up his mind. If ever there was a moment to take it all in stride, it was now. Rather than suffer through Marilyn's party, he was determined to make it a good time. But this wouldn't be possible with Gary Richards as his sole tagalong. More than likely, Brigitte would be preoccupied with Marilyn, so it only made sense that he would invite some of his own friends.

With the entitlement only a Battenberg could feel, he invited Chandler to the party. Then he phoned Ted Sanderson to extend yet another invitation. He had barely seen Ted since the New Orleans attack. Why not use Marilyn's celebration to reconnect with him and other friends? While it was certain things would never be the same, he had to try and reclaim what he could of his former life. The idea of a return to normalcy comforted Max, but there was just one problem. He wasn't entirely convinced he could actually pull it off.

CHAPTER 42

*A*fter his bath, Max dressed in jeans and a T-shirt. For more than a minute, he stood staring at his reflection in the large mirror that doubled as a vault door to his panic room. Superficially, he appeared the same, tall and slender with his unusual but appealing facial features. But he was different now. Max had received his initiation into the league of the unbelievable.

Only an hour before, by using the Anti-k Mechanism, he had been transported, somehow made witness to a history that most would never believe. Max studied the contours of his face, aware of the truth he would have to own one way or another. His family was more than just wealthy, and they were shrewder than expert businessmen. These were the realities Max was desperately trying on for size.

On some level, the truth felt liberating, but there were also conse-quences to pay. As his knowledge expanded, Max felt increasingly alienated from those he considered friends. To share details of the things he had learned with anyone seemed unthinkable.

With the best of intentions, he tried to appear normal, but more and more, he was finding it a struggle. With each passing day, it seemed the fun-loving playboy who had flown to Mardi Gras no longer existed. Yes, he laughed at jokes and contributed to conver-sations, but he did so without the conviction or presence of mind he had possessed before the initiation. In the face of psychic powers and alien planets, anything worldly or mundane seemed impossibly trivial. And those who knew Max well were starting to see through his facade of normality.

He snapped from his trance. Turning from the mirror, he rushed from his room, skipping down the steps to his garage. Tonight, he would try with everything he had to release his anxieties and tension. There would be no facade of forced interest or levity. If this was his life, he would embrace it and enjoy it.

Brigitte had finally decided what to wear to her best friend's twen-ty-fifth birthday party. The winning outfit was a navy blue baby doll dress with white trim that she had purchased nearly a year earlier at the French Open in Paris. Until now, she hadn't found the right occasion to wear it.

When the doorbell rang, she quickly slipped on the dress, pivoting back and forth in the mirror. She wanted to be certain all of her angles were just right. After the bell's second ring, she sprinted toward the front to answer it. She yanked open the door to see Max looking stylish in jeans and a simple v-neck T-shirt. He was leaning against the doorjamb with a boyish grin she hadn't seen since the Money Pit.

"Sorry, I was just getting dressed."

From top to bottom, Max admired the entirety of Brigitte's body. "You look great."

She wanted to blush but stood guard in the doorway instead, blocking it like a sentinel. She stared at Max, unsure if she should embrace him or perhaps return his things.

He flashed his best show of dimples. "Did you miss me?"

Brigitte barked out a laugh. "I should be asking you that."

"No, no, we're not talking about any hard stuff. Not tonight. At this party, we're going to be normal and have a good time."

"Really?" Brigitte challenged, slightly amused by Max's upbeat disposition.

"Of course."

She studied him, searching his face for a glimpse of his truth.

"Well, are you going to let me in?"

Finally ready to oblige, Brigitte stepped aside to allow Max entrance. He had no doubt she was losing patience with all of the adjustments he was going through, especially the ones he could never tell her about. In view of his recent behavior, he couldn't really blame her. He kissed and hugged her, gestures she always found reassuring. This time, she broke away from his embrace and closed the door.

"I'm just about ready." Brigitte continued staring in an attempt to analyze his mood.

"What?" Max questioned with a mischievous grin.

"I was sure you weren't coming." Brigitte was sheepish as she averted her eyes. "I asked Bertrand to come in case you flaked. He's on his way."

"All right, if you want him there, that's fine. But I am here." Max took his turn to stare at Brigitte with just a touch of incredulity.

"What?"

"You really thought I'd cancel? I mean am I that bad? I'm already in hot water, I wouldn't flake. I even invited people. Ted. Chandler."

"Max, no, things were so awkward earlier. I figured we'd keep it small."

"But they're not awkward now, right? Plus neither of us has seen Ted. And you're going to be with Marilyn and 'Bertrand' the whole night anyway."

For more than a few minutes, Max remained playful and upbeat, almost like his former self. But Brigitte knew him too well and was absolutely the hardest to fool. In spite of his best efforts, there were signs of his apprehension beginning to seep through the cracks.

"You sure you're okay?"

"I'm fine, Bridge." Max realized his response was too swift and matter of fact. Just as he suspected, she frowned, unconvinced. He looked away.

"Now, I know you're lying. You don't want to go to this thing, Max. I know you."

He looked her in the eye. Deep down, he wanted to share just a smidgeon of the things he'd been living, but he didn't dare.

"I feel like you want to say something but you won't." Aware that he might be on the verge of a confession, Brigitte suddenly grew emotional. "There's something going on and honestly, it's better if you just say it."

Max felt his concrete demeanor beginning to fracture. So much had happened, there was no way he could keep it all in. He crossed to the window to see if Bertrand, or anyone else, was parked outside. When he recognized that the coast was clear, he turned to Brigitte. "Turn the music up."

Brigitte did as instructed and raised the volume on her stereo. The chants of Enigma's "Mea Culpa" resonated across the room. He gestured for her to turn the volume up even further, which she did. With the music on high, Max removed his cell phone and powered it off. He turned to her ready to spill the beans, or at least some of them.

"Dance with me." Max embraced her and could instantly feel the contours of her physique pressed firmly against his. He sensed

Brigitte's confusion in the rigid awkwardness of her body. Still, he led the dance, urging her to sway from side to side. He placed his mouth beside her ear.

Brigitte giggled as his lips gently brushed the side of her face. "That tickles," she squirmed.

He clung to her tightly and proclaimed, "You smell good." Although he couldn't see it, she was smiling from ear to ear.

"That's not what you wanted to tell me." These were the types of moments Brigitte cherished, when Max was attentive with both playfulness and charm.

"I'm sorry if I've been acting strange." He shifted his hand, sliding it down her lower back. With his voice at the low end of a whisper, he continued, "The initiation... let's just say it shook me up."

Brigitte was still smiling. "You wanna talk about it?" In her mind, the dance and whispery voice were all a part of Max's seduction. But this could not have been further from the truth. He was worried, even scared that the slightest breach of secrecy could be discovered with regard to his initiation. He paused, still rocking her back and forth as if in a slow dance.

"Nothing's as it seems. Down in Mexico—"

Before he could say another word, his cell phone came to life, both ringing and vibrating in his pocket. Max froze in place, paralyzed. Only minutes before he had powered it down. Just as he was convincing himself that it couldn't have been his phone, it rang again.

"Didn't you shut that off?" Brigitte questioned.

He released her and took a step backward, staring for a brief moment into her eyes. Then he lied. "I thought I put it on silent." Still in disbelief, he fished the phone from his pocket and saw Battenberg Industries flashing on the screen. "It's someone at the office." Max answered the call as he walked away from Brigitte toward the window. "This is Max."

"Mr. Battenberg, this is Rosalee from your father's office."

"Yes, Rosalee, what can I do for you?"

Rosalee hesitated a beat. "I was just calling to let you know that your father has asked me to be your aid for anything you might require. A reminder just popped up on my PDA, so I figured I'd give you a call. If there's anything you need to discuss or talk about, I am at your disposal."

The gears that were Max's thoughts ticked forward on over-drive. Yes, he had powered down his phone, but it had come to life at a time that could not have been coincidental. He was unsure if Rosalee even knew herself that she had intervened. "I understand. Thank you for the call, Rosalee."

"Not a problem, Mr. Battenberg. Again, don't hesitate to call if there's anything you need."

He clicked off the call, then contemplated what had just happened. Somehow, his phone had reactivated just in time to prevent him from divulging anything to Brigitte.

She stared at Max, who appeared dazed and just a little baffled. "Max? Is everything all right?"

Once again, he found himself needing to pretend everything was fine. As it turned out, the tiny microchip around his neck was not the only leash at his father's disposal. There were apparently other controls in place.

"Yeah. That was my father's office." Max tried but could scarcely hide his surprise. "There's a situation I have to deal with. It can wait until tomorrow though."

"Are you going to finish what you were about to tell me?"

Max stepped to Brigitte and kissed her gently. She immediately understood the meaning of the embrace. Any chance of her learning what Max was about to reveal had just vanished with the business call.

"I just realize with everything that happened down in Mexico that I need to get more serious about life. There's my job at Badem and now a baby. Maybe I need to get more serious about us."

"That's sweet, hon." Brigitte knew this wasn't what Max had intended to say, but in her mind it was good news nonetheless.

"Where is that brother of yours? Are we waiting here for him or meeting him there?" Max was still thrown by Rosalee's call, but managed to cover enough to avert Brigitte's worst suspicions. Rosalee's intervention made it clear that any sense of privacy was potentially nonexistent.

"Let me get my shoes and we'll call him. Marilyn'll kill me if we're late."

"I'm ready when you are." Max smiled as Brigitte pivoted on her bare feet and dashed back into her room. Full of angst, he crossed to the window and peered out onto the quiet street. Nothing looked out of the ordinary, but Max still couldn't shake the nagging notion that somehow he was being watched.

CHAPTER 43

*M*arilyn's birthday party took place at Chicago's Aragon Ballroom. The Aragon, built in 1926, had ultimately become one of the Windy City's traditional hot spots. Inside, a large ballroom dance floor was encircled by architecture that resembled the courtyard of a Moorish castle. Archways, verandas, balconies, Spanish tiled rooftops and towers gave patrons the illusion of being in a castle's inner square. And when properly lit, the ceiling mimicked a true night sky.

Upon entering the Aragon, club-goers crossed onto a huge staircase that split, descending on both sides to meet again at the dance floor. At the bottom of each staircase, black painted Greek statues, each larger than Da Vinci's David, stood like sentinels to the faux courtyard. The gaudy style was very much old Europe. It didn't surprise Max that Marilyn, a true socialite, had chosen such a venue for her birthday festivities.

The celebration was already in full swing when Max and Brigitte stepped onto the landing at the top of the stairs. Brigitte, waif-like and feminine, clung tightly to Max's chiseled arm. They hadn't intended to coordinate their outfits, but his dark jeans and white T-shirt perfectly matched her navy blue dress with white trim. In some ways, the two resembled models at a fashion shoot.

An outsider looking in would never have known that there was any tension between them. Max was well aware that Brigitte didn't appreciate his answers earlier that day with regard to her pregnancy. A failure to reconcile the misstep would only result in weeks of persona non grata status, something Max desperately wanted to avoid.

When he thought about it, he was perplexed that they were attending the party at all. The news of Brigitte's condition was shocking to say the least. Max would have been foolish not to question what else could go wrong.

Without a word, Brigitte unfolded herself from his arm and fished her phone from the small bag across her shoulder. Within seconds, they were both typing text messages to announce their arrival and coordinate locations. From the top of the staircase, there was a perfect view of the ballroom, where hundreds of people were already dancing and moving about.

The music thumped loudly as Max finished his text message to Chandler, Ted and Gary. It read rather simply, "Just arrived. u here yet?"

Max slid the phone in his pocket just as Brigitte was finishing her messages to Bertrand and Marilyn. Together they descended the stairs, passing the enormous statues as they entered the main floor.

Max spotted a bar at the other end of the dance floor. Turning to Brigitte, he yelled over the music, "Come on, let's get a drink." He took her hand and led her through the crowd. "Bertrand here yet?"

"Let me check." Brigitte reached in her bag and retrieved her phone. Her eyes lit up at the flashing message from her brother. "He sent me a message." She opened and read her brother's response, then looked up to the staircase where they had just been. "There he goes." Brigitte bounced up and down yelling across the crowd, "Bert. Bert. Over here."

"Babe, he'll never hear over this music."

Spotting Max and Brigitte, Bertrand made his way down the steps. Suddenly, a girl's scream rang out from across the bar. Max spun around, looking for the source of commotion, when Brigitte burst into a banshee call of her own.

"Oh my God! Happy birthday, girl." Brigitte cut through the crowd and hugged Marilyn, who raised her champagne glass to prevent any spillage.

"I am so glad you're here," Marilyn explained. "I need help with this crowd. Would you believe that bitch Veronica showed up?"

Brigitte shook her head in disbelief. "Forget her. This is your party. Why shouldn't she see how fabulous it is?"

Marilyn turned up her glass and drank down a huge gulp of champagne. "You really aren't gonna drink, are you?"

"I can't. And you know why."

Marilyn's infectious smile turned to a frown, barely comprehending how her best friend had managed to get herself pregnant. She swung around to Max, "I see you got him to come," and added with a coquettish wink, "Hi, Max."

Max didn't particularly dislike Marilyn, but she wasn't his favorite either. Tonight's festivities were not his idea of fun, but he forced a smile nonetheless. "Happy birthday, Marilyn."

Marilyn gestured around the ballroom. "Isn't this great?" Max wasn't her favorite person either, but she often looked to him for the Battenberg stamp of approval.

Bertrand slid up behind his sister and hugged her from behind. "Hey, sis. Everything good?"

More subdued than normal, Brigitte nodded to her brother's question. His presence, while comforting, only reminded her of the unfortunate circumstances between her and Max.

With a nod, Bertrand acknowledged Max and Marilyn. "Happy birthday, Marilyn."

"Thanks, B. Glad you could make it." Marilyn flipped her hair to the side and smiled at the sole heir to the Battenberg fortune. "How are you, Max? I keep telling Brigitte I think you two are broken up. You're never around."

Upon hearing Marilyn's words, Bertrand narrowed his eyes at Max, but remained silent.

Marilyn, upon spotting a server, snapped her fingers as she yelled out for his attention. The young man turned and approached with a tray of champagne flutes. Marilyn grabbed two, handing one to Brigitte and the other to Bertrand.

Left to fend for himself, Max took a glass from the tray and smiled at Marilyn. "Well, as you can see, I am still in the picture."

"I heard about that whole psychic thing and your friend getting attacked down in New Orleans. You gotta admit that was fuckin' trippy."

Max turned to Brigitte, who looked completely embarrassed. "Yeah. That day was unfortunate. And the psychic... pretty fascinating."

"Max, you hated her," Brigitte added.

He didn't dare reveal that he now believed Indigo was the real thing.

"Well, my dear," Marilyn chimed in, "if you're interested in a second opinion, I have a great gal right here in Chicago."

Marilyn was an interesting specimen of a woman. Her hair was a peculiar shade of reddish-orange. It looked very unnatural, as did her skin tone, which appeared like an artificial tan, also in the family of orange. Unusually, Marilyn didn't have a freckle in sight. The combination of flawless, unblemished skin and bright-colored hair made her seem exotic. When she and Brigitte were together, they turned heads, each one of them gorgeous in a completely different fashion. Already intoxicated from sipping champagne, Marilyn rattled on about dresses, outfits, hairdos and such. Max found the chatter useless and mundane. Just when he thought he couldn't stand another word, his phone started vibrating with text replies from Gary and Chandler. Both were inside the building and asking for Max's location. He replied, and within minutes Chandler appeared.

Max offered dap, greeting him in a macho fashion. "Bridge, you remember Chandler, right? My editor over at Badem."

Brigitte did remember, but there was something about Chandler she didn't like. She could never truly put her finger on it. Because Max rarely brought Chandler around, she had honestly forgotten about him. "Of course. Hi, Chandler, this is the guest of honor, Marilyn Bornkamp. And my brother, Bertrand."

With a cheery smile, Chandler offered a friendly wave. "Hey, everybody," then he turned to Marilyn, "and happy birthday to you."

Marilyn tried to return Chandler's smile, but it was more a smirk than she intended it to be. After an awkward pause, Gary appeared, pushing his way through the crowd. Brigitte noticed him behind Max, but figured he was trying to pass. She urged Max aside with a nudge.

"Hon, he's trying to get by."

Max turned and noticed who it was behind him. "Hey, Gary, you found us."

Brigitte stared quizzically at Gary, trying to figure out who he was and why Max had invited him. Max made another round of introductions followed by obligatory nods, smiles and handshakes. There was an immediate shift in Brigitte's demeanor but Max tried to ignore it.

"Gary lives in DC. He's only in town till tomorrow." Max turned to Marilyn. "I hope it was okay to invite him."

Marilyn tossed her reddish-orange hair to the side and smiled. "The more the merrier. Thanks for coming, guys."

Most times, Max found there was a phoniness to Marilyn's demeanor, which is why he wasn't a big fan. The night had just started and already he was regretting being there. Maybe inviting other people hadn't been such a good idea after all.

Brigitte finally left her brother's side and grabbed Max from behind. She hugged him close and whispered in his ear, "Who's this Gary guy? It's one thing inviting people we know..."

Max smiled to make it seem like Brigitte had whispered sweet nothings in his ear. He turned and planted a kiss on her cheek. "Just wanted back up. In case you needed space."

Brigitte smiled, but it was a contrived Cheshire-cat grin. She studied Max's face, concerned that a stranger was emerging from the man she thought she knew. "I just thought—" Brigitte faltered before continuing in frustration, "whatever."

Max was genuinely perplexed by her point of view. "What are you saying? You wanted quality time at a huge party where you invited your brother."

Brigitte was caught off guard by Max's saltiness. While she may have been pregnant, he was the one who seemed hormonal. She struggled for a retort that wouldn't start a fight. Before she could find the words a handsome, well-built man slipped by on his way to the bar. The rugged party guest didn't go unnoticed, as Chandler and Gary exchanged innocent yet playful glances. Because they were his guests, the move was a bit more obvious than Max would have liked.

Just then, Ted burst through the crowd, with a Superman-like entrance to save the day. "Max, Brigitte!" He high-fived Brigitte with one hand while guarding a cocktail in the other. "What's up, babe?"

"Hey, Ted, oh my God." Brigitte shot Max a quick glance. "I didn't really believe Max when he said you were coming. I'm glad you did, though."

"Abso-fucking-lutely. It's been too long since we partied. And no, I'm not counting Mardi Gras." Ted turned to Max. "The way you described it, I thought it was gonna be some rinky-dink function. It's a huge bash, dude."

A few weeks had passed since Max or Brigitte last saw Ted. While his injuries were healing quite well, a large scar, much larger than the one Max had, was stretching from the right side of his mouth to his right ear.

Brigitte approached and hugged Ted. "It's good to see you." When she drew back, she examined his scar. "It's healing pretty well, Ted."

"Yeah, in a few months I can decide if I want plastic surgery or not. To be honest, the scar's kinda growing on me."

"Dude, I feel the same way," Max interjected as he high-fived his friend.

Ted puffed his chest out with pride. "Battle wounds are sexy, right?"

Both Max and Brigitte were pleased to see Ted getting back to his old self, especially after such a brutal attack. Max placed an arm around his old friend in a warm embrace.

"Good to see ya, man."

"Well, guys," Marilyn continued, trying to switch gears. "Enjoy the party. I need to greet my other guests." She grabbed Brigitte's hand. "You wanna come with?"

Brigitte, who was quietly irritated, twisted her hair in a bun as she did only when annoyed. "Yeah, I wanna see the rest of this space." She turned to Bertrand. "You want to come or hang with the boys?"

Bertrand flashed Max a dissatisfied glance. "I came to hang with my sis."

Sporting a false grin, Brigitte looked to Max. "I'll catch up with you later, okay?"

Max leaned in to kiss Brigitte then whispered in her ear. "Are you mad I invited them?"

"Kinda late to ask now, dontcha think?" With a tilt of her head she disappeared into the crowd behind Marilyn and Bertrand.

Ted, although tipsy, could feel the tension in the air. "Dude, what the fuck just happened? Did I do something wrong?"

From the start, Max hadn't wanted to attend Marilyn's party. Now, he was certain the decision to come had been a mistake. "No, dude, it's Brigitte. She's pissed at me. It's a long story."

Chandler, completely oblivious to the awkwardness, finally chimed in, "So, how do you know Gary?"

Max gulped down his flute of champagne, trying to dull his own aggravation. "Come on, let's get another drink."

For the remainder of the evening, Max and his friends circulated through different rooms of the Aragon. From what Max could gather, everyone was having a good time but him. More than a few times Chandler flirted openly in the crowd, but was for the most part on his best behavior. At the same time, Ted would vanish only to text Max ten or fifteen minutes later requesting his location. At one point, after Ted's third disappearance, Chandler noticed a handsome man and excused himself, leaving Gary and Max alone.

Gary gestured at Chandler as he departed. "Didn't quite think that was your style."

"He's a good guy and a super employee."

"Hm," Gary responded, studying Chandler across the way. "Okay." Realizing that he had Max alone, Gary finally opened up as to why he had contacted him. In the last months, he had been experiencing trouble with an issue he was lobbying for in DC. He needed to exert pressure to make things go his way. He thought maybe Max could get one of Battenberg Industries' higher-ups, if not Demetrius himself, to assist.

Max listened, mulling over the expansive scope of Demetrius' influence. He'd always known his father held a power position, but he had no idea of the degree until recently. In a friendly gesture, Max agreed to make inquiries. He promised Gary that he'd get back to him within a few weeks. In truth, Gary's issues were microscopic compared to the ones Max was dealing with.

Max had hoped that hours of drinking would help to improve his mood, but alcohol didn't change the fact that he found the party dull and inconsequential. He apologized to Gary and then excused himself to find Brigitte and say goodbye. Neither she nor Bertrand had softened in their demeanor. Both were still offering cold shoulders to his attempts at conversation. Rather than deal with their attitudes, he turned and promptly left Marilyn's infamous birthday bash.

CHAPTER 44

The moment he exited the Aragon, a sense of relief washed over Max. He contemplated what a failure the disastrous evening had been and his bad judgment in having agreed to attend the party. As he crossed the street toward the valet kiosk, he noticed Gary trying to hail a cab.

"Mr. Richards, I don't know why I didn't ask, I just figured you rented a car."

Gary, who was standing in the street, stepped up onto the sidewalk. "I decided it didn't make sense to get one for a day and a half. Besides, I hate driving."

"Need a lift?"

"Who knew it'd be so hard getting a cab," Gary looked at his watch, "at two o'clock in the morning? If you don't mind, a ride would be great."

Seconds later, the valet arrived with Max's Range Rover. He and Gary climbed in. Neither had their seatbelts buckled when Max punched down on the gas, putting as much distance as he could between himself and the Aragon. For several blocks they rode without conversation. At the very best, things were awkward, since neither of them had fully addressed what had transpired between them more than a year before. Finally, Max broke the silence.

"The Aragon's pretty well known, but the area's a little sketchy these days. It's probably not a good idea hanging around for a cab at this hour anyway."

"Ah, okay."

"So, what time's your meeting tomorrow?"

"Breakfast at 9:30. If I'm careful I still have about six hours to sleep."

"Yeah, maybe if you were heading to sleep now." Max could tell there were at least a half dozen things that weren't being spoken between them. But it was hardly the time to invite further confusion into the picture.

There was another awkward silence before Gary chimed in. "What's going on with you and Brigitte?"

Max thought about the question. Why had Gary all of a sudden reappeared in his life asking for political favors? And now he was asking personal questions. "What do you mean?"

"Not to pry, but there was some serious tension between you two back there."

Even as the words flew from his mouth, Max regretted saying them. "There's a chance she might be pregnant."

Gary turned and stared at Max while Chicago's night lights flashed by outside. "Wow, that's big. A little Battenberg."

Max was remorseful at having brought Gary into his confidence, but he was also relieved to have told someone something of his complicated personal agenda. "We haven't a hundred percent confirmed, but it has us both on edge."

Gary pivoted in his seat, pressing his back against the passenger door as he faced Max. "I wouldn't think you'd worry about that kind of thing."

Max shot Gary a glance, then returned his eyes to the road. "Yeah, well, you were wrong."

"Max, you gotta relax." Gary reached across to squeeze Max's shoulder with a gentle massage. "Take the edge off, pal. I give great back rubs by the way. In case you forgot."

The direct nature of Gary's advance caught Max off guard. "It's late, Gary. When I offered to drop you off, that's all I had in mind."

"There's different ways to let go, that's all I'm saying. If I'm not mistaken I did a pretty decent job of that in the past."

Max frowned at the gauche nature of Gary's declaration. "Afraid I'll have to take a pass. There's too much shit..." Max didn't bother to complete his sentence since Gary's hotel was only a few hundred yards away. He pulled into the circular driveway and brought the car to a stop. "It was good seeing you though. Sorry if the night was crappy."

"I didn't think that at all. It was a nice party."

"This week I'll check if anyone at Battenberg can help with the lobbying thing."

Gary held his gaze on Max with his back still pressed to the door. "Okay, great. I'm glad I came out. I doubt we would've been able to see each other tomorrow. So, can I get a hug?"

While Max didn't want to, it somehow seemed rude to admit

it. After all, at one time, he and Gary had been close friends. He unbuckled his seatbelt and came around to the passenger side for a goodbye embrace. Even at the late hour, valets and bellhops were scurrying about the driveway.

Gary embraced Max tightly and lowered his voice to a whisper. "You're awfully tense. You sure I can't help with that?"

A zillion things rushed through Max's head as he broke from Gary's embrace. "Dude, I was serious. I'm only here to drop you off."

Sexually, Max and Gary were no strangers to each other. For the most part, their tryst had been rather harmless, at least until Demetrius found out about it.

Switching gears, Max changed his tune. "You know what? I am going to come up. Just for a drink though."

Max took a ticket from the valet and followed Gary up to his room on the twenty-third floor. The plush suite was less modern than Max liked and had the traditional appeal of a law office. The tables and nightstands were made of cherry wood while the couches and armchairs were just a tad overstuffed. The room offered a great view of the city. It wasn't nearly as stunning as the one from the Spire, but it was breathtaking nonetheless.

Gary opened the wet bar and made Max a drink. After securing a beer for himself, he crossed the room and handed Max the glass. "I take it you still drink G & T's?"

"Thanks." Max raised his glass and clinked it against Gary's beer bottle. "To brighter days."

Gary chuckled at Max's toast. "Is there any other kind in your family?"

Gary leaned in for a kiss, but Max promptly withdrew.

"You thought I was kidding when I said just a drink?"

"Okay." Gary stepped away, perplexed. "Maybe someone should've explained what a drink means nowadays."

Desirous of his space, Max crossed to the couch and took a seat. He flipped on the television using the remote. "Look, I realize it's confusing that I came up. But I really did want to talk. I shouldn't have told you that little sound byte about Brigitte being pregnant. I'd appreciate if you didn't mention it to anyone. We're not really sure anyway."

Using his thumb and index finger Gary motioned as if he were zipping his lips. "It's like I never heard it."

The old flame approached and planted himself beside Max on the sofa. For a short while, they sat in silence, sipping drinks and watching an infomercial on youthful skin.

Gary reached over and playfully wrestled the remote from Max's hand. "Last I checked we weren't in need of wrinkle cream. Not yet anyway."

Gary began flipping channels: commercials, "I Love Lucy" reruns, a fundraiser for underprivileged children in South America, local news and a reality show competition. In the brief glimpses of imagery, Max noticed the name Battenberg flashing across the screen, but Gary had already advanced to another station.

"Hey, what was that?" Max questioned. "Turn it back."

Gary did as requested and flipped back to the news. To Max's disbelief, a photo of Demetrius was on screen. The breaking news story provided details of a serious accident. His father had been gravely injured in an explosion at one of Battenberg Industries' manufacturing plants in Brazil.

Max's mouth dropped open. "Fuck. Turn it up." Not even realizing it, Max snatched the remote from Gary's hand and cranked up the volume.

The report continued, but disclosed very few details about Demetrius' current condition. A clandestine source had leaked information stating that Demetrius was hospitalized in an undisclosed location. Some believed he had even been evacuated to Argentina, but such news was entirely unconfirmed.

As soon as the story ended, Max began flipping through stations, hunting for another report. When he didn't find one, he tossed the remote at Gary. "See if you can find something. There have to be other reports."

"Oh wait, here it is."

Gary had located another station with breaking news. Investigators were searching for the cause of the explosion, but it was not yet known whether the incident was deliberate or an accident.

"I gotta go." Max grabbed his things and rushed to leave. "I'll call you later, okay?"

Gary nodded as Max disappeared through the doorway. Within minutes, he was standing at the valet kiosk, urging them to hurry with his car. During the wait, he made several calls, desperately trying to get information on his father's condition. At every juncture he hit a brick wall.

Max, having barely been initiated and just months shy of his twenty-fifth birthday, didn't have nearly the experience necessary to fully grasp just how complicated his life was about to become.

$\mathcal{M}$ax was frantic during the drive home from Gary's hotel. His tires screeched and the Range Rover leaned as he cornered through intersections along the route back to his neighborhood. He dialed every emergency number he could think of while he drove. Finally, he got Rosalee on the line.

"Hi, Rosalee, this is Max Battenberg. I'm trying to get information on my dad. Is he okay?"

Rosalee sounded strangely calm. "He's in intensive care, Mr. Battenberg. That much I can confirm. I don't have much more to give you, I'm afraid. In scenarios like these, your father established a very clear disclosure process. We won't likely have much information anytime soon."

Rosalee's matter-of-fact demeanor immediately aggravated Max. He continued grilling her with dozens of questions but Rosalee worked for Demetrius and was accustomed to pressure. With no cracks in her disposition, she assured Max she would be in contact with any updates as soon as she knew more.

His panic was swiftly turning to resentment at being put in such a position. Here was his father, badly injured, but no one could tell him how badly or even what hospital he was in.

When he hung up with Rosalee, he was only blocks from his house. Max swung the car around and quickly headed to his father's high-rise. From there he might have a better chance of ascertaining exactly what was going on.

Within minutes, Max skidded into the Spire's underground parking structure and came screeching to a halt. He jumped from the car and threw his keys at a valet as he ran into the building.

To his dismay, the concierge at the front desk had already heard about Demetrius and immediately began to grill Max for information. He paid little attention as he entered his father's private elevator and keyed in the access codes. The doors closed and Max shot toward the penthouse.

Sadly, his theory was false that Demetrius' staff might know more than he knew. In the end, they were just as unhelpful as everyone else had been.

He excused himself to the same waiting room where he had patiently awaited Demetrius only weeks before. He remotely lowered the flat-screen television from the ceiling and immediately began surfing news stations for any updated reports.

Because it was breaking news, it wasn't long before he found another account of his father's accident—if that's truly what it was. Max had spent his entire life erroneously believing his mother's death was an accident. Now, it seemed Demetrius may have fallen victim to a similar fate.

He removed his cell phone from his pocket and crossed to the huge wall of glass overlooking the city. Hopeful, he redialed the emergency number Demetrius had given him. Again it went to voice mail. In frustration, he flung the phone, smashing it into pieces against the inner wall.

Completely drained, Max leaned back against the glass, allowing himself to slide down it until he was seated on the floor.

In Max's childhood, Demetrius had been mostly absent as a father. Even present day, more often than not he was emotionally unavailable, but he was still all Max had. And there was so much he didn't yet know that would require Demetrius' mentoring. Max drew in a breath and tried to exhale his tensions. The news story echoed in his head, but a tiny voice continued whispering, *This isn't happening. This isn't happening.*

After a while, Max wasn't sure how long, he dragged himself to the couch and stretched out across it. Somehow, in spite of himself, he managed to sleep, if only for a few hours.

At dawn, the morning light stung his face awake. He had failed to dim the windows, a function without which the room took on the full effect of the morning sun.

He glanced at a clock and noticed it was 6:30 a.m. He had not forgotten why he was there. Stretching, Max reached for the house phone and tried once again to call his father's emergency number. When voice mail picked up, he hung up and dialed Rosalee. After a few rings, she answered.

"Battenberg Industries."

"Rosalee, it's Max Battenberg again. I know we just spoke, but have you had any news on my dad?"

"I know this must be frustrating, Mr. Battenberg. All morning I've been monitoring the information channels. Until now, there are no updates."

"You'll make sure to call if you hear something?"

"I promise you'll be the first number I dial."

Rosalee's demeanor was so controlled Max couldn't distinguish if she was being kind or flippant. He thanked her nonetheless and hung up. Waiting games were not his strong point, and sitting around made him feel as if he could jump from his skin.

Slowly, he began to realize there was no purpose in waiting at the penthouse. After an hour of contemplating whether to stay or go, he grabbed his things, stopping at Demetrius' front desk to secure and activate a new cell phone.

The moment he walked in his front door, both his landline and cell phone began to ring. Brigitte was the first call. She had gone to sleep angry and was determined not to be the first one to reach out. But because she had neglected to switch off her radio alarm, she had awakened to the story of Demetrius' accident. Max explained that he had been unable to get any updates on his father's condition.

Brigitte knew Max well. She could tell he was understandably freaking out over his father's situation. "I'm so sorry, Max. If you want I can come by, maybe make some calls for you."

"Thanks, but I need to get out... maybe go to the gym. Hopefully, a workout will help me relax. I'm fucking going crazy with this radio silence thing. My father could be dead and I wouldn't even know it."

"Max, don't say that. Your dad's gonna be fine. Wherever he is, you know he's getting the best care possible."

Max stood by quietly, hoping and praying that Brigitte was right. The only consolation for his father's predicament was that he was now off the hook for the previous night's episode at Marilyn's party.

"I'll call you later, okay?"

As soon as he hung up, more calls began to flood in. One by one, people were waking up to the breaking news. With no updates to share, he forwarded each call to voice mail. In the last weeks with all the remarkable stresses, only one thing had relaxed him in an extraordinary way. He needed to revisit the yoga studio whose address corresponded to the special number Indigo had given him: 7129.

He showered, changed into sweats and pulled the car out for the trip across town. In her predictions, Indigo had explained that he would struggle to remain centered. Only now did he fully comprehend what she meant. He maneuvered onto the yoga center's street with the white building labeled 7129.

After parking, he hopped out and was surprised to see the same homeless man across the street. The vagrant was propped against the wall, wrapped in the same dirty, red plaid blanket. At first, it appeared the down-on-his-luck man was asleep, but he came alive as Max approached. Sitting up, he straightened the blanket that was carefully draped across his legs. He studied Max as he neared the yoga center.

Situated directly in front of the man's blanket was a cup filled with change. Max looked up from the makeshift till and noticed the man's smile. It was warm and inviting. Still, he was in no mood to be panhandled. He stepped onto the sidewalk, already aware of himself relaxing, perhaps in anticipation of the class. Without a word Max walked by the beggar and entered the building.

At the front desk, Max discovered the selection of classes he could attend: Kundalini, kickboxing, Hatha yoga and Pilates. He remembered the Kundalini poster with its seven energy centers. If the class had anything to do with things he had seen during his initiation, he definitely wanted to know more. But Max was desperate to work off steam. He felt a need to punch something—perhaps a wall, a person, it didn't matter what. Today, both Hatha and Kundalini would have to wait.

Max signed into kickboxing and was outfitted with boxing gloves and protective headgear. The spacious sparring studio was square in shape with long rectangular windows near the ceiling. Rust-colored mats covered the floor and a row of ten punching bags lined the wall on the far side of the room.

After a brief warm-up, the class dispersed to spar against the punching bags. Max unleashed on his, socking and kicking until he felt out of breath. The instructor, and maybe a few students, observed him with concern.

"Okay, people, don't burn yourselves out on the warm-up." The instructor spoke as if to the entire class. "Remember kickboxing is also about endurance."

When the time came to spar with other class members, Max was teamed with a striking, athletic African American woman. An expression of disappointment crossed his face. The woman shrugged as if to question, *what's the problem?*

Max scanned the other students and spotted a burly Asian man who stood nearly six feet tall. "Team me with him," he requested of the instructor.

The burly Asian smiled with a shrug of compliance. Max's request may have been unusual, but it wasn't totally unorthodox. To avoid any awkwardness, the instructor stepped in to speak to Max's current and proposed partners.

"You guys opposed to switching?"

Upon their agreement, the Asian man and the African American woman traded places. Max nodded to acknowledge his new opponent. Before they could exchange a word, the instructor yelled out.

"Spar!"

The second he assumed a fighting stance, Max's punch connected with the Asian man's cheek. The man stumbled back a step. "What the fuck, dude!"

Max motioned him forward as he continued his attack. The man immediately defended using a combination of fighting techniques. He dodged to the left, then roundhouse kicked, connecting fully with Max's protective mask. Max spun and stumbled, but he didn't fall. With each step, memories of childhood training resurfaced in his mind. Although he wasn't aware of it, other class members had ceased their own matches and were now observing from the sidelines.

Max was fighting like he meant to hurt his opponent, but his Asian adversary was no stranger to martial arts. The burly man quickly switched to attack mode and landed several punches. The hits stung, but Max wasn't deterred. He wanted a fight.

He closed his eyes and was instantly able to access a warehouse of his childhood fighting lessons. When his eyes snapped open, time seemed to have slowed.

The Asian man was approaching, his fists raised as he swung. Max easily sidestepped the punches as he rained down a series of his own jabs. Then he roundhouse kicked exactly as the man had done only minutes before. Max connected fully with the man's mask. His foot was perfectly positioned and entered the space where his opponent's face resided. The man quickly spun and fell to the floor as blood splattered across the mat.

"Whoa!" the instructor yelled as he rushed to intervene. "We're in class here, not a street fight." He quickly knelt to investigate if the man was okay.

"I'm fine. I'm fine," the man assured, retrieving his towel to dab at the blood on his face. "You're way too intense, dude."

"I'm sorry," Max explained, "I just... I guess... I'm sorry." While he sounded apologetic, Max wasn't truly remorseful. They may have been displaced, but unleashing his frustrations felt liberating.

The instructor sighed as he viewed his student on the floor beside a pool of his own blood. "This has to be a safe place, even when it's kickboxing. I can't have you beating up on people here."

While he knew he had been out of line, Max wasn't accustomed to be spoken to in such a manner. "Are you asking me to leave?"

The instructor turned to query other members of the class. Max spotted his original sparring partner, the African American woman. She was silently nodding her head. The instructor assisted the Asian man to his feet before he turned to Max.

"I think it might be best. Lift weights, go for a run, do some yoga. But beating up on my class is not an option."

Max was rarely ejected anywhere he went, but today his emotions were too raw and unreined. "Fine."

He lifted his fists before the instructor, who in turn helped to remove his gloves. With his hands free, he removed his protective headgear. Refusing to make a scene, he turned and marched through the studio door. As the door swung shut, his embarrassment lifted, leaving behind the same bitter sense of aggravation he had so desperately wanted to emancipate.

Max passed down the lonely corridor before the door to the Hatha class. Peering through the glass, he noticed a peaceful tranquility in the room.

The Hatha instructor was sitting on a yoga mat cross-legged. On his right, smoke from a stick of Nag Champa incense snaked its way into the room. To his left, a boom box played soothing Eastern music. The lights had been dimmed to create a relaxed mood.

Even with the door closed, Max could hear the instructor. He pointed out that yoga was all about breath and breathing. His voice had a calming quality.

"Let's start in mountain pose. Place your legs hips' width apart.

Let your arms and hands just hang, relaxed. Feel the connection through your feet to Mother Earth. Inhale." The instructor drew in a deep breath along with the class. "And exhale." A hissing sound filled the room as everyone released their breath.

Feeling completely extraneous, Max returned to the lockers where his things were stashed. He immediately retrieved his phone to verify if Rosalee had called with any updates. He scrolled through a list of missed calls as he stepped outside the building. None were from Rosalee.

Max had promptly forgotten about the homeless man until he exited the building and spotted the vagrant on the street. Still seated in lotus position, he gazed at Max with an unsettling intensity. Max shook off his feelings of apprehension and headed toward his car.

The seemingly destitute man got to his feet and stood in the center of the sidewalk. His legs were partly spread and his arms gently resting at his sides. Max thought of the mountain pose instruction he had seen only seconds before in the yoga studio. Now, more than ever, the term made sense. The man's hulking frame would be hard to get around without stepping off the walkway. As he attempted to pass, the loiterer sidestepped deeper into his path.

"Top of the morning to you, sir," he offered with a smile. "How's your day so far?" The man's voice was melodic and soothing, not unlike that of the yoga instructor inside.

Max was thrown by his demeanor. There was a quiet elegance to his enunciation, which he had forgotten during their last interaction. None of it fit with the image standing before him, from whom he might have expected slurred and drunken speech.

"Not really in the mood today, friend."

The intensity of his gaze burned through Max. "You're driving the large SUV, right? The black one."

"Excuse me?" The question caught Max off guard. Suddenly, he felt cornered. "Why does that matter?"

The man was still smiling as he continued, "Some might expect brighter moods from men in shiny cars."

Max wasn't sure how or why, but it was the man's presence more than his body that was creating a blockade. While he saw a clear path to his car, he couldn't manage to actually pass.

Growing serious, the homeless man glared more intently.

"People coming from yoga generally have a stronger connection to themselves."

The more the man spoke, the more impressed Max became by his eloquence. The stranger continued, hypnotizing Max with his words.

"The more connected we are, the easier it becomes to understand others and their needs."

Max didn't like feeling caged in. Part of him wanted to listen while the rest of him yearned for the stranger to step the hell aside. "Okay. What is it you understand about my needs?"

"You're in the wind, my friend, searching for tranquility in a storm that somehow seems endless. But the calm you seek has been elusive. This is why you're here."

Max squinted at the man, perplexed by the accuracy of his words. "Who are you?"

With a shrug, the vagrant continued, "In the end, we're all very much one and the same."

Everything about the man confused Max. He was big and well spoken. He seemed healthy, and there was a charm and charisma about him. From everything he could see, the man should have been a success, not a homeless person on the street.

"I don't really have time for this," Max exclaimed, finally summoning the courage to pass.

As he strode by, the homeless man grabbed him tightly by each arm.

"Wake up, fella! Time for others is time for yourself!"

Max was stunned by the man's antagonistic move. His mind told him to break away and strike the beggar so he could get to his car and leave. But his body refused to obey. Instead, Max experienced an unusual sensation, something he'd never felt before.

It started at the base of his spine and felt like high voltage electricity coursing through him. Max had never been tasered, nor did he have an idea how it felt to be struck by lighting. But somehow it seemed he was experiencing just that. The electrifying sensation instantly traveled up his spine, paralyzing his limbs, radiating out into his extremities. When it reached his head, his vision blurred, burning out into a blinding, white light. What happened next was entirely unexpected.

CHAPTER 46

*E*nlil could not have wished for a better scenario. He had not even seen his first sunset on Earth and already he had succeeded in evicting his older brother from the royal quarters. Of course, he had maneuvered to make sure Enki surrendered the beautiful master chamber and its huge veranda to their father.

The younger Enlil knew there was a chance that their father was partial to Enki, who was his firstborn. But the great Anu favored no one over himself. Enlil had expertly used this to his advantage.

The grandiose palace had more than a few apartments on each of its levels. His nemesis had chosen to relocate his quarters a floor below to avoid him. As it turned out, Enlil preferred the new arrangement. It gave him the perception that Enki was beneath him, just where Enlil felt he belonged.

The newly arrived Prince Enlil moved swiftly, taking the apartment adjacent to Anu's quarters. He wanted access to their father so that whenever the possibility arose, he could influence him against Enki.

Enki may have been the firstborn, but Enlil considered himself the shrewdest and most determined of the two. When it came down to it, Enlil was prepared to lie and cheat, but Enki foolishly had created circumstances in which he really didn't need to. In fact, Enlil could not have crafted a better circumstance for his brother's downfall. Signs of trouble abounded in nearly every aspect of the mining operation. Everyone knew the shipments were too few and the quality of gold was not always up to par.

To make things worse, because he was a slave driver, it was virtually impossible to find Igigi who spoke well of Enki. No, in this setting sabotage wouldn't be necessary, thought Enlil. All he needed was to show Anu around. Enki, as a result of the distance, had grown accustomed to complete autonomy. This was obvious since there had been no effort on his part to mask his shortcomings as a leader. Everything needed to bring down his brother was out in the open for anyone, including their father, to see.

Just before their seventh sunset on Earth, Enlil made an appointment to meet with Anu. A week had been more than enough time to report on everything he had discovered about Enki's operation. If asked, he could weigh in with suggestions on how to improve things and make them more efficient. Poor, unsuspecting Enki was still scrambling around in an attempt to fix things, not realizing he had already been replaced. In fact, Enlil wouldn't be surprised if Enki were on the next transport back to Nibiru.

Such a punishment would only be fitting, as it might allow Enki to see the true impact of his poor performance back at home. From the date of his brazen departure, the atmosphere on Nibiru had only worsened. Oxygen was now being removed from the planet's vast oceans only to be rationed to the youngest, the sickest and the most elderly.

In the middle of Enlil's scheming, a transmission arrived. Back on Nibiru, a typical procedure had taken place when a premature infant was removed from life support. Within hours, the small child had succumbed to what was believed to be their homeland's deteriorating atmosphere. Enlil rejoiced, unable to conceive of a better time for such news. The infant, according to record, was the first true casualty of Nibiru's failing skies.

As his plan came together, Enlil didn't feel the slightest remorse for initiating his brother's downfall. The successful coup against Nibiru's prior ruler, Alalu, had been his personal brainchild. But, somehow, Enki had maneuvered to improve his own position while he sat idly at home. In Enlil's mind, he was only claiming the glory that had rightfully been his all along. Soon, everyone would know of his station as the next heir to Nibiru's throne. At that point, even Enki would bow at his feet.

Filled with an emotion best described as glee, Enlil felt entirely incapable of waiting till sunset. He was giddy with anticipation and wanted to meet with their father as soon as possible. He gathered together each report on Enki and included the Nibiru news transmission. Then he made his way onto the famous, sunny master veranda where their father had begun receiving his afternoon meals. It was the same veranda where Enki had enjoyed the light of dawn, the veranda that would soon be Enlil's along with the rest of Eridu.

Enlil walked to a huge stone table and spread his reports across it. He had already perused them many times to insure their flawlessness.

With a performance he considered one of his best, he pretended to be engrossed in the paperwork. In truth, he was simply soaking in the sun. The rays of light warmed his skin, lulling him to sleep. A moment later, Anu's booming voice awakened him.

"Why have you come when our meeting is set for later?"

Enlil jumped to attention. It was always his plan to feign surprise, but he was genuinely startled, since he had dozed off. He turned away to hide his smile from Anu, quickly fumbling the papers into a messy pile.

"Father, I apologize." Enlil turned and bowed respectfully to his father. "I had hoped to prepare my presentation before your arrival."

Anu studied his son, furrowing his brow. It was true, Enlil was shrewd, but he had inherited the trait from Anu. While Enlil didn't fully realize it, Anu typically knew his true intentions.

"I will take my meal here shortly. What is it you wish to discuss?"

"Father, if you prefer to eat—"

"Sit." Anu's voice thundered across the veranda. "Next time, you will use appropriate channels to advance our meeting."

Enlil bowed his head, "Of course, father," before they each took a seat at the stone table. "I fear there isn't much that's favorable in this report." Trying his best not to smile, Enlil reorganized the reports across the table. Bit-by-bit, he updated Anu on the Earth operation and its varied mishandlings by Enki. Throughout the presentation he would glance at Anu to gauge his reaction. There was no doubt his plan could not have come together in a more expert fashion.

As the presentation wrapped up, Enlil stole a final glance at his father. Anu was silent but a hurricane of rage was evident on his face. For the first time that day, Enlil was unable to hide his smile.

He had already gone over it twice, but Enki mulled over more than a dozen Nibiru transmissions for a third time. There was no sign in any of them that Anu or Enlil were slated to visit Earth either individually or together. The moment he spotted Anu exiting the transport, Enki knew he had miscalculated. There were hardly any elements of his mining operation that were functioning properly. He had requested replenishments of Igigi in hopes of solving the major issues, but the arrival of his father and brother had only exacerbated them.

Anu he maybe could have managed alone, but Enlil was uncaged, running rampant like an animal. There was hardly a difference between his younger brother and the primitive beasts that wandered the plains of the small blue planet. For seven Earth days, Enki had been attempting damage control, but he was certain Enlil would strike like a venomous serpent at the first opportunity.

The worst of his fears was to be sent back to Nibiru. If this occurred, Enlil stood to inherit everything he had built. There was no way Enki could allow an injustice of such magnitude. If it came down to it, he would level Eridu, tearing it stone by stone to the ground.

For an entire week, Enki had enjoyed the solitude of his own wing just a floor below the master apartment. He had needed the space to think and formulate damage control that would minimize his brother's interference. Suddenly, he found his quietude interrupted, his worst fears materializing at the sound of Enlil's voice in the corridor.

"It's this way, father."

The muscles in Enki's neck seized up as he heard his brother's voice reverberating through the hall. He readied himself for battle.

With a smirk across his face, Enlil pushed open the door. "There you are."

An instant later, Anu swept into the room, his face drawn with fury. With no hesitation, he crossed to Enki and plucked him off the ground. Anu swung him around and slammed him against the wall. "Is it true what I see in these reports?" He fixed his gaze on Enki the way a predator does its prey. "The misuse of Igigi for your comforts is unforgiveable while the denizens of Nibiru wither in the wind."

Even though the breath had been knocked from his body, Enki glared at Enlil, who was still in the doorway watching. He managed to blurt out, "Father, you mustn't listen to him. Enlil poisons your mind for his own gain."

Anu removed Enki from the wall and tossed him like a ragdoll into the corner. "This is not about him. Nearly half your resources went toward the construction of Eridu in direct opposition to my orders for increased production. Such insolence will not be tolerated." Enlil's reports were balled up in Anu's fist. He threw them at Enki in a rain of papers. "When you asked for command of this operation I thought it wise. Clearly, I was wrong."

Enki quickly got to his feet, feeling too vulnerable on the floor. "Enlil feeds you half truths." Enki glared at his traitorous sibling. "He has no understanding of this planet's limitations."

Unable to hold his tongue, Enlil interjected, "Perhaps they are your limitations, brother."

Spinning around, Anu silenced Enlil with a stare. The father turned back to Enki. "When Alalu discovered the ore, it was for the salvation of our great planet. In distance, your judgment has grown poor. It is Enlil's wish to run this operation."

"No, father! You cannot." Enki gestured at the gorgeous palace around them. "I built this. Eridu is mine, and Planet Earth I understand better than anyone."

The hulking mass that was Anu approached. "Do you question my authority?"

Immediately backing down, Enki answered, "Of course not, father."

"Back home, the council wishes to be impressed by gold, not by a fortress. You, my dear Enki, have fumbled your command. As a result, we have seen our first fatality at home. This and any other deaths I fear are on your hands. Perhaps you will return so you might see for yourself."

It was Enki's wish to bolt across the room and strangle Enlil. But he knew that if he tried this, he would be massacred. Of the siblings, Enki was the least conniving, but what he lacked in deviousness he made up for with finesse. Bowing to Anu, Enki continued.

"Your highness... I offer the humblest of apologies for the condition of these operations. If I miscalculated, it was to create something worthy of your presence. This I believe I have done. I would ask you to consider that I have developed a certain expertise in my years here."

While Enlil's plan had seemingly been executed without a hitch, he hadn't counted on Enki countering with humility. His heart sank as he saw faltering in his father's resolve.

Enki sensed the tension dissipating in the room and continued, "While Enlil may not wish to acknowledge it, I have obtained a true proficiency with regard to this planet. This he would need many suns to acquire."

For Enlil, the only victory would be to send Enki home. "This is laughable, father. In seven suns I have decoded this operation and all of its flaws. In no time, I will see the ore's production brought to acceptable levels."

"Enough." Anu's voice reverberated through the apartment. "What the two of you wish is of little import. While you bicker, the warship we call our home withers. It is checks and balances we need." Anu gestured toward Enlil. "You will stay to insure operations are to my liking. This is the only way our sacred Nibiru might be saved."

"But father—" Enki interrupted.

"Silence," Anu bellowed, nearly rattling the walls with his roar. The father held Enki in his gaze with seeds of doubt still germinating in his mind. "You will stay as well, but not to enjoy the luxuries of Eridu. You will see a new operation south of here in the Abzu."

Protests rattled in Enki's throat, but he didn't dare utter them. He was losing Eridu, but only for now. Yes, a battle lost, but the war had not yet ended. Enki threw a smile his brother's way, pausing to bow to their father.

The more Anu spoke, the more convinced he became. "In this manner we will see increased production of the ore."

Still scheming, Enlil felt incapable of biting his tongue. "Father, so we are clear, I am to oversee the current operations here in Eridu as well as any new operations in the Abzu."

"Until I am satisfied Enki understands his role, you are to insure all is in alignment with the council's initiatives."

At first, Enlil had been angry at the prospect of Enki remaining on Earth. But realizing he was now in charge of his older brother completely changed the playing field. The idea that Enki would report to him seemed just a bit attractive. "As long as we are both clear on our roles."

Anu turned to Enki. "Before nightfall, you will organize a team of Igigi. At sunrise you will travel to the Abzu on the southern coast. There, you will build a new production facility for the ore."

With a nod of respect Enki bowed to Anu. "As you wish, father." Rising up, he turned Enlil's way with a look that shot daggers. For now, he would cooperate in an effort to save Nibiru. But one day soon, he would make sure of it, Enlil would pay for his impertinence.

CHAPTER 47

*I*n a flash, Max became aware of himself again outside of the yoga studio, in front of building 7129. The mysterious man still held him in his clutches, but quickly released him.

Max trembled and shook as he fell to the ground, his body wracked with convulsions. He had no idea how, but the stranger had somehow accomplished what only the Antikythera Device and the elixir had done, and he had shown Max another piece of the Anunnaki puzzle.

As his vision cleared, Max realized he was on the ground, sprawled across the sidewalk and curb. He wanted to stand, but found he had little control of his limbs. As a sudden wave of emotion struck him, Max began to laugh maniacally and uncontrollably.

The homeless man reached down and grabbed him beneath the armpits to drag him to the wall next to his blanket.

Shivers and spasms rocked his limbs as the fit of laughter continued. After several minutes of unbridled guffaws, Max's body finally settled into a semblance of calm. He chuckled and twitched before attempting to speak.

"What did you do to me?" Max could hardly catch his breath.

"You should go, my friend. There are long days ahead."

Max stared at his arms and legs, which continued to spasm as if they were not his own. "What the hell did you do to me?"

"Your body's trying to tell you something, my friend. From here on out, I suggest you listen. It's information you might need."

The mystery man picked up his blanket and draped it across his shoulders. After three backward steps, he turned and strolled away.

Max, still not in control of his body, watched helplessly as the man departed. From where he sat, the stranger's silhouette appeared that of a warrior. Like a superhero's cape, his soiled blanket wafted in the wind.

"Where are you going?" Max questioned weakly as mini convulsions rippled through him. "Don't leave me here like this."

A new and unexpected round of laughter overcame him. The harder he laughed, the more he felt strength returning to his limbs.

He attempted to stand but quickly collapsed against the wall.

Max grew more horrified as people began exiting the yoga studio. One by one they spotted him against the wall in the homeless man's spot. He tried desperately to quell his laughter, but was unsuccessful.

By the time he could stand, Max was unsure how long he had been against the wall. It may have been ten minutes or an hour. As if inebriated, he stumbled toward the car. Max was overcome with relief as he got in and slammed the door. He lowered his head to the steering wheel only to be hit with another fit of chuckles that lasted nearly ten minutes. As they subsided, his cell phone came to life. He grabbed it, struggling to stifle his laughter.

"Hello."

It was Brigitte on the other line. "Max, what's so funny?"

He took a deep breath and paused, managing somehow not to laugh. "Nothing, really. It's just if I don't laugh, I might cry." The laughter removed all seriousness from his voice.

"Okay." More than ever, Brigitte was concerned for Max. His behavior was growing more and more peculiar. "Have you gotten any news on your dad?"

He tried to respond but instead ended up choking down his laughter. Unable to speak, he removed the phone from his face and covered the receiver. With renewed composure, he returned the phone to his ear.

"Max, are you there?"

"Yeah." He exhaled, trying to maintain a normal tone. "I haven't heard anything. I'm just leaving the yoga studio now."

"Yoga? I thought you were at the gym."

"Yeah, it's a long story."

Brigitte could tell there was something wrong, but given Max's irregular behavior she was terribly confused as to what it might be. "I'm coming over. You shouldn't be alone right now."

On the surface, Max displayed a lighthearted demeanor, but it was a poor facade. Deep down, he was relieved that Brigitte had offered to stop by. "I'm heading home now. Should be there in about fifteen."

"All right. I'll meet you there."

After ending the call, Max burst into laughter. He wasn't sure why, but the more he laughed the more he felt a return to normalcy, as if pressure were being released from his body. He finally started the car and began to drive, first circling the block in search of the homeless man. Unable to locate him, he continued to his house, laughing all the way home.

As he pulled onto his street, he noticed two black Town Cars with windows tinted as dark as the paint. Both were parked in front of his house. Max rolled to a stop beside one of them. It was clear to him why they were there: either his father was dead, or Demetrius had finally sent for him.

He placed his car in park just as Rosalee exited the first Town Car. A well-fitting designer skirt suit hugged her slim figure. As his father's top assistant, Rosalee was always exquisitely put together. To accept anything less from his staff was not in Demetrius' mindset.

Max prayed he wouldn't have yet another fit of laughter in front of her. As Rosalee stepped to the driver's side of the car, he lowered his window.

"Hello, Mr. Battenberg. I know this is short notice, but—"

"My father sent for me."

"Correct. For reasons of security his location remains undisclosed. He has, however, requested that you be escorted to him."

"Okay, great." Max could barely contain his relief. "When do we leave?"

Rosalee cocked her head to the side with a smile. "We need to get going now, Mr. Battenberg."

"Oh." After hours without an update, Max felt thrown by Rosalee's request for an immediate departure. "All right, um,... just let me grab a few things."

Rosalee respectfully shook her head. "I'm afraid there isn't time. Your jet's already been scheduled for takeoff," Rosalee glanced at her watch, "in just under forty-five minutes. Already, we're cutting it close. I have all the codes to assure that the house and car are properly secured."

The response wasn't natural, but Max chuckled, trying desperately not to laugh. Rosalee noticed the outburst but her expression remained blank. Max grabbed his phone and wallet and stepped from the Range Rover.

Like a game show beauty, Rosalee gestured toward one of the delivery vehicles. "Please, sir, if you'd just step into the second Town Car we can be on our way."

"Thank you, Rosalee. I was wondering how long it would take to get news."

"I promised you'd be the first to know."

Max quickly dialed Brigitte as he crossed to the second Town Car. When she picked up, he immediately questioned, "Babe, where are you?"

"Almost there. Just two blocks away."

The driver of the second Town Car opened the door for Max. His heart sank as he realized he wouldn't be allowed to wait. "Don't hate me for this." Stifled chuckles escaped into the phone as he continued, "I just got home and my father has a car waiting for me. I have to catch a plane."

Brigitte remained silent for longer than was comfortable. "Max, I'm turning onto your street now."

Noticing Max's hesitation, Rosalee approached. "Mr. Battenberg, I'm sorry, we need to get going."

With her urging, Max stepped into the Town Car. The chauffeur shut the door, then climbed in the driver's seat. Within seconds, the car was moving. Max yelled to the driver, "Can we wait two seconds, please?"

In spite of his request, the Town Car continued accelerating. The chauffeur had Demetrius' instructions and Max had no authority to override them.

"Bridge, they're not even letting me pack a bag." Max watched as Brigitte's luxury sedan approached from the opposite direction. He lowered his window and leaned out. "I'm sorry, babe."

Brigitte turned to stare at Max, her face etched with incredulity and disappointment. As their cars passed each other, she spoke into the phone, "You're kidding me, right?"

"I swear this wasn't my plan. A plane's been cleared and I have to be on it."

Max turned to see Brigitte's car come to a full stop in the middle of the road. Her brake lights remained illuminated like miniature twin stoplights.

As the Town Car turned off his street, the phone went dead. Max was certain Brigitte had hung up. When he dialed her again, her voice mail kicked in, confirming her anger. Even though he didn't mean to, Max laughed out loud.

He settled into the back seat. Outside, the streets of Chicago whizzed by along their route to the airport. He knew he should phone Brigitte back, but the strange laughter made him decide against it. While he felt rotten, Max had to look on the bright side: his father was still alive, and he would finally be able to see him and determine exactly what state he was in.

CHAPTER 48

With only minutes to spare, Max's Town Car came screeching to a halt beside one of Demetrius' private planes. He stepped from the vehicle, feeling trapped in a whirlwind, as security ushered him across the tarmac to the plane's entrance. Its jet engines were already engaged and a blast of air whipped through his hair and stung his eyes.

The sleek, pewter-colored aircraft had the company logo of Battenberg Industries snaking across its tail section. Max climbed the steps and entered the fuselage just as the other Town Car arrived. With a cell phone pressed to her ear, Rosalee exited and pursued Max into the plane. Once inside the cabin, she quickly stowed her things before approaching Max.

"I'm sorry, Mr. Battenberg, but do you have any electronic devices with you?"

"Just my cell," he replied.

"I'm afraid I'll need it for now. I promise I'll return it safely."

Max was hardly thrown by the request, figuring it a necessary safety precaution. "Okay." He removed the phone and handed it over.

"No other devices, correct?"

A desire to protest arose in Max, who was unaccustomed to following instructions from anyone but Demetrius. Choosing instead to cooperate, he squashed down his feelings of belligerence. He needed answers and would facilitate anything to see Demetrius sooner than later. "No. Just the phone."

Rosalee removed her own phone and passed both handsets to a member of the crew. Before Max knew it, they were all seated in the signature jet. More like a small living room than a plane, the cabin's interior was plush with hardwood flooring and designer Italian furnishings. Toward the rear of the plane, two cream-colored leather sofas ran parallel to each other and were separated by a coffee table that was mounted to three metal bars in the ceiling.

In front of the sofa section, there were two sets of reclining armchairs on each side of the aisle for a total of eight individual seats. They were each crafted of the same soft garment leather that

Demetrius surrounded himself with.

Max grabbed a seat in one of the individual armchairs. Before he knew it, the plane was taxiing down the runway, and within seconds they were airborne. Max took a deep breath, relieved by the break in his causeless laughter. While not especially religious, he prayed that the strange symptoms would not return. *What did he do to me?*

He had no idea where they were headed or how long it would take to get there. As the plane continued to climb, he turned to Rosalee, who was on one of the sofas behind him. "Where are we headed exactly?"

Rosalee, now wearing glasses, was flipping through Vanity Fair magazine. She looked over her spectacles at Max. "Las Cruces, New Mexico."

"I thought he was in Brazil?"

She closed her magazine and gave Max her full attention. "He was, Mr. Battenberg. But he's been moved to a secure location. We should be in Las Cruces in a couple of hours."

Max sighed deeply. In Las Cruces, he would have answers. Somehow, the stress he was feeling about his father felt lightened by the plane's sheer speed. Hurtling through the air gave him the sense of movement and action, which was preferable to sitting at home, waiting. His last memory before drifting off to sleep was of nestling in his seat and giggling.

The remainder of the flight was smooth and allowed Max needed time to rest. He was bumped awake when the plane touched down. Opening his eyes, he gazed out on a sunny New Mexico day. He stretched and turned back to see Rosalee on the airphone. It seemed there was no rest for her as his father's assistant.

Max felt calmed and a little disoriented from the brief nap. Gathering himself, he gazed more attentively through the cabin window, only to be completely taken aback by what he saw.

They had landed in a desolate airfield that resembled an abandoned military outpost. For miles, there was nothing but dry desert terrain. It appeared they were on an old, dusty runway without an airport. As the private jet continued to taxi, a large, rusty hangar came into view. The jet disappeared inside while shutting down its engines.

Rosalee grabbed her briefcase and stood. She gestured for Max to disembark. "After you, Mr. Battenberg."

"You didn't forget our phones, did you?"

Rosalee generated a smile that was neither friendly nor cold. "We're not quite cleared for those just yet. Security measures, I'm afraid."

Max considered the protocol. Outside of Indigo's request, he had never been asked to relinquish his phone. He understood the concern since he didn't ever remember having it remotely activated, as he had experienced at Brigitte's house.

When they stepped from the plane, a dark blue Mercedes SUV was waiting in the dusty confines of the immense, rickety hangar. Rosalee herded Max inside and they were promptly chauffeured from the airstrip. Roughly a mile away there was a chain link fence topped with barbed wire. The barrier seemed to surround the entirety of the airfield.

They drove through an unmanned guard station and proceeded roughly thirty miles into the desert. The ride was smooth, but Max was certain the Mercedes was traveling at a minimum of ninety miles per hour. After another ten minutes, he noticed a rocky hillside coming into view. As they drew nearer, Max realized it wasn't so much a hill as a hulking piece of solid rock.

The SUV drove straight toward the sandstone monolith until they reached another guard station. Two men exited the small booth, each carrying a large assault rifle.

Max felt the urge to laugh, but he was in much greater control than he had been earlier that morning. He turned to Rosalee. "I thought we were going to see my dad?"

"We are."

She maintained a professional manner, but Max could tell Rosalee was losing patience.

"What is this, some kind of military installation?"

"I know this is all new for you, Mr. Battenberg. For the time being, your father is being held in a secure medical facility, which we are arriving at now."

The security guards waved them through the first gate. A quarter of a mile ahead, they encountered a second gate with more armed guards. After clearing the second barricade, Max noticed an entrance tunneling into the rocky hill. More guards were there, also armed with rifles.

The Mercedes drove past the final guard station into the large mountain of rock. Inside, a spacious and well-organized hangar was busy with activity. Workers circulated about. Some were driving forklifts loaded with large containers that they stacked in various quadrants of the spacious depot. Max couldn't distinguish if the crates and palettes were being shipped away or delivered in.

Positioned diagonally across the floor, there were a half dozen golf carts. They were all parked in tandem beside two enormous drilling machines, the kind used to excavate bedrock. The car finally came to a stop before an enormous metallic door.

Rosalee offered Max a friendly smile. "Here we are."

He stepped from the Mercedes and looked around, astonished. He was standing in a huge, fully functioning warehouse that had been carved from the mountain itself. Strangely, there was no sign of a hospital in this facility that seemed entirely industrial.

Directly in front of them, there were two enormous steel doors that appeared to be cargo elevators. Rosalee gently touched Max's arm and led him across the hangar to an adjacent wall. Lined up in a row were three small passenger elevators. Just like their larger counterparts, they had been constructed by burrowing deep into the mountain.

Rosalee swiped her badge, keyed in an access code and the doors to one of the people movers slid open to invite them in. Inside on the right wall, there were three buttons. From top to bottom they were colored red, blue and green. Using the buttons, Rosalee punched in a sequence that prompted the doors to close.

To Max's surprise, the elevator's fluorescent lighting blinked out. A moment later, a red light bathed the room and the entire chamber began to vibrate. To Max, it felt like standing before a gigantic nightclub speaker thumping with bass. The vibration rang in his ears, radiating through his legs and into his pelvis. He turned to Rosalee, feeling awkward and uncomfortable.

"What's going on?"

"There are no contaminants allowed in this facility. Infrared and high frequency are extremely efficient at wiping out anything unwanted."

After a minute or two, the elevator ceased vibrating and its normal fluorescent lighting resumed. Rosalee keyed in a different combination code, and the elevator dropped like an amusement park ride.

"Whoa!" Max exclaimed, caught off guard by the elevator's descendant velocity. "This feels faster than the ones at my father's penthouse."

Even Rosalee, whose resolve was like steel, appeared unsettled. She turned to Max in confirmation. "I'll never get used to that."

It was clear the elevator was traveling at a high rate of speed. Given its acceleration, Max didn't think they would be on it for long. But nearly two minutes passed before the elevator slowed to a stop. When the doors opened, Max was flabbergasted once again.

Expansive marble floors in beiges and yellows stretched across a palatial hallway with thirty-foot ceilings. Off to the left was a large, circular sitting area with contemporary seating, just as one might find in the lounge sections of an upscale shopping center.

He and Rosalee stepped from the elevator into the wide, open space. Oddly, there was music playing as it might be piped in at a popular mall. Without thinking Max spit out a laugh.

"What is this place?"

A number of windows and doorways ran along the corridor that looked to be a mix of offices and storefronts. With a few exceptions, they were obscured by blinds or opaque glass. In the areas that were visible, he could see people going about their everyday routines in what seemed to be ordinary desk jobs.

"This, Mr. Battenberg, is just one of several underground installations. Much of what you see was actually built by Battenberg Industries."

"This is crazy. It looks like a shopping mall."

Rosalee motioned for Max to begin walking. "The goal is to replicate comforts we enjoy above ground, with the security and sterility that only a few miles of solid rock can offer."

People crossed back and forth through the hall while others lingered casually in storefront doorways. Max peered in several windows and could see people working on computers or conversing on the phone.

He and Rosalee passed by a second sitting area on their way down the main hall. After roughly five hundred feet, Rosalee crossed to a set of double doors. In a chivalrous move without need of access codes, Max pulled open the doors, allowing her to enter.

As they passed through the threshold, Max realized they were now in a hospital wing, clearly where his father was being held. Together, he and Rosalee approached a heavy metal door with keypad access. Rosalee entered a code and they passed into a huge hotel-like suite.

Max looked around the room with an immediate sense of déjà vu. A huge window boasted a view of Chicago's skyline. This was of course impossible. Not only were they not in Chicago, they were two miles within the Earth. Max realized the room was the clone of a room in Demetrius' penthouse, with every detail perfectly replicated. Upon this realization, he spotted his father across the room.

Demetrius was completely immobilized in a large hospital bed adjusted to its upright position. The bed had been placed against the wall facing the virtual window. It allowed Demetrius to gaze across Chicago as if he were at home in the Spire.

Max was shocked by his father's appearance. His head was twice its normal size and his face, black and blue. A couple of clear tubes descended from behind his head down into his lap. A pinkish-brown fluid trickled through them and was captured in small plastic receptacles. The elder Battenberg appeared to be sleeping soundly.

Rosalee gently touched Max's arm. "I know how this must appear, but he's recovering quite well. I'll give you a moment alone." Rosalee's smile was warm as she excused herself and left the room.

Max stood in one spot, staring long and hard at Demetrius. He had been anxious to speak with his father, but now that he was in his presence, he didn't want to wake him. It was also a shock to see a man so powerful brought so low. After several minutes of surveying his injuries, Max crossed to the virtual window. Up close, he realized the view was significantly better than he had imagined. Gazing down on the streets, he could actually see there were cars driving and pedestrians on the move.

The large window was a huge flat screen monitor connected to a live feed. It allowed Demetrius to see exactly what he would be seeing at home. Max reached out and touched the makeshift window, which was strangely cool.

The silence shattered as Demetrius spoke, his voice humbled and broken. "How long have you been here?"

Max spun around to see his father making the saddest attempt at a smile. "Hey, pops." He approached the bed and sat in a chair beside it. "You look like shit."

Demetrius shifted slightly, making it clear what a tremendous effort it was for him to move at all. "I'd say that's a great way... to describe how I feel."

Max tried not to stare. It was awful, seeing his father's cranium swollen to such a degree. It was obvious the tubes were draining fluid from his brain. Demetrius closed his eyes as a wave of pain washed over him.

"What happened, dad? Who did this to you?"

With a grimace Demetrius spoke. "What happened... is they got to me."

"Who, pop? Who did this?"

Demetrius coughed and grimaced. After a brief pause, he found a cord beside him and depressed a button to dispense additional morphine. "I'm sorry this is how you're learning things. I should've shared more... before now." Demetrius stared into his son's face and could see his hunger for an explanation. "Your initiation, and mine... and my father's before me..." Demetrius paused to catch his breath, "The responsibility... of the bloodline... must be passed along."

Max tried to finish his father's thought. "The Nibiru bloodline, you mean?"

Demetrius scowled and Max understood it was an attempt at a smile. "Very good... You've done your homework I see."

"You could say that. I'm still going to have a hard time saying Anunnaki."

Demetrius frowned once more before continuing. "Our legacy is one of supremacy... and strength... we must keep it that way."

Something in Max was afraid to ask, but stronger than his fear was his desire to know. "I've seen so much, I need you to tell me what that legacy is." Max studied his father's pained expression.

After a bout of wheezing, Demetrius continued, "Enlil... We are Enlil's bloodline. His is the legacy we must preserve." A trail of dribble ran down his chin.

Max took a cloth from the bedside and wiped his father's face. During the initiation he had felt Enlil's rage. Now, he understood why. He had somehow merged with his ancestor. On one hand, he was exhilarated by the idea, but he also felt shame. Because he had experienced Enlil's essence, Max knew his ancient relative possessed a myriad of negative traits, including pettiness and jealousy. For the first time in his life, Max feared those qualities. Had they been passed down to him over the generations?

Demetrius gargled saliva in his throat before he spoke again. "There is another bloodline..."

"Enki," Max spoke the word aloud as if he had stolen it from his father's lips.

"Yes," Demetrius whispered. "Enki. We are all cousins really. But just as it was with them... there exists opposition in the bloodlines today... conflicting views."

"Are these the people who did this to you, these cousins?"

"So much is done in secrecy, Max... it's hard to know. Since your mother's accident, I have always been careful, you know this. But this time they got to me. Just like they got to her."

"These are the same people who killed Mom?" The reality of his mother having been murdered still hadn't settled with Max. Being made witness to the broken wreckage that was now his father didn't make this circumstance any easier to digest. Without warning, Max felt rage building inside of him. *Is this Enlil stirring inside of me?* "Dad, listen to me." Max scooted closer to his father's bed. "Can you tell me who did this?"

"I have theories, but it's hard to know for sure. They conceal themselves, Max. Just like we do. But over time, we all come to know who the players are... and the nature of our conflicts... Whether it be Israel or the Arab world, communism or democracy..." Demetrius attempted a laugh but a cough is all that escaped him. "The North and South in the Civil War. In time, we will know all the answers."

Max stared long and hard at his father. In spite of himself, a lone tear meandered down his cheek. "What did you do when they killed Mom and Christian? Was somebody punished?"

This time, Demetrius managed a laugh, which caused him immense pain. He coughed and grimaced before continuing, "So rarely are any of us the casualties of our own conflicts, Max. Back then I was sloppy. And they were brazen... Not unlike this time I suppose. Our debts, typically, are paid... and messages are sent... in collateral damage."

Max looked around the replicated room, incensed that his family was being picked off one by one. "I suppose they'll never get to you here."

Demetrius waved his hand dismissively. "There are many of these places. We aren't the only ones who have them." With tremendous effort, Demetrius shifted again. "But I'm going to be here a while."

"I get that, pops."

"One of us... a Battenberg... must be present." Demetrius swallowed hard before continuing, "Without that our position will be considerably weakened."

"What're you talking about? Present where?"

Demetrius closed his eyes, but this time it was more from disappointment than from pain. "I know this is all new to you. And there isn't much time for you to get up to speed. There are too many commitments... I need you to fulfill them... in my stead."

Max glanced through the window. For a split second he forgot they were deep underneath the state of New Mexico. "What do you need me to do?"

Demetrius fell silent with all the misgivings of his current circumstances. Just as Max was growing concerned, he spoke.

"There's a meeting... there's a meeting a month from now. The Rizick Group. There's no way I'll be able to attend..." Demetrius' voice was growing throatier with each word. "Not like this. I need you to go instead."

"The Rizick Group?" Max recalled having heard the term somewhere, but he couldn't remember exactly where or when. Then, after a delayed reaction, it came to him — *Rizick!*

He had seen the word twice before, once in Chicago, in the back alley of the club where his father's guards had abducted him. *The black stencil.* The word "RIZICK" had been spray painted along with the image of George W. Bush. He'd seen similar graffiti outside the club in Mexico City.

"Rizick is where we, and others like us, come to meet... once or twice a year. For me not to be there... would be a huge blow... to the stability I've worked too hard to establish. You must go... and make our presence known."

"Okay. Just tell me what I need to do."

For the first time, Max felt fully empowered by his father. It felt good, like they were a team, but only for a fleeting moment. Suddenly, he could hear Indigo's voice in his head, telling him everything would be revealed and that a burden would soon be placed upon him. It would be Max's decision whether or not the domination continued of the few over the many.

In an uncharacteristic move, Demetrius reached for Max's hand and squeezed it. "The next weeks are crucial. Your preparation... you must know everything. At Rizick, our determinations... those decisions, which benefit our interests... they must be swift, and more important than that, firm. Battenberg ideals must be made clear... even with me in this bed." With these final words, Demetrius began to cough as an accumulation of fluid slowly choked his lungs.

"Pops, you okay?" Alarmed, Max ran from the room and found Rosalee outside with a male nurse. "He's having trouble breathing," Max interrupted, looking urgently at the nurse. "I need you to check on him."

The nurse quickly reentered to evaluate Demetrius, who was still coughing and gagging for breath. The health worker grabbed an aspirator from beside the bed and inserted it into a tracheal tube that Max hadn't even noticed. "It's okay, Mr. Battenberg." He suctioned off the fluid and Demetrius immediately began to breathe more easily. The elder Battenberg motioned for Max to approach, but the nurse protested.

"I'm sorry, Mr. Battenberg. I'm going to have ask your son to step out."

Demetrius took a labored breath. "I just have a few things... to discuss."

The nurse glanced at a monitor over the bed and noticed a dip in Demetrius' vitals. "I'm afraid I can't allow that, Mr. Battenberg. Once you're stabilized, your son can certainly return."

Max couldn't recall ever having heard his father take instructions, but Demetrius simply closed his eyes and sighed. His father's caregiver removed a syringe from a bedside table and injected something into the I.V. Within seconds, Demetrius relaxed.

The nurse paused to observe his vitals again, then crossed to where Max and Rosalee were standing. "He just needs rest is all. You're welcome to come back the moment he's stronger."

Max and Rosalee smiled before turning to quietly exit the room. In signature fashion, Rosalee remained pleasant and professional when she spoke.

"His injuries are pretty extensive, but they aren't life-threatening. Knowing Mr. Battenberg, he should be on his feet in no time."

While he wasn't fully convinced, Max did feel hopeful. Demetrius, if anything, was a fighter. In the back of his mind, Max prayed his father would recover before the upcoming Rizick Group meeting. For him to step into his father's shoes and learn everything there was to know felt overwhelming. At best, Max worried he was about to bite off more than he could chew.

Rosalee removed her Blackberry and read from it briefly. "My instructions are to put you in contact with Mr. Khrzinsky."

"Otto?" It had been a while since Max spoke with his father's trusted advisor and friend. Of course he would be somewhere nearby.

"Mr. Khrzinsky is in the District of Columbia right now. Per your father's instructions, I am to put you on the next train to DC."

Max couldn't remember ever having been on a train in the United States. "I'm sorry, did you say a train?"

"This one you'll want to take, Mr. Battenberg. It's quite preferable to an airplane. I suggest you buy a suit, maybe a pair of jeans. There are shops down here and you may need a few things for DC."

Anxiety and a little excitement flooded Max's mind as he considered this. Like Alice, he had been dropped down a rabbit hole, an analogy made ironic by his presence deep in the Earth.

Indigo had suggested that what he knew was only the tip of the iceberg. It seemed that the iceberg was coming to the surface. She had also predicted he would understand everything before year's end. From what he could gather, it would be only a matter of weeks before much was revealed. Max pondered this reality and took a deep sigh, just as his father had done only minutes before.

CHAPTER 49

*A*fter pointing out his need for clothing, Rosalee had ushered Max through the underground facility. He now had a garment bag with several thousand dollars worth of purchases slung over one shoulder. To his surprise, Rosalee finally returned his cell phone, which had been wiped clean of any spyware or other suspicious downloads.

With her as his guide, Max strolled through the underground complex, amazed by the array of amenities that were more typically found above ground. Escalators and moving sidewalks were strategically placed about the complex. There was also an occasional golf cart that would drive by on the shiny marble floors.

Just when Max thought he couldn't be more astonished, Rosalee escorted him to the underground train system. The platform resembled one of London's tube stations. Its tunnel was circular and covered in polished stainless steel plates. Illuminated crystals similar to the ones in the pyramid of Teotihuacán were strategically placed about the station and brightened the entire area with a soft white glow.

Max gawked. "It's like a miniature city down here. How is all of this powered?"

"Extremely clean and efficient technologies. Each of these complexes is designed for complete self-sufficiency."

Max frowned at Rosalee's explanation. "You mean none of this is plugged in to the power grids up there?"

"That's correct, sir."

"Why aren't these technologies being used above ground?"

Rosalee raised an eyebrow at Max's statement. "I'm sure you know why that is, Mr. Battenberg. The existence of these locations and the technologies used within them are on a strict need-to-know basis. They were created solely for people of the highest caliber."

The Anunnaki. Max gestured to the only bench he could see. "Shall we sit?"

"It'll hardly be worthwhile. The trains are extremely punctual here. And they only stop when signaled for pickup. The next one arrives," Rosalee glanced at her Blackberry, "in about ninety seconds."

Max wracked his brain, trying to ascertain how so much could have existed without his knowledge. There was an entire invisible world that he and many others had never even imagined. "How many of these places are there?"

"Dozens. And that's only on this continent."

Just as Rosalee had predicted, a series of green lights began flashing along the spine of the tunnel roof.

"That would be the train, Mr. Battenberg."

Before he could gather himself, a strong wind gusted through the station. Rosalee's hair whipped about as Max's garment bag flapped up and down against his shoulder. She urged him forward on the platform.

Chasing the wind, the most aerodynamic transport vehicle Max had ever seen came rushing down the platform. Max was astonished how much the train resembled a giant snake. Its head, or the engineer's cabin, was slightly larger than the body, which glistened a metallic silver. Unlike conventional trains, there didn't appear to be separate cars, but rather a continuous serpentine body. Other than the whistling of the wind, the locomotive didn't make a sound.

Max stared at the tunnel floor in amazement. *There are no tracks!*

As if riding on some invisible cushion, the train was simply floating above where the tracks should have been. What seemed a large portion of the vehicle shot by and vanished into the tunnel ahead. After nearly a minute, the state-of-the-art vehicle slowed. Its hull was constructed of large metallic pieces that fit together like scaly armor. There were no seams or rivets evident on the individual pieces that Max could tell, but long rectangular windows appeared intermittently along the train's length.

The train continued to slow, allowing Max a better view of its passing compartments. He peered through a lengthy rectangular window and was stupefied by what he saw. Inside, there were rows and rows of benches, like church pews. Attached to every bench were multiple sets of chains and shackles. He did a double take as the cars in question disappeared into the tunnel.

Max was certain Rosalee saw his reaction, but his father's assistant remained stone-faced and silent. Without skipping a beat, she removed a deck of papers from her satchel.

"As you know, Mr. Battenberg, there is a delicate nature to everything you're seeing. To call it top secret would be an understatement
at best. Also along that line, it is customary that we provide you
with a list of associates it would be advisable to avoid. This is of
course based on our best and most current intel." Rosalee handed
the deck of papers to Max. "Should you want to discuss any names
on the list, by all means let me know."

Suddenly, Max could see the silhouettes of people through
obscured translucent glass. As the train came to a stop, he realized
it must be private cabins he was seeing. He lifted the deck of papers
before Rosalee. "So, is this some kind of blacklist?"

She escorted him toward the train. "The list is a simple recom-
mendation of people it might be advisable to avoid. At the end of the
day, the choice is entirely yours." Rosalee's disposition was pleasant, albeit cold and impersonal.

One of the train's large metal pieces slid forward to expose an
entrance.

"Your room is twenty-two B. Should you need privacy, the code
is zero-one-seven-six. You'll arrive in DC in about two hours."

"What?" Max was amazed by such an absurd time frame. "DC's
got to be nearly two thousand miles from here."

"As I mentioned, the trains are very quick. This is what makes
them convenient. Go on—you should get on. My contact numbers
have been added to your phone if you need to reach me."

"Thank you, Rosalee. For everything. I'm sure I'll be in touch."

She smiled as Max boarded the train. Seconds after his entrance,
the armored door slid shut. Almost instantly, they were on the move.
Being a passenger on the train was even more remarkable than
watching it approach. As the high-tech vehicle accelerated, Max
had the distinct feeling they were standing still. The only sense of
movement stemmed from the fact that Rosalee was disappearing
out of view. In the blink of an eye, the windows went dark as his
compartment was swallowed by the underground tunnel.

Now the train was hurtling toward DC. Max walked down the
corridor and found compartment twenty-two B. It was a plush
room with a soft cushioned bench, a table and a flat screen monitor against the opposite wall. He hung his garment bag on the door,
then fidgeted with the TV monitor. He couldn't get it to work, but
didn't care since it was such a short ride.

Settling in, Max stretched out along the comfortable bench and considered the futuristic feel of the underground train. The sense of privilege he enjoyed as a Battenberg only felt further enhanced by his access to such a clandestine facility.

As he rocketed toward DC at nearly a thousand miles per hour, Max removed his cell phone from his pocket. More than likely, it would function magically in spite of their intense depth beneath the ground. Yes: to his bewilderment, he had full reception. He dialed Brigitte's number and waited several rings until voice mail kicked in.

Staccato laughter escaped him. Max didn't know if it was due to the absurdity of his circumstances, or whether it had more to do with the whammy he had received from the homeless man outside of the yoga studio. After the beep, he spoke into the phone.

"Hey, babe, it's me. Just finished seeing my dad. He's in pretty bad shape." Max unfortunately chuckled. "He looks terrible in fact. But he is expected to survive. It was difficult seeing him like that." Max struggled to find the right words. "Listen, I'm sorry about last night and earlier today. I hope I didn't ruin the party for you. I swear when I spoke to you this morning I didn't realize a driver was at my house. I tried getting them to wait..." After a long pause, Max continued, "Anyway, call me. I miss you."

He hung up and opened the blacklist Rosalee had given him. He was curious, and maybe a little annoyed, by the audacity of such a list. Still, he wanted to know which associates were being deemed unsuitable for him. Max flipped through several pages and noticed the names of people who were acquaintances at best. With a sense of growing relief, he browsed further until a name caught his eye. *Gary Richards.*

Gary was number two fifty-five on the roster. Max stared at the name, wondering what he had done to make the list. And ironically, Gary was in DC. Max immediately felt his defiant side beginning to surface. He wondered if he would try to see Gary. As he continued through the list, he made a mental note to investigate why Gary was on it.

Growing bored, Max laid the blacklist on the table. Until now, he hadn't noticed his own exhaustion. He leaned back, settling in to the comfort of the climate-controlled cabin. It was the first time in a long while that he wished for a longer journey if only to allow for a moment's rest.

In the far recesses of his mind, Max still had a zillion questions. He wondered and even worried what might await him at the upcoming Rizick Group meeting. Too much weight, he felt, had now been placed on his young shoulders. There was an enormous amount he didn't know, yet here he was, about to play substitute for Demetrius.

Max closed his eyes, and a desire to sleep immediately enveloped him like a warm blanket. As the train snaked through the earth, he had a final conscious thought before drifting off to sleep.

What explanation could there possibly be for a train full of shackles? With this in mind, he lapsed into a state that could best be described as dreamscape.

CHAPTER 50

*F*or many a decade, Enki walked with anger. After centuries of autonomy, his younger meddling brother had traveled all the way from Nibiru to successfully usurp everything he had built: The palace and pyramid complex of Eridu, the glory of the mining operation — everything he had created had been lost to Enlil's reprehensible plan for control.

Enki knew on an intellectual level, however, that the laws of impermanence were on his side. *Statistically*, he thought, *nothing can remain the same. Everything must change.* Just as he had fallen from grace, it would only be a matter of time before Enlil got what he deserved.

After their father's reprimand, Enki had been permitted to remain on Earth. But he was more or less in exile in the Abzu, five thousand miles away. In his new home on the southern coast of the lower continent, he had been tasked with developing a new mining operation. With the combined efforts of two sites, both Eridu and the Abzu, gold shipments to Nibiru were expected to double.

Soon after he took command, Enlil had learned of the many challenges Earth presented. Of course these were all things Enki already knew well. From the start, his Igigi work force had been delivered from Nibiru in increments that were too few and too far in between. At its best, the fleet of Nibirian workers on Earth remained in limited supply.

When Enki was in charge, he had struggled to placate the Igigi, doing whatever it took to maintain production. Now, under his brother's rule, the Igigi were more disgruntled than ever. *The virtue of patience*, Enki thought, *is the greatest prize. For many decades I have waited for Enlil's humiliation.*

Over time as Enlil gained expertise, Nibiru had expected a dramatic boost in Eridu's gold provisions. But instead they had diminished. Under Enlil's cruel and unforgiving control, gold production in the north had finally ground to a halt. Fed up with their work conditions, the Igigi had mutinied, something Enki could easily have predicted had he not been banished to the Abzu.

Now his day had come. With production rising in the Abzu, Enki would soon be restored as Earth's master and commander. For the time being, he would lay low while quietly examining his younger brother's comings and goings.

Enlil was still in command and would stop at nothing to sabotage Enki's reputation in the south. He had purposely supplied him with fewer workers than needed. To make things worse, the operation in the Abzu was every bit as backbreaking as it had been in Eridu and perhaps even more so.

But Enlil, in his arrogance, had missed the source of Enki's true advantage. The older brother had been on Earth longer and was infinitely more familiar with the terrain. The small, blue planet was overabundant in a variety of resources other than gold. Enki used these resources to keep his own Igigi satisfied, even when they were unhappy with their work.

The use of Earth's animals, fruits and vegetables enabled Enki to prepare lavish meals unlike any seen on Nibiru. He bestowed weekly parties upon his Igigi, allowing them to gorge themselves as never before. Because of their sugars, many fruits were easily distilled into intoxicants that helped the Igigi forget their woes for a while.

For a time, Enki produced the gold demanded of him, at times even outperforming Eridu. During this quiet time of waiting, as he thought of it, he followed orders from both his father and Enlil. But when Enlil least suspected, he would strike the way a panther ambushes its prey. His foolish brother didn't realize it, but his tactics were so dictatorial that they had already boosted Enki's popularity among the Igigi. Already the workforces of Eridu were more than happy to be reassigned to the Abzu.

If everything went as planned, Earth would provide yet another asset to save Nibiru and to further humiliate Enlil. Until now, the planet's primitive beings had remained entirely unharvested. To his credit, Enki had already mapped a tremendous range of terrain upon which he had located numerous tribes of the indigenous creatures.

Many of the humanoids, he found, were in vastly different stages of development. The most advanced had developed a rather crude use of language and seemed more suited toward hunting and agriculture than mining. Enki, who had been a skilled geneticist on Nibiru, had recognized an opportunity that his brother was too unwise to realize.

Why should I not use them? he thought. *They are here for my bidding.*
Enlil may have denied him the troops of Igigi needed in the Abzu,
but the beasts of planet Earth were in ample supply. His younger
sibling's sole expertise found its footing in his brutish nature and
was often accompanied with violence and aggression: coups, uprisings and domination were his field of excellence.

Enki, on the other hand, was skilled in areas of a more intellectual
nature. Aware that he would need help, he sent word to Nibiru with
a request for Ninmah, his half sister, who happened to be Enlil's full-
blooded sibling. Ninmah, as it turned out, held an affinity for Enki
that was deeper than the connection she felt for her own full brother.
As peers on Nibiru, she and Enki had studied the intricate workings of bio-genetics and were both considered experts in the field.

To assure her passage, he had asked Ninmah to arrange her
transport through Enlil. This was not from necessity, but more
because Enki preferred that Enlil participate in his own downfall.
In the end, everything transitioned smoothly, with Ninmah's arrival
on the first transport from Nibiru.

After several months in Eridu, she had taken leave for the Abzu
under the guise of "we need to keep an eye on Enki." At the very
moment of her arrival, Enki ushered her into his new laboratory.
He had secretly commissioned the workspace, which took nearly
two years to build.

Full of smiles, Ninmah hugged her half brother, looking about
the room in awe. "This is amazing, brother. How have you procured
such a space in this place?"

"Patiently," Enki explained, inflating his chest with pride. "With
each transport, I request one or two things. Other elements I have
assembled while here."

The large L-shaped lab was fully operational with plumbing
and electricity. In the top portion of the "L," an extensive shelving
unit housed a series of glass bottles, jars and test tubes. Beside it,
an enormous stone basin was divided into two sinks with running
water. Covering the adjacent wall, there were nearly a hundred
compartments, each the size of standard post office boxes. Ninmah
wondered what was housed inside of them.

Startled by sound and movement, she spun around to the far
corner of the room in the lower section of the "L." Her eyes widened
with excitement as she spotted the source of commotion. "Are those

what I think they are?"

Enki's expression softened into a smile. "I told you they'd be ready by the time you arrived."

Ninmah rushed toward the far wall, but stopped a few paces shy of a caged enclosure. Inside the pen, she beheld a collection of eight ape-like beasts who were the planet's indigenous beings. Earthlings. The dark-haired humanoids cowered in the farthest corner of the cage.

Enki sensed his half-sister's apprehension. "Go ahead, you can approach. They're more frightened of us than we could ever be of them."

Ninmah stepped to the cage. The creatures kept their distance against the far wall, clinging to one another for comfort and protection.

"Where did you find them?"

"Not far from here. To the north is where the cleverer ones reside. Notice I have procured four males and four females. We'll need variety in the gene pool."

Ninmah studied the beasts in amazement. Brown and black coarse hair grew on every part of their bodies, including on their faces, upon which flat, wide noses spread. Ninmah took note of their hands and sinewy elongated digits.

"Look at their fingers, they're so long. It's strange, don't you think?"

"Much of the time they walk on all fours."

"And their hairiness is peculiar." For nearly a minute, Ninmah stood at the cage, mesmerized. "I was about to ask how you tell the males from the females." But Ninmah spotted the breasts of a female. On an adjacent male she could see the faint outline of a penis hidden in tufts of hair. "At least we know their organs are situated similarly to ours." Ninmah turned to Enki, full of hope. "That will make things easier."

"I extracted blood before you got here." Enki gazed longingly at his half sister, unsure what was turning him on more—her, or the prospect of vengeance against Enlil. "We can start as soon as you like."

Ninmah grabbed Enki in her arms with a loving embrace. Their passion, striking like a powerful wave, swept them off their feet, and

Enki and Ninmah fell to the floor, ripping at one another's clothes. Without shame, they began to make love in front of the caged beings, who watched, still in fear and awe.

In the months following Ninmah's arrival, both she and Enki worked feverishly in the covert laboratory. They harvested a small collection of ova from the captive females as well as spermatozoa from the males.

They deconstructed the creatures' genetic coding, identifying each unique element of their DNA. With a recipe thus in hand, they began tinkering to remove the parts they wished to omit. *They have no need to utilize the full capacity of their brains*, Enki thought. *This is not necessary to work the mines.*

At the same time, the creatures' need for language was paramount if they were to follow instructions. Enki and Ninmah toiled to strip down the animals' genetic code to the bare essentials. Conversely, they added desired elements from their own Anunnaki DNA.

When they were finished, Enki implanted a triad of hybridized embryos in Ninmah's womb. She carried them for a nine-month term before climbing on the laboratory birthing chair. With ease, she pushed each triplet from her womb, only to be dismayed by their condition. Each was more imperfect than the one before: the first deaf-mute, the second blind and the third stillborn.

Enki cringed at the sight of each infirm baby, but took the two surviving offspring and placed them in the cage with the captive humanoids. He and Ninmah watched as two females sheepishly moved forward to investigate. One at a time, they took the newborns and retreated to the back of the cage, cradling each infant with maternal care.

Ninmah rose from the birthing chair and covered herself as she crossed to Enki. "We will try again, brother."

She and Enki returned to the laboratory to further adjust their hybridized code. They repaired defective chains, continuing to add and remove elements of their choosing. But after another failed batch, Ninmah grew weary.

"Brother... I cannot carry on much longer. With each essay, I can feel my life force draining."

"Ninmah," Enki assured, "we'll be heroes when we perfect the code. I promise, down the road, we'll find others to incubate the progeny." Enki knew very well that Ninmah found him seductive. He would use this every bit to his advantage. "We're very close, I know it. Shall we try once more? This will surely be the last time."

Reluctant, Ninmah nodded in agreement. "All right. This time, we shall only try one. I can't bear the idea of more."

On the third occasion, a single male embryo was created and implanted in Ninmah. Once again she carried the hybrid throughout its gestation. When it was fully developed, she climbed onto the birthing chair and pushed it from her womb.

"Well?" Ninmah asked, locked in suspense.

Enki, with a startled look on his face, removed the child from between her loins. He lifted it into view. When she saw the infant, Ninmah gasped with surprise. The olive-complexioned baby had beautiful hairless skin. In many ways, it appeared just as an Anunnaki child.

Enki handed the newborn to Ninmah. They stared wide-eyed at the male hybrid, whose blood contained a mixture of human and Anunnaki DNA. Patiently, they stroked the infant, waiting for him to open his eyes. As if on cue, he opened them and looked from Enki to Ninmah.

"He can see!" Ninmah screamed, full of excitement. "Look at his body, Enki. It is so beautiful! Without the hair."

Enki hardly took notice of Ninmah as he studied the tiny creature, who finally opened his mouth and screamed at full volume.

Enki's eyes grew large with joy. "He speaks, Ninmah, he speaks."

Ninmah pulled the child to her breast, gazing down with pride and joy. "We have done it, brother. This time, I believe we have done it."

Enki kissed and hugged Ninmah before taking the baby to examine him more closely. "He looks so much like our own."

"In our image," Ninmah muttered, spellbound.

Filled with pride, Enki counted the child's fingers and toes before turning his attention to the infant's genitalia. A puzzled look crossed his face. "Although there is one thing: no child on Nibiru is born with this."

Ninmah followed his eyes to the newborn's foreskin at the tip of his penis. "How peculiar. Such a strange fold of skin."

"It is of little import," Enki declared, "Such a thing won't affect work in the mines." Enki looked up, his mind unbound by the possibilities. "We will create others to increase production in the Abzu. When it is double that of Eridu, I will resume my role as master and commander. Then I will make you my wife. And together, we will show Enlil his place."

Unable to stop smiling, Ninmah questioned, "What shall we call it, brother?"

Enki studied the child. After a moment's consideration he spoke. "We will call him Adamu. Through him, a new race of Igigi shall rise."

CHAPTER 51

Was it true sleep or the strange, induced dream-state that enabled Max to view yet another piece of the Enki and Enlil story? Only weeks before, the white powder from his initiation had triggered something extraordinary, allowing Max to gaze deeply into the past of the royal half brothers. Later, through a similarly unexplained phenomenon, the Antikythera Mechanism had accomplished the same thing. And then the homeless man had flipped a switch in him, triggering another vision in front of the yoga studio. Whatever the man had done, there were also other residual effects like the uncontrolled laughter and muscle spasms.

Am I dreaming now?

Stuck between sleep and wakefulness, Max mulled over the events of the past month. It was only after he recovered the dial from the Money Pit that he had begun to see the woman and the midget in his dreams. The nightmarish scenes of the tall blonde and her miniature cohort felt terribly realistic, much like the visions generated from his initiation and the Antikythera Device. As more time passed, he was having an increasingly difficult time distinguishing the real world from his dreams.

Suddenly, he felt a hand shaking him, jarring him from his semi-slumber. Max jumped up in a startle. "What? What?" When his eyes came into focus, it was Otto Khrzinsky staring back at him.

"Wake up, sleepy head."

"Otto." Max took a few seconds to get his bearings, then inquired, "What are you doing here?" Max hugged his father's friend and advisor.

"You're in DC, pal. And we're holding up this ride."

"Oh, shit." Max was still a bit fuzzy. "We're here?" He stared in disbelief, clicking into his phone to see the time.

"When I didn't see you, I had to come looking." In a friendly gesture, Otto grabbed Max's garment bag from the door. "We need to get going."

Together, he and Max crossed into the corridor of the train to exit.

"Otto, wait." Max, finally waking up, realized he had questions for his father's friend.

"Max, we've already thrown the train off schedule, which we're only getting away with because of your dad."

"I need to show you something. It'll only take a second." Max grabbed Otto by the sleeve and led him down the corridor. He had never seen architecture such as that used in the train. The corridors were long and sleek with the same enormous panels of pewter-colored metal. In addition, there were occasional pieces of thick rectangular glass as on the outside.

Several cars of the train must have been in a curved portion of the tunnel, since he and Otto were veering to the left in what should have been a straight corridor. Somehow, the metal and glass were malleable in each of the cars, allowing them to twist and contort as they snaked through the subterranean pathways.

As they entered their third compartment, Otto protested, "Max, if we don't get off now, they're taking us with them."

Max broke into a jog, pulling Otto down the corridor until they crossed into yet another compartment. Harsh, fluorescent lighting splashed against Otto's skin, making it appear even more weathered and sallow than usual. Otto looked around and immediately guessed the nature of Max's question. They were standing in a section of the train that was dramatically unlike the others. Dozens of seats like church pews were equipped with shackles and chains.

Max stared at his father's right-hand man as he motioned toward the metal restraints. "What's all this?"

With a slight nod of his head Otto acknowledged the question. "Can we discuss this outside? If we don't, we'll be in Denver in a couple of hours."

While Max was anxious to hear Otto's answer, he didn't care to be stuck on the train. "All right."

Together, he and Otto hustled to the nearest exit, where the train's paneled doors were already open. Otto nevertheless placed his hand against the adjacent window. A keypad similar to the one in Max's panic room became visible in the glass. Otto quickly entered a sequence of numbers and the keypad quickly faded into its original transparency.

Max followed behind Otto, stepping from the train onto the secret underground platform. Within seconds, the doors to the train snapped shut and the serpentine vehicle slithered ahead, silently disappearing into the forward tunnel.

Otto turned to Max, still carrying his garment bag. "Is this all you have?"

Max offered a simple shrug. "They wouldn't let me pack anything before we left Chicago."

Otto's mood grew somber, as if he were a balloon being deflated of its air. "Understandable, I suppose. How's the old man?"

On some level, Max was surprised how emotional Otto's question made him feel. He pushed the sentiment aside as usual. "I hardly recognized him. No one thinks this was an accident, right?"

"I think that's pretty safe to say, although they're still determining what happened. Sadly, the Battenbergs have always been and will likely forever be targets."

A feeling of complete powerlessness enveloped Max. "So, what? Are we supposed to always look over our shoulders?"

"I'm afraid so."

"Fuck." Max stared down the train's empty tunnel. "If I didn't believe that New Orleans attack was about me, I'm pretty damn close to believing it now. Otto, just tell me people were punished for what happened to my mother and brother. And whoever did this to my dad, they should be punished too."

"This is why you're here, kiddo. To learn the ins and outs, and who the players are. Not to scare you, but that attack in New Orleans, if it was about you — more than likely they're going to try again."

"Yeah, I'm starting to get that."

Otto studied Max, looking for a reaction of some kind. "How're you holding up with all this?"

"All right, I suppose." Max was unsure how to answer, so he side-stepped his nervousness. "My dad's more resilient than we knew. Even in his condition, he's still giving orders."

Otto took note of Max's demeanor, searching for cracks in the veneer of a stoic facade. "It's more than just your dad. You received your initiation, Max; that's no small thing. Now, your father's in this situation... it's a lot."

Max pondered Otto's words. "If only you knew." Finally, some-one was saying what he had hoped to hear from his father. "The entire last month has been off the fuckin' charts." As Max finished his sentence, a bout of uncontrolled laughter came rushing from his mouth.

Otto frowned, finding the outburst peculiar. But given the circumstances, he dismissed it as stress on Max's part. "C'mon, let's get above ground."

Otto led Max through a maze of hallways. In Las Cruces, the underground complex felt every bit like the commercial centers found above ground, complete with marbled floors, brightly lit grand hallways and background music.

Here, there was no mistaking they were in a subterranean facility. Gray concrete floors gave the installation a dark and cave-like feeling. The halls and passageways felt more like mineshafts. The ceiling and walls were covered with dull white tiles like those found in antiquated school bathrooms or old subway stations. Where Las Cruces had been shiny and new, the DC installation felt outdated and unfinished.

Finally, Otto and Max stopped before a single, stainless steel elevator door. Otto pressed the call button and machinery roared to life from the interior of the elevator shaft.

Max felt a little spooked by the mechanized groans and squeaks that brought into question the elevator's safety. "How long's this place been here?"

"A bit longer than Las Cruces. That place has been there a few decades. Here," Otto glanced around at the capitol city's aging walls, "we're talking centuries. Just like the rest of DC."

Max stared about the corridor, noting the areas in need of repair. Finally, the elevator doors slid open to reveal the most ordinary compartment of scuffed-up stainless steel. "Where's this thing go?"

Otto smiled at the question. "There are a few options. I'll show you the one I like best." Using a ten-digit keypad, Otto punched in a sequence of numbers. The steel doors closed and the elevator jerked upwards. For more than a minute they ascended until the elevator came to an abrupt halt.

Fearing some type of malfunction, Max turned to Otto, full of concern. Otto started to speak when the elevator snapped into motion again. Only now, Max was sure it was moving horizontally instead of vertically. Otto smiled again as if to confirm his suspicion.

"There's a maze of elevator shafts. The one we're about to access might surprise you."

The elevator rattled to a stop. After a brief moment, it began to rise vertically again. Another minute passed before the doors opened to a hallway full of people, most of them in suits. Max stared at Otto in awe.

Otto led him from the elevator as a horde of people piled on. Somehow, they had accessed the elevator shaft of a public building.

"Over the next month or so, we'll be spending quite a bit of time here. That's when we'll go into detail about what you saw on the train. Something big's on the horizon. It's going to require more than a few people down there. We're anticipating not all of them are going to go willingly."

Max considered the shackles and wondered with trepidation what that implied. "From the looks of that train, we're talking more than a few."

"It'll be clear soon. This is why you're here. Your training for Rizick will illuminate a lot of things."

Max remained hesitant. He was hoping life would slow down, but this didn't seem to be the case. If anything, it was speeding up.

Otto took his turn to chuckle as he patted Max on the shoulder. "Don't look so shell-shocked. It's my mission to get you up to speed. I'm guessing neither of us is planning to let your father down on that front. Especially not now."

As hard as he tried, Max couldn't keep his game face on. Indigo had spoken of a huge weight he would carry, and now that Otto was talking, her words were ringing in his ears.

He followed Otto from the building and halfway down the steps toward the sidewalk. Together they turned to gaze up at the monolithic structure whose front was decorated with a series of eighteen stone pillars. Eight of them were centered perfectly above the stairs. Carved above those eight were the words, "Archives of the United States Of America."

They had just exited the National Archives Building. All around them, researchers, tourists and employees were rushing about.

Otto seemed impressed by his personal choice of exit. "Unless you have something else in mind, I've already arranged accommodations."

"No, of course not. Whatever you chose I'm sure is fine."

"It's just a few minutes from here." Otto smiled, bursting with pride. "Another Battenberg comes into his own." He leaned in and hugged Max. "Tomorrow, at nine o'clock sharp, we'll meet right here in front of the building. Then you'll get your first glimpse of how the world really runs."

"Thanks, Otto. For everything I mean." Max meant what he said. He was grateful to Otto even if deep down he felt a strong discord about the things they were seeing and doing. While he wasn't fully aware of it, tension was creeping up his back like a virus.

He and Otto skipped down the final steps to the sidewalk, where two Town Cars waited at the curb. Otto motioned toward the lead car. "Take the first one. And try to enjoy your first night in DC."

"You do the same, Otto. I'll see you in the morning."

Max jumped in the first delivery car and turned to see Otto disappearing into the second. Both cars pulled out and merged into traffic.

Max still had not connected the dots concerning his channeling of emotions from other people. Now again, he was channeling negative energy. Perhaps it was from Otto.

As his Town Car sped down Constitution Avenue, he gradually felt his uneasiness dissipating. He wondered if the relief was somehow connected to the growing distance between his car and Otto's. *No, I'm just stressed.*

He turned to see Otto's car at a stoplight. His car continued, creating an even greater distance. When he looked to his right, he could just make out the White House and its majestic south lawn. To his left, the Washington Monument towered against the grass of President's Park. For a fleeting moment, the giant structure brought to mind the obelisks of Egypt. Then Max thought of the amazing architecture he had seen on Nibiru during his initiation.

As his vehicle crossed 17th Street, Max became aware of his reflection in the window. He didn't recall ever looking so haggard. He studied his likeness in the glass, as the car passed before the pond of Constitution Gardens. A beam of sunlight reflecting off the water blinded him ever so briefly. In the flash, his image in the glass morphed. If only for a moment, he saw Enlil's face staring back at him.

Max sank deeper into the Town Car's back seat, stunned and even exhilarated. For the first time, he had recognized his uncanny resemblance to *Enlil*. He removed his phone and dialed Demetrius' emergency number. After several rings, his father's voice mail kicked in.

"Dad, I just wanted to call," Max hesitated, trying carefully to choose his words. "I know things are pretty messed up right now. But I thought... I wanted you to know there's no need to worry. There's a lot I have to learn, but I understand better now. I'm clear what it is I have to do." Max took a breath. "When you're better and feeling up to it, give me a call. All right, pops. Get well soon."

Max clicked off his phone and nestled again in the leather seat. Minutes earlier, Otto had promised he would see how the world really runs. Gazing outside at the passing streets, he wondered just what undiscovered things the capitol city held in store for him. Max also feared that more than likely, he was about to find out.

TO BE CONTINUED...

Coming soon

THE **UNVEILING** 2.0

GLOSSARY OF TERMS

Abzu – This region, as told in Sumerian mythology, is believed to be the area known under modern appellation as the southern coast of South Africa.

Adamu – The very first man of a genetically created race of hybrid workers.

Akasha – Sanskrit word meaning Ether, the fifth element after air, fire, water and Earth.

Akashic Record – Believed to be a library of everything ever created in human existence as well as the history of the cosmos. The Akashic record does not exist in the physical plane, but is found in the ether.

Anunnaki [Best translation = "those of royal blood"] – A race of beings that came to Earth from the planet Nibiru as described in Sumerian Mythology.

Antikythera Mechanism – An ancient device discovered in 1901 in the Antikythera shipwreck off the coast of Greece. The mechanism, believed to have been constructed between 100 and 150 BC, is historically out of order, as its technology was not considered existent before the 14th century.

Anu – Sumerian deity considered to be the Supreme Leader of the royal race of Anunnaki.

Chakras – Concepts that originate in Hindu text. There are seven power centers or vortices that exist along the spine, each are considered portals that channel energy from the spiritual world into the physical world.

Enki – Sumerian deity, considered a prince as the first-born son of Anu and his second wife, Antu.

Enlil – Sumerian deity, considered a prince as the second born son of Anu and his first wife, Ki.

Eridu – The first city on Earth to be created by the Anunnaki. Eridu is believed to be in ancient Sumer or what is also known as Mesopotamia. Today this region is known as parts of Iraq, northeastern Syria, southeastern Turkey and southwestern Iran.

Hatha Yoga – In Sanskrit, the word "Ha" translates to sun and "Tha" to moon. As with night and day, Hatha is a system of yoga that unites opposites.

Igigi – The Anunnaki workforce brought to Earth from Nibiru.

Ki – Sumerian deity, first wife of Anu and mother to Enlil.

Kundalini Yoga – The yoga of awareness. Kundalini is a practice that attunes the physical body with spiritual awareness. Kundalini activation is the process of fully activating each of the seven chakras.

Money Pit – The site of the world's longest running hunt for lost treasure. The booby-trapped pit has drawn treasure hunters to Nova Scotia's Oak Island for nearly two centuries.

Nibiru (or Marduk) – Believed to be the 12th planet of our solar system as referred to in Zecharia Sitchen's book "The 12th Planet." Modern appellations include Planet X, Eris.

Ninmah – Sumerian deity, daughter of Anu and his first wife, Ki; full sister to Enlil; half-sister to Enki.

Sumerian Mythology – In the vein of Greek Mythology, Roman Mythology and Egyptian Mythology... Sumerian Mythology recounts the story of gods from the planet Nibiru as told by the culture that is modernly known as Iraq.

White Powder of Gold – The byproduct of gold that has been vaporized by heating it to the temperature of the sun. It is a superconductor with monoatomic properties.

www.ingramcontent.com/pod-product-compliance
Lightning Source LLC
Chambersburg PA
CBHW030414180626
46812CB00005B/2007